GOLDEN DAWN

Thomas M. Kostigen

A TOM DOHERTY ASSOCIATES BOOK
NEW YORK

GOLDEN DAWN

Copyright © 2012 by Thomas M. Kostigen

A Forge Book
Published by Tom Doherty Associates, LLC
175 Fifth Avenue
New York, NY 10010

www.tor-forge.com

Forge® is a registered trademark of Tom Doherty Associates, LLC.

Library of Congress Cataloging-in-Publication Data

Kostigen, Thomas.
    Golden dawn / Thomas M. Kostigen.—1st ed.
        p. cm.
    "A Tom Doherty Associates book."
    ISBN 978-0-7653-2933-2 (hardcover)
    ISBN 978-1-4299-4319-2 (e-book)
    1. Hermetic Order of the Golden Dawn—Fiction.   2. Prophecies—
Fiction.   3. Nuclear terrorism—Fiction.   I. Title.
    PS3611.O74924G65 2012
    813'.6—dc23

                                                                        2012019939

First Edition: October 2012

Printed in the United States of America

0   9   8   7   6   5   4   3   2   1

For Dorothy, Katherine, Patricia, Joanne,
Susan, William, Robert, and Richard

ACKNOWLEDGMENTS

As always, I need to thank Susan Raihofer for believing in me and pushing my career in new directions. Her support and tenacity always go beyond the expected.

Margaret Riley, too, has my back and never quits.

At Tor, Tom Doherty, Linda Quinton, Karl Gold, Heather Saunders, Kevin Sweeney, Jane Herman, Andrea Wilk, Seth Lerner, Whitney Ross, and Bob Gleason pushed, pulled, and literally laid this book out.

My family is my net. I may live and travel far from them, but they are always near when I need them most.

Many of my friends are writers, and their understanding of the wicked ways in which words get put together keep me from believing that I sit alone in the grandstands.

In sketching out *Golden Dawn*'s story lines and characters, I relied on actual people, places, and things, which meant traveling to many of the locales mentioned.

To get to the places I couldn't get to, I leaned on and learned from other journalists, authors, and academics, as well as the occasional religious scholar. Given the nature and potentially sensitive and controversial content of this novel, I won't name names. But you know who you are— and I thank you: to the gent who bought me far too many Guinesses and shots of Redbreast in that dark bar in Northern Ireland and described the *real* IRA to me; to my guides and hosts in Istanbul who helped me see the sites and trace what would become Michael Shea's steps; to my Persian friends who rolled their eyes and talked through history and their language; to a certain biblical scholar in Italy who opened my eyes to the Vatican's Secret Archives; and to the network of people I have become so fond and friendly with throughout the Middle East—thanks for showing me how to sneak in and out of countries.

The technical aspects of bomb-making are widely available on the Internet, as are many of the details of Iran's nuclear program. Omagh's place in The Troubles has been chronicled from a variety of points of view, including that of the victims' families. My sorrow is for them and everyone else who suffers at the hands of murderers (with or without political cause), no matter where in the world.

I don't like to use books as reference points. I find news accounts far more useful. Indeed, some of the more lively and sprightly accounts of happenings in the book came from news reports—read, watched, or listened to on the road.

The Golden Dawn is an actual spiritual order. And Zoroastrianism is a faith whose basic tenets we should all be able to relate to: the constant fight between good and evil. I have meant no disrespect to Golden Dawn adherents or Zoroastrians in the writing of this book.

Along with some of the spiritual facts and practices, I have taken liberties with some of the geographic places mentioned to accommodate the narrative. Of course, the political dynamics of Iran are sometimes even more fantastical and fanatical than as described in this novel. This should not be construed as a reflection of the people of Iran, rather as a lens on the government and certain religious leaders.

Now about Scripture: it's all there ready for interpretation. The Vatican Secret Archives are actually available online. The Third Secret of Fatima was kept under lock and key for much of the twentieth century—until the New Millennium. And the Mahdi is a well-known figure in Islam.

What you choose to believe is a matter to sort out for yourself.

GOLDEN
DAWN

PROLOGUE

HE SOMETIMES COULD ALMOST FEEL THE HAND SMACK HIM ON THE
back of his head. He'd catch himself inadvertently rubbing the nub on
the base of his skull where the ring—that damned ring!—over the years
had stopped drawing blood and instead formed scar tissue—so much so
that in primary school he was taunted for the constant welt he wore. "That
your twin growin' in there?" his schoolmates would harass.

Child services had even come knocking once.

They never came back.

The first smack that he could remember came when he wondered
aloud who a certain man was at his uncle's door. "Never ask that question, Mikey. You hear?" his uncle, the man responsible for raising him, if
you wanted to call it that, after his parents died, had said. "It's for your
own good." Another smack came as reinforcement.

More men came and went over the years—usually late at night and
through the back door of the house. He could never recall anything about
them: their faces were hidden under caps or the hoods to their sweatshirts.

What he learned as he got older was that their visits were timed exactly to the bloodiest bombings in Northern Ireland:

July 21, 1976. The British ambassador and his secretary were assassinated by car bomb. The ambassador's car tripped a land mine loaded with hundreds of pounds of explosives, and he was blown to bits in front of his residence.

February 17, 1978. Twelve people were killed and thirty injured at a restaurant bombing outside Belfast. The explosive device was an experimental design of homemade napalm intended to stick to whatever it hit, causing severe burn injuries to its victims. It worked ingloriously.

November 14–19, 1978. Fifty bombs exploded across the country, injuring thirty-seven people. The random timing and locales were meant to strike fear into the hearts of people along with a severe message: no one was safe anywhere.

March 22, 1979. The British ambassador to the Netherlands was assassinated and twenty-four bombs were exploded in various locations. The ambassador was shot point-blank in the head and the bombs were meant as a war cry.

Twenty-two more bombings would take place over the following twenty years, each explosion another sign of bloody rebellion. And every time different men would come and go from the house.

Then the worst incident of them all occurred. He couldn't bear to think of that one; the memory of it was kept buried deep inside. It was then that he left the house for good.

THESE TIMES WERE CALLED THE TROUBLES, AND THEY LIVED UP TO their meaning in almost every sense of the word for Michael Shea.

Now, whenever he found himself rubbing the back of his neck, it usually meant that he was on to something, something that inevitably led to blood and . . . trouble.

PART ONE

"DON'T LOOK
BACK"

THE VOICE WAS AS SCRATCHY AS THE STATIC ON THE TELEPHONE LINE that connected them across continents.

"I never make a mistake. I know it is him; your uncle. He's working for us now." The voice was rushed. The information came in staccato-like bursts.

British News's star foreign correspondent Michael Shea gripped the phone in his hand tight and pressed it hard against his ear. The noise of the London newsroom that usually reminded him of why he liked to report from the field was lost, shut out. He was focused on the words coming through the phone. Shea was consumed by the possibility that for once he might be able to catch his uncle, Sean O'Shaughnessy, in the act, the act of terrorism.

"My uncle is in Chechnya?" Shea asked quickly, fearful the line would go dead.

He needed a location. He began to write things down. He'd get there, wherever his uncle was.

"*Dac*, no. He's in Iran. A meeting is set. I have the details. I can tell you . . ."

HE WAS STANDING ACROSS THE ROAD. IN PLAIN SIGHT. SEEMINGLY unarmed. An easy target. After more than a decade and through the dozen countries he had been chased, Shea's uncle now stood within a stone's throw.

His informant had been right. "*Lake Urmia. Northern Iran. Just over the Turkish border.*"

Shea had sneaked into the country easily.

His uncle was standing next to one of the more powerful Chechen rebels, the commander, it was reported, who was directly responsible for the infamous Moscow subway bombings.

It was no secret within certain underground circles that Iran was supplying Chechen rebels with arms and training. But why remained something of a mystery. Moscow had been a staunch ally of Tehran in the face of international criticism over Iran's nuclear power program. And as the world knew, Russians and Chechens were enemies.

Shea snapped another photograph of the Chechen commander, Alu Abramov, standing next to his uncle. It was difficult to see much of the Chechen's skin. He had a full beard that curled down to his chest. His dark hair covered much of his forehead, too, touching down to meet his unibrow, and fell below his shoulders. His eyes looked black. The fur on his hooded parka blended in so much that Shea had to focus his lens on Abramov's flat nose to find anything remotely light-colored on the Chechen's face.

He pressed the shutter on his Canon PowerShot SX20 that he had switched off auto mode to make sure he got the shot. Click, the face. Click, Alu shaking hands with his uncle. Click, his uncle.

He and his uncle looked frighteningly alike, despite the twenty-year age difference. Shea, thirty-three, his uncle fifty-three years of age. They both had dark brown wavy hair. They both were six feet tall and about the same weight: one hundred eighty-five pounds. Solid. Muscular. Their strength also resided in their chiseled cheekbones, and their eyes. Their eyes were deep-set and smoky. They were tools that could stare a man down with a flash, or, with a twinkle, catch a woman's fancy.

Shea zoomed in on his uncle's. He tried to gauge them. *Chariots to the soul,* he thought.

His uncle's eyes were searching.

SHEA OFTEN WONDERED HOW TWO PEOPLE WHO PHYSICALLY LOOKED so alike could see the world so differently: Shea, a prominent correspondent for the leading British news service, and his uncle Sean, one of the most famous terrorists alive. One trying to enlighten the world, the other trying to light it afire.

He zoomed the lens back out and took another wide shot with his camera. Click—nothing but black. Shea took the camera away from his face to see what had blocked his view.

A twenty-four-vehicle motorcade had arrived in front of the single-story brownish stucco building that looked as if it dated back to the Ottoman Empire. Shea's uncle and Abramov were standing in front of it, and a motorcade had pulled up. The black cars waving the Iranian flag and the black sunglasses of the security team that jumped out were giant clues to who had just arrived.

The Iranian president's arrival was unexpected and just landed Shea the biggest story of his career. It also put him at unexpected and extreme risk.

Shea began to rub the back of his neck.

"DOWN!" SHEA BARKED, SLUMPING IN HIS SEAT. MUNJED, HIS CAMERA-man, was seated next to him on the driver's side. Shea pressed on Munjed's shoulder, urging him to quickly duck low.

He and Munjed had been almost inseparable for the past three years, coworkers and best friends. An unlikely pairing—Munjed being a short, fat, and disheveled Palestinian whereas Shea was obsessively neat and well dressed—they covered each other's butts. They had saved each other's lives too many times to count—one cautioning when the other became careless. In the Middle East, danger, like a desert wind, was sudden. And it often took more than one set of senses to feel it, see it, or hear it.

Munjed did what he was told and crouched lower in his seat. "Wow, is that who I think it is?" he asked.

"'Tis. The president of Iran. In the flesh."

Munjed whistled softly. "And here during Ramadan when he is supposed to be at home with his family praying. Tsk-tsk. What a bad Muslim."

"I hear he is really a secret Jew," Shea quipped.

Munjed laughed. "Don't let him hear you say that."

Shea thought, *If he could hear me I'd say something much more offensive. Perhaps I'd ask him if he's ever visited a concentration camp.*

Shea's mind sometimes wandered like this. He'd have entire conversations in his head.

Shea angled his camera lens so he could see across the street. The battered old Mercedes he and Munjed were in was parked no more than fifty yards away from the motorcade on the roadside. The Iranian president had stepped out of the back of his car and was standing on the road.

Shea and Munjed were vulnerable where they had parked. They had picked a location appropriate to spy on a clandestine meeting between two terrorists, not one that would hide them from a presidential security detail. And if they were found, they were as good as dead.

Munjed decided that he just couldn't sit there without filming. Shea apparently was thinking the same thing. "Too bad we aren't getting this," he said to Munjed, lightly masking his request.

"You got it, boss. Let's show the world." This was something Munjed said whenever he and Shea uncovered a big story. And this was no doubt the biggest story they had ever uncovered: the president of the Iranian Republic clandestinely meeting with two very dangerous international villains. The world would demand to know why.

Shea had in mind a different demand: retribution.

5

MUNJED SAT UP, TURNED, AND REACHED TO THE BACKSEAT FOR HIS camera. It was over before his fingers made contact. Bullets sprayed the inside of the Mercedes. They ripped Munjed's chest wide open, and his guts began to spill onto the floor. Shea froze, but only for an instant. He reached over for Munjed and yet another bullet spray landed. He slumped back down in his seat and looked at the man who was the closest thing to family he had in the world. "Munjed!" Shea reached for his friend. He knew it was too late. Munjed was dead and gone. His eyes were wide open in the death stare. Another short burst of gunfire hit the windshield and forced Shea to scramble out of the car. He would have to leave Munjed behind. Now he had to save his own life.

Shea stayed low and out of sight as he ducked out of the passenger's side of the Mercedes. They had parked next to a brick wall and Shea's choices of escape were limited. There was nowhere to run in front of him—the presidential security detail had parked one of its black SUVs ahead and agents were scrambling out. But behind him he had noticed an alleyway. He slinked along the ground to the rear of the car to get a better view. When he peeked his head up over the trunk to gauge just how far away the alley was, an elbow caught him in the face. A left hook then crushed his temple, and he stumbled onto one knee. The blows, though, weren't hard enough to put him down, and he steadied himself as he stood. Facing him was an agent of the Iranian Secret Service, the agency known as SAVAMA. The agent was dressed in the secret agent uniform of dark suit and sunglasses. The agent paused, and this was his first and last mistake—not continuing the assault on Shea.

In a flash, Shea pushed off his back foot, lowered his hips, and landed a front kick to the agent's groin. He then landed a brutal punch to the man's skull. A left knee to the face sent the agent to the ground.

Shea knew how to fight. As a brawler growing up on the mean streets of Belfast to the many war zones he covered as a foreign correspondent to the Krav Maga studio where he learned the technical aspects of that brutal Israeli form of self-defense, he was well schooled in close combat. Shea also knew when it was time to run. And that time was now.

He spotted the alley's entrance and sprinted for it.

Go! Go! Go! Run, Michael. But don't look back. Don't look. Just run.

Shea turned his head to see if he was being chased. He met those searching eyes.

Idiot! He chastised himself. He snapped his look away.

Three SAVAMA agents, now in V-formation, were running after him. Shea focused. He figured he had ten seconds to get lost.

He made it to the alley in five seconds flat. A staircase was just a few feet to his right, and he made his way up two steps at a time.

From his perch on the rooftop, Shea, breathless, could see down to the road and the alley's entrance. They would be coming. It would be just a matter of seconds before he was found. There was only one way to escape.

Don't think. Just do it!

Shea stood at the roof's edge on the opposite side from the stairs.

Footsteps.

Do it. Do it now!

He jumped.

Midflight, he ignored his own advice again and thought about what he had just done. Words didn't come this time, only fright. He crashed onto a corrugated-steel overhang below and crashed again onto the ground. Nothing broken, just bruised; he stood and brushed himself off. When he looked up, a SAVAMA agent was looking down at him from the rooftop. It was a brief stare, not more than a second, but it sent a chill down Shea's spine. *Darkness.* Then the agent was gone.

Shea had landed in yet another alleyway. These old villages and towns were full of them, and some dated back to 2000 B.C.

Nice going, Michael. You jumped straight into the cradle of civilization and you don't know your way out.

The place he was in looked as if it hadn't changed in centuries. It was all dim, dank alleyways that stretched thirty or more feet high.

Shea sprinted as far as the alley would take him. He ducked right where the alley came to a T. This is what he needed—choices. The more choices there were the better possibilities he had for losing his pursuers.

Left. Go left. Jesus, you're like a rat caught in a maze. Run, you fuck, run.

He ran for several hundred feet. Then the alley came to a dead end. He heard running feet behind him. The SAVAMA agents would close in on him at any moment.

He couldn't go back the way he came. Shea's escape route was limited to finding an open door. Having spent a significant period of time in the Middle East, Shea knew that apartments lay beyond those doors. And usually the homes built into the walls of ancient cities had doors on both sides. If he could get into a home from this side of the wall he could get out the other side.

It's your only chance. Use your strength.

Shea tucked his arm into his side and put his chin against his shoulder. He pounded on several of the thick, medieval-looking wooden doors. Dust flew onto his sweat-matted hair and face, but none of the doors would budge. He had only one chance left—and he saw it.

ACROSS THE NARROW ALLEY SHEA HAD FOUND HIMSELF IN, A DOOR was ajar. He sprinted for it and without losing stride crashed through.

This better not be a closet were the last words he thought before he barreled in.

He rolled and then stood up. He saw an arm and grabbed it. The room was pitch black. He wrenched the arm back while simultaneously turning the wrist. Wrist pressure he knew was enough to make even the toughest of men give up. He pushed the body against the door, slamming it shut and pinning this person to it. A yelp. A small cry. It was a woman he had pushed against the door. He took a quick look around. His eyes adjusted to the darkness. There was no one else in the room. He could make out a living area, a kitchenette. "Shh" was all he said. He heard footsteps outside. He cupped the woman's mouth with his free hand. The footsteps stopped, shuffled, and then moved on.

Shea spun the woman around and looked straight into the dark brown eyes of the most perfect face he had ever seen: her cheeks high, her lips full, and those eyes dancing underneath a dark, wavy mane. She was beauty defined.

He couldn't think. He couldn't speak. His mouth went agape. Hers didn't: "How dare you touch me! How dare you break into my . . . this place!" the woman yelled. "Shh," Shea said again, regaining control of her and cupping his hand over her mouth. She struggled madly. He stared at her until she relented. His eyes. She stared into them. They weren't kind eyes. Yet they weren't murderous either. They were the type of deep-set brown eyes that drew you in. They stirred emotion.

At that moment, Neda Ghazali couldn't be sure what emotion she was feeling: fear, or some type of relief. She had been locked up inside this apartment for weeks. Shea couldn't know it yet, but he was just as much a salvation to her as she was to him.

Shea removed his hand from her mouth.

"Stop doing that!" she said, this time more quietly.

"I'm sorry. I am trying to . . ." He paused, not knowing how much to say. ". . . get safe." He noticed that she spoke English to him, and asked her why she had.

"Well, Persian isn't your color," Neda said. "Now what are you doing here? What do you want from me?"

"Don't worry. I'm not going to hurt you. I just need to get out of here. Is there another exit?" He stepped back and away from her to show he meant no harm. At the same time he checked her out some more. She was five foot eight and dressed in a loose-fitting black skirt. From the thinness of her neck and shoulders, he could tell that she was petite. Without staring, he glanced at her chest, too. It didn't disappoint.

He caught himself and looked past her and noticed on a table by the door a burka, the headdress leaving only a small slit for eyeholes.

Shame. A face like that should never be covered.

8

NEDA INTERRUPTED HIS THINKING. "AGAIN, COULD YOU TELL ME what the hell you want? What are you doing here?" she asked loudly.

Shea gave her the simple answer: "They killed my . . . friend." The emotion almost broke him, but he suppressed it for another time, another place. "And now they are trying to kill me."

"Who?" Neda asked.

"The SAVAMA."

Neda's eyes went wide. "The SAVAMA are here?! Why?"

"The president is here. I saw something that I wasn't supposed to. And now . . . they are after me."

Many thoughts ran through Neda's mind, but she said only one out loud, and she put it into the form of a question. "If I get you out of here, will you take me with you?"

"Lady, that wouldn't be good for you or for me."

"Are you CIA or something? A spy?"

"No," Shea said, a bit too forcefully. "I'm a journalist."

A smile swept across Neda's face. She looked up at the ceiling. "Praise Allah."

Shea shook his head, "Allah's got nothing to do with this, just so you know." He moved back even farther from her and walked behind a small table with chairs that had been set up between the living area and kitchenette. Nothing in the place looked too personal. Besides the door, the only source of air was the tiny window over the door. The windows above the sink were bricked over. Something wasn't quite right but he couldn't place his finger on it yet. Shea stole another look at the door and listened hard for any movement outside; there was none.

"Why would you want to come with me?" Shea asked.

"My name is Neda Ghazali. I am being held captive. And the president, you see, wants me dead."

AT THE SOUND OF GUNFIRE, IRANIAN PRESIDENT MAHMOUD TALIB had been covered and physically bulldozed by three SAVAMA agents into the domed building he was standing in front of. It wasn't difficult to physically maneuver the president. He was a small, gnomish man who hadn't exercised a day in his life.

His official bio would have a person believe that the president was a star athlete. That fact, among many others, was fabricated. It was meant to make the president seem strong.

Talib went to great lengths to make people believe he was powerful. He only allowed his photograph to be taken when he stood on stairs above others. Otherwise he was photographed alone or with others in close-up shots. He staged action shots of himself on horseback, on the football field, or at various sporting events. He was one of those men who suffered from a Napoleon complex—a victim of numerous compensations for the fact he was short. From a psychological perspective his insecurities may also have been part of the reason he wanted so desperately to acquire nuclear weapons for his country. He said it was imperative for Iran to possess nukes to fend off the evil warriors of the West.

Talib was a master at twisting his logic to suit his own goals and to support his own conclusions. This was evident when, at a speech at the UN, he claimed nuclear weapons destroy mankind and the environment, and then went on to say that the only way to defend the world against those who already possessed nuclear weapons was for countries to possess such weapons themselves. He was a frightfully curious man well adept at doublespeak. He had even gone so far as to theorize that the Holocaust had never occurred. "There was no genocide" he had said in numerous media interviews. He then made vague assessments of history and claimed facts had been distorted.

The president's remarks had stuck with Shea—and with much of the rest of the world.

Still, the one issue the president of Iran was singularly obsessed with was obtaining nukes. Most heads of state realized what a lunatic he was and refused to grant him nuclear concessions. That's why Talib was forced to acquire the nuclear materials he needed through back channels and underground groups. He set up front companies in places like Taiwan to buy components from Europe and Asia. He used stooges and shells and transported materials over his country's border in the dead of night. And he had amassed a massive arsenal.

Yet he needed a triggering device. And the two men he was about to speak with, Sean O'Shaughnessy and Alu Abramov, could get and assemble it for him. It was the last piece of weaponry needed to literally trigger a power the world had never before seen. A dangerous, unremitting power aimed at world domination.

10

TALIB SHOOK OFF THE SECURITY AGENTS SURROUNDING HIM AND found the Irish terrorist and bomb maker O'Shaughnessy standing off in a corner looking as if he had just seen a ghost. Across the room the Chechen rebel Abramov was standing among the SAVAMA agents, pistol drawn and ready for action.

The gunfire that had drawn them so quickly inside was a surprise to them all. But O'Shaughnessy's reaction was even more shocking to the Iranian president. He had heard that O'Shaughnessy was a hardened Irishman and a veteran of terrorist attacks and conflicts around the world. Sure, bomb makers like O'Shaughnessy rarely faced aggressors firsthand or experienced attacks themselves. They were usually long gone by the time the bomb went off or were far removed. But the president had expected that O'Shaughnessy would at least be a man about experiencing direct conflict.

What Talib didn't know was when Michael Shea had sprinted for the alley and looked back to see if he was being chased, he had also glanced across the street—and locked eyes with his uncle. The gaze transcended time and space. It ripped open a Pandora's box of emotions and feelings. And in that instant, an infinitesimal amount of time, conditioned them all into one—love's twin: hate.

It was the fear of that, not the gunshots, which showed on O'Shaughnessy's face.

11

"GENTLEMEN," TALIB SAID, DIRECTING HIS ATTENTION TOWARD BOTH Abramov and O'Shaughnessy, "my apologies. My security did not do as detailed a sweep as usual because of the last-minute scheduling of this meeting. I can assure that you are safe here. I was just informed that two men had breeched the security perimeter and they are now being taken care of."

Talib, Abramov, and O'Shaughnessy were standing inside the entrance to an old domed tomb. It had been converted into a public building and was now used for government meetings. Its dome was said to be perfect, a perfect oval through whose epicenter a single light shone. Archaeologists had recently found an astounding history to the building through artifacts in the area. It was for this reason that the building was closed off, and it was for this reason that Talib had chosen it as a meeting place.

Archaeologists were laying claims that the domed building was at the center of what was perhaps the most famous historical place on Earth: the Garden of Eden.

Talib stood directly under the light that beamed through the dome's apex when he spoke. He looked more at O'Shaughnessy than Abramov. Whereas Abramov seemed relaxed about the incident and what Talib was saying, O'Shaughnessy hung on every word the president spoke. He was like a distraught parent who had just lost his child at the mall; O'Shaughnessy was yearning to hear something. He was looking for meaning behind the words.

Talib said, "Mr. O'Shaughnessy. I am Mahmoud Talib, the president of Iran. Welcome to my country and thank you for meeting with me." O'Shaughnessy stared deep into the eyes of the president and saw nothing. No emotion. More than that, they were dark, like an abyss. If O'Shaughnessy was already feeling as if he had seen a ghost in the form of his nephew Michael, looking into the president's eyes made him feel as if he had just seen evil incarnate. He shuddered.

"Are you all right, Mr. O'Shaughnessy?" Talib asked. "You seem shaken."

O'Shaughnessy recovered fast. "I am fine, Mr. President. Thanks. And thanks for your hospitality."

"*Baleh*," Talib said, slipping into Farsi. The president let his hand linger around O'Shaughnessy's a tad longer than usual. It sent another shudder down his spine.

If there was one thing the Iranian president prided himself on it was intuition. And he felt something just wasn't right about Sean O'Shaughnessy. He'd look into that later. From all accounts, the Irishman was the man for the job. If there was anyone on the planet who had the technical know-how and the means to get what was needed, it was O'Shaughnessy. He knew how to build a trigger for a nuclear bomb.

12

TALIB TURNED HIS ATTENTION TO **A**BRAMOV. **T**HE BEAR OF A **C**HECHEN almost crushed Talib's hand in his giant paw when he shook it.

"*Salaam alaikum*," Abramov said, almost shouted.

"*Salaam*," Talib said, returning the greeting in the more casual Persian manner followed by a single kiss. *These radicals always get so hung up on us all being Muslim,* Talib thought. *They are not truly worthy to be followers of Islam.*

Still, Talib knew that he needed the Chechen connection to execute his plan, and even more than that: to execute Allah's will, the word of God.

"Come," Talib said, as he walked toward a large door to the left of the room in which they stood. We can speak better in here." Then he turned to one of his SAVAMA agents. "Zhubin, I trust all is being taken care of."

The agent nodded his head. "All is secure," Zhubin said.

Both Abramov and O'Shaughnessy had taken notice of Zhubin. The man was built like a pit bull. He had a shiny, bald head and he didn't wear sunglasses like the other agents. That made his piercing steel blue eyes all the more noticeable. They cut through people like lasers.

"Gentlemen," Talib gesticulated when he opened the door to the adjourning room, "please take a seat."

The room had twenty-foot-high ceilings, ornately designed in flower-like patterns typical of the Ottoman style. No human figures were ever the subject of calligraphy, according to the strict rules found in Islamic art, but exquisite geometric patterns adorned the walls. The windows stood more than ten feet tall and were draped by black-and-beige-checked leather curtains. The marbled walls and floor were equally rich-looking. A long table sat in the middle of the room and O'Shaughnessy and Abramov took seats on the opposite side of it from Talib.

"Gentlemen, let me be direct. I invited you both because I need your services. It is important that we meet and understand each other. My mission is much higher than merely defending my country. We must defend the world against the Western powers before it is too late. The time is approaching. You can join me in this revolution and I trust that you will. We are the saviors."

Talib took the opportunity to pontificate whenever he could—even if there were just two people in the room and they already knew what they were there to discuss. O'Shaughnessy, in his coarse and direct Irish way, was already thinking, "Okay, let's get on with it then." He was eager to find out what happened to his nephew, track him down if necessary. *What in the world was he doing here?* If he were found, it would crater O'Shaughnessy's deal with the crazy Iranian president. Further, if they found out Shea was his nephew, good night Irene, he'd be a dead man.

In a room close by, however, that family connection had just been discovered.

TALIB SPOKE ABOUT HIS PRESIDENCY, HIS PEOPLE, AND THEIR plight—all because of the West. Western powers just didn't trust Iran nor like its people. "It will be just a matter of time before they invade my country. We must strike first!" Talib said, snapping O'Shaughnessy out of his daze.

Talib smiled, and the gap between his two front teeth showed through. He looked across the table at O'Shaughnessy and Abramov to gauge their reactions. He had been so lost in his personal thoughts that he had almost forgotten they were in the room, and what they were there to discuss.

Abramov took the pause as his cue to concur with Talib and punched his fist on the table. *"Allah Akbar!"* he said. This startled the president. His security agents momentarily reached for their guns before they realized the giant Chechen was just being effusive.

Meanwhile, O'Shaughnessy sat in his chair stoically. Talib decided to address the issue. "Mr. O'Shaughnessy, are you well?" As he posed the question, Zhubin came into the room and placed a file down in front of the president, who opened it as O'Shaughnessy answered.

"Yes, Mr. President, just taking it all in," O'Shaughnessy said.

"Well, Mr. O'Shaughnessy, when I first saw you I thought that you looked, as they say in your language, 'like you had seen a ghost.'" Talib paused for effect. "And now I know that I was right." He paused again and slid the file he was looking at across the table. "I believe that I have just discovered the ghost in you."

Shea caught the file as it slid toward him and looked at it. On top was a photograph of Michael Shea that was obviously taken by a security camera. It was a shot of Shea sitting inside the Mercedes across the street just before the gunfire erupted and Munjed was killed.

"Quite a resemblance, don't you think?" Talib asked.

14

GREAT WORK, MICHAEL. OF ALL THE DOORS IN IRAN TO BARGE *through, you end up with a wanted criminal. Excellent.*

"What do you mean the president wants you dead?" Shea asked Neda, as he continued to look around the apartment for a way out.

He saw on a shelf behind where Neda was standing a photo of her and a man. They were touching the sides of their heads together and smiling at the camera. It was clearly a photo exhibiting a loving couple.

"My husband was murdered," Neda said. "His family believes that I am responsible. But as his widow, I must mourn according to Muslim law. I cannot move out of here, do nothing, really, for four months and ten days, if you know anything about the religion. I had just managed to unlock the door when you came barging in. But tomorrow my time is up and they plan to take me to Tehran, to turn me in—"

"You killed your husband?!" Shea almost screamed.

"No! He was shot by—" But before Neda finished explaining there were three rapid knocks on the door. Keys jingled. Shea and Neda snapped their attention to it.

"Quick," Neda said. She gave a look to the bathroom door just a few feet away.

Shea didn't know if he could trust her. But he didn't have a choice in the matter. He raced to it and closed the door as a stocky, bearded man about twenty years old, wearing a keffiyeh, a black-and-white-checkered scarf, loosely around his neck, stepped into the apartment. He left the door open behind him. The evening air and the darkness it represented spilled in.

The man looked around without saying a word.

"What do you want, Hussein?" Neda asked.

"I heard voices. Who were you speaking with?"

"I don't know what you are talking about. There is no one here."

Hussein looked at her strangely when she said that. "Do you have a phone? Are you speaking to people?" He grabbed her arm and began to twist it. Then he heard a creak come from the bathroom.

He noticed that a chair across from her at the kitchen table was pushed back. The bathroom door was shut. He looked directly at her, accusingly.

Neda tried to distract his attention and slapped him across the face with her free hand, but Hussein barely felt the blow and threw her to the ground. He stepped quickly toward the bathroom and approached the door as if he was going to walk straight through it.

"Look out!" is all Neda managed to yell before the door opened quickly—from the inside.

15

HUSSEIN DISAPPEARED FROM HER SIGHT.

Using his formidable Krav Maga fighting skills, Shea pulled Hussein in by one arm and used the momentum to shove him into the mirror over the sink. He kept hold of Hussein's arm and wrist. He snapped the wrist up and Hussein's knees buckled. Shea then swept Hussein's feet out from under him. With his other arm, Shea put him into a headlock. He released the wrist and worked his arm into a "carotid sleeper" hold. Shea squeezed his arms tight around Hussein's neck and pushed his head over the rim of the tub. In six seconds, Hussein was out cold. Shea kept squeezing for a few more seconds then released his grasp. He stood up and could see Neda through the cracked mirror. She was standing in the doorway holding a frying pan. For a second, he thought the pan might be for him. He took a quick look at himself. Dust-covered and sweat-stained, his scruff covered in white stone dust. He wouldn't blame her for thinking him a mad man.

"Is he dead?" she asked.

"No, just unconscious. He will wake up in a couple of minutes, maybe less. I've done this before." His eyes dropped to the pan in her hand.

Neda noted his glance and let the pan fall to the ground. It made a deadening clang. Hussein's body began to convulse. Shea stepped back over him, formed a fist with his right hand and then lifted the middle knuckle of his middle finger from the clench to form a point. He cracked

Hussein in the temple and the convulsing stopped; Hussein was out cold again.

When Shea looked up this time, Neda was no longer at the bathroom door. He leaped out to see where she'd gone. She was closing the front door. "They'll come," she explained, "when he doesn't return."

She didn't leave Shea any time to query further. "I almost made it out of here," Neda said. "I managed to unlock the door and then you came running down the alley. I thought one of them had seen me."

Shea thought for a moment. "And there is no other way out of these alleys besides the way I came in?" he asked.

"Not from this side," Neda said as she walked past Shea to Hussein. She began to pat him down. She reached into one of his pockets and pulled out a set of keys. Shea wiped himself off as best he could with a towel he had grabbed. He stood behind Neda and watched what she was doing.

"What are those for?" he asked, pointing to the keys.

"Our way out."

16

SHEA HAD LATCHED ON TO THE WORD *OUR* IN HER DECLARATION, "our way out," and had no choice except to go along with her.

Let it play out, Michael. Just get out. Get out and then you'll be on your own again. Like you always are. When you're safest. She'll be safer without you. People who get close to you . . . die. Like Munjed. Like the twenty-nine others who were killed. Then, back then. The blood on your hands.

Neda walked to the rear of the apartment and pulled back a rug hanging on the wall that revealed a door. The door had three metal buttresses across heavy wood slats. It looked like something out of a medieval dungeon. She put one of the keys into the lock and turned it. The door creaked open. The smell of must entered the room followed by a waft of cold air. "Come on," she said.

They stepped into a dark stone passageway. It was completely black. The opening was so narrow that Shea, with his broad shoulders, had to turn sideways to shimmy behind her.

"Don't shut the door yet!" she barked, then explained: "We won't be able to see."

"What is this place?"

"We are behind the *kiblah* wall of the village mosque."

"*Kiblah?*"

"It's the far end of the mosque, across the prayer hall from the exit."

Shea knew it was the second day of Ramadan, the sacred Muslim holiday that lasted for a full month. "We'll be walking straight into the most crowded place in town," Shea whispered, but with urgency in his voice.

"No. They had the *iftar* dinner here last night after the meal to break the fast. People will eat at home tonight. My husband used to sneak me into the apartment this way when we first started dating. Then one day I saw the key on one of his brother's chains." She held up a large skeleton key. "Can't mistake it for another." She opened another door and peered through. Some light spilled in. "Okay, shut the other door and come on."

They entered the small, candlelit prayer hall of the mosque. To their right was the *minbar*, the pulpit. The ablution fountain was at the doorway across from them and they headed straight for it. They took a few quick steps toward the exit, and then Shea grabbed Neda and spun her around.

17

"**What?!**" **Neda asked, startled by Shea's firm grasp.**

"It's not safe for you out there."

"It's not safe for me in here."

"I can't be responsible—"

"No one is asking you to be. I can take care of myself. I can get us out of here. Do you want to come with me or not?"

Shea didn't want to be led around by Neda, but he needed more time and direction. He looked at his hand. It was still gripping her arm tight. He didn't mean to hurt her, but he noticed that she was wincing.

Shea released his grip and Neda headed for the door. He followed her a few steps behind. He knew full well that they could be stepping out into danger, but now there was no choice, there was no going back. In the distance, behind walls, he heard banging. It was coming from the apartment they were just in. Whoever it was in the apartment would soon be coming for them.

Shea's hope of staying alive was now pinned to the woman whose back he was looking at, and who the president of Iran apparently wanted dead.

Of all the doors in the entire world you had to crash through, it had to be hers, he thought.

Shea couldn't yet know it, but in fact it had to be hers, it had to be—for higher and more mystical reasons than his own.

And more blood would be on his hands.

18

SHEA STEPPED OUT OF THE MOSQUE INTO THE TWILIGHT AND SAW
that the village streets were deserted. Across the road was a series of
shops. A row of cars was in front. At the end was a motorcycle. And that's
all he needed to see.

"Come on," he said to Neda, who was standing at the mosque door
waiting for him. "Fast." He buttoned the top button to his shirt and
tucked his shirt into his pants.

They broke across the road. A shadow. Someone? Something? It was
far away, but he sensed it—movement. He could see a flicker somewhere down the road, but he didn't look hard or long. He learned early
during his career as a war reporter that you didn't look to where the
gunfire or conflict was coming from—you just ran.

"No way," Neda said, as he took hold of the bike. "No way. I am not
getting on that with you." A car engine started. Headlights. He looked.
Damn! The lights caught them. Shea kicked away the bike's stand
and hopped on, praying that it would start. It did, with one kick. Neda
looked at him and gave in. It was their only means of escape. And they
needed to escape. Now. Fast.

They were off in a swirl of dust. Doors opened. People stepped out
onto the street to see what was going on. A black SUV gave chase and
kept the bike in its sights as it gained on them. Meanwhile, Shea was
trying to find the gears. Neda held on tight, her arms wrapped around
his waist. The bike bucked and revved high.

"Do you know how to ride this thing?" Neda asked.

"I hope so," he said, "or we're both in a lot of trouble."

It was a dirt bike. The gears were one up, four down, and Shea was finding his way through them as he tried to put distance between them and the fast-approaching SUV. He wasn't straying off the main road, which he could have easily done with a bike like the one he was riding. If he did he would have had to have to put on his headlight and they'd be too easily spotted.

Shea didn't immediately recognize the first popping sound. The second, though, caught his ear and the possible meaning of it formed. The third pop confirmed the sound of gunshot.

"They're shooting at us," he said, his head turned slightly so Neda could hear him.

"Really? I hadn't noticed," she said, sarcastically. "Ride faster!" She was anxiously looking at the car behind them. It was gaining on them.

19

SHEA TRIED TO FIGURE AN EVASIVE PATH FROM THE CAR BEARING down on them. The rows of shops and apartment buildings faded into one lone building every half block or so. It was typical zany Middle East architecture, building, and urban planning. Effectively none. Roads were a maze. Buildings crowded together threatening to topple. Instead of urban sprawl, it was countryside concocted.

Shea saw an intersection ahead. It was where the road forked. He broke left.

The days of evading the Belfast police when he was young came rushing back. His adrenaline was pumping.

Evade. Don't get caught. They'll beat you like your uncle Sean. They'll imprison you like your cousin Stephen. They'll kill you—like your da and mom.

A flash of Munjed's chest blown open entered his thoughts. The image of a severed hand. Blood. The anger gripped him fully and he steered hard to the left at the fork at the last second, hoping the SUV wouldn't have time to make the turn as well. But it did. It closed in. Neda didn't shift her weight properly and they almost wiped out. Shea had to steer hard to recover. Three more pops came. Then Shea made the move he had planned when he saw the fork in the road: he skidded and careened through a space at the back of a building and zipped onto another road heading in the opposite direction. The SUV braked and had to back up. The move put more distance between them. A quarter mile later, Shea raced up the side of a hill. A few seconds after that Neda informed him: "They went straight. You lost them."

"Really? I hadn't noticed," he said, downshifting and repeating her words. He wondered if she could sense the smirk on his face.

SHEA FELT NEDA'S ARMS WRAPPED AROUND HIM AS HE RODE TO A safe spot on the hill, and her embrace felt good.

Now is not the time, Michael. Now is definitely NOT the time.

Despite the circumstances, he felt a connection with Neda. She took his breath away and it took every bit of concentration he had not to lose focus, not to allow that ineffable feeling that beauty inspires to enter his consciousness.

He shut the engine and glided to a stop behind a massive stone structure. They got off, looked around, and listened. They had gotten away—for now.

Shea knew it wouldn't last. An alert would go out and they'd be hunted. A Westerner in this part of Iran was a rarity and there were few places for him to hide. Unless he could dye his hair black from light brown, unless he could change his skin tone to olive from pale white, and unless he could grow a dark beard from his three-day scruff, he'd have to flee the country the same way he came.

He and Munjed had sneaked over the border from Turkey. He could retrace their steps, but it would be risky. Granted, the dirt bike would help his cause. The mountain roads were better suited to travel via bike than car. That's probably why the region was popular among mountain bikers. Travel clubs frequented the Zagros mountain range that ran along the border between Turkey and Iran because of their spectacular beauty and relative ease to climb. They were then treated to a flat plain and Lake Urmia, of course. Still, he was a long way from the Turkish border now, about ninety miles. He could make it in less than two hours—alone.

Alone, Michael. Remember your past. Remember the bodies.

Shea looked over at Neda. She turned from examining the landscape and looked back at him. "I know what you are thinking," she said. "Now what, right?"

He said, "Read my mind," even though his thoughts were of people and a place far away. He flipped the subject to her: "But you are a mystery. I want to know more . . . like why your president would want you dead and what happened to your husband?"

NEDA LET OUT A SIGH AND SAT DOWN ON A ROCK. THE SUN WAS AL-most gone over the plain and a few sparkles of yellow skipped along Lake Urmia before they hid themselves from view. An orange glow was all that was left as a reminder that the sun had been there.

Neda picked up a small stone and rubbed it between her fingers as she took one last glance at the sunset and began to explain. "Do you remember the violence during the presidential election here?"

"Sure. The whole world was watching."

"I was one of those protestors. There were many of us, of course, but only a few groups were organized. My husband was the leader of an opposition group. We had traveled down from here to Tehran to take part in the opposition and the rallies that questioned the results of the election."

Neda tossed the stone aside, and continued. "My husband was one of those killed."

"I'm sorry . . ." Shea paused. "But I thought you said *you* killed him?"

"I said his family thinks that I killed him. They think I got him in-volved in politics and corrupted him. Nothing could have been further from the truth. In fact, it was the other way around. But they are pro-vincial, and I could never have disparaged their son by accusing him of anything."

Shea stepped closer to her, wanting to put his hand on her shoulder or at least show some type of comforting gesture. But he couldn't make that offer. He knew that Iranian women, even the modern ones, were extremely modest and sensitive around men. "I didn't know," Shea continued, "that the SAVAMA was still hunting protestors."

Neda scoffed. "They aren't. They're just after me."

22

NEDA LOOKED HARD AT SHEA. HER REVELATION HAD UNEARTHED A more serious tone in her voice and demeanor.

"Why are they just after you?" Shea asked.

"My husband wasn't killed randomly. They sought him out. They knew where we'd be and when. Someone turned us in to the secret police and told them what we had, and what we were about to do."

"And what was that?"

"Announce that Mahmoud Talib wasn't who he claimed to be. And that we had evidence of that as proof."

"What do you mean that Talib isn't who he claims to be? Do you mean that he isn't the president of Iran? That he is a fraud? You had proof the election was rigged?"

Neda began to laugh. She laughed hysterically until she was bent over. Shea didn't know what to do. It looked as if Neda had gone mad. And he thought to himself that this is just what he needed: to be stuck in a hostile country with some crazy woman as his only lifeline out.

Nice going, Shea.

Neda finally held her hand up, as she was bent over. She stopped laughing and sobered. "I am sorry," she said. "This is so crazy. But I am not. Really. Crazy, that is. It is just that so few people know. And it does

sound mad even though he has said it publicly: Mahmoud Talib believes that he is the Mahdi. My husband was a religious scholar. We had
proof that Talib was not who he claimed to be, as I said. That's what I
meant."

Shea blinked several times and searched the recesses of his memory,
but he didn't know what the word *Mahdi* meant. He finally had to admit this to Neda.

"Are you Christian?" Neda asked.

"Yes, Catholic, Irish Catholic."

"Then you would know the Mahdi as what he foreshadows: Judgment Day, Armageddon, the end of times as we know it."

Just then, Shea's head snapped away from Neda's gaze. He saw headlights approaching.

SEAN O'SHAUGHNESSY PICKED UP THE PHOTOGRAPH FROM THE FILE
Talib had slid across the table and stared at the picture of his nephew,
Michael Shea.

O'Shaughnessy could feel Talib's gaze upon him. He could also feel
the warm breath of the giant Chechen next to him; Abramov leaned in
closer to look at the photo.

"He's my nephew," O'Shaughnessy said, cutting the thickness of the
moment. Talib's security had made sure that both O'Shaughnessy and
Abramov handed over their weapons, and if O'Shaughnessy had had a
gun, he would have reached for it. The tension in the air was thick, like
the moments that preceded violence: there was a sort of stillness to it.

"What was he doing here? You were to be alone. Is he working with you?" Talib asked.

"No," O'Shaughnessy continued, keeping his eye on the photo. *Damn, Mikey, this time you might have gotten us both killed.* "He's a journalist. We haven't spoken for a long, long time."

O'Shaughnessy lifted his eyes from the table and met Talib's. The president could tell that O'Shaughnessy wasn't lying. O'Shaughnessy's answer was too layered with emotion. No one could fake that.

"So why is he here?" Talib asked again.

"He looks just like you," Abramov said, stating the obvious and munching down on the food that they had been served. He shoveled food into his mouth, chewing with his mouth open, ready for more. He was primitive in almost every aspect of his being.

"My men are after him now," Talib said. "We will catch him. Our mission, Mr. O'Shaughnessy, I want you to remember, is higher than family. It is higher than anything."

"Aih," O'Shaughnessy said curtly, "kill him. You'd be doin' me a favor. The hate runs deep in that one."

"You don't seem fazed," Talib said, surprised at the coldness with which the Irishman spoke.

"He's been hunting me for years. See, it's me he wants dead," O'Shaughnessy said.

"Bad blood," Abramov said, his mouth full. "It is like this in all of my country."

Talib looked over at Zhubin and nodded. The pit bull SAVAMA agent understood his orders perfectly and walked out the door. O'Shaughnessy understood, too, that the nod was an order to assassinate.

24

"**How did your nephew find out about the meeting, Mr.** O'Shaughnessy? Only two people besides me knew of its location: you and Mr. Abramov," Talib asked.

"I wouldn't know," O'Shaughnessy said. "Last I heard of him he was hunting for me in Grozny." He stared deadpan at Abramov.

Abramov's chewing slowed, and O'Shaughnessy drew out his next word for effect: "Chechnya."

The Chechen swallowed his last bite of food and wiped his mouth with his sleeve. "Are you accusing me?" he asked O'Shaughnessy.

"I am indeed," O'Shaughnessy said. "I work alone. No one knows my comings and goings. The whole feckin' world knows what the Chechens are up to, however, because you let 'em know. Make announcements, even . . ."

Abramov grabbed O'Shaughnessy by the throat. But O'Shaughnessy took the outside of the Chechen's gorilla-sized paw and, standing up, twisted Abramov's arm onto the table. He took a sharp steak knife from the place setting and raised it high in the air over his head.

"Stop!" the president of Iran yelled, as O'Shaughnessy was aiming to stab Abramov. "Don't."

O'Shaughnessy stole a glance at Talib and put the knife down at the same time that he released Abramov's arm.

"I need you both," Talib said. "My men will take care of your nephew, Mr. Shea, if they haven't already. I need you two to continue to work together. Soon none of this will matter. We will have the world's attention and make them understand. They will know there is accountability, that there is a new force in the world to judge their evil . . . in the name of Allah."

Abramov bowed his head at the name Allah but he kept his eyes on O'Shaughnessy the entire time.

25

"MR. ABRAMOV, ARE YOU IN CONTROL OF WHAT I NEED?" TALIB asked, after O'Shaughnessy and Abramov had settled back down in their seats.

"We have the rods of 239," Abramov said, finally looking away from O'Shaughnessy. "They just need to be shipped."

"Where are they now?" Talib asked.

Abramov put on a wide smile and just touched the right side of his nose with his index finger. "We have. Don't worry."

Talib squinted his eyes at Abramov to show his displeasure at the Chechen's vague response.

"They are the ones from Rostov, as we said, Mr. President," Abramov continued, answering more completely. Rostov was the region in southern Russia that housed the Volgodonsk nuclear power station.

Various Chechen factions had paid off unscrupulous Russian officials to obtain nuclear materials after the downfall of the Soviet Union. The bolder Chechens, such as Abramov, stole material from nuclear power plants—Rostov being one of them—and sold it on the black market.

Recently Abramov and some of his thugs had launched a raid on the Rostov plant and stolen a variety of nuclear materials, including caesium, strontium, and low-enriched uranium. None of these were weapons-grade materials. And, in fact, Abramov had only expected to obtain metals that could, when properly put together, make "dirty bombs." But it turned out that the Volgodonsk station was also in possession of plutonium 239, the holy grail of nuclear material because it's rare: it can't be found naturally—only by processing uranium through a nuclear reactor. With Pu-239, as it was called, far less material was needed to create a nuclear explosion than with highly enriched uranium, which was the more commonly sought-after material by those seeking to make nuclear weapons. Uranium had the advantage of being easier to detonate, but Pu-239 could create more bang for the buck. And because of its compact size—Pu-239 was usually stored in rods—could be more easily transported. The only problem with Pu-239 was triggering it; its implosion was more complex. It required a more sophisticated design, as well as designer. That's where Sean O'Shaughnessy came in.

26

TALIB TURNED HIS QUESTIONING TO O'SHAUGHNESSY. "MR. O'Shaughnessy," he began. "You understand your role is critical. Without a triggering element, all the nuclear material in the world is useless. Will you have the trigger ready?" Talib asked.

"Aih. Just need me lenses and me switches. Then we're set to go," O'Shaughnessy said.

"How much time will that take?" Talib asked.

"How much time do I have?" O'Shaughnessy shot back.

"One hundred sixty-eight hours, Mr. O'Shaughnessy. One week," Talib said. He looked up at the giant clock on the wall in the dining room. It read seven o'clock, exactly sunset time for that day.

"If I can get what I need from this moose," O'Shaughnessy said, indicating Abramov, "you will have what you need."

The Rostov theft had also provided Abramov with beryllium, an element O'Shaughnessy needed to complete the bomb's trigger. The bomb they were building was a version of the "Fat Man" bomb used by the United States at Nagasaki. It had a spherical core of Pu-239 jacketed by conventional extra-high explosives, which were imbedded with thirty-two explosive caps covered by lenses. These would reflect the blast down into the bomb's plutonium core causing it to implode. The design was relatively simple, but its effectiveness all hinged on the millisecond timing of the triggers. And trigger timing was what O'Shaughnessy excelled in.

Talib hadn't welcomed dealing with O'Shaughnessy, and his antics now tested Talib's patience. Since the mission was in motion, he cut the meeting, and therefore having to deal with the Irishman and the Chechen any longer, short.

"I suggest we get moving," Talib said, disregarding O'Shaughnessy's last potshot remark at Abramov. "We have much work to do." He stood, signaling an end to the meeting.

"Your rewards will be even more than you could imagine," Talib said to O'Shaughnessy as he shook his hand good-bye.

"As long as my bank account doesn't imagine anything and the money is there for real," said O'Shaughnessy, shaking the president's hand.

Talib didn't bother to respond to the snarky answer. He moved on to Abramov. "And Moscow shall be yours," he said to the Chechen.

Talib stayed at the head of the table as Abramov and O'Shaughnessy walked to the door. O'Shaughnessy turned around. "My nephew. He's . . . he's a tough catch. It may not be as easy as you think," he said.

"Leave that to me," Talib said.

O'Shaughnessy repeated, "I'll have the trigger ready for your test next week."

Talib narrowed his gaze. "Mr. O'Shaughnessy, this is not a test. I plan to strike. All should be as it should be. And all must be ready."

O'Shaughnessy nodded and stepped out of the room, closing the door behind him. He stepped into the domed room exactly when the last ray of daylight flickered out—and Abramov punched him out cold.

It was only in the darkness of his mind that he could go there, experience it. All of it. Over and over. How he had become this man.

'Twas a journey into the depths.

At first, o' course, there was good reason for the killings. Oppression did that. Gave a person their just cause. Subjective. But justification all the same. Then it turned into something else.

The trigger at Omagh had done it. Innocents, all of those killed. Civilians.

The trigger. He had timed it right. He had set it up perfectly, per usual. Always the same. Timer Power Units. They were the key. They fired the detonator which set off the explosive. Fixed it right, he did. The location, though. That was confounding.

The white flash of the explosive morphed—even through the blackness of his unconsciousness—to a hanging bulb. The interrogation room. There and then there was no sleep. Iron cuts into wrists and ankles. Harsh blows aimed to inflict the most pain. Bats to shins. Clubs to fingers. The dull, round end of a baton just under the ear, where skull and neck met. And ribs. Cracked, every one of them. Like a good butcher filleting a plump breast for his favorite customer. Delicate. Artful. Snap. Snap. Snap.

They could break his bones, not his resolve. Even during these dark thoughts—his unconscious—he never spoke.

His legend grew and found an audience. Far away. In Pakistan. A.Q. were the initials of the man who had contacted him from that country. They met in the Netherlands. It wasn't technical know-how the man was after. In fact, A.Q. later would become O'Shaughnessy's mentor. It was something much more powerful A.Q. wanted: understanding of the dark side of the soul.

A.Q. suffered from a complicated morality. He designed and built nuclear bombs in Pakistan. He was defiant of powerful Western nations, abhorred the Taliban, sought to empower Muslim countries with nuclear capability, and believed wholeheartedly in saving the natural environment from man's destruction.

O'Shaughnessy offered A.Q. something he could only know through massive death tolls: what it was like to live with the blood of so many on one's hands.

The flashes of images continued in the dark depths of O'Shaughnessy's mind while he was still passed out cold from Abramov's blow.

Meetings in Pakistan, in Libya, in North Korea, all rushed through his brain. Remembrances of the secret network that had been established came forth. Technology and know-how traded among the group. And he had become part of the "know-how." It was how the president of Iran came to contact him.

His unconscious began to catch up to real time: Talib. Abramov. Their meeting and shaking hands. Just moments ago. Then an image blazed fully.

Michael.

28

THE HEADLIGHTS WEREN'T MORE THAN A QUARTER MILE AWAY. THEY were far enough in the distance so that Shea and Neda couldn't be seen, but close enough to cause them to duck for cover.

Shea knocked over the bike so it lay flat on its side, flat as could be, and out of sight. He and Neda hid behind the giant stone Shea had been sitting on. They squatted low. Shea put his arm around Neda to keep them close—and unseen. Neda leaned in tighter and they formed a sort of ball. Their heads touched. Their breath—which they could see in the cold, night air—became one. The electricity between them was palpable. Neither dared look at the other for revealing the look of attraction and want that anyone observing the two would recognize.

Neda, in turn, placed her arm around Shea. And they just squatted like that, breathing hard and listening to the sound of the engine approaching. It was getting louder. The shine the headlights produced was getting brighter. Their shadows appeared on the rock and, in miniature, on the ground next to them. Their breathing became faster, and faster. Fear was gripping them and they held each other more tightly. Then, just as quickly as the headlights appeared, they were gone. The vehicle headed in a different direction.

Whether the people in that vehicle were out looking for them didn't matter anymore. Shea and Neda had to face the mix of circumstances that had brought them together—and they needed to get the hell out of there.

They continued to hold on to each other after the vehicle had gone.

Their streams of breath slowed and they finally turned to face one another in the darkness. They didn't have to verbally acknowledge the feeling between them; they both just knew.

They could have, had the scenario been different, ripped each other's clothes off and made mad, passionate love on the ground. And they each, for the briefest of moments, thought of that and how good it might feel to escape, at least momentarily, to a place where it was warm and safe.

But that was not the hard reality. Pleasure wasn't in the cards for them at that moment. They needed to move and get somewhere that was truly safe, somewhere where they could figure out a way to get out of the country. Whether Shea knew it—or liked it—or not, Neda was going with him.

His internal monologue and usual self-editing was off. He was open, blank, looking at nothing in particular, but feeling every bit of her closeness.

They stood up together and looked out at the plains below. The area comprised a small group of hills that were several hundred feet tall and as much wide. Lights from the villages below shone sporadically as the area wasn't very populated. The lights that they could see were therefore scattered like stars.

Slowly, from the empty space of paranoid existence that occupied both their minds, they colored in the world and began to shape it. Their thoughts returned to the present. Shea and Neda took their arms from around one another and said at the same time, "Now what?"

29

SHEA SPOKE FIRST. "WE HAVE TO FIND SOMEWHERE SAFE TO SPEND the night. It's too risky out here. And I have to get back to Turkey ASAP. If what you said is true about Talib thinking he is the— What did you call it again?"

"The Mahdi," Neda reminded.

"Yes, the Mahdi, some guy who appears at the end of the world, then I have a pretty good idea of why he was meeting with my uncle and a Chechen commander."

"Wait, now I don't understand. There was a meeting with your uncle?"

"Yes. That is why I went to Urmia. It's a long story. Right now we need to find someplace safe."

Neda thought for a moment. "I know of a place. It isn't too far from here. If we can get to him, he can help us, I am sure."

"Him?"

"Yes, a friend. He can be trusted."

"How far away is he?"

"The way you ride, not far. And we can take the side roads. It will be safer."

Shea eagerly accepted Neda's offer, not so much because it provided safety for him, but because it provided safety for her. He could not at the moment—in good conscience, anyway—dump her, and get the hell out of Dodge. He loved that saying. It was something he and Munjed used to say often when things got unhinged and were unsafe. Munjed. He'd miss his friend dearly. Perhaps he could avenge his death and at the same time avenge the long list of sins his uncle had committed, as well as the one sin in which he felt complicit, which haunted him every night and every day.

Twenty-nine people dead.

He wished he had a videotape of the secret meeting he had stumbled upon. The only evidence he had of the meeting were the photographs he had taken. And those were still inside his camera, which he had left behind inside the Mercedes.

He'd have to find another way to track his uncle down, or better yet, flush him out with the information he had. Knowledge of the meeting was his asset. That was his ammunition. And he planned to use it.

SHEA WALKED OVER TO THE MOTORCYCLE AND RIGHTED IT. "WHAT are we waiting for?" he asked Neda, who was standing still. "Let's go."

"Not so fast," she said, turning from him.

"What's the matter?" Shea asked.

Neda was standing with her back to the valley below. The sun had fully set and she was but a shadow before him.

"My friend," Neda said. "He is unusual . . . you should know."

"I am used to the unusual. I mean, I've gotten used to you."

He smiled. Wisecracking was in his genes. Just like the drink.

Neda ignored his remark at her expense. "My friend is a Zoroastrian," she said, turning back around to face him. "And a dervish. Just so you are aware."

"A dervish?"

"It's not as you think. He is not a whirling dervish. A dervish can be a wise person, a religious person."

"As long as he isn't wearing a fez and balloon pants . . ." Shea said.

"Actually—"

"Never mind. I get it. I don't care, and we don't have much time or many choices right now. Why are you telling me this?"

"Gaspar. That is his name. He is an archaeologist. These hills, you know, are sacred. They were once fire temples. That is why they rise high out of the ground. It is not natural. These are the ashes of the temple fires. Zoroaster, the great prophet, was born here. That is why this is considered the center of Zoroastrianism. Ancient Persians believed that they were the bearers of the torch of Zoroastrian heritage. They held many rituals here. King Solomon's prison is nearby. It's where he supposedly kept monsters hidden. And his mother, Bathsheba's throne is located in these hills. Gaspar, he studies these things. That is why he is here."

"And he is a revolutionary on the side?"

"We are all revolutionaries on the side, no? Mister . . . I am sorry, I don't even know your name."

"Shea, Michael Shea."

"I am Neda Ghazali."

"You told me already, but nice to meet you, Neda. So if the religious tour is over, can we go?"

"Yes." She looked hard into his eyes. "I see that I can trust you." She smiled. "No matter what you learn, Michael. No matter what you discover about us, you must never betray our trust."

Shea nodded, not quite comprehending but wanting to get a move on.

31

Neda turned away from Shea again and took one last look out toward the lake and spoke softly to it, chanting, *"athā ahu vairyo athā ratush ashāt chit hachā, vangheush dazdā manangho shyaothana-nām angheush Mazdāi, khshathremchā ahurāi â yim dregubyo dadat vāstārem."*

She hopped onto the bike and wrapped her arms around him from behind. She put her lips to his ear. "There are many more things that need to be explained to you, Michael Shea. I ask only that you open your mind as easily as you opened your heart to me."

She knows how I feel. How? Does she feel it, too?

"Come," she said, tapping his chest, "we haven't time to waste."

Shea didn't want to waste time discussing strange things and feelings with this woman. Instead, he merely asked, "Where am I going?"

"Down the hill, Michael. Down the hill."

He started the engine and began to think of why Talib was visiting Lake Urmia and meeting with his uncle here when they could have met anywhere in Iran.

He looked over at the lake. It was massive, the largest lake in Iran. And then he remembered that it took a whole lot of water to build anything nuclear.

32

THERE WAS A TIME WHEN SHEA AND HIS UNCLE HAD GOTTEN ALONG.
That was when Shea was just a boy and before he knew what type of
man his uncle had become. Even when Shea was a teenager and knew
that his uncle was a violent criminal of the worst sort, he and his uncle
left each other alone. They lived separate and distant lives, never speaking to or seeing each other. Then came the bombing at Omagh and all
that ensued.

Everything changed.

Shea couldn't bear that his uncle was let loose on the world, not after
what he had witnessed up close and personal at Omagh. And certainly
not after Shea himself was implicated and used in the plot. That's
when the epic battle between them had begun. In the typical tradition
of the Irish, the drama unfolded with a mix of curses, blame, violence,
and revenge. The battle between them had become, in the true sense
of the word, a saga. And it all went back to the bombing of Omagh.

On August 15, 1998, just after Shea had graduated from Queens
University and begun working as a producer at British News in Belfast, twenty-nine people, fourteen of whom were women, one of whom
was pregnant with twins, were killed in the Omagh blast. More than
three hundred were injured. "An appalling act of savagery and evil,"
Tony Blair had described it as. And Gerry Adams and Martin Mc-
Guinness, Sinn Fein's political leaders, had agreed. The Real Irish
Republican Army had taken credit for the horror. Sean O'Shaughnessy
was its leader.

O'Shaughnessy and his men had placed five hundred pounds of explosives in a car and parked it on a street in Omagh that tended to be very crowded with pedestrians. A phony warning named another spot nearby. That call had come from Michael Shea.

33

SHEA HAD BEEN DRIVING PAST HIS UNCLE'S HOUSE DEEP IN THE Catholic section of Belfast when he had seen a group of men coming out the door. Although he hadn't seen or spoken to his uncle in years, he knew who these men were: RIRA terrorists. He had grown up with these type of men coming and going from the house.

Now that he was older and was in a position to do something about his uncle's shenanigans, he had decided to take action. He stopped and went inside.

Sean O'Shaughnessy was sitting in his usual place at the kitchen table and didn't look particularly surprised to see his nephew enter the room. "Best be off" was all O'Shaughnessy had said, not even looking up. But O'Shaughnessy knew and Shea himself knew that leaving wasn't an option. Not at that point.

O'Shaughnessy rose from the table to show his nephew out the door, but Shea wouldn't budge. "Not until you tell me what this is all about," he had demanded. That's when his uncle hit him—hard. He nailed Shea in the gut and knocked the wind out of him. "Told yah, Mikey," he had said, "never go askin' . . ." Then he walked away, out of the room.

As Shea was bent over the table trying to catch his breath he heard his uncle say something to one of the other RIRA men in the house.

The only word he heard clearly was "courthouse." Then he spotted a piece of paper on the kitchen chair where his uncle had been sitting. On it were written two words: "Omagh" and "Main Street."

Shea beat it out the back door, hopped the fence, and cut through the yard to the street. He caught a bus back to British News headquarters. There, he told his editor about Omagh, the courthouse, and the suspicions he had about his uncle. But without anything more, any proof, they couldn't run a story. That's when Shea called the Royal Ulster Constabulary, the local police. This would be the dreaded call that would send people to their deaths.

Other rumors of a bomb threat in Omagh had come in, and the police began scrambling teams to move people away from the suspected bomb site. Ulster Television was dispatching reporters there, too.

Shea drove to Omagh. He was standing at the police barricades when he saw one of his uncle's men get out of a car nearby. Shea gave chase . . . but it was too late; the car exploded. Shea's information had led the police to direct people right to where the bomb was—instead of away from it. The police had him arrested. His uncle had used him.

Eventually Shea was cleared of all charges, and Sean O'Shaughnessy was the only man convicted of involvement in the plot. But he was let go on appeal. There simply wasn't enough evidence to hold him.

After that, O'Shaughnessy had disappeared and his nephew's hunt for him had begun..

34

She said, "I'm in love with a woman." Next came her familiar scornful smile. Then, "I'm leaving you."

As a foreign correspondent, Shea moved around a lot. Sure he was based in Tel Aviv, but he was usually on assignment in some remote and dangerous place on the planet. "It shouldn't be a surprise, you're never home," his wife at the time said when she shut the door for the last time on her way out.

Relationships had never come easy to Shea. He chalked it up to having lost his parents when he was just three years old. And a relationship at this point in his life would have been futile. He was committed to just one thing: finding his uncle Sean.

After Omagh, Shea had tracked his uncle to Peru on information that he was working with the Shining Path terrorist group. By the time Shea got to Lima, however, it was too late: a car bomb had exploded outside the U.S. embassy just before a visit by U.S. President George W. Bush. Nine people were killed and thirty were injured.

He next tracked him to Africa, where his uncle was rumored to be working with the Mai Mai groups in the Democratic Republic of Congo near the Rwandan border. Again he just missed him, and ended up in the aftermath of a genocide campaign that had taken the lives of thousands.

The closest he had come to finding O'Shaughnessy was on the West Bank in Palestine. Shea had traced his uncle to a refugee camp run by Hamas just outside Bethlehem. He made his way there, avoiding the

Palestinian spotters on rooftops and donning a *keffiyeh* as a disguise. This was his turf, his terrain. Shea knew the West Bank well. His uncle had erred. His location had been found.

Munjed drove Shea to the camp's entrance. Stones bounced against their car as a warning signal: stop or get shot. Shea looked up at the rooftops. On each corner a thin tube extended into the air. He blinked several times to clear his vision. The barrels of rifles were pointed down on them. They were surrounded.

Munjed rolled down his window and shouted in Arabic. *"Brothers,"* he said in a native tongue that was understood, especially the dialect. *"It is me, Munjed."*

Shea looked up and saw that the barrels receded. He got out of the Mercedes and ran in to the camp. It was a solo mission. Munjed wouldn't—couldn't—go. It was personal, even if it was business.

Shea ran past the graffiti. He ran past the market and the looks and the stares and the high-pitched warning sounds that rolled off old women's tongues. He knew where his uncle was. His source was positive.

On the far side of the hill on which he had just run up, Shea saw a blur and a car peeled off. He didn't see the man, he felt him. He went into the compound where his uncle was supposed to be, but he knew O'Shaughnessy wasn't there any longer. When he reappeared outside, an Uzi met him.

35

A COMPANY OF ISRAELI SOLDIERS HAD SEEN SHEA ENTER THE PALES-
tinian refugee camp and followed him in. "Are you crazy?" they asked,
when they had finally tracked him down. "You could have gotten yourself killed."

It was a question and a warning Shea had gotten used to over the
years. He wondered, sometimes, whether he was actually trying to get
himself killed—to rid himself of the pain and the guilt of Omagh. He
was responsible for all those deaths, in his own mind anyway. One way
or another Omagh would have to be redeemed. And it would have to be
his blood or his uncle's that would become the redemption.

When rocket attacks and suicide bombs rocked Jerusalem and Tel
Aviv that same day, the Israeli border was shut. Shea was stuck on the
wrong side, and he heard from a source that his uncle had just gotten
out . . . and away.

That was the last lead Shea had on his uncle until he received the call
in London linking O'Shaughnessy to a Chechen rebel group. The lead
had brought him here, to Iran, and he wasn't going to let his uncle slip
away this time.

Shea was now the only one in the world who knew that his uncle was
in cahoots with the Chechens and Mahmoud Talib—and that the
threat of global nuclear war had just been ratcheted up several notches.

Shea would have to impart what he knew as best he could to his
editors back in London. He hoped Neda's friend, or whatever he was to
her, had Internet service or at least a mobile phone he could use to call

the London office. All his communication equipment, including his sat phone, mobile phone, and laptop, was back in the Mercedes. He'd have to report Munjed's death also, he knew, but personally—to Munjed's family. Himself.

Munjed. He got too close. I got too close. Too bloody close.

Sadness began to overtake Shea. He repressed these thoughts. He'd have to keep the past where it belonged. He would have to focus on the present—and survival.

Shea shifted into fourth gear and revved the engine when the bike hit the plateau of the Iranian plains.

Neda's arm stretched past his head and pointed due west. He accelerated knowing that every second counted in the race to find his uncle and what he was up to.

I am become death, the destroyer of worlds.

The quote from physicist Robert Oppenheimer, who created the world's first atomic bomb, entered Shea's mind as he nodded, acknowledging Neda's signal. Oppenheimer had been quoting a Hindu god, Shiva.

Shea couldn't let his uncle become death anymore.

PRESIDENT TALIB WAITED FOR THE ECHO OF THE DOOR SHUT BY O'Shaughnessy to quiet before placing the call to Qom, the holy city just ninety minutes outside Tehran. It was in Qom where the Haghani school resided and where its founder, Ayatollah Mesbah Yavari, lived.

Mesbah Yavari had created the school to be a sort of Islamic academy.

Young and old scholars mixed, sharing ideas, debating different parts of the Koran, and seeking out new meanings from the *hadith* narrations originating from the words and deeds of Muhammad.

Shia and Sunni Muslims had different sets of *hadith* collections, and Mesbah Yavari wanted to have his come out on top, with his interpretations being considered the most elegant.

The school was strict. It imposed a dress code for students and teachers alike. All wore black crochet *taqiyah*, or prayer caps, as well as black tunics stretching down below their knees. Black pants and black slippers were also mandatory. At first glance the academy members looked as if they belonged to a martial arts school. Mesbah Yavari had that in mind when he created the place. He believed in the connection between mind, body, and spirit and enlisted everyone, students and teachers, in a very difficult physical regime daily. That is, for all but one student in the school's history. This student was weak and couldn't keep up with the others. He didn't have the energy to complete even the most modest of exercises never mind the full contact fights many students engaged in. In fact, this student was set to be expelled from the academy—until Mesbah Yavari had sat down and spoken with the boy. That was more than forty years ago.

It was then that he saw the signs of the Mahdi, maybe wanted to see signs of the Mahdi in the boy. Especially after the student told Mesbah Yavari his name and his family's lineage. That plus the fact that the student's physical features matched the description of the Mahdi in the *hadiths* reported by Imam Abu Dawud in the later part of the first century.

Mesbah Yavari took to personally tutoring the boy. He wanted to raise him in perfect accordance with the prophecy. The boy, of course, was Mahmoud Talib, and the time for the prophecy to be realized had come.

37

Mesbah Yavari was without doubt President Mahmoud Talib's ideological mentor and spiritual guide, if not a father figure. The Ayatollah not only taught Talib Islamic philosophy and shaped his radical views of the West, he coached Talib on his speeches and public comments. To that end, he was the power behind the scenes within the Iranian government.

Mesbah Yavari was also quite vocal about his personal views. It was Mesbah Yavari who had, for instance, called for a *fatwa* on a famous author. And it was Mesbah Yavari who advocated suicide bombings and the killing of any person who insulted Islam. He believed Zionists were the fundamental source of evil on Earth and those in the West were followers of the damned Satan. He made these pronouncements publicly, sometimes even issuing press releases.

Quietly, however, Mesbah Yavari was engaged in another mission. He had dedicated an entire department at the Haghani seminary to the study of the imminent coming of the Mahdi. His students researched the Koran and the books of *hadith*, of which there were hundreds, to interpret text, fashioning it to suit the Ayatollah's timeline and his secret plan to announce to the world his find, that Mahmoud Talib was, in fact, the redeemer of Islam, the one who would rid the world of injustice, tyranny, and wrongdoing before the Day of Judgment.

Even though the *hadith* predicted the Mahdi wouldn't arrive on Earth for another century, Mesbah Yavari believed that he had found ways to speed the Mahdi's coming, and with the theological seminary, with its highly regarded Islamic scholars available to back up and support his subjective findings, he knew that he could enlist all of Shia Islam to join in his cause—especially when he announced who the Mahdi was. And especially since the Mahdi would be a familiar and popular figure to the hard-line, right-wing community.

Sunni Muslims didn't believe in the Mahdi. Their own *hadith* interpretations made no mention of an Islamic savior who would rule the world, rid it of infidels, and become the judge to heaven as the Shia's books did. Mesbah Yavari would have to find some other way to convince the Sunnis that the Mahdi indeed was the real savior. And if he could enlist the rest of the Muslim world this way, a new day would dawn.

THE AYATOLLAH ANSWERED HIS PHONE ON THE FIRST RING. TALIB didn't need to identify himself or greet Mesbah Yavari in any way. They knew the sound of each other's voices well.

"The time has come," Talib said.

Mesbah Yavari's voice was usually gruff and low. His answer to this news, however, lifted it up an octave. "It is Allah's will," he said. He took a deep breath that Talib could hear even through the static on the line. "Are you sure, Mahmoud?"

"Yes, Ayatollah. The pieces are in place. All is as planned."

"It must be next week."

"And so it shall be. *Inshallah.*"

"Not *inshallah*—God willing. It *is* God's will. As it was written fourteen hundred years ago. We have the proof. The book makes it so. You will make it so . . . Imam Mahdi."

Talib smiled at the sound of that title administered to him by the cleric he held in such high esteem. "I have you to thank," he said.

"You have Allah," Mesbah Yavari said. "You are the chosen one."

"But it was you who found me and showed me the light. You led me on the path."

"It was always in you."

When Talib was a boy about to be expelled from school, he told Mesbah Yavari that his family was from the line of Fatima, that he was an only child, and that he was orphaned, and had been born in an even-numbered year. Talib had said that the only thing in the world that he wanted to do was good. The broad forehead and natural mascaralike rings around his eyes were also characteristics that Mesbah Yavari noticed about Talib and which the Mahdi was said to exhibit as well.

Talib paused after making his pronouncement to the Ayatollah and thought back on how far he and Mesbah Yavari had come in their plan to name him as the chosen one. He then turned the conversation from flattery to business.

"I have located the book, the original texts, as you had predicted," Talib said.

"They were in the place as I said? Solomon's prison?" the Ayatollah asked.

"Yes. They are being examined as we speak. I should have them tonight."

"Bring them to me."

"Of course, Ayatollah."

Mesbah Yavari knew that before he could convene the Assembly of Experts, the body that elects the Supreme Leader in Iran, and get their approval to have Talib named the chosen one, he would have to produce the part of the secret Zoroastrian scroll known as the Avesta that named and described the Mahdi.

39

ZOROASTRIANISM WAS THE FORCE BEHIND THE POLITICAL POWER OF the pre-Islamic Iranian dynasties, and Mesbah Yavari wanted to call upon its prestige and power to secure the backing of the Assembly. The secret scroll would also be the evidence he could use to convince the Sunni Muslim population of the Mahdi's existence. To be sure, in public, imams condemned the Zoroastrian religion, but in private they had used its texts to inform their own sacred Islamic texts.

Zoroastrianism was the primary religion in Iran before the Arab conquest of Persia more than a thousand years ago. Then, forced conversions and harassments divided and forced out much of the religious population to India, among other places throughout the world. Still, many Zoroastrians simply pretended to convert to Islam, while others began to adopt the mystical aspects of Zoroastrianism into the Muslim faith. These mystic branches sprouted into Sufism and other more esoteric practices. In fact, a select number of Zoroastrians helped the imams interpret Islamic text. Historical dates, places, and references were well documented in the Zoroastrian canon. Using these as a guide, imams were better able to explicate the Koran and put it into context for their Muslim adherents.

This group of Zoroastrian interpreters had its own secret agenda, however. They were the original "people of the book" as anointed spiritual guides. The Koran itself even recognized these "people of the book" and recused them from discrimination. Tolerance and autonomy, the Koran said, were to be given to Zoroastrians. The Koran also recused

Christianity and Judaism in the same manner. *"Do not dispute with the followers of the Book,"* the Koran said. It cryptically goes on to say, *"We believe in that which has been revealed to us and revealed to you, and our God and your God is One, and to Him do we submit."*

Few knew of this. And most people assumed that Islam was "anti-Western" and that it also held the same views against Christians and Jews. Not so. The original "people of the book," the Zoroastrians, knew why. They knew what the Koran meant when it said to "believe in that which had been revealed." There was a purpose for them all, all religions *"of the book."* Each would play a role in the Apocalypse. It was written, and they were the first to write it . . . in the texts that comprised the *Zand-i Vohuman Yasht.*

WHEN TALIB HAD HEARD THAT AN ADDITIONAL ZOROASTRIAN TEXT had been uncovered by an archaeological team near Lake Urmia, he called Mesbah Yavari. The text was a compendium scroll to the *Zand-i Vohuman Yasht*, and it provided new dates when the Mahdi would be recognized. One for the current year, the year Talib ruled. The other was some thirty years away.

It was all that Talib and Mesbah Yavari could do to wait and see the scroll for themselves. In fact, it had driven Talib almost to the point of madness knowing that the texts existed and could lay claim to him becoming what amounted to be the ruler of the world. But it had taken him months to get to Lake Urmia. Riots had broken out throughout Iran on claims that his election as president was rigged. He was forced to remain in Tehran at the presidential palace for fear of being assassinated and to prevent what he believed to be a coup mounted and funded by Western powers.

Others had also heard that certain missing pieces of the *Zand-i Vohuman Yasht* had recently been found in the temples surrounding Lake Urmia. But all those people along with the archaeologists who had first discovered the scroll had been killed by the SAVAMA.

"I am in Urmia now," Talib informed Mesbah Yazdi. "Tonight the Book shall be ours. I have the text from the *Zand-i Vohuman Yasht.*"

"Then you shall come home?"

"Then I shall come home."

"*Mibinamet.*"

"*Mibinamet.*"

Talib put down the handset and looked up at the clock. He wondered if Zhubin had killed the Irishman yet. The journalist was the only thing standing in his way of becoming what he believed he truly was: a god.

As it was written. In the Book.

41

ZHUBIN, TALIB'S SPECIAL SAVAMA AGENT AND PERSONAL ASSASSIN, combed the road leading from the small lake village toward the hills. He had lost sight of the motorcycle in the dust and cursed himself for it. Zhubin always completed his missions. Telling the president that he had failed was not an option.

He pulled over to the side of the road and watched as a flare burst from the ground into the night sky. These were common in the area.

Natural gas wells were scattered throughout the region. In ancient times, Zhubin knew villagers took these flares as a sign from the gods. They had concocted many stories about them, too. Many of the gas wells were even converted into temples. Crazy, he thought, those rituals. Never once had he questioned his own faith in Allah or even some of its more perverse teachings; he was a devout Muslim.

Zhubin's mobile telephone had a strange ring tone: it was Madonna's "Like a Virgin." He liked it because when he killed, he believed that he was doing it in the name of Allah and that he would one day be rewarded . . . with seventy-two virgins.

He didn't expect to be listening to Madonna so quickly however. He had left the president not more than an hour ago. Could he already be expected to have completed his mission? Zhubin answered just as Madonna began to sing. It wasn't the president on the line, though, it was Arman, another SAVAMA agent.

Arman informed Zhubin that he and the others agents had completed a sweep of the village. No one had seen the Irishman. But there was something strange: a woman, Neda Ghazali, had gone missing.

"Repeat what you just said," Zhubin ordered. Arman did as he was commanded. "And you are sure that was her name?"

Arman was a new SAVAMA agent and Zhubin didn't trust the rookie's information.

"Yes, I am positive," Arman said, slightly defensively. He may not have been a SAVAMA agent for long, but he could get a name straight. "Why?" he asked the legendary Zhubin. All the agents feared Zhubin. They had heard of his methods. They also knew that he was the president's personal assassin and had the freedom to kill whom he wanted whenever he wanted, without consequence.

"I know this woman," Zhubin barked. "She is on our wanted list. You should have known that. We have been after her for some time. Who named her?"

Arman's face turned beet red and he swallowed hard. He was

nervous that he had screwed up. "Her in-laws. They said she was responsible for their son's death. They were going to turn her in to us . . . after the required mourning, of course."

"Of course," Zhubin said, sarcastically. "Do they know anything more?"

"I don't think so," Arman said, knowing at once that he should have been more declarative. "I mean, no, I questioned them at length and that is not my assessment."

Zhubin smiled. He knew the young agent was shaking in his boots. "What about the Irishman. Did they know about him?"

"No, definitely not," Arman said, this time confidently.

"Ask them if Neda has any friends or relatives in the area."

"I did," Arman said with a degree of pride. "They said she is friendly with a man from the town of Shiz, an archaeologist."

Zhubin smiled again. He had her, and if his gut instinct was right the Irishman would be with her.

"Thank you. You have done well. Now kill them and come meet me in Shiz."

"Yes, sir," Arman said. It would be his first assassination. If he were a good agent, it wouldn't be his last.

ZHUBIN TOOK OFF HIS SUIT COAT AND HUNG IT NEATLY FROM THE hook above the backseat in the SUV he was driving. He checked his leather holster, loosened it, and then lifted up the backseat itself. The cache of arms hidden there would have suited a company of men. An

AK-47, or what the Iranians call a Kalesh; a G3 assault rifle with gre-
nade launcher; handguns of every sort; an RPG; and a special container
of plastic explosives.

Zhubin took off his sunglasses, which were custom designed and featured special night vision, and tossed them in with the guns. He wouldn't
need to mask the direction of his eyes for anyone. He only used the
glasses when he was in close proximity with the president. That was the
only time he really needed to look at people without them knowing that
he was staring.

After making himself more comfortable for the hour-long drive to
Shiz, he called Talib.

"Have you taken care of him?" Talib asked excitedly.

"Not yet. I am on my way to him now. He is with a woman, I believe,
a familiar name to us: Neda Ghazali."

The blood drained from the president's face.

"How did they come to meet?" Talib asked.

"I don't know how they know each other," Zhubin said. "That is why
I am going to Shiz to find out."

"Shiz!" Talib jumped out of his chair. "Why Shiz!"

"That is where I am told she has a friend. It is the logical place she
would hide for safety. And if she is there, the Irishman will be there, too.
Whatever it is they are up to, I will put a stop to it."

Talib was apoplectic. "You must take care of them, Zhubin. There is
a lot at stake. And when you have located them I want you to call me.
There is something else there I need you to take care of."

"*Inshallah.*"

"No," Talib said, imitating Mesbah Yavari's chastisement of "God
willing." "Make it happen," he said.

Talib hung up and paced the marble floor of the domed building.
What were the chances that the Irishman and Neda were friendly.
And what were the chances that they would be headed to Shiz, where
the secret Zoroastrian scroll was at the moment.

That archaeologist had better have the scroll someplace safe, he thought. Then he thought even better of it. He needed to make sure. Talib called the archaeologist. He told him to secure the text and that Zhubin was on his way to pick it up.

43

ZHUBIN STARTED THE ENGINE AND ENTERED THE LOCATION "SHIZ" in the GPS. He had driven these parts many times in the past. Many of those resistant to the president, those known as "reformers," lived in these parts. Many of the residents here didn't consider themselves Iranians as much as Azerbaijanis. It was a tribal culture. Hence, many of the Azerbaijanis didn't consider Talib their true ruler. They only adhered to local elders. Still, Talib needed their votes in the election. That was part of Zhubin's job, too—rounding up votes for the president. He handed out cash to these village elders, and when that didn't work, he let them know what fate could befall their entire community: he killed someone brutally before their eyes to get the message across.

The worst thing he ever did was pluck a teenage girl from a village and rape her before the elders. He held his Kalesh on them the whole time and forced them to watch. Then he stopped, put the machine-gun barrel into the girl's other orifice, her mouth, and pulled the trigger. Presto! Several hundred votes for President Talib.

That village wasn't more than a mile from the road he was driving on now. Zhubin reflected on that and shrugged. It was his job, he told himself. It was for the higher cause.

He turned on the radio in his black SUV and whaddya know: Madonna's "Like a Virgin" was playing. He turned up the volume and drove as fast at the SUV would take him into the night.

44

THE MOON SHONE OFF THE SMALL POND THAT LAY BEFORE THE conical mound known as Solomon's prison. Next to it a patch of building structures could be made out through the oblique light.

"That is Nosrat Abad," Neda told Shea as they dismounted the motorcycle and turned off its engine. "It's the village where Gaspar lives."

"This friend of yours, Gaspar, are you sure that he is okay? It's one thing for him to take you in, but it's another for him to take me in. I'm a Westerner, remember, and I'm not exactly a welcome one. He'd be putting his life on the line by helping me. You could always just go and I—"

"No!" Neda said, cutting Shea off. "We are in this together now. You saved my life."

"And you saved mine."

"We're even then."

They shook hands, but the electricity was too much for them to ignore this time. Shea's internal monologue was screaming, *No!* Alarm bells, warning lights, and all sorts of mental dissuasions ran through his brain. None worked. They were trumped.

I want this. I want her. I need her.

He didn't let go of her hand. Shea pulled Neda closer, and she didn't resist. She looked up at him. Her eyes batted. A flush came into her cheeks and they sealed their agreement with a kiss. At first it was a light lip smack. Neither could pull away after that, however. The second kiss was longer and they opened their mouths to let each other know just how much they wanted one another. It took all their strength to stop.

A final warning shot inside his head made Shea pull away.

Don't get close. She'll die, too. If you like her, if you love her, you'll leave her behind.

"We have to get safe," Shea said, breathing in the silent lust between them.

"I feel safe now," Neda said, hugging him and turning toward the village.

They were standing on the ledge of a mountain pass looking out onto the valley where the temple site was.

"We'll wake the entire village if we ride this," Shea said, kicking the bike and using that as an excuse to step away from her.

"We can leave it here. Gaspar has a car. He is the one who drove us to Tehran for the election demonstrations," Neda said.

It was getting cold as the night began to set in to its deepest hours. Neither was dressed for the weather. Shea was wearing jeans, boots, and a light flannel jacket. Neda was still wearing her long black dress.

Their bodies were numb from the ride. They began to walk down the hill toward the village in the distance.

45

WALKING BEGAN TO WARM THEM, AND THEY HEADED TOWARD THE
sparkle of lights ahead. Thankfully, the moon was almost full and they
could make out a path with the help of its light. Others clearly had used
the path in the village to get to and from the mountain pass because it
was well worn and well marked. They met the outer wall of the village. It
rounded in a semicircle past which was a pond. It stunk.

"Is this the village sewer?" Shea asked. "And if it is, what are these
people eating?"

"It's sulfur," Neda explained. "From all the gas wells beneath."

"Remind me not to drink the water."

"Once you smell it, you won't need any reminding. Even the streams
around here run yellow."

Ahead was a small section of trees that stood between them and the
village itself. Here and there stood structures that looked like Stone-
henge, and Shea asked about those, too. Neda told Shea that the entire area of Shiz was known locally as Takht-e Soleyman. "It means the
shrine of Solomon," she said. "The volcano is over there"—she pointed
at the conical mound just past the village—"and is called Solomon's
prison, the place I told you about before. Next to it is the tomb of King
Cyrus, known as Cyrus the Great. Inside it is a cylinder that was used to
produce tablets on which were written the law of Cyrus. They describe
how Cyrus liberated ancient Babylon. They are very sacred."

"Cyrus was the founder of the Persian Empire, right?" Shea asked.

"Yes, he was the first Zoroastrian emperor."

"See, I'm not so stupid."

"No, Michael, you are not," Neda said. "But, then again, we just met."

Neda stepped into the patch of trees and Shea followed her, choking back a laugh.

Midway through the wooded area, Shea heard it: an engine. The valley was dead quiet so any noise at all was noticeable.

They picked up their pace and made it to the edge of the trees. An open patch of land stood between them and the village gate. Shea stepped out into the opening and looked for the source of the engine's noise. Then he saw it: two headlights approaching the village from the mountain pass. The vehicle was far enough away so Shea couldn't be seen, but that wouldn't last long. They'd have to run now, and fast, before the headlights stood the chance of catching them.

It didn't matter to Shea who was driving the approaching vehicle. He couldn't risk being seen by anyone. And at this time of night, nine o'clock, anyone seen out and about would raise suspicion.

Shea signaled to Neda. She joined him out in the open area. "We're going to have to run," he said. "Look." He pointed to the headlights. "It's a couple of hundred yards from here to the gate," Shea continued. "If we move it we can get there before we are seen."

Neda nodded.

"Is this guy's house far from the gate?" Shea asked.

"We're not going to his house. He'll be at the temple working. That is where he always is. It's just inside that gate," Neda said.

"Let's move." Before the words had even left Shea's mouth, Neda was sprinting past him.

46

ZHUBIN SAW THE VILLAGE IN THE DISTANCE AS HE MADE THE FINAL turn on the mountain pass. From there it would be all dust and dirt as the road's surface changed. It wasn't the way he liked to roll up to a place—announcing his arrival with every sound. But he had no choice. He needed to get to the village quickly. He couldn't afford to lose the trail of Shea and Neda again.

As he turned on to the dirt road, Zhubin turned off his radio. He took his *tasbih*, prayer beads, from the rearview mirror on which they had been hung and began reciting, *"yatha ahu vairyo . . ."*

Zhubin understood that this was ancient and holy ground. And while he wasn't afraid of evil spirits or anything that reeked of superstition, he figured a quick prayer to his God would remind Allah whose side he was on. Besides, it was all the backup he had at the moment.

47

Inside the stone gate, Shea and Neda hugged close to the cobblestone that was to their left. Another wall stood directly in front of them and the L-shaped configuration of the entranceway gave them cover. It also blocked any light and allowed them to stand unseen in the shadows—which was a good thing.

Two elderly men dressed in the traditional garb—wide trousers and gold embroidered caps—strolled by. They were speaking softly and walking at a slow pace.

Shea listened for the sound of the approaching vehicle. It was getting closer. He needed for these two old men to move faster. But there was little he could do about that. He had to stay put. He listened to the sound of the gravel being torn up by the vehicle's tires. Neda heard the sound of the engine, too, and she grabbed Shea's hand and seized it.

Shea thought of springing out from the dark and taking out the two old men. He could have knocked them both out in two moves.

What were we taught in Krav Maga training? Never telegraph your moves. Never announce your intent. Just do it. Strike. Use everything to your advantage. There is only one goal. There is only one aim depending on the circumstance: Disarm. Disable. Or . . . Destroy.

Neda must have sensed what Shea was thinking and she held his hand even tighter, holding him back and preventing him from stepping into the direction of the old men.

In thirty seconds the old men were out of sight and Shea and Neda made their way along the L-shaped wall. They entered the veranda of the temple and slinked up to its massive door. It must have stood fifty feet high. Neda was about to knock on it when Shea stopped her.

The sound of tires screeching to a halt caused them both to look back at the village gate. They had little time to hide. Shea hoped the door was unlocked, and with a shoulder shove pushed it as hard as he could. It creaked open.

48

SHEA CLOSED THE DOOR BEHIND THEM BUT NOT BEFORE HE AND Neda both heard the engine they had been listening to turn off and a car door slam shut.

Inside the temple there were stone benches next to each of the four corners of the room. Other than that the room was bare. The vaulted ceiling was several feet taller than the door through which they had just come, and it looked as though gaps had purposefully been left in certain areas to let light in. Shea could see the white face of the moon.

In front of them stood a stone arch and yet another door. This one was much smaller—about six feet high—and was partially belowground. Neda went straight to it. "I've been here before," she said. "Come."

Shea followed Neda's lead and advanced down the stairs, careful not to smack his head on the stone doorway. Partly below the ground, and made from bricks nearly a foot square, there were two arched portals, after which was a vaulted brick chamber below. The walls were four or five feet thick, and inside the chamber were arched wall recesses.

At one of these recesses, standing by a burning torch, was a tubby man dressed all in white and wearing a fez cap. He stood hunched over and was concentrating on what looked like a large beehive placed on the table in front of him. He was scribbling notes on a pad. He was concentrating so fully that he hadn't noticed Shea or Neda enter the chamber.

"Gaspar," Neda whispered at the man in white. He turned quickly, startled, so much so that his fez fell off his head.

"Neda," he said. "What are you doing here?"

She stepped quickly to him and they embraced.

The man in white continued to talk. "Where have you been? I called and called. No one knew where you were." Then he noticed Shea step from the shadows.

"It's okay, Gaspar. He saved my life. This is Michael Shea, a journalist."

Shea stepped up to Gaspar and shook his hand.

"I've heard a lot about you, Mr. Shea . . . from the president of Iran. He just called to see if you were here."

They all heard the giant temple door creak open.

ZHUBIN HAD ONE FOOT IN THE DOOR OF THE TEMPLE WHEN HE heard footsteps behind him. He left the door ajar and scampered to the side of the building. He unclipped his PC9 combat pistol from its holster and unlocked the safety. He raised his arm to shoulder height and took aim. The gold embroidered hats diffused the moment, however, and Zhubin quickly discerned that the two men approaching were local villagers. Just as quickly as he had unholstered his weapon, he holstered it again.

Zhubin stepped out onto the veranda of the temple area and addressed the men.

"*Asr be kheyr!*," Zhubin said, greeting them formally.

The two men stopped and looked at each other. Just one look at Zhubin and they knew he was SAVAMA. They responded hesitantly, "*Mitoonam ke komaketoon konam?*"

"I am looking for a man," Zhubin said. "An archaeologist. Does he live near here?"

Both the men pointed in the same direction in unison. This left Zhubin with no doubt that they were telling the truth. "Please show me," he asked, although the two old men knew that it was more than a request he had put to them. They knew better than to refuse.

SHEA, NEDA, AND GASPAR STOOD SILENTLY AND LISTENED FOR FOOT-steps. There were none.

Gaspar walked to the small, stone door that led from the chamber to the temple's front room and peeked out. He saw that the door was ajar but no one was in the temple area itself. There was no room to hide within the four walls, so he was sure.

Gaspar shut the door and put his back to it. "There is no one there," he announced.

Shea had picked up a metal bar from the floor. It looked like some type of archaeological tool, sharp and pointed on one side and flat like a small shovel on the other. He held it in his right hand with his wrist cocked back and his elbow pressed tight into his body. He was ready to strike. The chamber was small and there was no other exit. Shea was prepared to fight his way out.

Use whatever you can to your advantage. There are weapons all around. Rocks. Tools. Sharp objects. They all can be used to accomplish your goal. Disarm. Disable. Destroy.

Neda stood to the side of them both, her eyes wide with expectation. She didn't want Shea to hurt her friend, but at the same time she was confused by Gaspar's revelation that he had just spoken with President Talib.

"Wait," Gaspar said, seeing the bar in Shea's hand and the look in his eye. "Please, I am on your side."

"Not if you are on speaking terms with Mahmoud Talib, you are not," Shea said, shuffling his right leg back into his fight stance.

Neda stepped between them. "Wait, let him explain," she asked Shea, and then turned to Gaspar. "Gaspar? Please tell me, tell us."

"It is why I was trying so desperately to get in touch with you, Neda. The president, he wants the texts from *Zand-i Vohuman Yasht* that your husband and I discovered. I think he wants to put it into practice . . . now!"

Neda gasped.

SHEA WAS UNMOVED BY THE JIBBLE-JABBLE BETWEEN NEDA AND GASpar. "Neda, please move out of the way. I need to get us out of here before it's too late," he said.

Neda turned to face Shea fully. She, all in black, and Gaspar, all in white standing behind her looked as if they were from another time, another age, especially in the torchlight. Shea looked on as Neda spoke.

"Michael, if what Gaspar says is true then it won't matter where we escape to. The world will end."

"Please," Gaspar said again, this time lifting his hands up in surrender. "I am trying to help, not hurt. The president doesn't yet know that."

Shea eyed Gaspar and dropped the metal bar. He actually knew that he wouldn't have needed any type of instrument to dispose of Gaspar. A quick front kick and a couple of blows to the right spots on the body—spots he was taught inflicted the most amount of pain—and Gaspar would be out of the way.

"Then could you please tell me what you just said?" Shea asked.

Neda interjected, "The *Zand-i Vohuman Yasht* is a secret Zoroastrian scroll that explains the Apocalypse. My husband had discovered it along with some other artifacts before he was killed. Only a few other people knew about his finding. Alone it doesn't mean anything. But there are other signs of the End Times. There are other connections that can be made. This could set off an avalanche of spiritual fanaticism around the world."

"All those who knew about the scroll are dead now," Gaspar said, stepping past Neda to the table at which he had been working when they entered the chamber. "I am the only one left who has seen it."

"But the president knows," Shea said, still standing in his fight stance, his right foot hip distance and at an angle to his left leg. His weight displaced mostly on the balls of his feet, ready to spring. Gaspar hadn't won his full trust just yet. "You haven't explained how and why he knows—and you had better . . . fast."

52

THE TWO OLD MEN'S BODIES WERE LEFT IN THE SHAPE OF AN X ON the ground in front of Gaspar's house. Zhubin had executed them professionally—quickly and silently. Each suffered a bullet to the back of the head. The suppressor on Zhubin's gun ensured quiet deaths.

Zhubin had searched the house thoroughly and come up empty. The search hadn't taken very long. There were only three rooms in the house and they were mostly filled with books, from floor to ceiling. Some strange-looking instruments were also scattered on the floor of each room. Otherwise, the house didn't look lived in. So beyond finding out the man's name and the understanding that Gaspar was a slob, Zhubin had no information to go on.

He was about to go door to door searching for Gaspar and eliciting, in his own imitable way, information that would lead him to the archaeologist and, hopefully in turn, the girl, when his phone rang in that familiar tone.

"Yes" was all he said. Talib quickly explained that he had just spoken with Gaspar. But the archaeologist hadn't seen the girl or the Irishman. Zhubin asked where the archaeologist was. Talib told him that Gaspar was in the temple—and that was all the information the assassin needed.

53

"SOMEONE LEAKED THE INFORMATION ABOUT THE SCROLL TO TALIB. I was in Qom visiting my brother when everyone else was assassinated," Gaspar said, looking at Neda with sorrow in his eyes. "He called me to come here and never suspected I knew about the find."

"Why would the president of Iran call you directly?" Shea asked Gaspar.

Neda answered for him. "Gaspar is a very well known archaeologist in Iran, Michael. It makes sense that the president would call him about something like an ancient scroll. But why do you think he wants to use it, Gaspar?"

"Because he wanted me to transcribe a copy . . . to make it look exactly like the original," Gaspar said.

"What for?" Neda asked.

"I have no idea," Gaspar said. "But we have little time. The president said that he wants the scroll tonight. He is sending one of his SAVAMA agents here to get it."

"He's already here," Shea said. "We heard him pull up to the gate."

"Then we must act fast," said Gaspar.

He picked up the beehive-looking item Shea had seen before. Shea now saw that it wasn't a beehive at all but a clay cylinder that had what looked like calligraphy written on the side. It was caked in layers of dried mud and dirt.

"This is the scroll. We must preserve it. We cannot let Talib get his hands on this," Gaspar said, holding the cylinder up for Shea and Neda to see.

"Why would he go through so much trouble for this? It won't make the world end. It can't help him do that. You and I both know what it says, Gaspar. He is not the one. It is not time," Neda said.

"He is closer than we thought to gaining such power. My brother told me that there are rumblings in Qom about a religious revolution. There is talk of the Mahdi appearing," Gaspar said. "If Talib can convince the Haghani Circle he is the one, he can exert his will upon the world."

"How?" Neda asked.

"That's where the nuclear bomb comes into play," said Shea.

They all heard the door creak open again. But this time, they also heard the sound of footsteps.

54

ZHUBIN STEPPED INTO THE TEMPLE AREA READY FOR ACTION. HE kept a firm grip on his PC9 as he crept on the balls of his feet past the first stone bench. The archaeologist might be expecting him but the Irishman and the woman would not—if they were here. And his gut told him that they were. He wasn't taking any chances with these two. He had heard what Shea had done with the SAVAMA agent back at Lake Urmia. That agent was in the hospital with a broken jaw.

Zhubin wasn't worried about fighting hand to hand. He was an expert in Pahlavani, an ancient Iranian form of martial art known as "the sport of the heroes." Still, all SAVAMA agents had basic training in self-defense so the Irishman must have been trained in some type of martial art, Zhubin thought, if he could defeat so easily someone from the secret service. Either that, or the Irishman had gotten lucky. And Zhubin didn't believe in luck. Fate, perhaps. But chance was something to be controlled.

He concentrated on the sliver of light coming from beneath the stone door in front of him, and headed for it. All his senses were alive. He heard a whisper. The light under the door went out. Zhubin then clicked off his gun's safety. The sound echoed.

He stepped toward the spot where there had been light but was now darkness.

THE TRUCK HAD PASSED THE NORTHERN TIP OF LAKE URMIA AND headed for the city of Khvoy. From here, a right turn could take travelers along the Silk Route to China. A left would land someone in Turkey. Due north was Russia.

It was rough terrain and the truck bounced up and down over bumps, rocks, and into holes. Khvoy may have meant "sunflower" but its environs were anything but sunny. Russian and Turkish invasions had established rubble as the most common sight to be seen. The area was mostly brown pastureland with few trees and even fewer buildings. At night, the area was "nowhere" defined.

Abramov looked out into the darkness from the passenger side of the truck he was riding in. Shortly they would be wheels up in the private jet Talib had provided. Soon he would be on his way from being a nobody in the middle of nowhere to being a somebody on top of the world.

Abramov glanced at O'Shaughnessy, who was still unconscious in the back of the truck. After he had knocked him out, Abramov had injected Shea with a sedative. The last thing he wanted was a prolonged battle with the Irishman. O'Shaughnessy had accused him of leaking information about the meeting. And that was probably true. Abramov had a big mouth and a tendency to run it a lot, especially when he was drunk, which was also a lot.

His mouth was part of the reason Abramov had never climbed high within the official ranks of the Chechen command. He was forced to splinter off and form his own rebel group. Now he would show them. He would become the Big Boss.

Abramov had justified his being ostracized from the Chechen high command by saying the command had gotten soft. They had kowtowed to the Russian government and even established formal relations with Moscow.

Still, he hadn't been invited to the party despite all he had done. Despite all the kidnappings and killings he had done at the behest of the high command. Two hundred million dollars. That is how much his kidnapping operation had fetched for the Chechen command back when they sorely needed funds. Then, when order was established after the millennium, the command all but forgot about Alu Abramov. He was to them a gangster. Never mind that he had sacrificed everything for them, and that his family had been killed by the Russians. His form of rebellion, the new Chechen commanders who formed the new Chechen government had told him, was a thing of the past.

56

ABRAMOV BEGAN A REBEL GROUP OF HIS OWN. THESE "REVOLUTION-aries," *his* revolutionaries, were thugs who'd enjoyed the kidnapping and killing of the late 1990s for the sport of it. When that dried up, they had few options. Abramov gave them one. He even gave them a new religious cause: Wahhabism.

Most Chechens and therefore most rebels were Sufi Muslims. They separated their religion from their politics. Wahhabism put the two together, melding religious orthodoxy with political fanaticism all in a march for power.

Wahhabism was a conservative sect of Islam based on the teachings of Muhammad ibn Abd al-Wahhab, an eighteenth-century scholar from Saudi Arabia. His teachings were radical and even militant.

Wahhabism had gained a sort of rebirth among orthodox Muslims, primarily in the wealthy Gulf states. And they were looking to spread its message elsewhere. Chechnya was a perfect proving ground for it. Alu Abramov the perfect liaison. He was desperate.

Wahhabism brought Abramov and his gang money and arms from the Arab states, even al-Qaida. They joined together and agreed to help change the Muslim world—Sunni style.

Sunni and Shia Muslims were always battling for control. Wahhabism gave Sunnis a leg up because it gave followers a cause: all non-adherents were evil and therefore their killings were justified. Shias had to make up other justifications for suicide bombings and the like; they typically turned to perverting the Koran's words.

Abramov had been recruited by a Sunni faction in Yemen to lead the Wahhabi cause in his home country. He had traveled to the Gulf state and been indoctrinated. It took six months. But he returned to Grozny with more money than he knew what to do with. He began to procure arms and men. That's when an Irishman named Sean O'Shaughnessy had come calling.

O'SHAUGHNESSY HELPED ABRAMOV MAKE BOMBS FOR WHAT WAS TO be a major coup in Chechnya. It never happened. Both the Russians and the Chechen high command had gotten wind of Abramov's plans and the coup was foiled. That had been just a year ago.

Abramov lost his money and his men. He had disappointed his Arab backers and they cut him off. Only two people had reached out and contacted him after the attempted coup: the bomb maker Sean O'Shaughnessy and Mahmoud Talib, the president of Iran.

Why Talib had contacted him, Abramov couldn't understand. Talib was an orthodox Shia Muslim and a Sufist to boot. Talib hated Wahhabism and the Sunnis. In fact, Talib had been waging a not so quiet war with the Sunnis within the Muslim community.

"I want to bring you back to see the truth," Talib explained to Abramov. He said he also wanted very much to help Abramov overtake the Russians. All this was too much of a good thing for the Chechen.

Of course Abramov knew there would be a catch. It was well known that Talib was seeking nuclear material. The other Chechen groups had refused to accommodate his requests. They wanted the nukes for themselves.

Abramov, however, agreed to help Talib procure what he wanted. He went back to Sufism. And if all went well he'd be sitting in the Kremlin in less than a week's time. The other Chechen commanders could kiss his boots. They'd see that he wasn't such a stupid *jiatt* after all. He'd get what they couldn't: Russia. He'd rule over them, too.

ABRAMOV HEARD SHEA GROANING IN THE BACK OF THE TRUCK. HE was waking, which was a good thing. They were approaching the tarmac. In a couple of hours they'd be back in Grozny. There they would have to agree to get along. They only had a few days to pull off their nuclear plan.

Abramov hadn't been exactly truthful with Talib. He was close to getting the nuclear material needed, but hadn't secured it yet. More important, he didn't have the material O'Shaughnessy needed to make the implosion bomb, the trigger for the nuclear blast. He needed to get O'Shaughnessy to cooperate. He began to regret punching him out.

The truck came to a halt in front of the black jet. "Wake up!" Abramov bellowed into the back of the truck. O'Shaughnessy groaned again. Abramov nodded to one of his men seated by O'Shaughnessy's side and the man began to shake O'Shaughnessy, trying to wake him.

As soon as the man touched O'Shaughnessy, Sean sprang up. He grabbed the man's arm and twisted it—then he snapped it, breaking it at the elbow. He next took hold of the man's chin and, taking a handful of hair from the back of his head for leverage, cranked the man's head violently. The man's neck broke. O'Shaughnessy reached down and took the man's pistol from its holster. He cocked it and held it to Abramov's face. The whole thing had taken less than a minute and neither Abramov nor his driver had time to react.

"Where am I?" O'Shaughnessy screamed. The death gurgle from the man at his feet ended. Abramov was aghast.

"Sean, please. I am sorry—" Abramov began.

O'Shaughnessy whipped him across the face with the pistol. "Feckin' answer me!"

"We're in Khvoy," Abramov answered.

"Why am I here?'

"I am taking you to Grozny with me."

"Fuck that. What for?"

Abramov shot a look at the driver. "Not here, Sean. I will explain everything. But in private."

O'Shaughnessy looked at the driver and then turned his pistol on him. He shot him through the ear. The driver's head fell on the steering wheel and the horn began to blast. O'Shaughnessy ignored it.

"Now we're in private. Talk," O'Shaughnessy commanded.

59

ABRAMOV LOOKED AT HIS DRIVER. HE WAS AN OLD FRIEND, A GOOD soldier. *Irish bastard*, he thought. Then he answered, "I couldn't say this in front of Talib, but we aren't as far along as planned."

"You don't have the nukes?"

Abramov was now staring at the pistol in his face. "Can you put that away?" he asked. O'Shaughnessy looked at him cross-eyed, but lowered his gun.

Abramov continued, "We had the Pu-239 stored along with the rest, but word got out—"

"Lemme guess, some other Chechens went after it."

"Yes—how did you –"

"Never mind. Where's it now?"

"My men held them off. They had to transfer the material to a new spot, however. And that is going to make transporting it even harder. They'll be on the lookout."

"Your other Chechen friends?"

"Yes. And there's something else." Abramov cleared his throat. "The material you need. It was left behind in the gunfight."

O'Shaughnessy looked down at the floor and shook his head. He was pissed.

"How am I going to build a bomb out of thin air? This ain't no feckin' fantasy. This is as real as it gets, Alu."

The horn had begun to gather attention and two of Abramov's goons started to walk over toward the truck from the jet. O'Shaughnessy pulled the driver's head off the wheel and the noise stopped. He motioned for Abramov to call off his men.

"What am I gonna do?" O'Shaughnessy asked.

"Don't you have any other sources?" Abramov queried.

O'Shaughnessy did, but there were dangers to that, dangers he wasn't ever going to let Abramov know about.

Meanwhile, what neither of them knew was that a welcoming committee was forming for them back in Grozny. Although its mission wasn't going to make them feel much welcome.

The Chechen command had found out about Abramov's nuclear theft and put a hit out on him. They wanted him dead. O'Shaughnessy would be along for much more than just a plane ride.

60

IRANIAN PRESIDENT MAHMOUD TALIB HAD HIS HELICOPTER STAND-ing by at the ready. He was waiting for Zhubin to call with news that he had (1) retrieved the Zoroastrian scroll from the archaeologist, Gaspar, and (2) he had taken care of Shea and Neda.

Talib was on edge. He drummed his fingers on the dining table and thought about the meeting he had just had with O'Shaughnessy and Abramov. A lot was riding on those two. He didn't trust either one. But each had their place, each had their role—more than they could or likely would ever know.

Talib looked around for something to occupy his time and his mind. He spotted the file on Michael Shea along with the photos on the table. The file was still placed in front of where O'Shaughnessy had been seated. Talib pushed back his chair and walked around the large table. He picked up the material and began to read.

Michael Thomas Shea. 33 Single (divorced). Male. Brown eyes. Brown hair. Occupation: television journalist. Birthplace: Belfast, UK. Father: William. Deceased. Mother: Helen. Deceased. Both killed by Blackwatch. Other living relatives: Sean O'Shaughnessy, uncle. Ex-spouse: Talia Cohen, Israeli national. Passport: UK. Iran entries: 0. Unofficial & undocumented: 3. Intelligence source briefings. Security threat: minor. Media.

Talib looked at the photos. *How could he have escaped?* He also began to wonder how in the world had Shea found Neda. He contemplated calling Zhubin and giving him different orders but decided against it. They both would have to die, no matter how he personally felt about Neda.

Neda, she was the key. Neda, she couldn't escape. It was time to put the last piece of the past to rest.

61

THE ROOKIE SAVAMA AGENT ARMAN RECOVERED FROM ALMOST driving off the mountain pass. He was close to Shiz, meeting Zhubin, as instructed.

This wasn't what he bargained for when he signed on as a secret service agent. He had grown up in a small fishing village in southern Iran. Police work was the only job he could find. And now, now he was involved in something beyond anything he could have ever imagined. Speaking with the president. Being ordered to kill in cold blood. And now who knows what? The night was still young.

Indeed, the night was very young for what it had in store for Arman.

62

THE SOUND OF GRAVEL SCRATCHING AS FEET SLIPPED ACROSS ITS surface emanated from the front hall of the temple. The sound grew fainter as it left the front door and made its way along the ancient walls of the village. Before any sound at all could reach a place where someone in the village might hear it, it was muffled sufficiently. It could be an animal burrowing, or a night bird flapping its wings against the leaves of a tree.

Shiz, the stone city, rarely let its secrets known. It held them tight within its walls, protecting the past as much as the future.

Zhubin pushed on the stone door but it didn't budge. He put his back to the door and pushed with the most powerful part of the human body: his legs. His might didn't move the door in the slightest.

In a flash, Zhubin ran out of the temple and to the other side of the building where any exit from the chamber itself might be located. There was none. There was absolutely no way for whoever was in the chamber to leave except through the temple area itself.

Zhubin had an idea. Remembering the plastique he kept stored in his backseat, he raced to the front of the temple itself. He made enough noise so that his presence was known. There was no way anyone could have escaped while he ran around the back. They'd have to be sure that he had gone. And he wasn't gone for more than two minutes.

Zhubin called Arman and asked where he was. The young agent could have simply shouted; he had just entered the village gate. Zhubin told him what to get from the SUV. It wasn't long before he was lining the crack of the stone door with C-4. If no one knew any better, they'd think he was filling in the cracks with putty. He next took what looked like basting needles and inserted them into the C-4. These were attached to wires that were in turn attached to a detonator. Zhubin flicked the switch. He and Arman turned away as the explosion rocked the temple. Boom! The door flew open.

Both Zhubin and Arman had their pistols and flashlights ready. They stepped into the dust that was blowing in from the doorway to the dark chamber. Down, up, side to side, they examined the room quickly and expertly for anything that moved. But the chamber was empty. Still, Zhubin was smart enough to know that it didn't mean no one was there.

63

AFTER THEY HEARD FOOTSTEPS IN THE TEMPLE, GASPAR DIRECTED Shea and Neda to the back of the chamber. He felt around and pressed on something that looked like a jagged stone but was really a secret door trigger.

"Through here," Gaspar whispered. Shea and Neda quickly followed him. Gaspar took the lit torch from its placeholder and then closed the door behind him. The light revealed a narrow passageway. Gaspar explained that they were in the vestibule of the temple area. If they followed the passageway straight into the next room they would find a stairwell that would take them downstairs; they could then find their way along an interior wall that had been built underground to preserve the temple. It would bring them to the temple's front entrance again.

"But that is where the SAVAMA agent is," Shea said.

"He probably won't wait there for long. He'll search for us. It's our only hope," Gaspar said.

That's when they heard the door blow open. They moved as quickly as they could. If they could get back to the village gate they had a chance to escape. "I have a car," Gaspar said. "It's not much, but we can get away."

They let Gaspar's torch guide them through the bedrock. They made it all the way to an ancient guardrail, a huge stone that served to protect passersby from falling into the open well below.

"These are natural gas wells. It's where they built fire temples. If we can make it to the floor, we can go under the temple," Gaspar explained. Then he stopped dead in his tracks. He signaled for Shea and Neda to be quiet. They strained their ears, the sense of sound more acute since their vision was partially hindered by the darkness.

The little tunnel's floor that they had just ducked through was lined with pebbles. Stepping on them made a crunching sound. And a fast series of crunches could now be heard. Someone was coming.

"Quick," Gaspar said. "Down."

He climbed over the ledge to the bottom of the well below. Neda went next, and then Shea. They all pressed up against the wall beneath the pathway above. Gaspar blew out the light. It was pitch black. The crunching stopped and a dull light illuminated the cavern. They were each careful to mind their breath and remain absolutely still. They heard the footsteps above their heads and they waited for them to pass by. But the footsteps didn't move on. The light remained. Clearly the person was standing right above them—not moving. But why? How would he (or she?) know that they had stopped and hidden below? The answer lay in the noise they heard next: crunch, crunch, crunch. More footsteps. The person above was waiting for someone else.

Gaspar felt the opening to the underground passageway and gesticulated his find to Shea and Neda. They silently entered the tunnel that led underneath the temple.

64

ZHUBIN WAITED FOR ARMAN TO CATCH UP TO HIM IN THE TUNNEL. He peeked over the giant stone that acted as a guardrail and looked down at the well below. It was too dark to see anything. He pressed against the stone to lean over farther—and it moved.

Just as Arman was entering the area where Zhubin was, he saw the stone fall from the ledge, Zhubin after it.

The rock crashed against the floor of the well and shook the whole temple. That wasn't what caught everyone's attention, however; it was Neda's scream.

When the stone had fallen, it caused other stones in the underground tunnel to cave in. The rocks blocked the entrance to the well. For all Neda, Shea, and Gaspar knew, they had been buried alive.

"Zhubin?" Arman shouted. "Are you all right?"

"Yes," Zhubin said from below. "Did you hear that scream?"

"Yes, it came from down there."

Zhubin flashed his light onto the wall. He could make out the small opening to the underground tunnel. But it was blocked. Zhubin ran to it and peered through. He could see a dim light. He started to remove the rocks.

"I'm coming down," Arman said.

But Zhubin warned him off. He told the young agent to go back to the outside of the temple. The tunnel, Zhubin knew, would pop out somewhere—and he didn't want to lose Shea and Neda again. He and Arman could block them in—if they were still alive.

65

Shea, Neda, and Gaspar waited for it. They stood still. And there it was, the sound of some one digging for them through the rubble. Their only choice was to push forward.

They were forced to crawl on their hands and knees single file. It was claustrophobic, and they couldn't know whether at any minute the tunnel's ceiling would collapse. Fear struck them all. They kept moving and then Gaspar stopped.

"What's wrong?" Shea asked.

"There's a grate in front of me. No way around it," Gaspar said.

Neda laid down flat on the ground so Shea could see. "Let me try," Shea said.

He crawled over Neda and then awkwardly over the back of Gaspar. He managed to turn his body around. He lay down on his back and brought his knees into his chest. He grabbed hold of the wall on each side of him and, using Gaspar's fat belly as back support, Shea kicked the grate open. When he did the floor underneath them all crumbled. They fell onto the ground outside the temple wall.

The young SAVAMA agent was standing there to greet them.

66

ARMAN WAS OUT OF BREATH. HE WAS BENT OVER WITH HIS HANDS ON his knees when he heard the noise. He thought it was a rat at first. Then the grate flew open and three people followed it onto the ground. A pile of dust plumed between them.

Shea had landed in a crouched position, and when he saw Arman standing in front of him, gun in hand, he launched himself onto the SAVAMA agent. Arman had raised his weapon, but Shea caught his wrist and pushed the gun onto Arman's left hip. This was a standard Krav Maga defense. It kept the gun out of firing range.

The surprise move gave Shea an advantage, which is what it was designed to do. Shea rabbit-punched Arman in the face several times. He then slid his striking hand down to the gun, so he had both hands on it. Holding it firmly against Arman, he snapped the barrel horizontally toward the ground. This broke Arman's index finger and he cried out. At the same time, Shea snatched the gun away from him. He reflexively stood back and cocked it. Arman was doubled over, holding his finger. Shea gave him a fierce upward kick to the face and then cracked him in the skull with the gun butt. The agent was out cold.

Neda and Gaspar stood off to the side. They were frightened and held on to each other during the fight. They were in shock and awe.

"Where did you learn to fight like that?" Neda asked.

"Never mind," he said, looking toward the village gate. The black SUVs were parked there as well as another vehicle.

"There's my car," Gaspar said. "Let's go."

Gaspar had pointed at a broken down old sedan. It looked like it would be lucky to even start. There was no way it could outrun anything that followed. And for sure, they would be followed.

"I have a better idea," Shea said. He raced to the SUVs. Both keys were in their respective ignitions. Who, after all, would mess with what were clearly government vehicles—SAVAMA vehicles, as everyone knew?

Shea opened the door to the first SUV. The backseat was up and he saw the cache of arms. He pushed it down and shut it, taking the keys. Next, he went to the SUV behind it and took those keys, too. He threw these as far away as he could. Then with Arman's gun he shot out all four tires.

Shea waved for Neda and Gaspar to get into the first SUV with him. He turned the ignition and looked over at the SAVAMA agent on the ground. Arman was moving, coming to. Shea suddenly had another idea. He stopped, hopped out of the vehicle, and whacked Arman again. Throwing him over his shoulder he dumped him into the backseat next to Gaspar. "Tie him up," Shea said, before peeling out and away. "And gag him."

ZHUBIN HAD MANAGED TO MOVE ENOUGH RUBBLE OUT OF THE WAY so that he could squeeze through the opening to the underground tunnel. Midway through it, though, he heard gunfire. By the time he came out the other side, Shea, Neda, Gaspar, and his fellow SAVAMA agent Arman were nowhere to be found. On top of that, his SUV was missing. The other SUV's tires had been shot out and he saw that the keys were gone.

Zhubin for the first time in a long time let his emotions get the better of him. He let out a long howl, like a wolf into the night.

68

INSIDE THE BLACK SUV THAT WAS RACING ON THE MOUNTAIN PASS with its lights off, the tension was high.

"How far is it to the Turkish border?" Shea asked. He didn't direct his question to anyone. He just wanted an answer. He needed one. Now.

"Fifteen kilometers," Gaspar said, piping right up. "That is, if you go off road. I know a way."

"Where should I go?" Shea asked.

"Turn here," Gaspar said.

There was only one way to turn, and it was to the left down an embankment. "Down there?" Shea asked to be sure.

"If you can, otherwise it is a long way," Gasper said.

"Hold on," Shea told them. And he turned the steering wheel. The SUV launched over the embankment.

Hoolyyyy shiiiiit . . . Shea thought, as he looked out the front window—below.

69

ZHUBIN IMMEDIATELY CALLED THE PRESIDENT AND LET HIM KNOW the situation: that Neda, Shea, and the archaeologist had escaped. He also called SAVAMA headquarters and had them jam all telephonic transmissions in the area. He ordered them to track the GPS in his official government vehicle. He was told they'd have a fix on its location in a matter of minutes.

The president wasn't so accommodating. He was furious. The only thing that saved Zhubin from being executed was the fact that he had the Zoroastrian scroll in his possession.

Talib ordered his helicopter to fire up. He boarded it and was airborne in less than ten minutes. If Zhubin couldn't bring the scroll to him, he'd go to the scroll.

70

BEFORE HE BEGAN HIS CHASE DOWN THE PASSAGEWAY FROM THE temple chamber, Zhubin had noticed something that looked like a beehive on a table in the back of the room. He examined it and realized that it was the scroll the president had instructed him to get from the archaeologist. He had gotten lucky. In the mayhem, the archaeologist must have left the scroll behind.

Zhubin should have known better than to trust luck.

THE SUV FELT AS THOUGH IT WAS GOING TO TOPPLE OVER. IT bounced violently down the hillside. Its front grill smashed into the flatland and everyone slid forward a foot.

Shea and Neda managed to avoid slamming into the windshield. Gaspar and the SAVAMA agent ended up on the floor of the backseat. Gaspar recovered but left the agent facedown in an awkward position. Arman was yelling through his gag. But no one paid him any attention.

Shea checked to make sure they were all right, and he drove on. "There!" Gaspar pointed toward a low-rising hill in the distance that looked like a camel's back. "That's the border," he said.

Shea gunned it.

72

TALIB'S HELICOPTER LANDED ON THE OPEN PATCH BETWEEN THE gates and the wooded area next to the pond at Shiz. The entire village, despite it being the middle of the night, turned out to see it.

Zhubin didn't wait for the rotors to slow before he ran to the helicopter door. Talib opened it, and Zhubin got right in.

"Let me see it" were the first words out of Talib's mouth. Zhubin handed the cylinder to him.

"We just got a fix on the SUV's GPS. They are heading toward the Turkish border," Zhubin informed the president as he handed over the artifact. But Talib wasn't listening. He was fixated on the cylinder, and what was inside.

Zhubin took matters into his own hands and order the pilot to lift off. The helicopter began to rise in the darkness. Its distinct silhouette appeared against the moon's face. And it flew away.

After the villagers spoke some, they disbanded and headed back to their homes. A few minutes later a woman screamed. The two old dead men had been found. Everyone stared at the blood and bullet wounds in the back of the men's heads.

People then began to wonder what happened to Gaspar, the strange archaeologist whose house they were in front of.

73

GASPAR HADN'T LIVED IN SHIZ LONG. HE HAD GROWN UP WITH HIS two brothers in Dalma, close but far in Iranian terms. (If a person wasn't your neighbor they were a complete stranger.)

To be sure, the villagers in Shiz knew of Gaspar, they just didn't know him. He didn't socialize with them. They couldn't know that Gaspar didn't socialize with anyone. Not since he was thirteen years old.

That's when his parents told him what his role in life would be. They let him in on the secret: he was to be a keeper of the light. And so, too, would his brothers.

From generation to generation the responsibility lay with the family. And next it would be up to him.

"What will be up to me?" young Gaspar had asked his mother as they both sat at the kitchen table in their home. His father was tending to the stove fire across the room.

His mother stole a glance at her husband. Then she spoke. "The future of the world, Gaspar. That is what will be up to you—and your brothers."

Her eyes began to fill up with tears. "Above all you must sacrifice everything for it."

He didn't understand. His father turned around and spoke. "You have been made part of a secret society, son. Fate has already determined your future. You are part of the Golden Dawn."

His father walked over to him . . . with a branding iron in his hand. It seared the flesh of Gaspar's forearm with the symbol.

AFTER MADLY CAREENING DOWN THE EMBANKMENT TO GET IN THE direction of the Turkish border, Shea finally turned on the headlights. It was the only way he could avoid the small mounds and ditches that were spread throughout the landscape.

If that gnome told me to go the wrong way, I am going to string him up by his prayer beads.

Shea looked in the rearview mirror at Gaspar.

And who wears all white besides brides, pretentious writers, and Brazilian revelers on New Year's Eve, anyway? Dervish, my arse.

They bowled over switch grass and barreled through puddles.

"Is the border guarded?" Shea asked.

"Only on the Iranian side. The Turks leave it to them. They go to bed early," Gaspar said.

Shea glanced over at Neda. She was holding on for dear life. He felt protective of her. He needed to make sure that she was safe. In the rearview mirror he could see that Arman the SAVAMA agent had managed to right himself and was now seated next to Gaspar. Shea looked at him, too.

"They'll never let us across," Neda said, stating the obvious. "There is no way around the checkpoint. We are better off staying in Iran. Gaspar and I have a friend who lives close. It is safe."

"I heard that somewhere before recently," Shea said, looking at Neda. It's what she had said about Gaspar. "And it's too late for that now, anyway."

"Why too late?" Neda asked.

"Listen," Shea told her. The faint whir of a helicopter could be heard in the distance. He stopped the vehicle. He got out and looked up to the sky. The helo's lights were there. It was only a few miles away. He stole a look inside the SUV through his open door. *Damn*, he thought. *The GPS. They are tracking us.*

"Michael," Neda said, "we must go."

"I agree," Shea said. He went around to the back of the SUV and pulled the young SAVAMA agent from it, throwing him onto the ground. He told Gaspar to get out as well. Shea then flipped up the backseat. He took out the RPG and the Kalesh machine gun that he remembered were stashed in there. Checking the tube to make sure it had a shell in it, Shea unlocked the red trigger. He put the RPG on his shoulder and took aim at the helo in the distance. He knew the shot would miss. The chopper was still too far away. But he also knew the helicopter would be forced to take evasive action, and that would buy him time, time he desperately needed. Shea had covered so many wars and seen so many RPGs that he knew how to fire one.

Shea pulled the trigger. The missile shot out of the barrel. He threw the RPG on the ground. Then he picked up the SAVAMA agent and took his gag off. He untied him. "If you want to live, I have a job for you," he said to Arman. Neda translated. A few moments later they were off again. This time Arman was driving.

75

IT TOOK A MOMENT FOR TALIB TO REALIZE WHAT WAS HAPPENING.
He was focused on getting the scroll out of the cylinder.

The helicopter banked severely to the right and then swept low to the ground.

"What is going on?" Talib shouted.

Zhubin knew exactly what was happening. "That's my RPG. Someone just fired at us."

"Where are we going?" Talib asked.

"After them, to the border. It isn't far," Zhubin said, instructing the pilot to continue to pursue the SUV. "They won't get across," Zhubin assured the president.

Talib had gone back to taking the scroll out of the cylinder. He managed to get it and unravel it. "Where is the other one?" he asked Zhubin.

"Other what?"

"Scroll. There should have been two in here."

76

SHEA WAS IN THE BACKSEAT WITH THE KALESH POINTED DIRECTLY AT Arman's head.

They were racing toward the checkpoint, but the helicopter was moving in quickly. There was no way they'd make it.

"Faster," Shea yelled.

Neda translated again. The young SAVAMA agent spoke up. "I speak English," he said. "I understand."

"Good," Shea said. "Then understand this. If we don't get across that border we are dead. And that means you'll die, too. Get us across and we'll let you go. You can make up whatever story you want."

Arman thought about his pregnant wife and young son. He nodded.

They were mere yards away from the checkpoint. They could see the guards at their post. The guards held up their rifles, not sure of what was happening or who was coming at them so fast.

The helicopter closed in—it was right on top of them as they pulled up to the gate.

Arman skidded to a stop. He rolled down his window and flashed his SAVAMA identification. "I'm dropping some things off where they belong," he said to the young guards. "President's orders."

The young guard looked up at the helicopter. It just so happened that the helicopter turned to its side at that moment, and the presidential seal could be seen on the door. Through the window, the young guards could see Talib. One of them saluted.

Inside the helicopter Talib was going ape shit. He told Zhubin to call the guard post and stop them from getting through. Zhubin reminded the president that they had blocked all telephonic transmissions in the area. There was no way to get a signal. Talib screamed at the pilot to put them down.

As the presidential helicopter landed, Arman drove Shea, Neda, and Gaspar through to Turkey. Shea told the SAVAMA agent not to stop anytime soon.

AYATOLLAH MESBAH YAVARI WALKED THROUGH THE DARK HALLS OF the *hawza*. The seminary was quiet. Wearing a black cap, shawl, and white tunic, he looked like a headless ghost from afar.

The Ayatollah couldn't sleep and had left his quarters to roam the grounds he had built with one purpose in mind: to welcome the coming of the Mahdi.

He had left half open the door to his ornate bedroom. On his massive four-post bed fitted with silk sheets and matching pillows, the young boy with whom he had been with slumped over the side—spent. The Ayatollah had been particularly lascivious and the boy had done his best to please, with his hands, his mouth, his backside, and his own member. The Ayatollah especially liked that—when the boy was in control from behind.

The door left open was a sign that it was time for the boy to go. By the time Mesbah Yavari got back to his quarters he hoped, indeed, that the boy would be gone. He had a lot to think about and such a young thing was a distraction.

The marble columns that lined the hallway down which he walked blocked every few feet the view of the golden dome of the mosque. Two of the columns matched perfectly the minarets. Mesbah Yavari had his residence built this way so that at the spot at which he now stood, he could look out unobstructed to the dome of the holy city below.

He thought of how he had almost lost it all. That was in the beginning when the seminary was called Muntashiriya and his "partners" tried to force him out because of his radical views. He looked at this time as his coming of age. He assassinated his two ayatollah partners and changed the seminary's name to explain to all who came exactly what they were being schooled for. The name left no doubt. He renamed the *hawza* the Shahidayh Seminary. It meant "martyr" school.

A flock of night birds swooped over the golden dome of the mosque and scattered onto the trees. The gold shimmered by the moonlight. The birds would rest now, and Mesbah Yavari was jealous. He could not rest. He could not sleep until the scroll was in his hands and the Mahdi could be revealed.

Decades of planning and plotting led him to this moment and he didn't want to let a minute go by without it being put to use. There was a lot to think through.

First, he needed to produce the scroll. The Haghani Circle, which was comprised of esteemed clerics and acted as a sort of board of directors to the seminary itself, would need to be convinced that it was authentic. No matter how much influence he had, he knew that he couldn't convince the other ayatollahs and theologians that the Mahdi's day had come without something material. Thankfully, Talib had the exact proof and artifact he needed.

Or so he believed.

78

MESBAH YAVARI TOOK HIS EYES FROM THE DOME. HE TURNED HIS back to the mosque and continued to walk down the wide hallway. He looked at the photos of himself on the walls. His white beard had gotten even whiter. His face had become even more wrinkled. And he had changed the shape of the glasses that he wore. Otherwise, Mesbah Yavari didn't think that he had aged all that much over the last twenty-five years since the school had opened. He was, in more ways than one, delusional.

The Ayatollah shuffled along and thought of that cartoonist who had depicted him as Professor Crocodile. He hardly looked reptilian, he thought. "Mesbah," his name, may have rhymed with crocodile in Farsi, but that was no reason for the depiction. Anyway, he wondered how that cartoonist liked the inside of his prison cell. *Let him draw all he wants about me in there.*

Mesbah Yavari's private prayer hall was to his right and he opened the door to peek inside. The pillows and mats were perfectly placed facing Mecca. Everything was a different shade of brown in the room. The pillows were velvet. Intricate calligraphy with the names of Muhammad, Fatima, Hasin, and Hussein surrounding the symbol for Allah were on the wall. He smiled and inhaled the incense they kept burning inside the prayer hall for him. He had no idea that they actually burned the incense more for themselves than for him.

Mesbah Yavari loved onions and tended to fart a lot. Students given the "privilege" to pray with him in private were honored but also left teary-eyed and horrified at the stench that came from the old man.

Mesbah Yavari shut the door to the prayer hall and walked on, deeper in thought.

After unveiling the scroll for the Circle he'd next have to get their endorsement in order to address the Assembly of Experts. This was key in getting the Mahdi movement accepted by the masses. The Assembly of Experts was comprised of eighty-six Islamic scholars who in turn represented different sects. If they abided by his conviction that the Mahdi was arriving, then the Supreme Leader would also have to abide—and that meant the whole of Iran would fall in line.

Mesbah Yavari stopped at the next opening. There was no door. This was where the young seminarians slept on bunks. One after the other, they slept covered only by the black loincloth Mesbah Yavari insisted they wear when they sleep. That only. There was nothing religious about it. He just liked to peer in at them at night. But now was not the time for that, he thought to himself.

Instead, he thought about Talib, how he, too, had once been so lithe and so young and so eager to please his ayatollah. He did so often and with vigor. There was a time when they stayed in bed together for a whole weekend.

79

HOLDING TALIB OUT TO THE SHIA COMMUNITY IN IRAN AS THE Mahdi would be the easy part, the Ayatollah figured. It was convincing the Sunnis that Talib was the chosen one that would prove tricky. He would have to call a summit and produce the truths. It was the only way.

What Mesbah Yavari didn't know was that the Sunnis as well as other religions from around the world were also looking for signs of the Mahdi's coming. And had found them. They were conspiring together already. Plans were being made. Evidence was being shared.

Mesbah Yavari could not know that he would deliver them the last piece of evidence that they needed to join together as one under one God and ruler. One judge.

He could not know yet what a crucial role he would play in the End Times.

It was not the role he had hoped for and intended.

80

THERE WERE NINE TRUTHS ABOUT THE MAHDI FOUND IN THE AN-cient and most sacred texts. Both the Sunnis and Shia agreed on these signs as well. They were what would pull the Muslim religion together into one, Mesbah Yavari believed. Indeed, if these signs came to be, all the world's religions would unite. And he would be in control . . . of them all.

The truths were:

1. The Mahdi will be a descendant of Muhammad of the line of Fatima.
2. His name will be as the name of Muhammad.
3. He will rule for forty years.
4. His coming will be accompanied by the raising of a Black Standard.

5. His coming will be accompanied by the appearance of the Great Deceiver.

6. There will be a lunar and solar eclipse within the same month of Ramadan.

7. A star with a luminous tail will rise from the east before the Mahdi emerges.

8. He will restore faith to its original form and eradicate moral corruption.

9. He will have a broad forehead, a prominent nose, and his eyes will be naturally mascaraed.

IN HIS MIND, MESBAH YAVARI WENT DOWN THE LIST THAT HE HAD long memorized. Talib was a descendant of Fatima. His name was Mahmoud, or Muhammad, just spelled differently. He was young enough to rule. The Black Standard, or flag, was the same color as al-Qaida's flag. To be sure, it had been raised in the name of Islam.

Painting the American president Barack Obama as the Great Deceiver had been one of Mesbah Yavari's personal favorite campaigns. It wasn't hard to challenge a man whose rhetoric was of hope and peace and change but whose actions amplified war and dishonesty. Even the American people themselves were starting to question Obama's motives. The Great Deceiver indeed. Just ask their Fox News.

The lunar and solar eclipse was what had prevented Mesbah Yavari from presenting Talib as the Mahdi before this. The newly found

Zoroastrian text, however, trumped this standard belief and time period; it lifted it. It was the ammunition they needed for the Mahdi to appear.

Mesbah Yavari's smile grew wider as he remembered watching Halley's comet zoom past Earth at night—from east to west—twenty-five years ago. It was then that he knew it was happening, that the time had come. It was the first sign he recognized and it had occurred at just about the same time as Talib had come to him before almost being expelled. The characteristics the boy bore—the broad forehead and nose—further excited Mesbah Yavari's belief.

The Ayatollah knew that he could help Talib with the penultimate sign, restoring faith to its original form and eradicating moral corruption. And it was this that could be done through force and violence.

He could see it now. He could imagine the congregation with all the ayatollahs, imams, and mullahs in attendance. Maybe it would be held in the beautiful gardens he had planted next to the Qom mosque, he thought. The area could hold thousands. After all, there were 45,000 clerics already living and praying in Qom.

Mesbah Yavari turned around and began to walk back to his chamber. He imagined Talib walking out onto the stage in the gardens. He imagined the crowd's reaction. The world would be forced to recognize him.

The Vatican story was even in place. He would make that connection next. The pope would want to know. It was something they had discussed between themselves for years. Quietly. Secretly.

According to the truths the Mahdi would rule with Isa for forty years. Isa was another name for Jesus.

Clouds covered the moon as Mesbah Yavari shuffled back to his chamber. The glow of the gold dome was gone. There was a bit more pep in his step. He was reenergized by all the thinking. He hoped the young boy in his bed hadn't left yet.

82

THE JET MADE A SMOOTH LANDING AT GROZNY AIRPORT. O'Shaughnessy and Abramov didn't speak for the entire length of the descent. Besides the pilot and the copilot, there was only one other person on the plane with them: Abramov's personal goon.

The ten-seat jet was narrow. To be sure, it was plush. Carrera leather seats and silk carpet. Burnished wood finishes. But the plane was small. Hence, Abramov's personal goon—who went only by his initials, B.A.D.—looked even more enormous.

B.A.D. had a long brown beard that he kept in a V by twisting elastics at its bottom. Dressed in a black three-quarter-length leather jacket, he wore black polyester pants and, curiously, traditional red-and-green-striped Bally loafers. He looked every bit the part of what he was: the muscle.

B.A.D. took up the front two seats of the plane. The seat belts wouldn't fasten around his large frame, so he had pressed his legs against the cabin wall for landing. Apparently B.A.D. didn't like to fly. He clutched the armrests and was pale and sweaty for the entire descent into Grozny.

B.A.D. had good reason to fear flying. Although he never spoke of it, he was one of the few who had survived detention during the "Dirty War" of 2001, when the Chechens suffered a spate of forced disappearances, torture, and summary executions at the hands of Russian troops.

It happened like this: B.A.D. and his cousin had gone to work at the car repair shop as usual. Then the power went off. They headed home.

On the way, a military truck pulled them over and seized them. B.A.D. and his cousin were both active in the Chechen rebellion and had long files. The Russians had scored two trophies. The military decided to fly them to Moscow for public trial and put the two cousins on display as case studies in terrorism and *casus belli* for their continued war with Chechnya. (B.A.D. was known for dismembering people with his bare hands, and his cousin had made an underground name for himself by specializing in military vehicle explosions.) The cousins were taken to Moscow. But on the way the plane crashed. B.A.D. had survived. No one else did.

That's why B.A.D. hated to fly.

These days, there weren't too many flights into or out of the Grozny Airport. Not at the late hour at which they had landed. Actually, not at any hour. Only a few daring commercial flights came in from Moscow. The city's name likely had something to do with its inhospitableness. Grozny meant "terrible." The famous Ivan the Terrible's name was, in fact, Ivan Grozny. And Grozny, the city, would more than live up to its name during this night.

THE JET DIDN'T TAKE MORE THAN A FEW MINUTES TO TAXI TO ITS SPOT next to the military hangar. Looking out of the window, O'Shaughnessy could see the Grozny Central Dome Mosque alit.

"Beautiful, isn't it?" Abramov said, standing over O'Shaughnessy and looking out at the city. "My home."

"Actually, it ain't," O'Shaughnessy said. "I've seen it in the daytime, remember."

For the last century, Grozny had been in almost a constant state of disrepair from all its wars and invasions. Out of more than sixty thousand apartment buildings and private homes that had been destroyed throughout the city, less than one thousand had been rebuilt. Grozny was a city of ruin.

Even before the jet had come to a full stop, B.A.D. had opened the exit door and pushed the stairs down. He was eager to get off the plane.

"Quite a stewardess you've got there," O'Shaughnessy wisecracked to Abramov.

"Don't be ignorant," Abramov said. "They're called flight attendants now."

They both chuckled.

B.A.D. had his gun out as he stepped onto the tarmac, scanning the area for any sign of trouble. He didn't notice anything out of the ordinary. He didn't see anyone or anything move. He gave the thumbs-up to the pilot who was standing at the jet's doorway. Then the sound of gunfire erupted. Sparks flew as bullets bounced off the plane. The inside of the plane lit up and the captain fell in, his body riddled with bullets. B.A.D., too, was hit and went down.

O'Shaughnessy and Abramov both looked outside. B.A.D.'s body lay still. A military jeep was approaching. A half-dozen commandos in blue fatigues were shooting at them.

Abramov raced to the front of the plane, raised the stairs, and shut the door. The copilot was still in his seat.

"Go!" Abramov barked.

"Where?" the copilot asked.

"I don't give a fuck. Just get us out of here!"

Bullets continued to spray against the plane. Windows were blown out. The jeep was almost on them.

84

THE GUNNER IN THE JEEP MANNING THE MOUNTED MACHINE GUN
had the copilot in his sights. That's when B.A.D. rolled over and fired.
He hadn't died quite yet. He'd kill as many as he could before he took
his last breath. He'd do it for his dead cousin's father, his uncle: Abramov,
the man who took care of him like a son after the plane crash.

B.A.D. hit the machine gunner in the neck and blood squirted
everywhere. He took aim at the driver and let off a few rounds. The
jeep swerved and smashed into the jet. Then one of the men in the jeep
grabbed the mounted machine gun and tore into B.A.D. It blew his
body to bits.

During the last round of shots a few ricocheted and the pilot's window got blown out.

"Sir," the copilot yelled. "We can't fly." He had fired up the engines
and was turning the jet away from the jeep.

"Then take us where you can," Abramov yelled back.

"On the ground?"

"Move this plane anywhere and anyway you can!"

O'Shaughnessy was ducking under one of the plane's rear windows.
Whenever he could, he let off a shot, but his efforts didn't amount to
much.

The jet began to move. Abramov ran out of the pilot's cabin and dove
down the aisle just as another pelting of bullets sprayed the main cabin.
"Hold them off!" Abramov yelled.

"Where are we going?" O'Shaughnessy asked.

"Anywhere but here."

The two began shooting at the jeep. The copilot drove the jet down the runway, past the military hangar and the control tower. Thankfully, because Grozny had been bombed so many times, there were lots of open spaces to maneuver the jet even outside the terminal.

Abramov and O'Shaughnessy managed to pick off two more commandos in the jeep. The copilot was doing the best that he could, but the track he was on was coming to an end. Abramov and O'Shaughnessy saw that, too. They nodded to one another and they each carefully took aim. *Pop! Pop!* They shot the last two commandos. But the commandos had done their job, as well: they had picked off the copilot. Now the plane was careening out of control.

THE COPILOT WHO WAS NO LONGER STEERING THE PLANE WAS slumped over in his seat. A bullet had again ricocheted, this time off the ceiling and had hit him in the left eye. Another caught him in the belly. His head was crooked to the right and blood was leaking out of his mouth.

The jet crashed into one of the burned-out apartment buildings by the airport. It stopped. O'Shaughnessy and Abramov scrambled to their feet. They had made it. Sort of. Two more jeeps were headed their way.

The two men jumped out of the jet through one of the windows. They managed to take a pistol off the copilot but there were no other weapons aboard. O'Shaughnessy only had half a clip left. Abramov, too, was almost empty. There was no way they could hold off the on-slaught with the ammunition they had.

"Who are those guys?" O'Shaughnessy asked as they made it into the crumbling building.

"Friends of mine," Abramov said sarcastically. "Good friends."

O'Shaughnessy had gotten mixed up in Abramov's personal war at home. It wasn't what he had bargained for. It put the deal in jeopardy and it compromised a very lucrative nuclear contract for them both. It did more than that, too: it interrupted a covert plan O'Shaughnessy was working on. For it to go off he needed Abramov alive—for now.

THE JEEPS PULLED UP IN FRONT OF THE BUILDING AND O'Shaughnessy and Abramov stepped out of sight. The commandos in one jeep jumped out and covered the front of the building, while the others stayed by their vehicle, crouching low beside it.

O'Shaughnessy and Abramov saw them and knew what they were doing. It was typical guerrilla strategy. The commandos were going to try to flush them out.

Two of the commandos took to either side of what used to be a door-way but was now just crumbling mortar. The third commando shot straight through the entrance.

O'Shaughnessy and Abramov also knew what would happen next: the other two commandos would fall in line behind him, then they would spread out again to either side of the commando in the lead position.

O'Shaughnessy looked at the back of the building they were in and noticed that a huge hole had been blown out of it. It looked as though there was another bombed-out building behind them. It would serve as better cover, or better yet, a way to escape.

They waited for the first commando to come through the door. They didn't fire. Then the other two commandos came through as predicted. This time they let off a round each and shot them both dead. The lead commando, however, had found solid cover.

"Alu," O'Shaughnessy said. "There." He pointed at the hole in the back of the building. Abramov saw it and immediately understood.

They hoofed it for the hole, fast.

O'SHAUGHNESSY RAN THROUGH THE HOLE FIRST AND MADE IT WITH-out attracting any gunfire. Abramov went next.

O'Shaughnessy watched as Abramov ran toward him. The Chechen's eyes were wide. His mouth was open and he was gasping for air as he sprinted as fast as he could. O'Shaughnessy saw a blur behind Abramov. He raised his gun and pointed it directly at Abramov's head and fired. Abramov ducked and fell onto the ground. He turned and aimed his weapon at O'Shaughnessy. Then he realized what O'Shaughnessy had just done: he had shot the commando and saved his life.

The other commandos began to spill into the first building. Abramov and O'Shaughnessy wended through the building they were in and out the other side to what looked like a promenade. It was lined by three-foot-high wrought-iron fencing. It was part of Grozny's effort to spruce itself up. O'Shaughnessy thought: *Long way to go for that to happen.*

O'Shaughnessy saw what looked like piles of sod grass ready to be placed between the fences. Not far off was the city's mosque. O'Shaughnessy looked at it, then back at the sod. He hoped a professional landscaper was taking care of the promenade. And it was the case. Midway down the promenade he saw what he was hoping for: a diesel generator and a plastic bag.

"This way, Alu," he said.

They went to the pile and O'Shaughnessy sniffed inside it. His hunch was right. He picked the bag up, as well as the small generator next to it. Litter was everywhere in Grozny and O'Shaughnessy told Abramov to grab some newspapers.

"What are we doing?" Abramov asked.

"You'll see," O'Shaughnessy said, noticing the cotton skullcap Abramov wore. "Just don't get religious on me."

88

ABRAMOV AND O'SHAUGHNESSY MADE IT TO THE ENTRANCE OF THE mosque. Several shots rang out. The commandos weren't far behind. The two terrorists crouched by the door. O'Shaughnessy went to open it, but the gunfire prevented him from getting even close to its handle.

"How much ammo do you have?" he asked Abramov.

"Three rounds, max."

"Use it."

Abramov began firing as O'Shaughnessy popped the door handle open. They made it inside and shut the door behind them. There was nothing to barricade it with. The best they could do was turn the lock.

"This is a holy place," Abramov noted.

"Like I said, don't go getting religious on me. You want to live?"

Abramov nodded.

"Is there a back way out of here?" O'Shaughnessy asked.

"Yes, through there." He pointed past the *minbar*, the pulpit, to a large wooden door.

"Got any fellas in the neighborhood?" O'Shaughnessy asked.

"My men are always close by."

"Yeah. I can see that. Call 'em and tell 'em to wait out back—but not too close."

"What are you going to do?"

"Make a statement."

O'Shaughnessy poked some holes through the newspapers and wrapped fertilizer from the plastic bag in them. Next he soaked Abramov's cotton skullcap that he had swiped off his head in diesel and then poured more onto the paper.

"Hey . . ." Abramov said.

There was banging at the door. It wasn't a solid door and it wouldn't hold for long.

Shots were fired. They wouldn't have much more than a minute to escape before the commandos came crashing in.

"Why don't you go out back," O'Shaughnessy suggested. "I'll be right there."

Abramov stayed for a few seconds and watched what O'Shaughnessy was doing.

O'Shaughnessy pulled down a curtain from the wall and ripped it into shreds. He took an end and placed it on the newspaper. Then he lined the curtain, which became a large fuse, with diesel.

"You sure about this?" Abramov asked.

"I am a bomb maker, you know. World's best. Now go."

Abramov lumbered out the back door. Just as he did, the front door blew open and a round of gunfire followed. The commandos all entered the mosque—as O'Shaughnessy had hoped.

89

O'SHAUGHNESSY LIT THE CURTAIN ON FIRE AND THEN FOLLOWED IN Abramov's footsteps out the back. He shut the door loudly.

The commandos followed the sound of the door shutting. By the time they reached the *minbar*, it was too late to escape. The mosque blew.

O'Shaughnessy was literally blown out of the door as he stepped outside. There, Abramov was waiting. He picked him up off the ground just as a black Mercedes screeched to a stop in front of them. They both got in the back.

They drove madly out of the grounds, almost running over the imam whose job it was to call for morning prayers. The imam grabbed hold of the hat on top of his head and turned to see the mosque engulfed in flames. He looked up at the minaret towers. One of them fell over.

Grozny's treasure, its new mosque, was blown to bits.

The imam spun and looked at the Mercedes as it sped away. He threw his hat on the ground and in a curiously Italian gesture, put his left arm in the crux of his right arm and lifted his right forearm straight up into the air.

90

HUNDRED OF MILES AWAY, IN TURKEY, ANOTHER SUV WAS RACING through the night. Shea was in the front passenger seat of this one. Gaspar and Neda were in the back. And the SAVAMA agent Arman was driving. Shea directed Arman to pull over and stop on the side of the road.

They were on the outskirts of the city of Van in eastern Turkey. A large lake was before them. Daylight allowed the lush and beautiful land they were in to finally be seen. They had driven through the dark.

Shea said, "I think I know where we are now. I drove past this on my way to the border. This is Lake Van. The city is close. The cafes will be opening soon. I can get online and get us in touch with some help."

Shea thought about the British News headquarters office in London. They would be none too pleased with him. He had gone to London from Tel Aviv for his annual review. But he had taken off before he received it. He hadn't checked in with his producers, or anyone else from the office.

I'll be lucky if they accept my call.

Neda and Gaspar looked at each other.

"Who are you going to get in touch with?" Neda asked.

"British News. They are my employers, after all."

"And what will you tell them?" she continued.

"Exactly what I saw and what happened," Shea said.

"There is more to do, Michael," Gaspar said. "The scroll Talib is trying to get his hands on could set off a religious war the likes of which the world has never seen."

"I am trying to stop a nuclear war, not a religious one!" Shea exclaimed.

"They are one and the same," Gaspar said.

"You are telling me that that scroll is just as powerful as a nuclear bomb?"

Neda decided to answer him this time. "More so, Michael. Even more so."

"Okay, well, maybe it's time you told me what this scroll says and why it is so important," Shea said.

"I will," Gaspar said. "But not here." He shot a look at Arman.

Shea still had his gun pointed at the SAVAMA agent in the driver's seat. He lowered it for a second and reached over Arman's shoulder, taking the keys from the ignition. He opened his own door and stepped out of the vehicle and called back, "Don't go anywhere fast."

Gaspar and Neda got out also. Shea had removed all the weapons from the backseat. There was nothing Arman could do but sit there.

91

SHEA COULDN'T SEE IT FROM THE OUTSIDE BECAUSE OF A SMALL LIP on the vehicle's door, but Arman had his window open a crack.

Standing by the lakeshore, Neda, Gaspar, and Shea gathered by a piece of timber someone had made into a bench. Shea noticed that people had scrawled initials and sayings on and into the wood. No matter where you were in the world, he thought, people acted the same. Signs of love. Signs of hate. Signs of existence: ". . . WAS HERE."

We all think we are so special . . . but we aren't. We just want validity that we exist.

"So?" Shea said to Gaspar. "Tell me. Unless, of course, you think the squirrels might hear." He stepped next to Neda and put his hand around the small of her back.

Gaspar stood in front of them both. Shea's gesture to Neda wasn't lost on him. He noted it and filed it away in his head. *Love,* he thought. *Good for you, Neda.*

"Here, I'll show you," Gaspar said. He removed the scroll from inside his shirt and unraveled it. "The first thing you need to know is that this is an Avestan text. That means it was one of the texts that the *Zand-i Vohu-man Yasht* is based on. Scholars know there is no such work. But it's easier to explain as a single book or work of literature. It's really a compilation of stories. Anyway, this scroll predates any other text known. From an archaeological standpoint this is a major find."

"What is the story?" Shea asked.

"I am trying to tell you," Gaspar said.

"No, not with the scroll. What is the *Zand-i* whatever you call it about?" Shea pressed.

Neda interjected. "It's an epic tale, like biblical stories and the gitas, if you know those."

Shea said, "I read the Bhagavad Gita in college. It boils down to a conversation on the battlefield before a war."

"Similar," Gaspar said, "from a storytelling point of view. But this story is of the aftermath of war."

"It is the story," Neda also explained, "of an immortal, Peshotanu. He ends up living in a fortress battling demons. During the fight, another god, Mithra—that is where some say the word *myth* comes from in English—comes to help Peshotanu. Together they drive the demons, or evil, back to the underworld."

92

GASPAR PICKED UP FROM NEDA THE EXPLANATION OF THE SCROLL'S story. "Mostly no one but scholars would care about another version of such a thing, so it was curious to me why Talib would take such a keen interest in it. Why would he have people killed over it?" Gaspar looked at Neda. "Again, I am sorry, my dear. I, too, miss your husband."

Neda acknowledged his sympathy and turned her eyes toward the ground. She stepped away from Shea's arm.

Gaspar continued. "It all came together for me when President Talib not only wanted me to authenticate the document and date it for him, but asked about a particular section of the text."

Shea began to bob his head and roll his finger in a circle. He wanted Gaspar to get on with it. Gaspar got the message and spoke more quickly. "What Talib was interested in were the lines: '*At the end of thy tenth hundredth winter . . . the sun is more unseen and more spotted; the year, month, and day are shorter; and the earth is more barren; and the crop will not yield the seed; and men become more deceitful and more given to vile practices. They have no gratitude. Honorable wealth will all proceed to those of perverted faith . . . and a dark cloud makes the whole sky night . . . and it will rain more noxious creatures than winter,*'" Gaspar recited from memory.

Shea asked with his facial expression more than his words. "Come on . . ." he said.

Gaspar and Neda shared another look. Gaspar explained, "This is a very important point in Zoroastrianism. It influenced Jewish and

Christian scripture and it is what the Sunni and Shia Muslims look to; it informs their specific religious beliefs."

Gaspar paused.

Shea said impatiently, "The suspense is killing me. Could you get on with it? This isn't a bedtime story."

Gaspar sighed. Clearly he had a flair for the dramatic. "The important phrases are '*the sun is more unseen and more spotted*' and '*a dark cloud makes the whole sky night.*' It means that there will be lunar and solar eclipses and they will both occur during Ramadan."

Neda drove the point home. "Those two signs are what Jews, Muslims, Christians—half the world's population—believe will begin the End Times, the Apocalypse. Zoroastrianism predates all those religions and it is said that the Avestan texts informed everything from the Bible to the Koran. All of these sacred books relied on the dates and references in one book."

"Let me guess," Shea said, "the *Zand-i* whoseywhats. That thing there in your hand."

"Yes. But this version of the scroll is different. It provides a new date for the revelation of the Mahdi," Gaspar said.

"When is that?" Shea asked Gaspar.

"Now," he said.

PART TWO

THE THIRD SECRET
OF FATIMA

IT TOOK EVERY BIT OF CONCENTRATION SHEA COULD MUSTER TO
follow what Gaspar and Neda were saying. He had been in such a
physical rush the last twenty-four hours, exercising his mental faculties
proved difficult. "Talib is Muslim," Shea said, trying to follow. "What
does he care about a Zoroastrian story and dates?"

Neda again interjected to make it clear to Shea. "Zoroastrian priests
were highly respected by Muslim imams. They were called the original 'people of the book.' Many take this to mean the book of prayer. It
actually translates better to the 'bearers of record.' In other words, the
people who held the book of time. And these priests were especially
helpful to one, Imam Abu Dawud. He is the imam who wrote the *hadiths,* or stories, about the Mahdi's coming and the Apocalypse. It is his
texts that the Muslims look to and interpret from."

"So if a new Zoroastrian text were discovered that predated any
other, it would be significant to Muslims as well," Shea went on, finally
getting it.

"Exactly. Them and every other religion," Gaspar said. "Previously, the Mahdi could only appear when a solar and lunar eclipse occurred during Ramadan. And that would only be scientifically possible in 2155."

"So," Shea said, still trying to get his brain around it, "the Mahdi can only come to Earth in a double eclipse during Ramadan. And that won't scientifically happen until 2155. The scroll gives a new date. But what about the eclipse? As far as I know there isn't supposed to be one this year."

Gaspar smiled, glad Shea understood. "That is the most misunderstood part of the prophecy. The text never uses the word for eclipse. It says something close: 'when the sun and the moon are in the same position in the sky.'"

"I'm not an astronomer, but isn't that what an eclipse is?"

"No," Gaspar continued. "The sun and moon are in the same position in the sky every month. It is what some people call a 'new moon' and others, the 'dark moon.' At this time the moon faces almost directly toward Earth, so that the moon is not visible to the naked eye." He pointed to the faint moon in the sky and then the sun as it rose. "There will be a new moon next week."

"And it is Ramadan now," Neda reminded Shea.

"You think Talib is going to say he has appeared so he can save the world? That he is this Mahdi character?" Shea asked, dumbfounded.

"That isn't really how it happens. The Mahdi actually, according to the texts, came to Earth hundreds of years ago and has been waiting here. It's when these signs occur that he will be revealed," Gaspar corrected.

"Have the other signs occurred?" Shea asked.

Neda and Gaspar stole one of their looks at each other again. "Yes," Neda said, finally.

"So that is why Talib is planning a nuclear bomb! This would give him the excuse to use it," Shea said. "Next week!"

"And there is one more very important thing," Gaspar began to explain—but he didn't get to finish what he wanted to say.

2

THE SUV'S ENGINE STARTED. SHEA, NEDA, AND GASPAR HAD BEEN so enrapt in the stories about the scroll that they forgot about the SA-VAMA agent. Arman had managed to hotwire the vehicle and was now driving straight for them.

Shea's fast reactions kicked in. He didn't panic. He took evasive action. His time spent in conflict zones and his Krav Maga combat training had indeed taught him well. He stepped quickly to the side of the SUV and pulled Neda out of the way with him. But Gaspar wasn't so lucky; Arman ran him down. Gaspar's body got stuck on the under-carriage and he was dragged several hundred yards. Finally, the SAVAMA agent stopped the vehicle and got out. He pulled Gaspar away and took the scroll out of his hands. Then he drove off again like a bat out of hell.

Shea reached Gaspar just as the SUV skidded on to the road. Gaspar's breath was short. He was dying. Neda caught up seconds later. Heaving, Gaspar said, "The Vatican, my brother. The Third Secret of Fatima. You must stop it. He will know. My brother . . ." Then Gaspar spoke no more. His mouth and his eyes remained open and still.

Neda leaned down and put his head in her arms. She rocked him like a baby.

Shea softened. He put his arm around Neda's shoulder. She had lost another person that she cared about. She needed comfort. But at the same time Shea wanted to know the meaning behind what Gaspar had said.

"Gaspar's brother is at the Vatican. He is part of the Iranian delegation. We must find him," Neda said.

"We will. We will."

Shea didn't bother asking anything more. He would find out in time. Instead he turned his thoughts to the office, to help. How could he reach British News? he wondered. He needed to let someone know what was going on, that he was on to the biggest story of his life, the biggest story in the world.

I've been in this position before. I won't lose another story like this. I won't allow it to happen.

And then his thoughts turned more personal. They turned back to that day in 1998 at Omagh. He thought of a hand, as he often did. Every night, if he really were to admit it. It was a little boy's hand and it was almost touching his, like the famous Michelangelo painting of the agony and ecstasy. Their fingers were tantalizingly close. Except there wasn't a body or an arm attached to the little boy's hand.

It haunted him through and through that day. It was a story, a story with a bloody consequence, and he had blown it. He wouldn't let it happen like that again.

I am a journalist. I am supposed to be objective.

He had thought that then. He thought those words now. It was too late. He was part of the story. It was no longer journalism. It was something else, another type of story in which he was involved. He couldn't describe it. But if he had the chance he'd report it. If he had the chance.

Shea looked around. There wasn't a phone or a store near the lake, just the road. He saw a bus go by.

Fifteen minutes later Shea and Neda were on an intercity bus headed to downtown Van.

Neda looked out the window as they drove away from the lake. She noticed a small, white cat wade into the water and begin to swim. It was headed toward Gaspar's body, which was floating and being pulled along by the tide.

3

ZHUBIN DIDN'T ASK EITHER OF THE IRANIAN BORDER GUARDS AT THE
Turkey checkpoint for a jeep; he commandeered one. The guards were
nervous for their lives, forget about the jeep. They thought they had
done the right thing by letting the SAVAMA agent and the black SUV
through with a mere wave. After all, what were they supposed to do?
The agent had flashed his badge, and it did look as if the president had
given them the thumbs-up from his helicopter.

Unfortunately for Zhubin the jeep was slow. It would gain little
ground on the souped-up SUV. Zhubin felt silly driving. The jeep was
like a toy, but it was his only chance to stay on the tail of the journalist.
It was him Zhubin was now focused on: Michael Shea. The woman,
sure, she was a problem, but she could easily be dealt with. As could
the archaeologist. Lock them up or kill them. The world wouldn't much
notice. An internationally known journalist with the ability to broadcast
to the world was a much bigger threat.

Anything could be made to look like an accident, though. And as
long as Zhubin reached Shea before he could communicate to anyone
else what he had seen, then an accidental death wouldn't raise many
eyebrows. Not in this part of the world anyway. It was the land of the
oppressed: Armenians, Kurds, and even Gypsies all jammed together
in a small vortex of land. Every once in a while one of them remembered just how oppressed they were and lashed out, and someone was
killed. Shea would just have to be that one.

Zhubin bounced along the countryside. He knew in which direction he was headed but had no idea where the journalist might be going. The road from the border only went toward one big city in Turkey: Van.

Zhubin placed his mobile phone in his lap. He was waiting for a call from SAVAMA headquarters. They had petitioned the Turks to get a satellite fix on the SUV's GPS unit. The Turks weren't being helpful enough, however. They had, after all, turned away the request for Talib's helo to enter their airspace.

Zhubin bounced hard over a hump in the road and his knees hit the steering wheel. His phone almost fell out of the jeep. He snatched it in midair. When he looked at it, it was ringing. He had to pull over to hear. The words to the song about making it through the wilderness were uncannily appropriate for his situation. On the second ring, he answered.

"Where are they?" he asked, his voice low, like a man who had no patience for anything but quick to the point information.

"We tracked them to Lake Van," the anonymous voice on the other end of the line said. It was a voice that changed with every eight-hour shift at SAVAMA headquarters.

I knew it, Zhubin said to himself. He was surprised by what he heard next, however.

"The target has begun heading back toward you. We have a fix on your vehicle. It's coming straight at you."

"How long?"

"Five minutes maximum, at current speed."

Zhubin hung up. He was confused. And he was rarely confused.

THE YOUNG SAVAMA AGENT ARMAN DROVE FAST AROUND A BEND IN the road and couldn't stop quickly enough to avoid slamming into the jeep that Zhubin had parked across it. Zhubin had staged the crash as soon as he had hung up with SAVAMA headquarters. With luck, he hoped it would buy him the opportunity to kill the Irishman and snag Neda alive.

The SUV flew into the air and rolled, miraculously landing on its tires again. But it had stopped as planned.

Zhubin came out from behind some bushes on the side of the road and opened the driver's side door. He kept his gun drawn. The door opened, and Arman fell out of the SUV onto the ground. Arman hadn't been wearing a seat belt and his head was smashed in from the impact. He was bleeding profusely. Zhubin didn't pay him much attention. He was focused on the inside of the SUV. But no one was there. He turned back to the young agent and bent down.

"Where are they?" he asked.

The agent was almost completely unconscious. He managed to whisper, "Lake." He coughed out another word. Zhubin couldn't be sure but he thought he heard the name "Fatima." The oozing blood slowed to a stop, and so finally did the young SAVAMA agent's breath.

Zhubin looked down and saw the scroll Arman was clutching in his hand. He was torn. If he called the president and told him that he had the scroll, the president would make him go back to Tehran. That meant he'd lose his tail. If no one knew that he had the scroll, on the other hand, he could continue on and catch the journalist.

He made his decision. Zhubin climbed into the SUV and turned it around. He headed back toward Lake Van.

SHEA AND NEDA WERE ANXIOUS. THEY WANTED TO GET TO VAN AS quickly as possible and get away. The problem, of course, was that Neda was traveling illegally. She had no passport or papers of any kind. Shea was hoping that he could pull some strings to help. He knew enough government officials in the Middle East. And he hoped the executives at British News would see fit to assist. Especially given the story he was working on.

Once they hear about this, they'll do whatever it takes. Ratings. This story will get them ratings. That's what the world is about these days, isn't it? Whether the number of Facebook friends or television viewers. It all means eyeballs. And eyeballs mean money. . . . I'll bring them lots of eyes.

But first he needed to get somewhere where he could communicate with the outside world. And that meant an Internet cafe.

The bus plodded along. It stopped, it seemed, every block. It wouldn't take a genius to figure they had gone to Van. The SAVAMA was one of the best intelligence agencies in the world. It wouldn't be long before an Iranian manhunt would begin for them.

Shea watched as a middle-aged woman wearing a red headdress that draped over her shoulders and hung down to her waist got off the bus. It was early and there weren't many people about.

There were just three people left on the bus—two burly men who looked like construction workers and a teenage girl carrying a knapsack full of books.

They rounded the lakeshore and began to enter the city proper. The bus line map above the windows displayed all the stops. He noticed a stadium to his left and matched it to the map. Shea figured out where they were. He had been to the city before on his way to Iran, but wasn't familiar enough with it to know where they were exactly.

He strained to see any cafe signs or spots where he might find an Internet hot spot. It all looked very residential. The streets were wide and the buildings they passed were clean and handsome. The facades were all washed cement and painted in muted greens and grays. Colorful Ottoman tiles stretched on many of them from the ground to the roofs. Van was a quaint city but not too friendly in terms of signage.

Neda was gazing out at the lake, which they skirted the whole way round to the city. She saw flashing lights in the distance. She knew Gaspar's body had been found.

Shea looked up again at the bus map. The line ended, he noticed, next to the international sign for railroad. Train stations were always hubs for Internet cafes, cheap motels, and pretty much anything one could want when on the lam. To be safe, they'd have to wait it out until the end of the line. It would turn out to be not such a wise decision.

6

POLICE CARS AND AN AMBULANCE WERE PULLING A BODY FROM THE lake. Zhubin stopped and got as close as he could to the action. He could see the body on the stretcher. It wasn't a Westerner, and that is all he needed to see.

Zhubin could see every street in Van on his GPS, but this was of little use to him. What he needed to do was to get inside the journalist's head. From the lake there were few escape options. The central city would be the best place to get in touch with people. He'd be looking to do that, Zhubin thought. *I would.* And where would be the easiest place to call or get online? An Internet cafe. He checked his GPS and found several cafes listed, thankfully not all that many for a city Van's size. He planned to visit them in order.

The last Internet cafe in the direction he was headed was located at the train station.

THE BUS STOPPED AND PARKED AT THE TERMINAL. SHEA AND NEDA got off, thanking the driver as best they could for taking them on their journey free of charge. Shea had Turkish lira—he had currency of all the surrounding countries. As one of his television producers told him early on in his career: "Money talks so you can walk." In dangerous places it was important to be able to "talk"—but he only had large bills. The bus driver had waived the fare for them both.

They walked across the street, which had so many electric wires stretched across it Shea couldn't count them all, and he saw the train station a block away. It was next to a ferry terminal by the lake.

The city was coming alive with commuters heading to work and kids to school. Again Shea thought of how similar people all around the world were in their day-to-day habits, functions, and tasks.

He spotted a small snack stand on the corner serving coffee and he couldn't resist stopping. Shea was starved and in need of caffeine. Neda indulged him and they got two large Turkish coffee and two *simits*—a donut-like pastry with sesame seeds.

They ate and drank right there on the street corner. Shea spit out the sediment in the bottom of the cup and Neda laughed. They both relaxed for a second. Their nerves had been on end for twelve straight hours. They needed a break. But they weren't going to get one.

The black SUV careened around the corner and crashed into the snack stand. Zhubin jumped out, his weapon drawn.

"Run!" Shea screamed to Neda.

Shea kicked the open door of the SUV into Zhubin's arm and he fired off a wild shot. People scattered like ants.

Zhubin recovered quickly but it had given Shea enough time to bolt to the other side of the SUV. They began to play what looked like a stupid children's game: Shea would run to the back of the vehicle, Zhubin would chase him from the other side. Then Shea would run to the front, and Zhubin would zip there. After a couple of back and forths like this, Zhubin ended the game: he shot straight through the door windows. He missed.

The coffee server got in on the act and threw an urn of hot coffee onto Zhubin from behind. Zhubin turned around ready to shoot him when four policemen came onto the scene. This was their favorite coffee spot. They brandished their weapons and Zhubin had to submit. They slapped the cuffs on him.

Shea slinked off across the street and got lost in the crowd of onlookers that had gathered. Almost all of them carried a newspaper under their arm and two out of three of them smoked. The men wore ties and the woman dresses or skirts. Turkey was like most Arab nations: proper, and that meant proper attire, too.

Shea felt a hand grab his and looked up to see Neda's face. That face. God, he loved that face.

They ran, holding hands, to the ferry terminal. A boat was departing. They didn't care where it was going. They hopped on.

SHEA AND NEDA WENT FROM ONE DECK TO ANOTHER LOOKING FOR
open space. They opted not to sit inside near any of the straggly passengers. Instead, they plunked down on two benches on the upper deck.
Finally they were alone. Finally they could sit. Finally they were safe.

The ferry cast off from the dock. Its horn blew twice.

"Where do you think we are headed?" Shea asked. He was one of
those types of people who always asked questions, almost reflexively,
sometimes even when he knew the answer, sometimes even when he
knew the person he was asking didn't have the answer. It made his profession a whole lot easier. Questions and questioning were natural to
him.

Shea rubbed the back of his neck.

Neda shrugged her shoulders in answer to his question. She looked
out at the platform. The people on it were getting smaller and smaller
as the ferry pulled farther and farther away from shore. To her, those
people represented the past. It, too, got smaller and smaller the farther
things got away.

The ticket taker came by to check their tickets. They had none, of
course, but Shea was able to purchase two for ten lira apiece. The ferryman spoke English.

"How long is the trip?" Shea asked.

"Two hours to Tatvan," the ferryman said. "American?"

"Irish," Shea answered.

The ferryman smiled and moved on as he made as if he was drinking an imaginary drink. "Good."

"Tatvan is directly across, on the other side of the lake. That much I know," Shea said. "We're heading due west."

"More of them could be waiting for us there, too," Neda said. Her voice was soft. She seemed depressed. Shea recognized the symptoms of shock and its aftereffects. He had seen it many times in violent situations. Hell, he had experienced these symptoms himself more than once.

He moved over and sat down on her bench, putting his arm around her shoulder to comfort her. "They don't know that we got on the ferry. No one saw us," he said.

"But they'll eventually figure it out."

"Probably. But by then, hopefully, we'll be somewhere where they can't find us. If I can get to a phone or get online I can get in touch with London. Once they know where I am I can have them call the embassy. We'll be safe then."

Shea hadn't wanted to ask Neda on the bus about what Gaspar had said about his brother and the Vatican. It hadn't been the place or the time to dissect it. Now was.

9

"WHAT WAS GASPAR TALKING ABOUT WHEN HE DIED? HIS BROTHER. The Vatican. The Third Secret of Fatima. All that?"

"I don't know what the Third Secret of Fatima is. But I do know Gaspar's brother is part of the Iranian delegation to the Vatican."

"I didn't know the Iranians had a delegation to the Vatican. That seems odd."

"Not really. Most countries do. The Vatican is considered its own nation and, just like the United Nations, countries have their own ambassador to it. What is strange about the Iranian delegation is how big it is. Most countries only have a token number of people at their Vatican embassy. It's not as if there is that much going on there in terms of Vatican relations. No passports, visas, or any mundane operational matters to deal with either. But the Iranian government has the second biggest Vatican contingent after the Dominican Republic—and that's a seriously Catholic country."

"Why?"

"I don't know. The only reason I even know that much is because Gaspar and I spoke about it when his brother was assigned to the embassy, which is also strange. Gaspar's brother—his name is Balthazar—is an archaeologist like Gaspar."

"Why would Iran send an archaeologist to the Vatican?"

"That's what Gaspar and I couldn't figure. But they stuck him in the archives and had him doing research all day, at least that was the last I heard. That was before . . . before I lost touch with Gaspar, before . . . my husband was killed."

"So you know him?"

"Balthazar? Of course. I know Gaspar's whole family. Even his brother in Qom. He studies theology there."

"Right, he said that."

"We were sort of one big family: my husband, me, Gaspar, and everyone. Especially since my parents died when I was young."

"When was that?"

"During the Revolution. 1979. I was three."

Neda choked back tears, but they forced their way through. "This has to end," she said. "They cannot force people to live like this, in fear. We are not hateful people but our government wants us to be hateful. I wish people in the West could understand that. Only a minority of the country is made up of religious zealots. The rest of us are like you. People are the same. Governments and religions corrupt people."

Shea laughed and Neda pulled away from him.

"You think this is funny, Michael? You think this is untrue?"

He cut her short. "No, Neda, I don't. I was laughing because I think those same thoughts all the time. We are all alike. My blood can be your blood. We are human beings and we forget that. We get so caught up in politics and hate that we forget that we come from the same gene pool— the same two people if you believe in that, which I don't believe you do."

"I believe in Ahura Mazda."

"Sounds like a car."

Neda looked at him, her head tilted. "Now you are being funny." She smiled a little and sniffled.

"Yes, I am. Trying, anyway."

"I am Zoroastrian. I believe in good, but I also believe that evil exists in the world. It is the foundation of my faith, the battle between these two forces."

"Well, we picked an interesting time to find each other then, because we are in the midst of exactly that: a war between good and evil."

"There always was and always will be such a war."

"Unless," Shea said, "there is no future."

Shea leaned against Neda. She turned her head to look out at the lake and the passing countryside. A mountain range rose in the distance. It was a crisp, clear, and sunny day. Lake Van glistened.

Shea reached over and turned her chin toward his. He kissed her. "I will take care of you."

"I know that you will, Michael. I know. But I can take care of myself."

Neda tilted her head and let it rest on Shea's shoulder. They were exhausted. They had been up all night and had barely eaten. The boat's rhythm rocked them both to sleep.

10

IT TOOK ALMOST TWO HOURS FOR ZHUBIN TO TALK THE TURKISH authorities into letting him call Tehran. Fifteen minutes later, he was released.

The SAVAMA agent was on a rampage. He got back to the area of Van where he had last seen Shea and Neda and went into the Internet cafe. The owner, his lapels held together with Zhubin's hand, said he hadn't seen anyone fitting their description. From the look of fright on the owner's face, Zhubin believed him.

Zhubin needed to get inside the journalist's head again. He heard a train whistle. He went to the station and looked at the schedule. The trains were heading east to Iran. The train schedule also listed the ferry schedule. The ferry headed west. Passengers could make the connections and take the train all the way to Istanbul. It didn't take long for Zhubin to figure out where Shea had gone.

Zhubin checked the ferry schedule against the time when he was arrested. A ferry had left for Tatvan about the same time. He bet that's where they were, or would be in a couple of hours. Obviously he couldn't be there to greet them, but he knew a couple of men who could.

Zhubin took out his mobile phone and dialed an encrypted number. "It's me," he said. There was silence on the other end of the line. These men were good. They wouldn't let their voices get out into the universe. Who knew who was listening? Zhubin spoke: "Two are coming from Van. I'll have the photos sent." The line went dead.

Zhubin next called SAVAMA headquarters and instructed them to MMS text photos of Shea and Neda to the contract killers he had just called.

Another ferry to Tatvan was leaving. He hopped aboard.

THE TWO KURDISH TERRORISTS THAT ZHUBIN HAD CONTACTED WERE twin brothers. They wore light blue blazers, even lighter blue open-collared shirts, dark pants, and black loafers. The only thing that didn't match were their socks—one wore black socks, and the other white. They had short-cropped black hair and thick mustaches.

They didn't have to travel very far to get to the location Zhubin had told them to get to; they worked at the Tatvan train station.

The brothers worked as clerks but were actually members of the PKK, the terrorist organization that had long opposed Turkish rule. The PKK bombed, kidnapped, and assassinated for much of the 1980s and 1990s. Then they ran out of money. Their secular ideology didn't sit well with any of the religious organizations that funded other terrorist groups. So they changed their ways. They embraced Islam. Along came Iran. Along came the money—but with a caveat: some PKK members had to work as contract agents for SAVAMA. The twins, Kendal and Kendo, known locally as "the two Kens," volunteered.

The twins had worked on their remote family farm for most of their lives. Working undercover in no matter what capacity allowed them to escape rural life. Their father, a senior member of the PKK, was proud and bid them farewell. They were eternally thankful to Iran for getting them out from under his harsh rule.

The twins trained diligently and became experts in all sorts of weaponry. Kendo became a serious martial artist, while Kendal focused more on becoming a sharpshooter. Between them they could handle just about any situation: close combat or long-range sniper assassination.

Zhubin liked how the twins complemented one another and he used them whenever he needed some "work done" in the area. They had never let him down. He hoped they wouldn't now.

12

SHEA LEANED OVER THE RAILING. TATVAN WAS DEAD AHEAD. HE turned to tell Neda but she was still asleep. The breeze had blown her hair over her face and she was curled up in a fetal position on the bench.

A pickle. A fine pickle, Michael. And now you've brought her into it. Another one. Another potential victim of yours.

He looked away from her. He could see the city pretty clearly now. *What a dump*, he thought, choosing to change the subject he was thinking about from the situation he was in to the location where he was.

He could see the yellow hotel and outlying buildings of town. Everything looked run-down. The bus station, the cafes, restaurants, and the hotel in the distance. It had a sign on top near the roof. Shea wondered what the name of the hotel was. He was always intrigued by hotel names. They were usually so boring—a street address, a family name. He relished the good ones. He stayed in a small inn called the

Pigsty once in Marseilles. The place unfortunately had lived up to its name. In Berlin he had stayed at a hotel called Aeroplane. It was an old airplane converted into a hostel. However, it was just as uncomfortable as sleeping on a plane—and it didn't take you anywhere. The best place he had stayed, though, was in Sweden, at a place called The Igloo. It was warm inside.

Shea looked farther off into the hills. They were rolling and beautiful. He took in a deep breath of fresh air and sat back down. He was satisfied that despite the looks of Tatvan he could find an Internet cafe there. He'd get in touch with London, check into the hotel, and wait for the cavalry to arrive.

He'd report on Munjed's death and tell the world what he had seen in Lake Urmia: the meeting between Talib, his uncle, and the Chechen. Then he'd have to see if he could find his uncle again. A worldwide report on O'Shaughnessy's whereabouts and doings wouldn't ingratiate his uncle to the terror group he was working with now.

Timing was important. He had to catch his uncle while his trail was still warm, while he could link him to Iran and the Chechens. While he had the chance. A chance, anyway.

Shea thought about heading straight to Chechnya from where he was. He could leave Neda in the embassy's care. He could get to Grozny quickly from Tatvan. It might make sense.

Expose, he thought. *Transparency is what keeps people honest and the world intact.* That is why he went into journalism in the first place . . . for the clear truth.

13

SHEA REMEMBERED SITTING IN THE DARK WITH HIS UNCLE AND LIS-tening to the BBC radio reports about the bombings throughout Ireland. He remembered watching the images of the bomb's destruction on television. He remembered reading about the violent acts and letters claiming responsibility in the newspaper. The stories, the comments, the way things played out in the media mattered a great deal to his uncle and his cohorts. That was power. It was more power than they had; it was judgment, the most powerful thing a human being ever had to face.

After the cover-ups and shady dealings at Belfast—his uncle's world—Shea wanted to get as far away from that as possible. He also wanted to do good. And he wanted power of his own. Besides police work, journalism was the next best thing. Or so he thought. He was soon schooled in the selective nature of the media. Stories of importance were often dropped for lighter fare, more appealing to advertisers. Political slants infected stories. The media had become, he learned, social, cultural, political, and business lobbyists. Hard news stories with "just the facts" didn't get ratings. Sex was what sold best. The thought jarred his mind.

Britney Spears. The two most searched words on the Internet last year: Britney Spears. Fuck all. What's the media come to now? What's the world come to?

Shea leaned down and brushed Neda's hair aside. He kissed her on the cheek. "Wake up," he said, as he shook her gently. "We're here."

The boat lightly banged into the dock and the crew tied it off. They stood on deck as the gangway lowered and passengers disembarked. Shea scoped the dock area for anyone or anything suspicious. All looked normal. He figured they had at least a two-hour lead on their pursuers. If things went according to plan, he'd have some type of protection before they were found out.

"You okay?" Shea asked Neda.

She yawned and nodded her head. "We just need to find Gaspar's brother, Balthazar, in Rome. He is our only link now."

She was right, of course. But Shea had another card to play with his Chechen source, the one who had informed him of his uncle's where-abouts to begin with. If he could find him, he could report all of the players in the plot and quash any nuclear ambitions Talib had. This, to Shea, was far more important than trying to figure out some religious nonsense. He kept these thoughts to himself, however. The task in front of him was to get safe.

They followed the other passengers off the boat and into the termi-nal. Many of the passengers walked straight through and boarded the train that was departing for Istanbul.

Inside the terminal building there were several wooden benches spread out within a few feet of each other on a scuffed-up tiled floor. The ticket counters comprised two Plexiglas windows. They each had a small slot on the bottom for customers to trade cash for tickets.

Shea looked at one window and then the other. He nudged Neda. "Look," he said.

Behind the two windows were two men who were identical twins. "Weird," Neda mumbled, and they walked to the tourist information board. Shea hoped he could spot an Internet cafe on the map. But it was he who was spotted.

14

THE TWO KENS HAD SEEN SHEA AND NEDA DISEMBARK. THEY DIDN'T look up when they saw them. They each took their weapons from their respective drawers and placed "Closed" signs on their windows. They walked around the counter to the lobby area.

Shea had seen a sign on the map for something that looked like an Internet cafe. It was in the hotel across the street. But he had to pee badly, and he couldn't hold it until he got to the hotel. He pointed to the men's room and Neda took his cue—she hit the ladies' room.

The two Kens followed them robotically. Kendal followed Neda into the ladies' room and Kendo went after Shea.

Shea raced to the urinal and was in mid pee when the men's room door opened. He turned to see that it was one of the goofy clerks he had just made mention of. *Looks like Borat,* Shea thought, and went back to concentrating on his whiz.

Shea's ears perked up when he saw that the man wasn't heading into a stall. Nor was he headed for the urinal to his left. The urinal to Shea's right was out of order. A clerk who worked at the terminal every day would know that.

Shea spun around. Kendo was standing directly behind him, about to try and choke Shea. Shea pissed all over him. This stunned Kendo. He looked down at his pants in disbelief.

Shea, cock out, popped Kendo in the nose. It sent Kendo back a couple of feet, and Shea kicked Kendo in the groin. This also proved to hurt Shea's own man piece—his zipper cut into him. Shea felt the pain and tried to zip up quick. But he wasn't fast enough. Kendo caught him with an uppercut. The blow hit Shea just right and knocked the wind out of him. Kendo kicked Shea in the shin and then attempted a knockdown roundhouse kick.

Shea had learned to fight with the wind knocked out of him. He was trained to fight with one goal: put the opponent down. In Krav Maga there was no fancy footwork. A fighter inflicted the most pain in the least amount of moves. Period. Game over.

Shea anticipated the kick and let it catch him in the left ribs. He wrapped his arm around Kendo's leg. This left Kendo hopping on one leg. He tried to punch Shea, but it was no use. There was no way that was going to happen.

Shea kicked Kendo's leg out from under him with a short sweep. He followed Kendo's fall to the ground and twisted his body so that his back was across Kendo's chest. As soon as Kendo hit the floor Shea knew what would happen: Kendo's head would snap up reflexively. The body does that. It tries to protect itself. Shea wouldn't let it.

Shea caught Kendo with the tip of his elbow as his head snapped up. He aimed it just under Kendo's nose and it crushed his nose bone into his brain.

Shea stood up, then Neda came running into the men's room wearing nothing but her underwear.

15

NEDA'S BATTLE WITH KENDAL KEPT REPLAYING IN FLASHY, SHORT clips in her mind as she ran:

Kendal had waited a few seconds before going into the ladies' room after Neda. He wanted her to be in a vulnerable position when he went in so as to avoid any hassles. Even though he was an expert shot, a sitting target was much easier than a moving one. He wanted to wait until Neda sat down.

Neda heard the door open and, still being paranoid, looked under the stall to see who it was. She saw a man's pair of shoes and she knew that meant trouble.

Neda slipped out of her long skirt and draped it over the seat so that its hem lay on the ground, as if she were sitting. She stood on the toilet and waited. When the man's head peeked under the door, she kicked it as hard as she could. It sent Kendal flying on his back and knocked the gun out of his hand. The gun bounced against the mirror and landed in the sink. The faucet turned on.

Neda tried to lunge over the fallen man but he grabbed her feet. She fell onto the ground and tried to twist loose. He was too strong. Kendal grabbed some of the flesh on her thigh and pulled her toward him on the ground. Neda dug her nails into the small grooves on the tiles but they were of no help.

Kendal now had both of her legs. He stood up and dragged Neda to the sink. He dropped her to pick up his gun and she quickly scrambled to her feet and stood facing him. He pointed the gun at her chest and fired. She heard it click. The water had damaged the chamber and saved her.

Neda didn't stick around for him to try another shot. She fled out the door.

The sink was overflowing and when Kendal took his first step to chase after her he slipped and fell.

16

NEDA WAS SO SCARED THAT SHE COULDN'T SPEAK. SHE WAVED HER arms and pointed as she ran into the men's room toward Shea.

Shea saw Kendal's arm and the gun before he saw the whole man. He shoved Neda into one of the stalls, took two long strides and a running jump. He landed square on Kendal's chest. The gun went flat against the floor.

Shea literally walked up him, stepping first on Kendal's chest and then his head. This pushed Kendal to the ground and left him with his head placed between Shea's legs.

Kendal managed to get hold of the gun on the ground and raised his arm to shoot. Shea grabbed the gun from his hand in a flash and used the butt of the gun to crush in the top of Kendal's skull. He exacted the blow on the softest part of the top of the head, midway between the crown and the forehead. Kendal died instantly.

Shea ran to the stall and found Neda curled up, wet and shivering.

"It's all right. I took care of them. You're safe now," Shea said, and bent low, placing his chin on her head and holding her.

"Michael," Neda said after a few seconds.

"Yes?"

"The man . . ."

"I know."

"He could have . . ." She broke down.

"He didn't."

Between tears she said, "They know that we are here."

Shea nodded so that she could feel it, and he continued to hold her tight.

IT TOOK A FEW MINUTES FOR SHEA TO CALM NEDA DOWN. THANK-fully, no one else had come into the men's room to see the two dead bodies strewn on the floor.

When Neda seemed as composed as she was going to get, Shea left her and dragged Kendo and Kendal into separate stalls, propping them up on the toilets. He needed to get Neda's clothes. He went to the ladies' room but a woman had just entered. She gave him a dirty look, and Shea backed away. He thanked God for what he saw next: a souvenir shop.

The old woman selling socks, gloves, and baseball caps was glad to sell Shea a white tunic. He purchased a new shirt for himself as well and let the old woman keep the change. It was a big tip and she smiled wide, insisting that he allow her to fold the garments properly and put them in a bag. Shea was impatient but didn't want to cause a scene. He waited as the old woman folded the items just so, and handed them back to him.

Inside the men's room, Shea ripped open the bag and gave Neda her tunic. They were outside of the terminal inside of two minutes, and Shea headed straight for the hotel.

"Michael, where are you going?" Neda asked.

"There is Internet service and a phone. We can call for help."

"But they know that we are here. More will come. This place isn't safe."

"The hotel is our only connection to the world. We don't have another choice."

Neda, however, was staring at her choice—the train. It was getting ready to leave.

Shea knew that Neda was right. Even if the embassy could be reached quickly it would take time for them to send assistance. By that time, the SAVAMA would likely send more assassins. He thought about the bald pit bull of an agent back in Van, and hoped he wasn't the one still giving chase. The agent was the meanest-looking man Shea had ever come across.

Neda had already begun walking toward the train. Shea hurried up next to her. He was carrying the bag the old woman had given him with his new shirt in it.

Let her go, Michael. Stay and let her go.

He thought the situation through. Neda had no money and no papers. If she got picked up by the authorities, she'd be sent back to Iran—and killed. He took her hand in his and they ran down the platform

On board the train, Shea paid for a couchette, their own cabin in first class. It had a small handheld shower inside its tiny private bathroom. It was awkward but it did the trick. Neda went straight to it after the train bumped to a start.

Shea kept his eyes on the platform. He was scanning to make sure they hadn't been followed. The coast looked clear.

18

WHEN SHEA TURNED AROUND NEDA WAS CLEANED UP, HER HAIR wet, and she was dressed in her new white tunic. She plunked down on the bench in the train cabin. Shea noticed that she wasn't wearing any underwear. Neda felt the material on the hem of her tunic. It was thick, white linen.

"Not bad, Mr. Shea. Not bad. You have some taste after all."

"You sound surprised."

"Well, I have noticed what you've been wearing."

"What's wrong with what I have on?" Shea asked and looked down at his soiled jeans, shirt, and mud-soaked boots. "Guess I could use a shower, too."

Shea washed himself and his clothes, leaving them hanging out of the train window to dry. He sat down on the bench opposite Neda wrapped only in his towel.

"Feel better?" he asked Neda. "I do."

"I'll feel better once there is no chance of Mahmoud Talib being named the Mahdi. We must stop him, Michael. If he rallies the Muslim population World War III will break out. There is already too much Islamaphobia around the world."

"There will be more resources in Istanbul for us to stop him. The embassy is there. I just hope we make it in time," Shea said.

"The Mahdi is said to rule for many years. There will be time."

"I meant time to stop his nuclear plans."

"Your uncle. Tell me, who is he?"

"His name is Sean O'Shaughnessy and he is a very bad man. He believes in fighting oppressors—violently."

"That sounds like a good thing."

"Depends who you consider the oppressors. He thinks they are governments—oppressive regimes."

"Then why is he working with the Iranian government?"

"Because he finally found a zealot crazier than himself. Talib upped the ante for my uncle. Talib's mission, from what I have seen and read, is to break the power structure of the world, specifically the Western power structure. The only thing that I can figure is that in some way this appealed to my uncle. That and the money. He was always looking for money. He believed that in the right hands money gave power to the people."

"He sounds more like a mercenary than a revolutionary."

"Oh, he would never keep the money for himself. Any money he got, he would give away to fund a new rebellion. It wasn't about the money itself, it was about the power of money. Taking from the rich and giving to the poor."

"A Robin Hood."

"How do you know so much about the West, even our fables?"

"There is this thing called the Internet . . ."

"Now you are trying to be funny."

They both smiled.

Neda went on, "I studied Western culture at school. That and politics. The world is at a critical juncture between the two right now, Michael." She looked off as if in a daze. "One person could light the world afire, and he happens to be the leader of my country."

"He scares you that much?"

"If you knew what I know, you'd be scared to death."

19

THE TRAIN BREEZED PAST LARGE STRETCHES OF FIELDS. SNOW-capped mountains and streams of white gave way to large patches of dark trees.

It was rugged terrain in a rough part of the world. A two-hundred-acre graveyard they passed by was testament to just how rough the environs were. In the distance were several large castles and mosques. There was no doubt as to what part of the world this was; all was Ottoman style. The only question that might be asked would be what period in time it was. Everything looked centuries old.

"Why does Talib hate the West so much?" Shea asked Neda, breaking the silence that had set in between them.

Neda sighed. "It goes back to the shah's regime. People forget what a tyrant the shah of Iran was. There were the very, very rich and the very, very poor.

"The shah and his friends lived an opulent lifestyle on the backs of his people. He spent millions on parties, drank from fine crystal, and was extravagant. People became outraged, especially when he libeled the clergy. We are a religious people.

"The president's own parents were very, very poor. And they were religious. They became part of the Islamic uprising and were killed along with many others during the Revolution. That's why he, Mahmoud Talib, blames the West for backing and supporting the shah. For him it is a personal vendetta."

"When did you suspect Talib's intentions? When did you begin to figure out that he wanted to become the Mahdi?" Shea asked.

"All along. All the students at the seminary he attended said Mesbah Yavari had discovered the Mahdi."

"Who is Mesbah Yavari?"

"He is a radical cleric who lives in the city of Qom and runs a religious school. He is the true evil behind Mahmoud. He is the one who must be dealt with—in time."

"Neda," Shea said, sliding closer to her, "how did you . . . I don't know, become you? Become a member of—what did you call it—the Golden Dawn?"

"That, too, Michael, I will tell you . . . in time."

20

NEDA STOPPED TALKING AND LOOKED AT SHEA. THE DISSIPATION OF fright had spun itself into another type of feeling, a sexual feeling. She looked at Shea wantonly, and they were both about to act on it when there was a knock at the cabin door. Shea figured that he had better answer it. He directed Neda to the bathroom, and she shut the door so she couldn't be seen.

A waiter appeared at the door. Room service for first class. Shea ordered almost the entire menu and a bottle of champagne.

Finally a drink, he thought. *Or six.*

When Neda returned from the bathroom, Shea was sitting where she had been on the bench. "Just room service," he informed her. "It's going to be a long ride to Istanbul."

She sat next to him. "We have a lot to figure out. How to stop them both: Mahmoud and your uncle."

"We have time for that." Shea placed his hand on Neda's thigh and she didn't resist. "Now, I think we better get something else out of the way," he said.

He leaned over and kissed her. They kissed again more passionately this time.

"Lock the door," Neda said.

When Shea went to lock the door Neda pulled up her skirt.

Trees flew by the window.

Shea undid his towel and lay on top of her. He was in fine shape and his back muscles bulged as he put the weight of his body on his hands.

Telephone poles. Wires. An old building. They whizzed by in succession.

He was already hard, but he looked down at her body again. "Take your clothes off," he said softly. And she did. They kissed again, and that was all the foreplay they attempted.

"I need you inside me. I need to feel you," she whispered.

They entered a tunnel and the cabin went black.

Shea felt her tingle as he entered her. She was wet.

The railcar shifted along the tracks. Rat tat tat, rat tat tat, the wheels held tight in the tracks as they chugged.

It was gruff, the sex. Hard. Fast, and without tenderness. They each wanted the end result. They weren't biding time, getting to know each other.

Rat tat tat. Rat tat tat. And then there was the hollow sound of the tunnel coming to an end.

A bright blast of sunshine lit up the cabin.

21

SEAN O'SHAUGHNESSY WAS MISERABLE. HE HAD BEEN STRANDED IN the same small, barrackslike room with Alu Abramov all day. They had made it to Abramov's secure compound in Argun, just ten miles east of Grozny—but a world away.

There was a virtual army defending the compound. But O'Shaughnessy wondered if that was even enough to hold off the full Chechen command for long, if indeed the full Chechen command was behind the assault at the airport. Abramov was making calls to find out if that was the case.

"Good news!" Abramov said, hanging up. "The ambush was not sanctioned." He had learned that a rival gang was behind the airport raid. A rogue commander had found out about Abramov's nuclear theft. The commander figured if he killed Abramov, he could enlist Abramov's men and get the nuclear material all in one fell swoop.

Abramov began to work the phones to plan an attack. He was going to fight back.

"Alu," O'Shaughnessy said, sitting behind an old metal desk in an uncomfortable chair. "We need to focus. The deal with Iran is more important than this."

But Abramov wasn't having any of it. He could do both, he said. He'd even use the funds from the Iran deal to fight this enemy. Abramov was stubborn, and O'Shaughnessy knew it wouldn't get him anywhere to argue more.

Personally, O'Shaughnessy didn't give a rat's ass about any rival gang wars. The only thing that he cared about was being stuck in Chechnya. Abramov had lied to him. He needed to finagle the materials to build the bomb trigger. Wasting time listening to Abramov wasn't helping matters.

O'Shaughnessy thought of the components he was most in need of at the moment, and those were specialized timing switches. In order for an implosion to cause the type of effect that was needed to trigger a nuclear reaction, he needed to build up enough pressure for things to blow—fast and accurately. The type of plutonium that was being used was extremely volatile. That meant the triggering device had to be accurate. Talib was building a fission-style bomb, therefore O'Shaughnessy's role was critical. If the trigger didn't set off the right shock wave . . . no ka-boom.

THERE WERE TWO TYPES OF NUCLEAR BOMBS. THE FISSION TYPE O'Shaughnessy was working on where explosion creates an implosion. The implosion creates a shock wave propelling the plutonium pieces together into a sphere, which strikes a pellet of beryllium/polonium at the center. If done accurately, the fission reaction can begin and the bomb explodes. The entire fission process takes a fraction of a second and there is no room for error.

The other style of nuclear bomb was a fusion bomb. These were more difficult to build, even though they were more lethal and accurate. To build one took some doing. And it was hard to hide or sneak the type of material needed.

For a fusion bomb, deuterium and tritium are needed as fuels for the fusion process itself. These are both gases and difficult to store. Also, tritium doesn't last long and needs to be continually replenished. Lastly, these two fuels need to be highly compressed at extremely high temperatures to initiate the fusion reaction. None of these could easily escape the eyes and ears of the world's intelligence services. Satellites monitor temperatures with extreme accuracy. A temperature flare is a big signal that nuclear activity is taking place.

O'Shaughnessy contemplated all the elements needed for the bomb. He knew that Talib had a team of nuclear engineers in place throughout Iran. If he didn't produce the right mechanism with the right capabilities, the engineers would see right through it.

The parts O'Shaughnessy needed were common enough: stock-in-trade for dialysis machine manufacturers and other high-tech equipment suppliers. But he'd still have to be discreet: the parts were strictly regulated.

O'Shaughnessy's portfolio of bomb making had taken him around the world, and he could—with a single phone call—get all the materials he needed. But that might tip someone off to his undertaking. Bomb makers knew that the most dangerous interference with their profession was chatter.

O'Shaughnessy knew that he'd easily be able to discreetly get the parts he needed most for the bomb in Belfast, where his network was the strongest.

Wouldn't be so if damn Abramov had done his bit, he thought.

In Belfast, he'd be an unexpected visitor—one who called the place home.

He just needed to get there—and back.

23

NUCLEAR REGULATORS KEPT A CLOSE EYE ON ANY MATERIAL THAT could be made into a bomb. Cement, certain types of glass, various chemical elements, pressure devices, and heavy metals, along with water use were all monitored by the International Atomic Energy Agency. Sometimes ridiculous stoppages occurred.

O'Shaughnessy remembered when Israel banned a shipment of cement from entering the Gaza strip for fear the Palestinians were building a nuclear bomb, as if any of the ragtag Palestinians factions had the means or the know-how to build anything nuclear.

The most famous case of impropriety and wrongful accusation, of course, had been in the lead-up to the Iraq War. The weapons of mass destruction that didn't exist could be partially traced to "uranium yellowcake" from Niger that Iraq supposedly smuggled in.

O'Shaughnessy or anyone else in the underground could have told the Americans that was bollocks. There were only two mines in Niger that contained uranium, and they were so zipped up and regulated that an ant couldn't leave the premises without being checked for radioactive material.

Still, there were parts of the world where the IAEA didn't have glasses. And the six-foot, two-hundred-forty-pound Chechen that O'Shaughnessy was staring at had found one of those blind spots.

24

ABRAMOV IGNORED O'SHAUGHNESSY'S HARD LOOKS AND CONTINued to work the phones. He was doing two things: preparing his turf battle and ensuring that the nukes were safe and on their way to him.

O'Shaughnessy meanwhile was devising a plan to get back to Belfast. First, he needed to make sure his nephew was out of the way. The only person who knew that for certain was Mahmoud Talib. O'Shaughnessy had to get in touch with him.

On the third ring, Talib picked up. O'Shaughnessy inquired about his nephew. If Michael reported the meeting in Lake Urmia, it could affect the whole damn plan.

"I am taking care of him," Talib said.

"You said that before."

"Your nephew is proving, as you had warned, trickier to catch than we imagined. He is now in Turkey."

"Turkey! How in bloody hell did he escape Iran? I thought your men were good? The best?"

"They are. And all shall be done. In fact, he may be dead already. One of my men is on his way to confirm the kill now. *Inshallah*."

This time Talib really meant "God willing."

O'Shaughnessy knew that his nephew was a tough catch and that if Talib hadn't caught him by now there was little chance he'd capture Shea outside Iran's borders. Shea was too good and had for too long been a journalist undercover in foreign territories. This is what his nephew did for a living. Talib's men would never get him now.

A small smile of pride actually came across O'Shaughnessy's face. If nothing else, he respected his nephew. Still, he needed him stopped and he decided that he would have to take matters into his own hands. He also needed to convey to Talib the situation in Chechnya. He didn't want to get caught up in Abramov's faults . . . again. That would alienate him from Talib for good.

"Well," O'Shaughnessy began, "it looks like my nephew isn't the only thing gone missing; so have the nukes."

O'Shaughnessy could feel the coldness come through the phone even before Talib's voice.

"What do you mean?" Talib asked.

When O'Shaughnessy was finished explaining how Abramov had been hijacked and how their jet had been attacked on landing, Talib was dead quiet. "Can it be fixed?" is all he asked.

"Yes," O'Shaughnessy said. "But there needs to be some changes." O'Shaughnessy outlined his plan to Talib, and they agreed on it.

O'SHAUGHNESSY HUNG UP THE PHONE AND LOOKED OVER AT Abramov to make sure he hadn't heard the call. Alu wasn't paying attention. He was pulling piles of cash from his desk drawers and putting it all into a suitcase. One of his crew came in and took the bag.

"All is good!" Abramov clapped. "All will go as planned." He rubbed his hands together giddily. "Now it is time to celebrate."

Despite the alcohol ban in the Muslim world, Abramov took a bottle of vodka out and had a shot. "Drink!" he said to Shea, passing over the bottle.

"Unless that's Redbreast Irish whiskey, you can keep it all to yourself," O'Shaughnessy said.

"Suit yourself then," Abramov said and had another shot. He clapped his hands twice and one of his lieutenants appeared in the room. "Bring in the women," he shouted to the boyish-looking man who had just come in.

Three attractive sluts entered the room and Abramov licked his lips. "What do you say, Sean? You like? Pick one."

O'Shaughnessy declined this offer as well and excused himself out of the room. He heard disco music begin to play as he walked to one of the SUVs in front of the compound. He got in and drove away.

O'Shaughnessy did what no one expected and that's why it was safe: he drove back to Grozny airport. He caught the next flight to Moscow. From there he'd make his way to Northern Ireland.

In Moscow O'Shaughnessy called a dark contact he had at MI6, the British Secret Service. He told the man that he had new evidence on his nephew to share about the bombing at Omagh. Michael Shea was soon to be a wanted man.

An Interpol alert went out.

26

MAHMOUD TALIB HADN'T GOTTEN BACK TO TEHRAN UNTIL CLOSE TO midnight. The helicopter landed at the presidential palace and he went directly to his residence. His wife and three children were asleep.

Talib didn't like political power. He didn't like playing politics and the trappings of government. He didn't like these things because they involved compromise—and Talib didn't like to compromise. Still, he knew political power was a necessary stepping-stone to the ultimate power that he wanted to achieve—supreme power.

Talib took off his trademark jacket and went into the palace's kitchen. The staff was asleep. It was just him and the night security. He opened the refrigerator and took out a Mecca-Cola. Zionists controlled Coca-Cola and he refused to allow it to be served in his country. Coca-Cola became Mecca-Cola.

Talib sat at the table reserved for the kitchen staff and thought of how his entire life's mission rested in the hands of two strangers. They had the power to help him change and redeem the world. Then there was that other one, the one in the way, the journalist.

Talib poured the cola over ice and listened to it sizzle and pop as the cubes cracked. He left the glass half empty and went to bed. His wife slept in a separate room. Talib was tempted to go to her and relieve the stress of the day. He could tell her not to speak. He could force her to turn over and do it the way he liked and the way he knew pained her most.

He decided that he was too tired to make the effort. He wanted to reserve his strength. He needed all the strength he could get.

Talib fell asleep in all his clothes facedown on the pillows. He didn't bother to get between the sheets. He dreamt strange dreams: clouds, men in bags, invisible ghosts, lances of blue flames, shields of pure white, a battle, the feeling of tension, pillars, lakes bursting from the ground, a ship sailing, the name *Nemed* painted on a hull, sails blowing, books, symbols, ancient texts, four signatures on a document, a one-armed man, an apple tree, a sea creature with tentacles coming out of its mouth like snakes, fright, a circle with winged feet, an oak tree.

Feelings and symbols combined in a flutter. At some point in the night he must have turned over for he sat up straight in bed. He woke at the *adhan*. It was the first call to prayer of the day and he duly washed and prayed.

Allah is greater than any description
I testify that there is no deity except for Allah
I testify that Muhammad is a Messenger of Allah
Make haste toward the prayer
Make haste toward the worship
Allah is the greatest!
There is no deity except for Allah

Throughout his recitation he kept thinking of his dreams. He had no idea what they meant.

Talib didn't know it, but he had dreamed an Irish dream.

TALIB HAD PROMISED MESBAH YAVARI THAT HE WOULD DELIVER THE scroll. But it wasn't in his possession. He would have to explain that. And he decided to do it face-to-face.

Qom was just a few hours drive from Tehran, but Talib decided to take the helicopter again for efficiency's sake. From above, Qom was quite a delight on the eyes, with its various mosques, museums, architecture, and layout around the river that ran through its center.

Talib never tired of the view. He loved the feeling he got when he zipped past the minarets. The city brought back such fond memories. It was where it all began for him.

After his parents died Mahmoud was too difficult a child to be put into the care of any family member. He had expressed a strong interest in religion, and when the new seminary at Qom opened it was decided that it would be best for him to board there. At first he hated the institution. The other students picked on him and he wasn't strong enough to defend himself. So he relied on the most ancient of powers—religion.

The other boys in the seminary hadn't read as much of the Koran as he. He read as an escape. It was the only way he could lose himself and deal with the pain of his parents' deaths. It also gave him comfort. It was as if the Koran were speaking directly to him. It became his guide. He found he could seek answers and get them through the various interpretations of the Koran by the imams. It was this that led him to explore more than just the teachings of the Koran itself, but the *hadiths*, the additional stories that complemented the Koran's text.

Talib was fascinated by the imams and the belief that they obtained supernatural knowledge. He read that there were twelve imams in the Shia faith and that the Sunni Muslims didn't believe in imams the same way. They believed that only the first four caliphs were Muhammad's successors and were the leaders of the religion. He couldn't understand that, not when all the imams became like superheroes to him.

From the first imam who was killed by a sword to all those who followed and were either beheaded or poisoned to death, Talib wondered what magical powers they held. Could they ward off enemies? Could they have their wishes become commands?

The more he read the more he discovered the power of the imams. He was, for instance, enthralled by the story of Hasan al-Askari, the eleventh imam who was imprisoned for most of his life in ancient Samarra and then poisoned by the Turks for fear that his power would usurp their rule.

Talib saw al-Askari's story as a metaphor. A young man whose father was killed and his legitimacy as a holy cleric questioned. He could relate to this: a young man whose father was killed. Also, like him, al-Askari took his pain and channeled it. He devoted himself to translating the Koran. Talib saw this as devotion, and he wanted to emulate him.

Talib even saw al-Askari's death as something to be honored. The imam had fought off the influence of the terrorizing Turks, who Talib likened to the West today.

However, it was the last part of the eleventh imam's story that captured Talib so. After al-Askari died, his possessions were seized and his followers disbanded into different sects. One of those sects began to gather in secret. They believed in the occult and the afterlife. Most important, what they believed was that Hasan al-Askari had returned to life.

This was the first time that Talib had ever heard of someone returning from the afterlife. He read that al-Askari was rumored to have a son and that his son's birth had been concealed from the Turks to save the boy's life. Then he read that this boy was al-Mahdi; the twelfth imam who would reappear at the end of times to fill the world with justice, peace, and to establish Islam as the global religion. He read of the Mahdi's powers and his ability to change the world, dominating all of mankind and judging it for all of eternity.

Talib decided that he was al-Mahdi, and that the boys at school would be sorry they ever teased him.

28

FROM THE HELICOPTER LANDING PAD IN QOM TO THE SEMINARY were winding paths through gardens and past fountains. Talib breathed in the familiar scents of plums, cherries, peaches, apricots, and almonds that were grown on the grounds. His memories came alive. Scents more than sights and sounds drove Talib back in time. He could for sure remember things from a look. He could remember impressions he had from a voice or a noise. But to actually feel the past it took something olfactory.

Talib walked up the two flights of stone steps that led to the wide terrace on which Mesbah Yavari stood. The old man was looking older and older, Talib thought. The white beard was looking yellow and the Ayatollah's skin was more wrinkled and flaky. Perhaps the old man would actually die before he had to kill him off, Talib thought. Wouldn't that make life easy.

The Ayatollah and his old student greeted each other in the traditional Persian fashion: they kissed and shook hands at the same time. "*Salaam*," they each said.

"Did you bring it with you?" Mesbah Yavari asked. The Ayatollah's eyes were alight.

The call to midday prayer saved Talib from having to explain things. They walked down the hallway past the old room where Talib had slept as a student. His happy thoughts turned sour. The pillow over his face. His shorts being pulled down. The feeling of helplessness as the other boys took turns on him. Talib found himself sweating by the time he finally made it inside Mesbah Yavari's private prayer hall. They prostrated and prayed. And the Ayatollah's chronic flatulence filled the room.

After praying, they remanded themselves to Mesbah Yavari's chambers to speak. There were too many students and teachers in the hallway. Talib's presence had them all in awe and many gathered around just to sneak a peek at the president. Talib secretly enjoyed this. How far he had come from being that awkward abused student.

29

MIDWAY TO MESBAH YAVARI'S CHAMBER, TALIB'S PHONE RANG. IT was Zhubin. He excused himself and went to the railing alone. People in the courtyard below were now hustling from their prayers and going back to work. It was like that in Qom. As a holy city it stopped whatever activity was going on five times a day for prayers, and then went right back to being a busy city of a million people.

"So?" Talib asked.

"The journalist and the woman were not there," Zhubin said.

Talib almost crushed the phone in his hand.

Zhubin let the bad news sink in and then added, "But I have the missing scroll."

This enlivened Talib. "Are you sure?"

"Yes, I am sure. It is the one."

"How do you know?"

"It was with the archaeologist and another SAVAMA agent. Both are dead."

Talib mulled over the meaning of this information but it wasn't the time for that.

"Bring it to me. I'm in Qom. Ayatollah Mesbah Yavari and I will be waiting."

When he heard the Ayatollah's name, Zhubin straightened up. He was at the Tatvan train station. Turkish police were everywhere examining and interviewing people about Kendo and Kendal.

"What about the journalist and the woman? Do we just let them get away?" Zhubin asked.

"That is also being handled."

Zhubin didn't like hearing that Talib, no matter that he was the president of Iran, had gone around his back to get Shea and Neda. This emboldened him to ask, "By whom?"

Talib was about to scream through the phone and remind Zhubin that he didn't ask questions, he took orders, but he needed the agent's cooperation at the moment.

"His uncle. Leave it to him. Bring me the scroll." At that, Talib hung up. He looked down at the courtyard and saw several young seminarians picking on a young boy. Talib yelled down at them to knock it off. When the boys looked up and saw who it was they were at first shocked and then ran off in awe. The boy who was being picked on was on the ground, his school papers scattered next to him and then blown away by the wind. The young boy fought to get to his feet. He stood and wiped the tears from his eyes. "Thank you," he said in Farsi. "You are like a god from above."

Talib smiled widely and walked to Mesbah Yavari's chambers. The door shut behind him, and he felt like an excited little boy again.

SHEA AND NEDA HAD MADE LOVE OVER AND OVER AGAIN, EACH time the hunger subsided and then rose again seemingly more powerfully than before. They had pulled out the two benches in the cabin so they laid flat and made one massive bed; they used every inch of it.

Shea had never been with a woman such as Neda before, someone so voracious in between the sheets. Yet the sex wasn't strictly carnal. There was a spiritual aspect to their pleasures that Shea couldn't figure.

As the train made its way past Ankara, Turkey's capital, Shea looked out the window. He could see what looked like a giant mushroom rising from the city. It was a tall building whose lights inside began to turn on. Lights everywhere began to shine from homes and they sparkled wildly through the rolling green hills. Ankara looked vast, a metropolis.

The sun was setting and the orange haze of the twilight streamed into the cabin.

Shea was sitting up with his back resting against the cabin wall. The crisp white sheets were tangled. They only covered his crotch and one of his legs. Neda was asleep on her stomach. One of her legs was bent and partially exposed. The cabin was warm and smelled of sex. Shea took a deep breath and sighed it out.

The train rocked some as it rounded a bend, leaving Ankara behind. Neda began to wake. Her bent leg moved first then her arms stretched and searched for the sheets to cover herself. She rolled over and her perfect breasts with their perfectly round nipples hung high. Shea couldn't believe it but he got hard again.

"Hi," she said, sitting up and scooting to the cabin wall opposite him. She leaned up against it, just as he was.

"Better cover your top or we are going to have a problem again," he said.

"I don't see it as a problem. But if you do, I will." She covered herself. "I'm all for getting into trouble." She then stretched her arms up over her head and yawned again. "Are we getting close?"

"Closer. We just passed Ankara. Istanbul is another few hours."

"Then what?"

"Then we get you safe."

"Michael, we have to get to Rome. We have to get in touch with Gaspar's brother Balthazar. We must stop the coming of the Mahdi. I still don't think that you understand."

"I understand that it is important to you—"

"It's important to the world."

"Look, Neda, I think that your heart is in the right place. And maybe this Mahdi thing is going on. But what I know for sure and what I know that I can stop is a bomb, a nuclear bomb, from getting built or perhaps even going off. That isn't some mystical bet. It's real and real people—a lot of them—might die if I don't do something about it."

Neda pulled the sheets up to completely cover herself. She bent both her legs and buried her chin in her knees. "I didn't believe in the Mahdi either," she said. "Then I understood. Then I believed."

Shea didn't respond. He believed that he had said all that needed to be said—from his point of view anyway.

Neda didn't look at him. She merely looked down at her feet and began to tell him a story: "I was born in the north, near Lake Urmia. That's where you and I met. After my parents died, I used to go for long walks in the hills near those temples I told you about."

"The fire temples," Shea affirmed.

"Yes. That is when I first saw them."

"Who?"

"The shadows of a secret sect of Zoroastrians known as the Golden Dawn. That is how I know that the prophecy is true. They are the guardians of al-Mahdi. And I became one of them."

31

Neda, at first, was hesitant about telling Shea her involvement with the sect. It sounded, she knew, far out for a Westerner, especially a nonspiritual Westerner such as Shea. But divulging who she was to him now seemed like the right thing to do. They had just made love. They had become cosmically entwined. Her heart had spoken to her. And then her brain followed. His understanding of Golden Dawn would keep him invested in finding out the truth, she thought. She had to make him understand that that was the end game of this battle between good and evil—the truth. Although she would still have to hold one bit of truth back. It wouldn't be wise to share that with him now. Her power, her secret, would have to wait.

At the right time she would reveal to him her identity. For now she could, however, relay her background. Who she was and what she was, of course, were two very different things. In time, he would come to understand.

Neda went on, "There was a *dakhma* near my town. It's a wide tower with a platform that is open to the sky and it is sometimes called the Tower of Silence. It is where Zoroastrians put the dead so they can be picked clean by vultures.

"Believers go to great lengths during this ritual to keep the body from corruption. The corpse is washed in bull urine and it is dressed in clean clothes. A dog is brought to the corpse to protect it from demons. This is called *sagdid*. Dogs are very special to Zoroastrians. No one but Zoroastrians can see the corpse or participate in the ritual or else the body is deemed corrupt. A fire is then lit in the temple and frankincense and sandalwoods are burned. It is a beautiful ceremony.

"Anyway, when I walking through the hills one night I saw the fire in one of the temples. I went to see what was going on and that is when I saw shadows picking at the bones of the dead person, preparing it for the ritual burial.

"I ran away, of course, not knowing what was going on, but I was caught. I didn't know it then but it was my future husband who had captured me."

"The shadows were people?"

"Yes. They were members of the Golden Dawn. Zarathustra was the founder of the Zoroastrian religion. His name means 'golden dawn.'"

She finally looked up at Shea. He looked confused. Interested and enrapt in her story. But confused.

NEDA EXPLAINED HOW CONFUSING THIS ALL WAS TO HER ALSO, AT first: "I didn't know any of this then. Nor did I know that I had committed a grave offense to them. They had already prepared the burial. My presence corrupted the corpse and damned its soul, I was told. The only choice was for me to become one of them. It was unusual. You can only become a Zoroastrian by birth. But I had unknowingly witnessed the burial of a high priest. His spirit they said became a part of me."

"So you converted to this religion?"

"I didn't have to. The Golden Dawn is an ancient sect. They bridged the conversions between Zoroastrians and Muslims. The sect rests somewhere in between. We report to the Secret Chiefs."

Shea raised his eyebrows.

Neda continued, "No one knows who they are, but they give us our orders."

"Secret Chiefs, really?"

"Yes, really. Muslims, remember, had tried to wipe out all of the Zoroastrians and convert them. Today there aren't that many of us left as a whole religion. There are people who want us all dead. Because it was the first religion, remember. All the others—Judaism, Christianity, and Islamic beliefs—followed. Some don't like that, such as the current president of Iran."

"So are all Zoroastrians after Talib?" Shea asked.

"No, just the Golden Dawn. We are a guardian sect. Others have different responsibilities. Ours is investigating signs of the Mahdi's presence."

"What signs are there that Talib is the Mahdi?"

"The Secret Chiefs tell us there are none. That is how we know he isn't the one."

"But there is one, a Mahdi?"

"Yes."

"Here? Now?"

"He is among us. He just hasn't shown himself."

"Won't he be a little pissed off when he finds out that Talib is pretending to be him?"

Neda laughed. "He knows when his time will come. Until then those who claim to be him will be . . ." she stammered, ". . . no more."

"They are killed?"

"They are given back to their rightful owner, Angra Mainyu."

"Who is . . . ?"

"In your faith he is the devil, Satan, call him what you will. He is the twin brother to all that is good."

"So who gives him back?"

Neda finally looked up at Shea. "I do. We do. The Golden Dawn."

SHEA SLID OFF THE BED AND STOOD UP. HE WAS NAKED AND NEDA liked looking at his body. It was muscular and tight. He didn't have a lot of hair. Most Persian men did. He had facial scruff but not a beard. And that was all she liked. She wished they could go back to making love again. But the story of the Golden Dawn needed to be told. He needed to become enlightened about this part of her.

"So why go to Rome? Talib is in Iran. Wouldn't it be better to get him there?" Shea asked.

"Gaspar—he was a member of Golden Dawn, too—said that his brother Balthazar knew something about the Third Secret of Fatima and how it was related to the Mahdi. We have to prove that Talib is not the Mahdi. If he were just killed he would be considered a martyr and that might be even worse for the world. That is why we must go to Rome."

"And this Secret of Fatima?" Shea asked.

"That is what we must find out—the connection."

Shea stepped into the bathroom. Before shutting the door he said: "If you can prove him wrong, then what? He can still blow up the world with a nuclear bomb. See my point?"

"Michael, if we prove that he isn't the Mahdi and he has been faking it, no one will have to worry. His own followers will kill him. The world will be safe until the true Mahdi is revealed."

Shea didn't answer. Neda only heard the toilet flush.

34

SEAN O'SHAUGHNESSY HAD SEVERAL PASSPORTS WITH DIFFERENT aliases at his disposal. He didn't need them traveling outside Ireland. Technically, he didn't need them while traveling in Ireland either. He was not a wanted man by the law. He was, however, a wanted man by the Irish Republican Army and the Real Irish Republican Army, as well as several other Irish nationalist splinter groups.

O'Shaughnessy had turned his back on these groups after the Omagh bombing in 1998. Sure he went to prison for the offense, but something never set right with the "boys" who had worked with him over the years. Why had he been let go? And then why did he so abruptly leave the "cause"?

There was a persistent rumor that O'Shaughnessy was a rat and that he had traded intelligence on the IRA and its underlings for his freedom. Although he couldn't be tied to any arrests or blown operations, there were rumblings. Rumblings in criminal circles were as good as truths.

O'Shaughnessy still had some loyalists, and this was who he was in Belfast to see.

He took a taxi along Dargan Road, where it passed by Buffer McMahon's Bar, an old haunt. He traveled down Dock Street to City

Center where the Belfast Big Wheel welcomed visitors to City Hall. (It surely wouldn't welcome him.)

He saw the gorgeous, palacelike City Hall that he would stumble by, drunk after carousing the bars around Donegall Square. They drove past the cafes along Howard Street and the Grand Opera House where he had experienced a different sort of culture, worldly culture. He peeked down Great Victoria Street where he could see the Europa Hotel, the most bombed in all of Europe.

And he had done most of the bombing.

SEAN'S OLD FRIEND TOMMY MCGUINNESS WAS WAITING FOR HIM AT the door to his Belfast home. Tommy took over O'Shaughnessy's house and cared for it. He had been O'Shaughnessy's number two man and best friend since just about forever. Neither could remember life without the other. Even after O'Shaughnessy left town, Tommy stood by him. He knew O'Shaughnessy would be back. It was just a matter of when.

Tommy had kept O'Shaughnessy's house just as it was. He took the occasional message and passed it along. He never asked for anything in return from O'Shaughnessy and he never ever asked him any questions.

"You're looking fit, Sean," Tommy said.

There was no handshake, no hug or embrace. They exhibited familiarity by their words.

"And you, fit as a fiddle," O'Shaughnessy responded. "It's good to see you."

"Aih, and you."

The house was exactly as O'Shaughnessy remembered it, standing in the shadows of St. Peter's Cathedral. The small gated garden. The brightly colored door. The only change inside, he noticed, was the umbrella stand had been moved across the hallway. The faded blue paint on the walls was the same. The furniture, except a new La-Z-Boy and flat-screen television, look exactly as he remembered, too. In the kitchen, the old table and chairs were still there. Even the odor that came with the house—black tea, musk, and sweat—was still in the air. It was a working-class man's scent.

O'Shaughnessy sat at the kitchen table. "Pint or a spot?" Tommy asked, inquiring whether O'Shaughnessy wanted beer or tea.

"Any RB?"

"Fifteen year. Just for you," Tommy said, disappearing to the cupboard room to grab a bottle of whiskey. He poured them both a shot. "*Sláinte*," they said in unison. The glasses hit the table.

"I know it's for sipping but it goes down so smooth," O'Shaughnessy said.

"Plenty more for sipping, Sean."

"Glad to hear."

There was a moment of awkward silence between them. This is when any other normal person would have asked O'Shaughnessy what he was doing in town. But Tommy just sat there looking at the bottom of the shot glass.

"I need you to ring up a couple of the boys. Quiet types," O'Shaughnessy said. Tommy didn't look up from his glass. "Got a job for 'em," O'Shaughnessy continued. "Any such fellas around?"

"There's a few. Disposable, or . . . ?"

"We won't be needin' after."

Tommy got the message.

"Also, last thing. Need you to ring up that journalist fella. One that works with Mikey."

Tommy nodded. "That it?"

"Aih."

"Then this one is for sippin'"

Tommy poured them two more shots of Redbreast.

MORRISONS BAR WAS JUST ACROSS THE ROAD FROM BRITISH NEWS headquarters in Belfast. A black van with blackened-out windows dropped O'Shaughnessy off behind it and waited idling, blocking the alley.

O'Shaughnessy entered the back door to Morrisons and found the person he was looking for upstairs at one of the tables overlooking Bedford Street. No one else was there, the upstairs section closed.

O'Shaughnessy sat, took his hat off, and fixed his hair. The jacket stayed on to hide the holster carrying a pistol under each armpit. He stared at the man across the table from him. The man was nervous.

"Not exactly feckin' discreet are yah?" O'Shaughnessy said to Willie Dyson, the British News bureau chief. "Pub is jammed downstairs." He wasn't looking for an answer, even though Dyson tried to give one: "I didn't know. I—"

"Doesn't feckin' matter," O'Shaughnessy said. "How's your brother doing by the way? Clear?"

"Yeah. Thanks for askin'. Police never pressed him on anything."

O'Shaughnessy nodded. He had done Dyson a favor by getting his brother out of a jam.

"Need you to know somethin' and I need you to hear it from me . . ."

O'Shaughnessy went on to claim that his nephew, Michael, was being investigated by MI6 for participating in the Omagh bombing. He told Dyson about the evidence, and that Interpol had a warrant out.

"Jesus, Sean. Watcha tellin' me this for?"

"Desperate people do desperate things. Michael and I had a falling out, as everyone knows. He'll likely try and stick this on me. Don't want him running his mouth off on the air. Can you fix it so he don't?"

"If there is a warrant out for him and he is suspected of a crime, I wouldn't worry about that. British News management won't let him near a camera never mind on air."

"Make sure."

Those two words uttered by O'Shaughnessy were dark. They held a threat and were intended to put the onus of the job on Dyson. The bureau chief got it: payback.

"Done," Dyson said categorically.

"Good," O'Shaughnessy said. "See yah around then, Willie. And next time it's The Laurel, or Shannon's after hours for a coffee. Remember that. Fancy place like this—" he looked at the sleek chairs, modern art, and fuchsia lights, and didn't even bother to finish his sentence. He just shook his head.

O'Shaughnessy put his cap back on and walked downstairs to the back alley where the van was waiting.

Phase one of his plan was done.

37

WILLIE DYSON SAT AT THE TABLE UPSTAIRS AT MORRISONS LONG AF-
ter O'Shaughnessy had gone. He drank and thought long and hard
about Michael Shea. The two had been colleagues since their days as
news assistants in the Belfast bureau. Both had gone to Queens University, although their paths had never crossed. It was their work that brought
them together as friends. They had opted to become foreign correspondents and on more than one occasion had collaborated on stories. It
gave them a unique bond.

Willie had just broken it.

38

SEAN O'SHAUGHNESSY GOT DROPPED OFF AT THE HOUSE AND MET
his new crew. He told them what he wanted: he needed exploding
bridgewire, a special type of wire designed to handle high charges of
electricity—as much as a lightning bolt—and then vaporize.

They thought he was cracked for having them burgle an industrial
plant and thieve a bunch of wire, but they were more than happy to
oblige.

He had just one thing to say when they left: "Don't fuck it up."

O'Shaughnessy sat at the kitchen table, bottle of Redbreast out, and called his Chechen friend. This was not Abramov. This was phase two of O'Shaughnessy's plan.

39

ZHUBIN HATED LEAVING THE TRAIL COLD. IT WAS OBVIOUS WHERE the journalist and the woman were going, he thought. The ferry they had taken had met with a train headed for Istanbul. They would go there. To be sure, they could get off at stations between— Eskisehir, Ankara, Kayseri, Sivas, Malatya—Tatvan and Turkey's largest city, modern Constantinople, but it was doubtful. The train gave them speed and shelter, two critical things people needed on the run. By this time the two would know they were being chased. Safety would be key. Efficacy would be sought. They'd want transportation and they'd want what Zhubin dreaded they'd find: communication.

Zhubin knew that Shea and Neda couldn't contact anyone from the train. But that would all change once they got to an urban environment. If he hurried, Zhubin could deliver the scroll to Qom and get to Istanbul before the train arrived. If he hurried.

To get back to Van from Tatvan by car would be arduous. The roads were rough and weren't even complete in some areas. They went in circuitous directions, making their way through small villages before moving in linear fashion from point to point. Travel by road was out.

The next ferry didn't leave for an hour and travel by boat would take far too long anyway.

Zhubin called SAVAMA headquarters. He needed intelligence on the nearest airport and he needed some type of aircraft—fast.

Tatvan was an agricultural community. It had a small airport for crop dusters. That's how he found himself on an open cockpit crop plane heading over Lake Van. He looked over the side of the plane and saw a castle in ruins. Several small islands popped up from the lake. On one he could see a large church.

The lake had always been between two worlds and two empires. Like Turkey itself, it was a bridge between East and West.

IF ZHUBIN DIDN'T KNOW EXACTLY WHAT HE WAS LOOKING AT IN LAKE Van, he knew exactly what he was seeing when he got to Qom: the Holy Shrine of Fatima. Fatima was the daughter of the seventh imam and the sister of the eighth. She was known not only for her piety but also for her transcriptions of the *hadiths*, Islamic stories.

Hadiths quoted by Fatima were considered among the most authentic of all *hadiths*. Her gravesite was revered because of the millions of miracles that have supposedly occurred there. Believers' wishes have been said to have been granted and those said to be incurably diseased have been healed. The Fatima shrine was a famous and holy site in Shia Islam. Zhubin revered it with all his heart.

It was this monument on the way to the Haghani seminary that the

SAVAMA agent who picked Zhubin up at the airport sped past. Zhubin had programmed his watch to the train's arrival in Istanbul. He had instructed the driver not to stop at red lights. He had three hours to make it back to Turkey. There was no time to be lost.

41

ZHUBIN HURRIED THROUGH THE GARDENS OF THE HAGHANI SEMInary and climbed the steps two at a time. Talib had ordered Zhubin to deliver the scroll personally to Ayatollah Mesbah Yavari's chambers.

At the top of the stairway, Zhubin knocked full on into one of the students. It was a young, overweight boy. His glasses fell off and his uniform tore. The student's papers went flying everywhere.

The accident had happened so quickly that Zhubin, too, had tripped and fallen. The scroll slipped out of his hands. He yelled at the boy to look where he was going. The boy was shaking and apoplectic. He tried to help Zhubin but that only made matters worse. The boy entangled himself in Zhubin's legs and caused him to fall again. Papers went flying once more.

Violent now, Zhubin stood up and kicked the boy in the head. "Stay down!" he yelled.

From the side of one of the archways, another young student was standing and watching. He was in his late teens, bald, and wearing a tunic, unlike the others. It had a hood and was chocolate brown rather than black. His beard, too, wasn't as full as the others. He shaved it low and thin so that it just shaped his jawline.

"Stop that!" the teen said. "He is just a boy!"

Zhubin threw a kick in the teen's direction to knock him out of the way. He didn't have time for this disruption. He needed to dispose quickly of these interferers, however innocent they were, and move on. Time was ticking away.

Surprisingly, the young man blocked Zhubin's kick. He stepped in and hit Zhubin in the head with an elbow. It caught Zhubin just right and sent him back a few paces. This angered the SAVAMA assassin even more. He put his chin down to his chest, tightened the muscles on his back, and got into his fight stance. He shuffled, faked a kick, and landed a spinning back fist to the young man's throat. The young man wasn't affected though. He also spun and threw a roundhouse kick in Zhubin's direction. It missed. Punch. Block. Kick. Block. Sweeps. Misses. They danced like this looking for openings to strike.

"Stop," came the shout. It was a familiar voice. It was Talib. He was standing in the doorway to Mesbah Yavari's chambers at the end of the long hallway.

Both fighters did as they were told.

"Zhubin" is all that Talib said. The name was enough to beckon the agent.

Zhubin brushed aside the young man's papers and spotted the scroll lying on the ground. He picked it up and brought it to Talib.

"This is not the time or the place for fighting," Talib said, taking the scroll. "Now leave. Complete your mission—in case the Irishman fails. We must make sure the journalist and Neda don't stop us."

Zhubin was happy to be given the chance to finish his kills. He ran past the two students who were gathering up the boy's papers. He muttered, "I will be back for you."

The young man with the beard looked up and smiled. It was an odd response, Zhubin noted. He had bigger things to concentrate on, though—and he was gone before the students stood.

They looked over the railing and saw the two black SAVAMA SUVs speed away. The students looked at each other and smiled.

42

INSIDE MESBAH YAVARI'S CHAMBERS, TALIB HELD ON TO THE SCROLL tightly. He unraveled it and looked at the words. He traced his finger across the lines from right to left. He caressed each character.

Mesbah Yavari was seated on a large chair by the window. It was as big as a throne. "Is it as you say?" the Ayatollah asked.

"It is as Allah commands."

The paper was crinkled and frayed. It looked burned at the edges. In studying the Avestan writings as long as he had, Talib had learned the language. This was the scroll he had been looking for his whole adult life. It lifted the time restriction as to when the Mahdi could appear. He had already submitted proof of all the other signs that he was the "one." Mesbah Yavari needed just this last proof, the last piece of evidence before he could hold himself out to the religious world as the anointed imam.

Not wanting to let go of it, but knowing that he had to, Talib handed over the only thing that stood in his way of becoming judge and ruler of the world.

Or so he thought.

43

NAKED, ALU ABRAMOV LOOKED LIKE THE CAVEMAN HE WAS ACCUSED of being. He had significant body hair and a potbelly that dipped below his crotch. There was a name for that particular paunch. It was called a "dick-do." It's when a man's belly fat falls lower than his *dick do*.

Abramov's belly wasn't in the way now: he was in midthrust with one of the most beautiful prostitutes he had ever been with when the tank came crashing through the wall. He pulled out of the hooker and stood back. She wasn't so fast—and the tank came rolling over her.

Abramov struggled to pull up his pants. The tank stopped. He ran for his desk and pulled out a handgun. He fired a couple of shots at the tank. The hatch popped open. A commando tried to get out, but quickly disappeared when Abramov began shooting.

Abramov pressed a button under his desktop and a panel opened in the narrow wall behind him. He vanished through it. The tank aimed its main gun at the opening and fired.

Boom!

The shell blasted into the wall, but didn't penetrate it. The panel closed.

Abramov had built himself an impenetrable escape route from the office to the rear of his compound. It led underground to a bunker filled with arms, a helicopter, military vehicles, a Ferrari, and pretty much anything anyone could think of to use in a getaway. Abramov chose an armored personnel carrier. It was an old Soviet model but virtually indestructible. Not even a tank's gun could penetrate its steel. Moreover, it was amphibious.

The bunker door opened. A ramp dropped out and a hydraulic lift brought the armored vehicle to the surface. Abramov drove it out slowly to the back of the compound. A tank shell immediately landed nearby. His men were in the midst of a gunfight. Already, a half dozen were dead on the ground.

Abramov could see through the scope a formation of jeeps approaching the compound. They were just outside the compound's perimeter, beyond the barbed-wire fence that blocked visitors.

As he watched he saw one of the prostitutes try to get away. She ran toward the fence in her high, see-through heels. She pulled up her skintight dress to run faster. A burst of gunfire dropped her.

Abramov about-faced and drove the personnel carrier farther to the back of the compound. More jeeps were headed his way from the rear. To his right was a small hill, tall enough so it couldn't be driven over. To his left a wall and more fencing. He knew other jeeps full of men would be coming for him from all sides. There were only two ways to get to him, however—from the front and from the back.

Abramov had picked this location because it was so secure. Now his own security was working against him—there was no way out.

44

ABRAMOV CHOSE TO KEEP DRIVING STRAIGHT THOUGH THE LINE OF
attack. He was equipped with RPGs and machine guns. Perhaps he
could take them, he thought. He was a fighter, the future commander
of this part of the world. Luck would be with him. It always had. Allah
would be with him. He would survive and conquer, just as he planned.
He would crush the Muscovites and the ego-driven Chechen command.
He would have his way. He would brute them as he always had—with
force.

In the distance he could see a caravan of trucks coming for the compound. "Not now," he thought. "Please, not now."

The caravan was carrying the nuclear materials for Talib. His men
were bringing it to him. They would have no way of knowing that he
was being attacked. The timing couldn't have been worse. *The timing*,
he thought as he drove on. The jeeps were almost on him. Someone
must have given him up—again!

He had brokered a deal. He had paid the right people and even
come up with a settlement for the rogue Chechen commander who had
attacked him at the airport. The commander would get a portion of the
fee Talib was paying for the nukes. In exchange, Abramov would get
clear passage to the Iranian border. No troubles. Instead of enemies,
they had become partners. They had agreed! It couldn't have been that
guy who sold him out this time. And no one else had the information
about the nukes, where they were and when they would be transported.

Except the Irish bomb maker Sean O'Shaughnessy.

The bullets bounced off the armored carrier's windshield. Abramov fired back. The armored carrier's machine gun took out a full jeepload of men.

Where was that Mick bastard anyway? Abramov wondered.

The jeeps continued to shoot at Abramov as they drove past him, splitting their formation around him. They fired at his tracks and the windows. All the shots pinged off. He scoffed at them.

Heh, heh. Fuckers.

Abramov opened the side guns and fired. They lit up both jeeps as they went by.

A new formation of jeeps and a tank came into line in front of him. The tank turned its canon and fired. It hit Abramov's right side and jacked the carrier to the left. He jerked the wheel as the carrier slammed back to the ground. He barreled on.

O'Shaughnessy wasn't in the compound. He had driven off. No one had seen him. *The fuck must have sold me out! Things were going so well. We were so close! Sure I punched him and kidnapped him. But that was payback.*

Abramov couldn't believe that O'Shaughnessy would blow a deal of this magnitude over some trifle like that. There was no reason for O'Shaughnessy not to want to get rich. No reason for him to take away from Abramov what he deserved!

Abramov got pissed thinking about this. He fired madly at the jeeps in front of him. The tank blew another shell at him. It landed in front of him and he swerved to avoid it.

I'll murder that Irish fuck! Why?! Why?! Why?! Moscow could be mine. O'Shaughnessy would get his money . . .

He ran through the reasons O'Shaughnessy might betray him again in his mind. None of them made sense.

He saw it as he was thinking. Overhead. A dot at first and then it became larger. It was coming straight for him. The cutting sound of steel through air. A MIG.

Shit, Abramov thought just as the missile left the MIG and made itself known by a white trail in the sky.

Abramov realized he was going to die. He also realized that Sean O'Shaughnessy wasn't in the terror plot for the money. It came to him clear as day what O'Shaughnessy was going to do. There had been talk about it. Abramov had always ignored it.

The missile hit the front of the APC. It crushed the steel and blew the vehicle to pieces. There wasn't a bit of Abramov's body left. He had been incinerated by the blast. He went literally up in smoke. He'd never be able to tell the world what he had figured out about O'Shaughnessy. He had been silenced.

Sean O'Shaughnessy had completed phase two of his plan.

45

As the train rolled into Istanbul station, Shea and Neda waited in their cabin. They looked out the window like wide-eyed children on their first day of school. They didn't know what to expect or whether someone might be waiting for them on the platform.

The coast looked clear from what they could see. Beyond the tremendous mayhem at the station—businessmen in suits barking into mobile phones, a Greek Orthodox priest carrying a bag, women in headscarves efficiently weaving their way through the crowds, tourists in tie dye, street vendors, and hustlers—there was no one nefarious-looking as far as they could tell.

Eyes sharp, Michael. You're the protector. You're her guardian. It's up to you. It's personal now.

The world, even if it were to explode, paled in comparison to the feeling inside him. It was like that, the weight of things. The most heavy—war, money, birth, death—were only really felt when they were made personal, relevant on an individual level. It was, Shea realized, the same with love. People could talk about these things in the abstract, but they could only really care when they were touched . . . on the inside.

Slowly they walked in line off the train. A young boy ran by and knocked between them. An old man pushing a kebab cart wouldn't let them pass. Try as they did, they couldn't get past him until he pulled to the side to serve a customer.

Shea had been to Istanbul many times. He knew the train station well enough to know that an Internet cafe was inside.

They were still on the Asian side of the city. They had arrived at the Haydarpasa station, the massive castlelike terminal overlooking the Kadikoy Bay in the center of Istanbul. This wasn't the terminal made famous by the Orient Express. It didn't exude glamour or style or mystery. That was left to the Sirkeci train station on the European side. The Haydarpasa was, however, monumental: its facade covered in textured sandstone, its roof slated, its interior lit by stained-glass windows under ribbed vaults. A clock tower rose in the form of a crest at its center. The design was meant to welcome those arriving from the east with a sense of awe, and to leave on those who departed Europe a lasting impression.

The east side of Istanbul, even though it held the city's highest point, had always been a shadow to the west.

It was a divisive and divided city, whether as Byzantium, which chose the wrong side in the Roman war and was toppled, or as Constantinople, which sided with the Germans during World War I, or as Istanbul, its modern name. There was a chasm that almost allowed East to meet West. Almost.

For Shea, there it was, Europe just across the small channel of Marmara. The British consulate and the British News bureau were on that side. Safety.

Almost.

SHEA LIKED THE FELLOW WHO WORKED IN THE RAGGED OLD ONE-man Istanbul office they called a "bureau" for British News. It was located in a low-income district of Istanbul called Güngören. The office had a lot Old World character and charm even if it was a bit grungy.

Shea had drunk many a pint with the British News bureau chief, Matt Beynon, at the taverns, or *meyhanes* as they were called, by the bazaar district. The *meyhanes* were a great place to people watch. Or get lost in the crowd. That thought stayed in the back of Shea's mind as he held the door open for Neda to walk through into the terminal station.

Get lost in the crowd.

Train stations were designed pretty much the same around the world: tracks ending at platforms that lead to a series of doors that lead people to a grand hall that always curiously echoed loudly of footsteps and voices. The halls were typically lined with ticket windows and shops and cafes.

Inside the Haydarpasa station Shea spotted what he needed and headed for it. He took hold of Neda's hand and managed their way through the crowd.

The kid working the Internet cafe gave Shea a pass code for the aged Apple Mac desktop near the restroom. The cafe didn't have any type of phone-for-hire service, but it did have headsets for telephone calls via Skype.

Shea logged on to his account and in a few minutes had reached Willie Dyson, his longtime mate who had just been promoted to Belfast bureau chief. Willie was the one man who could handle Shea's shorthand. And Willie had half-expected to get a call from Shea, especially since the Interpol alert went out and a warrant had been issued for Shea's arrest. The news bureaus were aflutter with speculation.

Willie could never give up Shea's uncle as a source. He owed that hard chaw big. Still, he knew Shea would push him to find out who had made the claims against him.

The business about Omagh was by now an ancient piece of history as far as the world was concerned. It was meant to lie buried along with its victims. It was a painful and ever-fading memory, never to be forgotten, just dulled into the lists of wrongs the world had seen. Except someone wanted to rekindle that time—and latch Michael Shea to it.

Shea, of course, had no idea that a warrant had been issued for him, or that he had been effectively disowned by British News while an investigation was launched.

But he was about to find out.

"MICHAEL, I THOUGHT I BE HEARIN' FROM YOU," WILLIE'S VOICE trebled through the line from Belfast. Internet calling might be cheap or free but it always made someone sound as if they were calling from the bottom of a sewer.

Shea was struck by Willie's expectation. "Why, Willie?"

"I am the Belfast bureau chief, you know," Willie went on, still believing Shea was calling about the warrant for his arrest regarding Omagh. "Likely suspect, I am."

Shea had no idea what Willie was going on about.

"Willie, what are you talking about? I'm in Istanbul. I need your help. The whole news organization's help, truth be told. I also need you to call the British embassy in Turkey for me. Get me out."

"Trifle not, Michael. They'll see to you, I am sure. Why don't you just go pay them a visit. I'm sure that would be best. Usually how these things work, you know."

Now Shea was truly baffled. "Willie, I don't think you are hearing me. We are being chased by the Iranian Secret Service. I am on to something big. I need to get the story out now. But I need to get safe first," Shea said as fast as he could get the words out of his mouth. "What's this you're going on about?"

Willie realized that he and Shea were speaking about two different things. He proceeded to fill Shea in on the accusations that had been leveled against him by Interpol. Of course he left out his own complicity in the matter when it came to British News finding out.

He told Shea that Interpol had an alert out for him and that British News had informed the staff that it would be working with the authorities to bring him in. This dashed any hopes of Shea himself broadcasting a story to thwart the nuclear plot. He needed, however, to inform Willie of what was going on.

"Willie, it's nuclear. And," he added, "it's Sean."

Dyson got it in two seconds. He knew O'Shaughnessy had set him up. He knew why now. He also knew that it was too late to do anything without clearing Shea's name first.

"Michael," Willie yelled, his voice scratching over the line. "Go underground. Run, and do it now!"

By the time Willie Dyson had finished his urgent plea for Shea to run, Shea already had. It wasn't words that prompted him, it was whom he had seen through the cafe window: two Brits in dark suits had walked by twice. MI6.

SHEA SMACKED THE KID MANAGING THE CAFE ON THE SIDE OF HIS head hard to get his attention and let him know that he meant business.

"Exit!" he yelled.

The kid pointed at the front door. Shea smacked the kid again. He pointed to the back. The kid nodded, scared shit.

The two MI6 agents saw Shea. They bolted for the front door to the cafe from across the hall. Shea and Neda scooted through the small kitchen in the back of the cafe to a hallway. Wood crates were stacked everywhere. Shea threw some of them against the door. It wouldn't stop the door from opening, but it would slow the agents down. He and Neda ran to another door at the end of the hallway. They heard the back door to the cafe being banged against and shoved open.

"Shea!" one of the agents yelled. "Stop! Stop!"

Shea and Neda ran out the door. The agents broke through and saw the hallway door shut ahead of them. They headed for it. Outside Shea and Neda found themselves in the front of the station where hordes of people were coming to and from terminals. Haydarpasa didn't have as many trains coming in and out of it as the Sirkeci station, but it was still packed with people at rush hour. Some would head for the ferries in back of Haydarpasa that went to the European side of Istanbul. Others would catch the buses out front that traversed the city.

Shea saw a bus coming down the station entranceway. If he and Neda could make their way through the crowd they could hop on. A grimy-looking hustler had grabbed on to Neda. He wanted to sell her a tour of the city. He wouldn't let her go. Shea was a few steps ahead and hadn't seen the man grab Neda. When he turned, he also saw that the agents were out the door and right behind them.

Shea pushed his way through the crowd of people. He got to Neda and rabbit punched the street hustler in the stomach and again in the kidneys. It sent the man to the ground. They turned to run. The MI6 agents were closer now, too close. One of them shouted, "I'll shoot."

Shea and Neda stopped dead in their tracks.

THE STREAMS OF PEOPLE WHO HAD BEEN RUSHING BY THE STATION suddenly stopped to see what was going on. The two MI6 agents who had been giving chase were about ten feet away from Shea and Neda. They had their guns drawn. "Turn around, Shea. You, too, miss," the agents commanded.

As Shea and Neda did as they were told, two shots cracked. Both MI6 agents went down with bullets between their eyes. Shea and Neda instinctively ducked low. The crowd dispersed in a frenzied chaos with people screaming and yelling and pointing at the two dead agents on the ground.

Shea saw the SAVAMA agent across the way. He was coming at

them full force. He still had the gun is his hand that he had used to shoot the MI6 agents.

Zhubin was running full out at them. He hadn't considered the crowd, though, and was swamped. He couldn't get by all the people. A bus stopped. Shea saw it. After the passengers loaded and it began to roll, he signaled to Neda. They ran for the door and caught it, standing on the rear stairs.

Zhubin finally broke through the crowd and watched them drive away. There was no way to catch them now. But he'd come for them. They were *his* prey. That is why he shot the MI6 agents. Shea knew this. He didn't know why he feared the SAVAMA agent so, but he did.

Shea looked out at the Sea of Marmar. He noticed a helium balloon moored on the shore. It was anchored tilting sideways and bobbing in the wind. It was an odd site. Shea couldn't figure it. It was a strange thing in a strange city.

He thought of his old chum, Matt, the Istanbul bureau chief. He'd have to get to him. Beynon always took a three-hour, three-martini lunch at the same place. And Shea planned on joining him.

Beynon was their only hope at the moment of getting out of Istanbul. Neda was right. They'd have to get to Rome.

50

MATT BEYNON WAS AN ECCENTRIC WELSHMAN. HE WORE A WHITE hat and white suit every day—no matter the time of year or the weather. He also always wore a black shirt. He sported yellow-tinted glasses and long sideburns.

Beynon had been British News's bureau chief for half a dozen years. Prior to this assignment he had been the bureau chief in Rome. And before that, a star correspondent, breaking big news stories and winning just about every journalism award there was.

It was in Rome that he had met a woman, a beautiful Italian woman from the south, Campagna. In short order Beynon was married and had a daughter. He wanted to spend more time with his family so he took a sabbatical to write a book. That didn't work out, and he ended up losing his position as bureau chief to an up-and-coming Australian, Marc Hardy. Hardy took over just when the famous Cosa Nostra trials were getting under way in Rome, and he did a bang-up job covering them. It put Italy back on the map as far as news went. When Beynon returned, he was pushed over to Istanbul. In truth, the ratty assignment of Istanbul couldn't have come at a better time for Beynon. His marriage was falling apart and he had begun to drink a lot. No one would much care what he did in Istanbul. He toiled away. And for the last six years the amount of airtime he got was less than a promo for a late-late-night talk show. Blink. Gone.

To his credit, Beynon commuted to Italy every weekend to be with his wife and daughter. He and his wife didn't speak, or anything else for that matter. But his daughter was the apple of his eye.

To bide his time during the week, Matt had taken up a couple of hobbies. One was opium, and the other was a nineteen-year-old named Esra. The two hobbies weren't exactly mutually exclusive. In fact, they usually took place together. Shea knew where and when. Blowing through Istanbul on his way to cover one of the "stan" countries, Shea had worked out of the Istanbul bureau a few times. He remembered Beynon's schedule.

He hoped it hadn't changed.

THE BUS FINALLY MADE IT SAFELY TO THE EUROPEAN SIDE OF THE city by bridge, skirting the Bosphorous on both sides. Giant tankers and ships looked as if they were stopped in freeway traffic; they were piled up, one after one, so close to shore it was all Shea could do to not stick his arm out the window and try to touch one.

He thought about where on Earth he was, and wondered if the path they had taken to the city's famous Horn was the same one the Greeks had in 600 B.C., the same as the Romans had in 324, or the Ottomans had nearly six hundred years ago. Albeit with less shipping traffic.

On land, the streets now looked the same as Athens, Rome, and nearly every major European city. The leather jacket, jeans, and sneaker manner of dress of people, too, were the same. Beneath, though, were dark complexions that looked almost like caricatured disguises: black hair and big mustaches. Big brand-name cars drove past luxury shops and expensive-looking restaurants that belied Istanbul's trampled-upon past. It was now what it had always strived to be: a jewel unto itself and under its own control.

Shea looked at his watch. He pictured Beynon and Esra at their favorite opium salon—a minimal but elegant place on the second floor of
an old Victorian-era-looking house near the British News bureau. Designed like a Chinese teahouse, the salon had private rooms separated
by slats and sliding doors made of rice paper. Low tables, cushions, and
a hookah for smoking opium were placed neatly in each room, Shea
recalled.

It would be on the pillows that young Esra, a stunning dark-haired
beauty, would lie, sometimes with her head on Beynon's chest and strok-
ing his hair—high as beejesus. Beynon mostly just sat there, dumb-
looking, drinking his martinis.

Shea had tried opium with Matt once but hadn't liked the high. He
didn't like to lose clarity or control. Opiates did that. Shea had tried all
sorts of drugs over the years—coke, pot, hallucinogenics. None of them
did it for him. He liked the drink; the Dark Stuff. Guinness is good.

52

IT WOULD BE MANY MORE STOPS BEFORE THEY COULD GET OFF THE
bus. Over the Galata Bridge through the spice bazaar and past Istanbul
University they went.

Shea caught sight of the Hagia Sophia, the former Byzantine church
and mosque, which, like Istanbul, had its roots firmly in the worlds of
Christianity and Islam. For a thousand years it was the largest cathedral in the world. For five hundred years it served as a principal mosque.
In every language its name translated to wisdom, holy wisdom. Yet it
now served as merely a museum, not a formal place to go and pray. Its

most renowned quality was not its size, however, but its light. It had a mystical quality of light that reflected everywhere inside.

Shea pointed it out to Neda, but she was already looking at it, entranced. She reached out her hand in the Hagia Sophia's direction and spread her fingers wide. She then closed her eyes and breathed deeply.

This was, in her mind, affirmation of her journey. She was enamored by the sights, smells, and sounds of Istanbul. Now another level of her senses had been aroused.

Neda had never been outside of Iran. The mosques, the streets, and the place were unlike the atmosphere of Tehran, which was stark and utilitarian, the people rigid. There seemed to be a sense of freedom in Istanbul. She loved it—all the different people, places, and things. Sparks of wisdom.

The bus slowed as it passed an Islamic cemetery and a park. The wonderful sights and sounds of the tourist areas had dulled into the everyday grim portrait of a city. The bus stopped at a pedestrian area. Shea and Neda got off and he quickly whisked Neda into a dark alley. The chances of anyone following them were slim. But Shea wasn't about to take any more risks.

The alley opened up to a bright street. Shea looked to either side. It was deserted. Shea took Neda's elbow and beat it across. They went into a Victorian-looking house and up a flight of stairs. Small paintings and calendars with Chinese characters lined the walls. Shea bowed to the hostess who greeted them when they entered the opium salon. He knew that he need only mention Beynon's name.

The hostess, who wore a fine silk robe, shuffled down the hallway taking the smallest of steps. She knocked and slid open a door to one of the private rooms. Beynon was in exactly the position Shea had imagined. He was in a stupor. Martini on the table. No Esra though. Just the faint, sweet smell of opium.

53

BEYNON RECOGNIZED SHEA THROUGH HIS HAZE. "SHEA," HE SAID, his eyes barely open and his tongue seemingly numb. "Shea . . ."

He didn't move to get up. Probably couldn't. Beynon raised his arm halfheartedly to wave hello. It flapped back on his thigh. "Shea . . ."

Shea shot Neda a look. Beynon was far too gone to speak. Shea put his arm under and around him, lifting his friend off the ground. Beynon could barely stand. Shea kept him moving, up, out the door, and down the stairs to the street.

Thankfully, Beynon lived only a few blocks away. Shea carried him down the alley and then down two more streets to a sprightly looking town house. Beynon had a good thing going with British News. He expensed his living—and they paid well. Correspondents got stipends and living allowances. Beynon had a full staff as well as a driver. He obviously was an expert in gaming his expense account. It was evident when Neda took the keys out of his pocket and opened the door to his home just how much Beynon had gotten away with over the years. Rare books and antiques were everywhere. It was spectacular.

The house was done in rattan and dark burnished wood. It looked like a set from the movies *Casablanca* or *Out of Africa*. Very British Colonial. Indeed, these movies must have inspired Beynon's decor for both movie posters were on the wall.

Shea put Beynon on the couch, where he immediately fell asleep.

"He'll be all right in a few hours," Shea said to Neda.

"We don't have time to waste," she said.

"He is our only chance. He knows all the right people in all the wrong places. If anyone can get us out, it's him."

"He doesn't look very helpful."

"Shame, really. He was the tops when he was on his game."

"What happened to him?"

"You saw."

"No. What caused him to start using drugs?"

"Who knows? Icarus probably would have been a drunk or a druggy had either vice been so available at the time. You fly high, you fall hard."

"What do we do now?"

"Wait."

54

THREE HOURS AFTER HE HAD PASSED OUT ON THE COUCH IN HIS LIVing room, Beynon came to. Shea and Neda were seated on two antique chairs across from him, sipping tea out of fine china.

Beynon woke as quickly as he had passed out. "Shea, right, I remember."

"Good to see you, Matt."

"I am sure I have looked better. Who's this?"

"Neda. A friend."

"Hello," she said, standing and leaning over to shake his hand.

"Don't get up on my account. Please," Beynon said. He looked over at Shea. "You're in a thick one."

"Like mud."

"I heard. Embassy wants you. So do the powers that be."

"I am on to something."

"Figured."

Neda watched as Shea and Beynon lobbed questions and answers back and forth to one another.

"Want to fill me in?" Beynon asked, sitting up and pouring himself some tea. Neda couldn't believe that a few moments ago he was completely drugged out. He looked clear and sharp. Opium must be a strange drug, she thought.

Shea answered Beynon's query. He told him about the meeting at Lake Urmia in Iran. The nuclear plot. His uncle. The chase.

"Any proof or sources I could use to get the story on the air?" Beynon asked.

"On the hunt," Shea said. "So far just me and her."

"You won't fly as a source. She would. Need more than that though, as you know."

"If we can get to Rome I can get you what you need," Neda said, interjecting.

Shea looked over at her. She hadn't told him this. As far as he knew, they were just going to question Gaspar's brother Balthazar about some secret connection. The religious story was still secondary in Shea's mind—at best. It was more of a story for the tabloids than a serious news organization.

But Neda persisted. "Balthazar has proof," she said. "I was going to show you when we got there."

"I don't know who Balthazar is but if he can prove any of this, it will save my career . . . and yours," Beynon said, taking a sip of tea.

"I was hoping you'd see it that way," Shea said. He turned to Neda.

"The truth lies in Rome," she said.

"To Rome then," Matt said.

55

Shea was thrown by Neda's talk of proof in Rome. He didn't know whether she was just saying that to get Beynon to help or whether she had been holding back on him. He'd have to ask her later. The important thing now was getting out of Istanbul.

"There's a small problem with leaving," Shea said. He reminded Beynon that Interpol had a warrant out for him, that the SAVAMA was on his tail, and that Neda didn't have a passport.

"Is that all?" Beynon said glibly. "Not a problem. I have some friends who can help."

Beynon drank the rest of his tea and stood. He put on his white suit jacket, pushed his fingers through his hair, and put on his tinted glasses. "Off we go," he said.

Shea and Neda looked at one another and shrugged. They followed Beynon out the door.

"Where's Esra, by the way?" Shea asked.

"Ran off with another man."

"Oh," Shea said, indulging in some honest reproach with his friend. "Sorry. Someone closer to her own age?"

"Far from it. Older. Her teacher."

"Guess she has a thing for older men," Shea said, smiling and trying to make light of the discussion as they walked out onto the street where Beynon hailed a cab.

"Wasn't the age," Matt said as he held open the taxi door for them to get. "She was turned on by learning. And I seem to have nothing left to teach her."

The taxi sped off. Across the street two cars pulled away from the curb.

SAVAMA and British Intelligence both had surveillance teams in place. Both had found who they were looking for.

AYATOLLAH MESBAH YAVARI READ THE FIRST WORDS OF THE SCROLL aloud: "*And he, Ohrmazd the propitious spirit, creator of the material world, the righteous one, even he put the omniscient wisdom, in the shape of water, on the hand of Zartosht, and said to him thus: 'Devour it.'*"

"And we shall devour it," Talib said. "We shall devour the world."

Mesbah Yavari smiled. He ran his fingers over the edges of the paper and rubbed the ink in his fingers. A curious look came over his face. He sniffed his fingertips.

Talib watched him closely. "It is the smell of victory, Ayatollah. We shall make the world according to Allah's will."

The Ayatollah put the scroll down on the floor. He and Talib were sitting on two large pillows facing each other. A pot of tea was on the ground between them.

Talib was horrified that Mesbah Yavari had placed the scroll on the ground. It was sacrilegious.

"Ayatollah!" he said alarmingly. "What are you doing? That text is sacred. How can you soil it on the floor?"

Mesbah Yavari sipped his cup of tea and looked down at the paper on the ground and then back up at Talib. He finished his sip and then poured the rest of his tea onto the scroll.

Talib sprang up. He waved the scroll in the air, trying desperately to dry it. He looked at Mesbah Yavari like he was crazed. All the while Mesbah Yavari remained calm. He took the pot of tea and refilled his cup.

"Are you crazy?" Talib shouted. "This is our proof. This is what will convince the other ayatollahs. It is what we have been working for all these years and you have ruined it."

Mesbah Yavari slowly put his cup down. "You have been fooled. That is not the original *Zand-i Vohuman Yasht*."

"It is! My agent just delivered it directly to us from the north. It has been authenticated."

Talib went to the table where he had placed the copy Gaspar had made of the original and compared the two. It was similar, but not the same. The scroll Zhubin delivered referenced a different date of the Mahdi's appearance than the copy Gaspar had made. Talib had the copy he had unsealed in the helicopter, but a copy would not stand up to close scrutiny. He needed the original scroll!

"That scroll is from my own library. We have copies. This"—he pointed to the wet scroll in Talib's hands—"was supposed to predate all the writings.

"It is a fake."

"How did you know it wasn't the original?" Talib sheepishly asked the Ayatollah, his eyes shifting from the scroll to the floor.

"We use a particular ink that has aniseed in it. I operate the printing press myself. We also use a different type of papyrus. I have felt thousands of pages of it. This is one of my own."

"Zhubin could not have made such a mistake."

"Someone did."

Talib looked at the scroll again. He sniffed it and felt its edges.

"Here, let me see," Mesbah Yavari said, snatching the scroll out of Talib's hands. "You see, we use an offset press. The boys also make paper. They pound strips that have been soaked in water for three days. The strips are then cut and laid on a cotton sheet. Other strips are laid over them so there is a very particular crisscross pattern. When the strips are pressed and dried it forms a single sheet of papyrus paper—exactly like this. That is why these edges are so thick and rough." He ran his hands over the edge again. "The boys then put this into a hardcover. Our covers don't extend past the edge of the pages we make. The paper sticks out a little—like this. The light ages the color along this border. It is the same here."

Talib looked at the thin discoloration on the scroll, his plan falling apart before his eyes. He watched as Mesbah Yavari poured the rest of his tea over the copy of the scroll Gaspar had made and handed it back to him. "Dry it by candle and be careful not to let it burn," Mesbah Yavari said.

Talib was confused. He took the wet copy of the scroll Gaspar had made and just looked at it as the Ayatollah walked to the door.

"Tea ages paper. It will look centuries old. Do as I say. We cannot let this opportunity pass."

Talib was shocked that the Ayatollah had agreed to forge the document.

"Where are you going?" Talib asked weakly.

"To see who has been in my library and who stole the text from the archives."

Mesbah Yavari exited and slammed the door behind him. Talib took a candle from one of the giant holders next to the bed and began to run it under the scroll.

"When it is the end of the time, those enemies will be as much destroyed as the root of a shrub . . ."

Talib thought his time had run out. But there was hope yet for the End of Times to begin.

ZHUBIN HAD MADE IT TO ISTANBUL'S BAZAAR DISTRICT. IT WAS THE most densely populated area in the city and he believed that Shea and Neda would probably try to lose themselves in it. He had already stationed agents outside the British consulate and the British News bureau. He even had a tail put on the British News bureau chief. Zhubin wasn't going to lose them again. Not this time. This time Zhubin was going to capture his prey. He could feel it.

The bazaar district was a massive place stretching from the Galata

Bridge all the way to the middle of the city. If they were in Istanbul, they would eventually have to come through here, Zhubin thought.

Immediately the smell of cinnamon and clove hit his nostrils. Hand-carts full of fresh fruits and vegetables were in front of small stores and kiosks. All sorts of spices, olives, and nuts were piled in mounds, out in the open.

Zhubin watched as old women haggled with vendors and teens stole pieces of candy and sweets only to be chased off by storeowners.

He strolled through the hidden Ottoman *hans* and labyrinthine streets—scanning robotically for any sign of Shea or Neda. He had made it all the way to where the bazaar ended near the university when his mobile phone rang and he wasn't yet "beat," as the lyric suggested, nor sad nor blue. It was one of his agents. They had found what he was looking for. The journalist and the woman were with the British News chief, the agent said. And they were being pursued.

"Where are they headed?" Zhubin asked. The agent told him. Turned out they were headed for his location: the Grand Bazaar.

59

THE *EZAN*—CALL TO PRAYER—BEGAN. PEOPLE BEGAN TO MOVE quickly toward the mosque in the center of the city. Zhubin would typically pray in private. But he was among a crowd. He noticed a headscarf turn his way. Eyes showed through the slit and caught his. He noticed that his breath was cut short.

Zhubin prided himself on celibacy. But this feeling caught him like a gust of wind. The headscarf turned and he followed her. She went through a door, pockmarked in gold. It was comprised of small squares of wood that created an ornate pattern. The door rose twelve feet high. Past the door he entered one of the most beautiful mosques he had ever seen. Several domes seemed to float in the air above gold-colored buttresses. Maroon columns rose from the marble floors and touched the bottoms of the domes. Natural stone colors blended with stenciled floral designs. Orbs of lanterns floated. The muezzin's beautiful voice as he continued the call to prayer sent chills down Zhubin's spine.

A feeling of love overwhelmed him. Zhubin had never experienced anything like it. It was happy. It was pure. It was good. He looked around the mosque and saw the headscarf. She disappeared behind a curtain to the women's side. Of course she would have to pray there, Zhubin thought.

The curves of the domes above his head went in semicircles. They looked like a bunch of balloons that had been cut in half. Tiny arched windows lined the center of the dome and allowed natural light to shine in. Stained-glass windows and ornately designed and hand-painted circles of what looked like stenciled butterflies were magnificently placed on the top of every column.

Zhubin knelt and prostrated. He performed four *ak'ahs,* or bows. Zhubin noticed that when he stood in *qiyam,* the basic standing posture, his knees were weak. He raised his hands to his ears and then folded them, right over left, upon his breast. He then bowed and placed his hands on his knees. Every time he stood to repeat the ritual, he noticed he was weaker. He said over and over, "There is no God but Allah."

For some reason he began to think of all the people he had killed.

60

THE FIRST TIME ZHUBIN HAD KILLED WAS WHEN HE WAS STILL IN SAVAMA training.

He hadn't known that the SAVAMA tested recruits by pretending to put them in life-threatening scenarios designed to look real.

One day after class, Zhubin and another recruit were walking to a cafe when a van pulled up next to them. Three men in hoods jumped out and tackled his friend. They dragged him to the back of the van. The men also tried to wrestle Zhubin into the van, but weren't so lucky. When one of the hooded men took out his gun, Zhubin artfully took it from him. Instead of holding it on him and demanding the release of his friend, Zhubin shot all three men through their hoods and took off. Only later did he find out that it had been an exercise—and three senior SAVAMA agents were killed in the process.

The agency realized it was on to something, a natural killer. They put him into special training for that one purpose. To kill. Zhubin learned all of the dark arts and became especially expert at close combat. He put it to use on his second kill.

Zhubin trailed a young engineer who was suspected of trading information with Iran's closest enemy: Iraq. The young man walked his infant son every morning through a Tehran park. One morning Zhubin waited in the bushes for the man. As the young father strolled by with his baby in the carriage, Zhubin stepped behind him and choked him to death with his bare hands. He left the baby crying in its stroller.

Next were two Chinese officials executed in Abu Dhabi. He gutted them with a steak knife. He killed his first female after that. He tortured her first. Then more men by knife, hand, and gun. After that came the elections. And the worst of things he did.

Tears came down Zhubin's face. He didn't bother to wipe them. They flowed out of him as he remembered all their faces; mostly their eyes. At last he thought of the woman in the headscarf . . . and the eyes that drove right through him.

When the prayer was complete, he felt refreshed, as if he had just slept. He walked to the forecourt and waited. But the woman in the headscarf did not come out.

Instead, the queen of pop beckoned.

He answered the phone before it rang a second time. The agent informed Zhubin that they were on Ordu Cad, not more than a few minutes away. Zhubin asked where a good location would be to pick him up. Satisfied that he could make it to Beyazit Square, he hustled off. He thought of the woman in the headscarf again. But he didn't turn around to look for her.

She was standing behind the drape of the mosque waiting for him to leave. She had felt her heart skip a beat, too. It wasn't love that she had felt, however. She was an intuitive. It was fear. Zhubin had the mark of death upon him.

61

SHEA LISTENED AS BEYNON MADE A CALL ON HIS MOBILE PHONE. They were still in the taxi headed toward the Grand Bazaar district and stuck in Istanbul's nightmarish traffic. Neda was squished between them. She was letting Shea take the lead in getting them out of Istanbul, but she was desperate to tell him something. She had been holding it back, waiting for the right time to explain it. Now she wished that she hadn't. She wished she had told him everything, just as he had been so open with her.

In the beginning she hadn't trusted him enough to relay the information she was pining to tell him now. After they had become lovers, she didn't want to tell him anything because she was being protective. It made sense to disclose everything now but there wasn't any time. She'd have to wait until they were with Balthazar in Rome. If they made it to Rome, that was. They could be killed at any moment, she knew. Then her secret would die with her. Their future, the world's future, rested in Shea's hands, well, his and the odd man in the white suit's hands.

Beynon spoke loudly, "Faruk? It's me, Matt. Yes, yes! I know. I haven't forgotten. What size are you again? . . . No, actually, not gay at all. I have a pair of espadrilles myself. Yes, very funny, Faruk, but I haven't been gay since the eighties. Ha, ha! Yes. Joking. Anyway, I'm hoping to leave tonight. You wouldn't by chance be making a trip? Ah, splendid. Usual place and time then? Fantastic. Yes. No. I won't forget. Indeed, same size in Italy as in Turkey. Right. Right. Cheers."

Shea looked at Beynon after he hung up. "So?"

"We are good. Be in Italy tonight. Rome by morning, I'd say. Unless you fancy a midnight run," Beynon said.

"Mind telling us how?" Shea asked.

"I don't have a passport," Neda reminded them both.

"Not to worry. We won't be going through customs. As you know, I commute every week to Italy. Well, so does my friend Faruk. He has his own plane," Beynon explained.

"And . . . something you aren't telling us? Even private flights have to go through customs," Shea said.

"He flies opium if you must know. Authorities look the other way. All fixed. Direct flight to Naples. You can guess who he flies for."

"The Mafia," Shea said.

Beynon put his index finger to the side of his nose. "There is no such thing," he said, and smiled mischievously.

"Grand," Shea said.

Beynon shrugged. "Better than coach class."

Neda asked, "So I don't need a passport?"

Beynon and Shea laughed.

"No, no passport needed," Shea said, smiling.

62

THE TAXI CLIPPED ALONG ORDU CAD AND THE NEIGHBORHOODS began to change. From low income and industrial, college students began to appear on the streets as they approached the university district. They passed Beyazit Square and the Grand Bazaar. The taxi slowed.

On every corner kids milled about. Across every street tourists bolted and were nearly run down by traffic. Apparently Turks don't brake for pedestrians.

Beynon remembered that he had instructed the driver to go to the bazaar, and that's why he had slowed. But they needed to travel on to meet Faruk.

"To Topkapi Sarayr," Beynon said, giving a new instruction.

"Now where are we going?" Shea asked.

"We'll meet Faruk just after sunset at the tip of the Topkapi Palace. There is a small park there. All the ferries pass it by. Only one stops. That's our man," Beynon explained.

"But I thought you said we are traveling by air?" Shea asked.

"We are," Beynon said. "The boat will take us to a private airstrip on the Asian side of the city. More relaxed there, I dare say. Then we'll be off and, Bob's your uncle, we'll be in Naples in a few hours time."

"Will Faruk be all right with us tagging along?" Shea asked.

"I'll get him another pair of shoes. Let me worry about that," Beynon said.

"Lately, I worry about everything," Shea said.

He could see the green park ahead. They were headed in the direction of the Blue Mosque. Its minarets began to peek at them. There were six tall and unmistakable minarets that faced the park. Below lay thousands of blue *iznik* tiles. Alit at night, they were spectacular. The mosque's beauty, Shea thought, rivaled even that of the Topkapi Palace, home to Ottoman sultans for centuries and displaying all their jeweled treasures and grandeur.

Lost in thought, Shea was unprepared for what happened next: a car slammed into them from the side—hard. It caved in Shea's door. Neda was thrown over Beynon and crashed into the side window. She bounced off it and landed on Beynon's lap.

Beynon had instinctively tried to block Neda from hitting the window. He had put his arm up to stop her. But the force of the crash was so hard that it broke his arm.

Everything stopped.

STEAM POURED OUT OF THE TAXI'S ENGINE. THE DRIVER WAS SLUMPED over the wheel. Shea felt it coming. He could hear the shots before they hit the car. He was still in shock from the crash. He couldn't speak. It took a few moments for the words to come. "Go! Go! Go!"

The bullets came through the rear window. Neda managed to open the door and climb out. She pulled Beynon by his lapel and he fell onto the ground. Shea pressed himself into the seat, leaning as far back and ducking as best he could. He was stuck. The door had him pinned.

The gunfire came from the front this time. The taxi driver's head exploded and blood splattered everywhere.

"Michael!" Neda yelled. "Come on!"

Shea couldn't get his leg pried loose from the door. The gunshots were coming from both directions. He couldn't see or know it, but the MI6 and SAVAMA agents were both exchanging rounds.

Standing on the curb, watching it all was Zhubin.

Shea's only hope was to get the door open and exit through his side. "Go!" he screamed to Neda. "Go! Get her safe, Matt!"

Beynon clutched his broken wing and took Neda's hand. She fought to get back to the car. But even with a broken arm, Neda was no match for Beynon. He pulled her between two cars that had gotten caught up in the crash.

"Stay low and when I give you the word you run after me, okay?" he said to Neda.

"No," she said, "I won't leave Michael."

"He'll find his way. Tough bugger, that one. He and I have been through a lot. I wouldn't leave him if I didn't think he could make it on his own. If one of us goes back for him, we'll be shot. Better to put the focus on us. And the only way to do that is to run."

Neda looked at him and realized he was right. She looked over at Shea. He had managed to get his door open. Beynon described him well: Shea was a tough bugger. "Okay," she said.

AT THE SAME MOMENT THAT NEDA AGREED TO RUN, SHEA FELL OUT of the taxi onto the ground. He had banged the door so hard that it fell off its hinges. He watched as another spray of gunfire landed on the seat where he had just been. In the exact spot. He had narrowly escaped death again. There were holes are big as eyeballs in the seat cushion.

On the ground he could see feet, ankles, and legs. He could see where Neda and Beynon were—skin and a white pant leg. Behind them were black pants and thick shoes. Two men. To his right were pin-striped trousers and highly polished leather monk straps. It wasn't hard to discern who was who in this gun battle: SAVAMA and MI6.

The gunfire stopped. Shea slid under the car next to him. And then under the car next to that. He was shimmying away from Neda and

Beynon. The curb was closer to him. If he could get to it, he could divert the agents.

He could see their feet move, step by step toward the taxi. The agents were closing in on where they thought he was.

Shea got under the last car before the curb. One of the MI6 agents got smart and looked under the cars. He spotted Shea. He took aim—and then he fell to the ground, the gun still in his hand. More gunfire began. Shea looked toward the SAVAMA agents. They both fell, dead. Eyes open. He could see Neda and Beynon's legs moving. They were still alive, slinking from car to car. Shea had to get up. He had to get away.

Before he climbed out from under the last car he looked back and saw the other MI6 agent. His body was on the ground. He, too, was dead. Who was doing the shooting now? He wondered. When he stood he looked across the wreckage and had his answer. It was the man he feared most—Zhubin. The assassin had a gun to Beynon's head and held Neda under his other arm.

Turkish cops pulled up on either side of Zhubin, sirens blaring and lights flashing. Zhubin looked in both directions. Then he looked directly at Shea. Shea knew the look.

"No!" he yelled. But it was too late. Zhubin pulled the trigger and Beynon fell to the ground, a bullet through his temple. Neda screamed and took his head into her hands. She tried to stop the blood. She tried to fool herself into believing that it hadn't happened, that Beynon hadn't been shot and killed in front of her eyes, that somehow it was her imagination or a dream. But the blood on her hands was all too real, and the arms that lifted her up were all too hard of reminders that what she was seeing and feeling was indeed real and happening.

The Turkish police jumped out of their vehicles. Shea tried to climb over the cars parked on the street and get to Neda, but Zhubin had already pushed her into an SUV that was waiting behind him. Like that, she was gone. They were gone. All was lost. And Shea was on his own.

65

O'SHAUGHNESSY WAS SITTING AT THE BAR IN THE LAUREL LEAF PUB just off Falls Road in Belfast. It was a bold move. Everyone in the place knew who he was. Everyone had an opinion of him. He didn't care. Pint of the black stuff and a shot of Paddy further numbed his feelings.

He was waiting for the job to be done. And the Laurel was only a few blocks from his house. Alibi was set. Couple more hours and the boys would be back, bounty in hand. They'd better.

O'Shaughnessy wiped the foam from his mouth and listened to the music. Wasn't U2, thank Christ. Local band, probably, he thought. Maybe Ash. But a little too hard for the environs. He was hoping for some of the more traditional folk music; he wasn't going to be staying long in Ireland. He wanted to take in, and take with him, as much as he could.

He finished his pint and put the pounds on the bar. It was when he was reaching into his pocket that he saw them in the bar mirror—two fellas. Beer buzzed. Standing tall. Swaggers on them. Looking for trouble.

O'Shaughnessy didn't stand up and turn toward them as they expected. He sat on his stool and spun around. "Help ya, fellas?"

One tall. One short. Both skinny. Both nervous. He laughed inside. A smile came across his face.

"Hear you got a job on tonight," the tall one said.

It wiped away O'Shaughnessy's smile. "Must be mistaken," he said.

Now he was angry. News of his heist had leaked. He had to get back and see that the job went off. He stood. "Excuse me, boys."

The short one addressed him. "You don't know who I am, do you?"

"No. But you sure as fuck know who I am. Now make way," O'Shaughnessy said, putting his scally cap on.

The two men stood together, shoulder to shoulder, blocking O'Shaughnessy from going anywhere. The short one continued. "Jimmy, Jimmy Fallon. Just like my old man. He did a job for you once. He's in the clink now."

"My sympathies," O'Shaughnessy said, putting on his peacoat. "Like I said. Excuse me, boys." He took a step, and the small one, Jimmy Fallon, put a hand on O'Shaughnessy's chest. "Says you ratted him out. Says you played both sides, my old man."

O'Shaughnessy looked down at the young man. "Then your father is a lying fuckin' bastard." He didn't wait for either of the two men to strike. O'Shaughnessy never waited. He grabbed the short man's arm, the one that was still pressing against his chest, and twisted it so he bent low. He kicked the tall one in the groin and then swiped his empty beer glass from the bar and smashed it into the short man's face. The tall man was still bent over and O'Shaughnessy picked up his stool and hit him over the head with it. He hit him again and again. It sounded like a melon being dropped over and over.

The pub was silent. The bartender wiped the spot on the bar in front of O'Shaughnessy. He said calmly, "'Nough, Sean. I'll clean 'em up but I won't bury 'em."

O'Shaughnessy stopped beating the tall man. He looked over at the short one: his face was cut to pieces. Shards of glass were in his eyes. He was bleeding profusely. "Enough then," O'Shaughnessy said. "Enough. You are right."

He walked out the door and the crowd's eyes followed him.

There was more violence to come.

66

O'SHAUGHNESSY SAT ON HIS COUCH IN THE DARK. HE HEARD THE familiar sound of footsteps on his porch. He heard three sets.

He opened the door and Tommy and two other men came through. Hoods were up. Their faces darkened. It was like old times.

"Downstairs," O'Shaughnessy said, not greeting them. None of them spoke.

He turned on the light to the cellar and they all went down. Musty. A furnace was in the corner. Cement floors. An old card table and chairs were at the base of the landing. The thieves removed their hoods.

"Get it clean?" O'Shaughnessy asked.

"Aih," Tommy said. "Without a hitch. Parked it by the Titanic, just like you said."

The *Titanic* was built in a shipyard by the Belfast docks. The ship itself, of course, rested somewhere at the bottom of the sea. But its reputation remained a part of Belfast lore. Especially where it was built. The place they still called the Titanic.

"Storage was open?" O'Shaughnessy asked.

"Aih," Tommy said. "Just like you said. Pat and Jack did a fine job of it, too."

O'Shaughnessy looked at the two other men for the first time. They were brothers. Black-haired. Dark complexions. Hence they were called Black Irish. Legend had it that Moors seeded the Black Irish. O'Shaughnessy just nodded at them.

"How many crates you get?" he asked.

"Six," Tommy said. The brothers apparently weren't much for talking.

O'Shaughnessy nodded again and went around a pole to a storage unit he had. It looked like a gym locker.

"Was down at the Laurel, and a couple of fellas said they heard about the job," O'Shaughnessy said with the tiniest bit of aggravation discernible.

The brothers looked at one another, their eyes bulged out of their sockets. "Guess someone chirped," O'Shaughnessy continued, as he took a shotgun out of the locker. "Anyone got anything to say?"

The men backed up a step. O'Shaughnessy cocked the gun and shot Jack and then Pat. He blew holes through their chests so wide you could see through them.

He placed the smoking shotgun on his shoulder.

Tommy looked down at the dead men. "Shame. Good boys, too. Happens. Sorry, Sean, thought we could trust 'em."

O'Shaughnessy looked hard at his old friend. "I think we could trust 'em. I don't think they said a fuckin' word."

67

TOMMY WENT PALE. HE SWALLOWED HARD. IT WASN'T THE KILLING that got to him, it was O'Shaughnessy's words and the meaning behind them; he knew.

"Cops heard about the bust, too, Tommy. Imagine that. After the fact. 'Twas leaked. Anonymous call. Just like Omagh. Still got my sources," O'Shaughnessy said.

"Sean, I—"

"Stop. Let me finish. I always wondered how the Omagh bombing got so botched. Was supposed to go off at the courthouse like we planned. All those people, though, dead 'cause the location got switched. I never could figure that out. Mikey, even, all these years, blamed hisself for it. All those people directed to where the bomb was not, where it wasn't. Cost lives, Tommy. Civilians. Now I realize it was you. You redirected the plot. It was you who changed the locale."

Tommy sat down on one of the folding chairs at the card table. He nodded his head several times. "Was always you, wasn't it, Sean? Never about me. The planning. The strategy. The glory, even, if you want to call it that. You. You, the general. But what about me? I did all the dirty work all those years. Where was my glory? I never asked for nothin'. I just wanted your respect. Anything you could have asked of me I would have done, Sean." He looked up at O'Shaughnessy. "Then I got to thinkin'. And I retraced all that we had done over the years. I examined all the bombings. I saw what was happening. I figured it out, Sean. See, I know. That's why I changed the Omagh location. That's why all those people got killed. For once, it was my game and my plan. You weren't the only one with a secret strategy, Sean. I had my own. Been planning it for years." He laughed and slapped his knee.

O'Shaughnessy looked down at his friend. He cocked the shotgun. "Set me up good then, Tommy, you did. Set me up good."

"Ain't nothing good about what either of us has ever done, Sean. Can't you see that? We play for the other side."

"It's time then, Tommy."

"Aih. 'Tis."

They looked each other in the eye, neither deviating from the stare—and O'Shaughnessy blasted a hole in Tommy's head, his best friend, the man he had known since forever, and a man he actually never knew.

68

MESBAH YAVARI WALKED DOWN THE WINDING STAIRCASE TO THE LI-brary and religious archives of the seminary. He had collected what he believed to be the most comprehensive Islamic texts in the world. What he didn't have in original form, he had transcribed and printed himself.

The library was located just under Mesbah Yavari's personal chambers, so he needed only to walk a few steps down the hallway to the staircase. Lights automatically went on in every area in the seminary. Mesbah Yavari was proud of his technologically advanced building and gardens. He had even installed rain sensors, a curious thing for such a dry place as Qom.

The library relied on the old-fashioned honor system. Students signed in by hand and noted which books they borrowed.

Mesbah Yavari walked into the library and the lights went on row by row. There were no windows since the library was belowground. There was a reading area with picniclike tables and benches. Then rows of books. He breathed deeply. He loved the smell of the leather, paper, and ink. A hint of licorice was in the air from the aniseed mixed in ink.

An entire section of the library was devoted to the Koran. There was a complete *hadith* collection. There were Sufi texts, including the *Masnavi* of Rumi, Sa'di's *The Gulistan*, *Salaman and Absal*, and different translations of the texts from the twelve imams. The only modern book in the room was a single copy of *The Satanic Verses* by Salman Rushdie.

Mesbah Yavari strolled past all those rows to the very end of the library. His robes draped on the ground covering his feet as he walked. The old ayatollah was like a ghost creeping around. The library was stone quiet. Students were in class.

In the corner of the library against the wall was a copy of the *Zand-i Vohuman Yasht*. The Zoroastrian texts informed the Islamic texts and the books were vital for scholars for all sorts of reasons: dates, locations, and derivations of certain ancient Muslim rituals and practices. Mesbah Yavari read them often.

He opened the Zoroastrian book and saw that a page from the binding had been torn out. He walked back to the sign-in sheet and looked for the last person to have checked the book out; it hadn't been signed out for weeks. Whoever took the page wasn't stupid enough to sign the book out. He probably took the page out right there in the library, the ayatollah thought. It's what he hoped.

None of the students knew it but Mesbah Yavari's technological obsession went beyond light switches and rain sensors. He had the whole seminary wired. Video cameras were secretly installed in every room. All the footage fed back into a security system. The control room was in the deep, deep basement a floor below the library. The students were afraid of that level of the building. They never went down there—by choice. There were rumors of bad things that happened to other students in the deep, deep, as they referred to it. A torture chamber. A prison cell. Mesbah Yavari never had to worry about the control room being discovered. The students were too scared to snoop.

Besides, the rumors happened to be true.

69

IN THE CONTROL ROOM IN THE DEEP, DEEP BASEMENT OF THE SEMI-nary, the ayatollah sat in front of a computer terminal. It was an odd sight, the old bearded man draped in robes and wearing a turban clicking away on a PC.

Footage of students coming and going played on the screen. Mesbah Yavari sat for more than an hour fast-forwarding through footage. He was able to narrow his search by limiting it to the one camera placed at the back row of the library.

Bingo!

Two students. A young one, pudgy and disheveled, stood while another, an older student with a trim and thin beard, took the page out of one of the books. It had to be the *Zand-i Vohuman Yasht*.

Mesbah Yavari froze the frame on the older student. He didn't know who this student was, and he knew all his students. This one was tall, handsome, fit, and trim. He definitely would have remembered him. He definitely would have *had* him.

The ayatollah let the tape play as he contemplated how an outsider could have infiltrated the seminary. *Were there others? What was their purpose?* Clearly they had known about the Zoroastrian text. They would also have to have known that Talib's assassin had a copy and was delivering it. Only a few people knew of the scroll's existence and even fewer knew that the SAVAMA agent was bringing it to Qom.

The thinly bearded student rolled up the page into its original scroll form as Mesbah Yavari watched and contemplated all this. The ayatollah looked at the time code. *They were bold, these two.* They had stolen the scroll just a few hours ago.

On the screen, the young man walked to the pudgy boy and put his hand on his shoulder. They had gotten away with their theft and he was signaling the boy to go. The younger boy then did something strange. He looked up and stared straight into the video camera—straight at Mesbah Yavari—and smiled.

Mesbah Yavari froze the frame. The boy knew the camera was there. *Yet he still proceeded with the theft!* The ayatollah looked more closely at the boy. He looked into his eyes. A pain ran deep through the ayatollah. It was as if someone was cutting out his innards with a knife, as if acid was running through his veins. He had to turn away.

Deep down he knew who he was looking at, but the other part of himself wouldn't let him see.

70

ZHUBIN HAD NEDA BOUND AND GAGGED IN THE BACK OF THE CAR that he had escaped in. A SAVAMA agent named Ray was driving. He was in his early forties, the same as Zhubin, and was also a veteran secret service agent. He knew his way around Istanbul and got them clear of the police and any tails with some fast maneuvering and good driving skills.

They were headed for the SAVAMA safe house in the east end of Istanbul. Ray stuck to side roads and alleys just to be on the ultrasafe side. The roads in some cases were so narrow the side-view mirrors scraped walls. Old men sitting on chairs covered by red cloths and smoking cursed them for driving so fast. The tires squealed as they flew around sharp corners and screeched when stopped hard for a woman and child crossing the street. This was the only time that Zhubin took issue with Ray's driving. He yelled, and Ray heard fear in his voice. Ray was surprised that the great agent was so shaken. Zhubin's head was shaking.

All day, Zhubin hadn't been happy. Not only had two SAVAMA agents been killed right in front of him by MI6, he had only fifty percent of his prize. He knew the president wasn't going to be satisfied with half his bounty. Neda was a priority, but Shea was still at large. That meant the prospect of a news story hitting the airwaves still hung in the air.

Zhubin had read the alert from headquarters about the Interpol warrant on Shea. That would explain MI6's involvement, he thought. It also might compromise Shea's ability to escape and perhaps even prevent him from broadcasting a news story. But Zhubin didn't want to take that chance. After all, he had found Shea with the British News bureau chief.

Zhubin resisted thinking about Ray's driving. About the woman and child he almost hit. About the woman and child he almost hit. About . . . the woman. A child. *No*, he forced his thoughts away. *No, not now.*

Instead, he went back to thinking like the Irishman again. It got him out of his own head.

Shea, Zhubin knew, wouldn't be able to fly or take a train across any border. He'd be stopped by customs. Sure, a journalist such as Shea who operated in war-torn countries all over the world might have alternative passports. But he was a journalist, not a spy, so that was doubtful. *How would he escape? Where would he go? To whom might he turn now that the British News chief was dead? Would he try to come after the woman?*

The woman. Who was she anyway? Not only to Shea, but also to Talib? The president was hell-bent on getting her.

Zhubin could hear the woman's muffled cries for help coming from the backseat. Getting her to the safe house was one thing, like taking a chess piece off the board. But the game still continued. He needed to get Michael Shea. He needed to affect a strategy. And every good strategy was driven by information.

Neda shrieked in a high-pitched noise that blistered throughout the vehicle.

Zhubin knew how he'd get his information. She was tied up in the backseat. She would take his mind off things.

71

THE SAVAMA SAFE HOUSE WAS LOCATED OFF THE BUSY ATATURK Bulvan next to the Aqueduct of Valens, the thousand-yard-long series of stone archways that was a city landmark and easy for any agent to recognize.

Ray checked the rearview mirror one last time before pulling into the garage of the house. He closed the door with a remote control device and it slammed shut. They were in total blackness. Zhubin pulled Neda with ease from the backseat and threw her over his shoulder. She kicked and screamed and tried to wiggle out of his grasp. But it was futile.

Zhubin took her into the house and placed her in the soundproof room next to the kitchen. The room was used for surveillance and recordings, among other things. It was painted gray. A fluorescent light gave the room a fuzzy brightness. More like a haze.

The recording and surveillance equipment were on one side of the room, and on the other was a bench. It looked like an exercise bench, with straps and stirrups to keep a person's feet in place. If someone were to walk in and not know what the bench was used for, they might think it was used to do sit-ups.

The rest of the house was different from this stark and clinical room. The town house was furnished in classical Ottoman antiques. Fine rugs and rich leather sofas went along with thick wood chairs that complemented the paneled walls and expensive-looking oil paintings. Whoever designed and furnished the SAVAMA town house had sophisticated taste and seemingly an unlimited budget. It was an ambience far different from the soundproof room where Neda lay on her back.

The town house had a small, enclosed patio out back with a capped cistern. Underneath the entire Fatih neighborhood there was a vast and elaborate system of water linking two hundred fifty miles of water channels. It was one of the greatest feats of ancient times. It was said in times past that people could lower buckets and even bring up fish.

Ray hoisted a water bucket from the cistern and went back inside. He passed through the kitchen and entered the security code for the soundproof room. Neda was strapped to the bench with the hood they put on her in the car still over her head.

Zhubin and the agent didn't speak with each other. They didn't need to. They were each old hands at the torture method they were about to use on Neda.

72

It worked like this: the bench would be adjusted so the subject's body was on an incline, head toward the floor. Water would be poured over the hood, until the subject choked. The method, "waterboarding," as it was commonly called, was effective. It caused the mammalian diving reflex to occur, which gave the sensation of drowning.

The method typically was repeated over and over until the subject was rendered unconscious, died, or talked. Subjects fell into two categories—those who spoke and those who didn't. The consequence of the latter was up to the torturer.

Zhubin took the bucket from Ray while Ray held down Neda's arms. Zhubin didn't bother to undo her gag under the hood yet. He wasn't interested in listening to what she had to say—yet. He wanted her to feel the pain.

Zhubin carefully poured the water over Neda's face. It splashed off the black hood and then sopped through. He kept pouring until her body began to convulse and she bucked. He waited a minute and did it again. She tried to turn her head from side to side to avoid the water, but Ray held it in place. She shook and shook. Finally he stopped. It was time to remove the gag and see which category Neda fell into.

Zhubin nodded to Ray. The agent untied the hood from Neda's neck and slowly took it off. He then untied her gag. She gasped for air. Zhubin readjusted the bench so she laid flat.

"Tell us where the journalist is," Zhubin said.

"You killed him," Neda said, still gasping and coughing.

Zhubin hadn't looked Neda in the face before. Too much was happening, and Ray had taken care of hooding her. He now saw how beautiful she was. It took him back.

"You know," he said, "who I mean. The Irishman. Michael Shea."

Neda turned her head away from him and began to chant. She said the same three words over and over again. *"Humata, Hukhta, Hvarshta."* It was Avestan and was the cornerstone of Zoroastrianism: "Good thoughts, good words, good deeds." Zhubin knew what they meant.

Neda's voice was melodious. Zhubin and Ray listened, almost pleasantly, forgetting their place and what they were there to do.

Neda had drifted off. She went to that soulful place in her mind that existed of peace, safety, and stillness. This was the place people who meditated or prayed frequently could find. It was a spot, the type worn on the outside by many Hindus, which shut out the world. It was an inner sanctum. All humans had the capability of finding it—if they looked for it. It was the place of dreams, of spirit, and most important of control. The center functions to all feelings and emotions existed there. It was a powerful place once found because it separated the mind from its vessel. And no matter what harm may come or what fright may be enlisted, the spot was safe. It was sacred. It was the inner god in all people. Neda called upon its power to shut out the evil being inflicted upon her. *"Humata, Hukhta, Hvarshta."*

73

Zhubin and Ray had, for a moment, fallen into a trance as they listened repeatedly to Neda's chant.

Neda then turned and looked at Zhubin. Ray was behind her so she couldn't see him.

It was the look, and the turn of the head that did it. Neda reminded him of the woman he had seen earlier in the mosque, the woman in the headscarf. It drove a deep pain into his stomach. He realized what the look represented and it took him back in time to when he was six years old.

Zhubin was standing on a street corner in Tehran. His mother was crossing the street to get him. He had foolishly dared traffic and almost been hit by a truck. His mother wasn't so fortunate. She got hit and landed on the hood of a car, smashing into the windshield and then onto the street. Zhubin just stood and watched. On the ground, she turned and looked at him. Blood dribbled from her mouth.

Neda stopped her chant. And Zhubin and Ray seemed to break out of their own trances.

"Should we go again?" Ray asked.

Before Zhubin could answer a vibration went through his body. He felt it tingle. It came in flashes. Zhubin didn't know what it was. Then he realized a mobile phone was ringing. It was inside his jacket pocket. Madonna wasn't singing. This was the British News bureau chief's mobile phone. Zhubin had taken it from him just before he shot him in the head. He had forgotten that he had slipped it in his jacket.

Zhubin answered. "Hello," he said, his English rough.

"Size forty-three!" were the words that came booming.

"Yes," Zhubin said, muffling the phone to disguise his voice.

"Okay. We'll be early. Be at the park early then, too, okay. Not after sunset, just before. We'll swing by and get you. By the way it's a new boat. Speedboat. You'll like it. Okay. I have to go. See you, okay."

Zhubin hung up. He now knew the bureau chief was going to meet a boat at a park. There couldn't be that many parks on the water in Istanbul. He needed to consult a map. He turned from Neda and headed for the door.

Ray asked, "Where are you going?"

"To get the journalist."

"What about her?"

"Call Talib. He'll tell you what to do with her."

Zhubin didn't turn around and look at Neda again. He couldn't bring himself to do that. He walked out of the room and shut the door behind him. For the second time that day the past came back to haunt him through a woman's eyes.

Zhubin didn't find himself thinking of Neda when he went into the garage and started the car. He wasn't thinking of the woman in the headscarf nor his mother. He was thinking of Fatima. She was regarded as the judge in the hereafter. In other words, Zhubin was thinking about his own death.

He was overcome with a feeling of darkness. He pressed the remote. Light began to come through in steady stages as the garage door opened. Then it was bright and he could see. He put the SUV in reverse and pulled out.

74

MAHMOUD TALIB HAD FINISHED DRYING THE TEA-AGED SCROLL when his mobile phone rang. He listened as the SAVAMA agent explained the situation. They had Neda. Now what should they do with her?

"Where is Zhubin?"

"He went after the journalist," Ray said.

Talib punched the floor. Shea had gotten away again. At least they had Neda, though. He needed her taken care of. He needed to speak with her. What he had to ask her, he needed to do in private.

"Bring her to me," Talib said. He instructed Ray to bring Neda to Qom. The agent was to gag and blindfold her. "No one should be allowed to speak with her, understand?"

"Yes, Mr. President," Ray said.

Talib ordered a jet to pick Ray and Neda up at Istanbul's private aircraft terminal. He'd have diplomatic cover for them waiting.

Talib hung up just as Mesbah Yavari came back into the room. He'd need to keep Neda's secret safe. He couldn't let the Ayatollah speak with her either. That would be too great a risk. Still, it was safer to have Neda brought to Qom rather than Tehran. There was too great a scrutiny already being waged at the presidency.

The Green Party movement still had its followers despite the draconian measures he had installed to quash it. Any person found to be aligned with the movement was to be shot or imprisoned. The international press and diplomatic corps had their fangs out for him, too.

Talib the dictator.

Talib the tyrant.

Talib the devil.

If they only knew. Still, the criticism was giving way to some dissent within the Iranian Parliament. As best as he tried not to antagonize these elected officials, it still was not enough to dissuade the questions about leadership. He could intimidate them with threats. Perhaps kill a few as an example. But he couldn't kill them all (yet). There would be another revolution. And that would prevent him from coming into power. The less Tehran knew, the better. Spies, of course, were everywhere. If Neda were seen, there would be questions and a formal interrogation. There might even be an uprising like the one during the election.

The uprising itself had been overblown, all because of technology. Some ridiculous thing called Twitter. Did the Western media not know the charges and the "tweets" were mostly coming from foreign intelligence agents amplifying claims of violence? Praise Allah he could not let that happen again. Nor could he let the Ayatollah know who Neda was. Just her existence was power. It was enough to end his campaign as the Mahdi.

Mesbah Yavari might forgive a forged document, but he would never forgive the information Neda had on Talib. She was his Achilles' heel. Everything else he could fake, forge, or force upon the masses—eventually the world. Just not Neda. Not now. Not ever.

75

"I HAVE FOUND THE DECEPTION," MESBAH YAVARI SAID, CLOSING the door to his chambers behind him.

Talib's head snapped up. For a second, he thought the Ayatollah was speaking about him.

"Here, these two. We must find them. They cannot have gotten far," Mesbah Yavari said, handing a printout of the frozen video frame of the pudgy boy and the young man over to Talib.

"Who are they?"

"They are the ones who switched the Zoroastrian scroll."

Mesbah Yavari and Talib figured that the scroll had been switched when Zhubin was fighting in the hallway. (The plan had been devised as a backup by Gaspar and his brothers to prevent the scroll from falling into Mesbah Yavari's hands.)

"I don't know who they are. They are not from here," said Mesbah Yavari.

Talib held the printout closer to his face. The younger boy had a broad forehead and a distinctively pointed nose. A shimmering light seemed to appear above his head. His eyes looked thick with mascara. But most shocking was what was on the boy's neck next to his shoulder. His uniform had flopped open and it could be seen: the seal of the prophet.

Talib had one, too. Although he had burned his own on when he was young.

The boy he was looking at was the Mahdi.

"He will have a broad forehead, a prominent nose, and his eyes will be naturally mascaraed. Al Mahdi will have a seal of prophethood between his shoulders, which can be clearly seen, just as that of the Messenger of Allah (praise and peace upon him)."

After Neda was taken care of, he'd have to send Ray to find and execute the boy.

Talib was happy that Mesbah Yavari hadn't noticed the sign of the revelation. He still needed the old man to believe in him.

What Talib didn't realize is that the Mahdi could hide in plain sight and reveal himself to only those whom he chose.

76

ZHUBIN WAS ALARMED TO LEARN THAT ISTANBUL WAS LOUSY WITH waterfront parks. He was in a predicament. He couldn't exactly call the man who said he'd be making the rendezvous. First, Zhubin's voice would give him away. Second, even if he could get away with faking that, asking which rendezvous point would be a giveaway in and of itself.

Zhubin looked at the GPS map of Istanbul. He looked at where the shoot-out had occurred. He traced that back to Beynon's house and stared at the line. He continued the line in the direction of the nearest waterfront location. It led him to Topkapi Palace . . . and Gülhane Park.

Zhubin knew from his training that when people ran, they tended to run in a straight line.

Zhubin drove past the large imperial mosque known as the Mosque of the Prince and saw that the police had the whole area where the shooting took place blocked off. He looked at the spot where he had killed Beynon and where several police officers now stood taking notes and photographs. The look on Neda's face flashed into his mind. Then the woman in the headscarf from the mosque. Then his mother. Zhubin swerved hard to avoid crashing into the car in front of him. He had zoned out.

He pulled over to the side of the road. His hands were shaking. Zhubin didn't know what was happening to him. He tried to put the thoughts out of his mind and concentrate. He focused on one thing: killing Michael Shea.

There wasn't a passion behind killing Shea. There didn't need to be a reason beyond what he was told, what he was ordered to do. That is what made sense of Zhubin's world: his was not to question why, his was just to do or die.

Orders also gave Zhubin an out when it came to responsibility. He was an agent of the state and therefore any blame, any regret, any guilt could be laid off on the government.

Lately, though, Zhubin was beginning to think for himself. He was beginning to wonder. He was beginning to question why.

77

THE WORLD WAS SPINNING OUT OF CONTROL. SHEA WAS RUNNING frantically away from the police. Neda was kidnapped. His friend, Matt, was dead. The circumstances were dire. Movement was his only friend now. He had to get somewhere safe to think and put a plan together.

Priorities, Michael. Get it together.

What he had learned from being a foreign correspondent all these years was, first, never freak out. Clear minds made good, lifesaving decisions. A rattled mind got you killed. He had seen more than his fair share of correspondents shot for running when they should have walked, or moving too fast when they should have remained still. Second, he learned that you always needed a plan.

The Turkish police blew their whistles. Shea bolted down a side street, Mithatpasa Cad—he saw the name as he ran down it—and then cut around a series of side streets. He was lucky. The small street he was running down intersected several others. He disappeared down one and ran into a rug merchant's store. He ducked behind one of the tall, hanging carpets as a policeman ran by.

The rug merchant was sipping tea at the counter in the back of the store. There was a backgammon board in front of him. He didn't say anything to Shea. Barely acknowledged his presence. The merchant turned his averted eyes back to the board. Shea had experienced this type before. They were called *keyif*. It was a cult of people who practiced quiet relaxation. They were often found playing backgammon in

parks and sipping tea—without a word to interrupt the game. Some sat
and watched the world go by, while others interacted with one another,
all without sound. They soaked in, rather than put out. It was a sopo-
rific society, the opposite of how Shea felt now; he was in a state of high
anxiety.

Shea heard the toilet flush and saw a man come out of the bathroom. It must have been the merchant's board game opponent. He was
a young man, dressed in a T-shirt, blue jeans, and work boots. He could
have been a teenager anywhere. He lit a cigarette, blew smoke in Shea's
direction, and went back to his game. Again, actions without words.

Shea pretended to eye a few rugs and then hastily beat it out of the
shop. He stood on the sidewalk and peered around the corners of the
intersecting streets. Policemen were everywhere. None had seen him—
yet. But they were closing in. He needed somewhere to hide. He looked
around for a cafe where he could blend in, but there weren't any. Directly across the street, however, was a *hamam*. The Turkish bathhouse
would provide the perfect cover for him, precisely because he and everyone in it would be . . . uncovered.

SHEA HAD BEEN TO TURKISH BATHS BEFORE. INDEED, HE AND BEY-
non went to them every time Shea was in the city.

Shea paid the attendant and went into the dressing room where he
took off his clothes and wrapped a *pestemal* around his waist. He put on
a pair of sandals and walked into the main room, the *sicakilik*. The heat
hit him in the face. He began to sweat immediately. The attendant

pointed to a spot on the marble platform on which he could lie down. A half-dozen men were already lying there soaking up the heat. Some were getting massaged, others scrubbed.

Shea looked up at the ceiling and thought about how he might get Neda back. The SAVAMA would probably whisk her back to Iran. No way he could go back there. There was only one solution for Neda's release and thwarting Talib's nuclear ambitions: he'd have to abandon any plans that he had to find his uncle. He'd have to get to Rome and discredit Talib. Finding his uncle might prove to satisfy his own ego, but following the lead Gaspar had given him might provide him with the hard evidence he needed to save Neda. The only thing he had now was conjecture. It was his own theory that Talib was in cahoots with the Chechens and his uncle to execute a nuclear plot. There was no evidence of it. And it was even a theory that Talib believed himself to be the Mahdi. Perhaps by uncovering the mystery of what Gaspar had said about the Third Secret of Fatima, connections of some ilk could be shown. If nothing else, he might be able to use whatever information he found in Rome as leverage for Neda's release. The key would be convincing Beynon's contact to take him to Italy—while explaining that Matt had been killed. And that it had been because of him, Michael Shea, that Beynon was dead.

See, Michael, another person who got too close . . .

Shea was holding himself responsible for the death of yet another human being. So far in his life, he calculated, he had killed hundreds.

79

Z HUBIN DROVE ALONG THE SMALL, CIRCULAR ROAD IN G ÜLHANE
Park. He pulled off to the side and killed the engine just before the
road ended. Armed with a scope rifle, he got out and slinked through
the trees. He found his way to another small road and followed that to
the end. In front of him was the Bosphorus Strait, the narrowest strait
in the world. It separated Asia from Europe and was the source for
many a myth, from Lo's travels where Zeus was said to have turned her
into a cow for her own protection to perhaps most famously where Jason and the Argonauts came upon the Clashing Rocks. Jason obtained
passage and the rocks became fixed. The Greeks gained access to the
Black Sea.

Zhubin did not know any of these stories. He didn't know that the
Bosphorus Strait connected Russia to the Mediterranean or that its
name came from the word *phosphorus*. The light-bearing stream that
ran through it could be seen from outer space; it then could be seen
abruptly dissolving into the Black Sea.

Zhubin knew only that he had to kill Shea. For that opportunity
he'd have to wait. He crouched down beside a large tree and took out
his binoculars. He scanned the water's edge and tried hard not to let
his mind wander. He was deathly afraid of the memories coming back.
A kill, he hoped, would keep them buried.

80

SHEA HAD NO WAY OF KNOWING THAT FARUK HAD CHANGED HIS PLAN and was going to the rendezvous point early. He had finished his Turkish sauna, stolen another man's clothes and cap, and, feeling better in his new disguise, hurried to Gülhane Park.

Shea was surprised to see an Irish name on the street he was walking along: Kennedy Cad. He crossed the busy road to the park and waited. He wanted to time things just right. His plan was to wait until the sun had set and then make his way to the water. The darker the better for him. It would have to be the last second before Faruk would realize he wasn't Matt. Then, hopefully, he could convince him to help.

He began to walk through the trees. He had chosen to walk along the left side of the tree patch. Had he chosen differently, he would have run smack into Zhubin.

ZHUBIN HAD HUNKERED DOWN BEHIND A TREE NEAR THE SHORE. HE watched and waited for the boat. When one broke away from the channel of traffic, he knew it was the one he was after. Shea would be close by.

Zhubin checked the shoreline but didn't see anyone. Could he have been wrong? *Maybe it wasn't the right park and the right spot where the rendezvous was set? Perhaps the Irishman wouldn't show?*

SHEA HAD SEEN ZHUBIN'S CAR PARKED ON THE SIDE OF THE ROAD. IT was the only one. It had blacked out windows and diplomatic plates. It wasn't hard to miss.

*   *   *

ZHUBIN TOOK THE RIFLE OUT OF ITS CASE AND ATTACHED THE SCOPE. He loaded the chamber with hollow bullets and clocked it as the boat tied up to shore. He was prepared, he just didn't know for what.

SHEA WATCHED FARUK STEP OFF THE BOAT AND LOOK AROUND. HE heard him call for Beynon. If Shea hadn't seen the vehicle, he would have missed the pickup entirely; Faruk was early.

Shea looked around but couldn't see anyone else in the small park area. But the car. His sixth sense told him that the SAVAMA agent was somewhere in the trees . . . waiting. He'd have to time his move to Faruk's actions.

"MATT!" FARUK YELLED AS HE WALKED ALONG THE SHORE OF THE park. He was younger than Shea expected. Dressed expensively in an open-collared shirt, black slacks, and gold buckled shoes, Faruk looked rich. His hair was thick with gel.

"Matt!"

No one appeared so Faruk turned around and untied the boat.

ZHUBIN HAD FARUK IN HIS SIGHTS. IT WOULD MAKE NO SENSE TO shoot him now, though. The shot would warn off Shea. He waited, exhaled, and waited. Shea would come. He sensed it.

THE BOAT'S ENGINE STARTED.

SHEA STEPPED OUT FROM THE TREES AND RAN FOR IT.

81

THE BOAT WAS PULLING AWAY FROM SHORE. FARUK HADN'T SEEN SHEA run for it. He was heading the boat out to sea.

Zhubin saw movement out of the corner of his eye. He put the scope on Shea. He was dressed differently, but Zhubin recognized him immediately. He aimed at Shea's chest. Normally he preferred to shoot at the head, but he wanted to be safe and aim for a bigger target.

Shea was taking long strides. He was two steps away from the dock. If he jumped, he could make it onto the boat. Maybe. He hoped. He'd have to.

Faruk pushed the throttle and the bow of the boat pitched high. The propeller would take a second or two before it caught water and zoomed the boat forward.

Shea jumped.

His mother's eyes stared at him and Zhubin's hands shook. He fired anyway.

Shea landed on the back of the boat just as it took off. Faruk heard him land and turned around.

The shot hit the windshield and cracked it.

"Go!" Shea yelled.

Another shot made Faruk obey.

They were halfway across the strait before Faruk killed the engine and pulled a gun on Shea.

"Who the fuck are you?!" he asked "And where is Matt Beynon?"

Zhubin kept the boat in sight. He saw which way it was headed. His only hope was that whoever had called him—the man on board that boat—kept his mobile phone turned on. So he could track it.

82

"MATT IS DEAD. I AM A FRIEND OF HIS. HE SAID THAT I COULD TRUST you. Please. I need your help." Shea tried to use as many key words and phrases as possible to disarm Faruk and show that he wasn't a threat.

The sun had almost set and the glare prevented Shea from seeing Faruk's expression. He put his hand over his eyes to visor the sun. He decided to press on with his case: "He was killed by the SAVAMA—Iranian Intelligence. That's also who was shooting at us."

"Why?" came the voice from the face Shea couldn't see.

Shea could have responded, *because of me. I got him killed because of something I got bungled up in.* Instead, he decided to give Faruk information, the truth. He knew from years of being a reporter that certain people responded to this. It built trust.

"Matt and I were working on a story about the Iranian president," Shea began, lying just a shade to win Faruk over.

"Matt was a good man," Faruk interrupted.

"He was."

"Mahmoud Talib isn't."

"I'd like to get revenge," Shea agreed.

"In that case, I will help you."

The silhouette that was Faruk appeared again as the young man Shea had seen. The glare faded into a gray backdrop, the type of light that remained just before darkness set in.

Faruk lowered his gun and got behind the wheel. He powered the boat as fast as it could go toward the Asian shore.

Zhubin relayed the exact time of his call with Faruk to SAVAMA headquarters. He gave them Beynon's mobile number and SIM card identification. Within a matter of minutes Faruk's mobile was locked on to an Iranian satellite. It tracked his location and transmitted the data directly to Zhubin's handheld device. He could see the boat's heading and watched the dot that represented it on his tiny screen move toward shore.

SHEA AND FARUK WERE IN THE BACK OF A BEAT-UP OLD VAN DRIVING toward the Sabiha Gökçen International Airport. A young Rastafarian-looking dude was driving.

"How was he killed?" Faruk asked.

Shea was trying not to choke on all the cologne that Faruk was wearing. "They shot him in the head," he explained.

Faruk shook his head back and forth and punched the side of the van. The van jerked to a stop. The driver had taken the bang as a signal. "It's okay, Ronnie," Faruk said. "False alarm." He stuck his head between the two front seats to tell Ronnie to keep going.

"You knew Matt well?" Shea asked Faruk, when the young Turk sat back down.

"Yes, he dated my sister."

"Esra?"

Faruk looked at Shea and tilted his head like a curious dog. "You know her?"

"We met a couple of times with Matt," Shea said.

"Why me? Why are you here with me?" Faruk wanted to know. He had gotten past his mistrust of Shea and was now moving deeper into his analysis of the circumstance. Now he wanted to know what Shea was after.

"Matt and I were on our way to see you when it happened," Shea explained. He left Neda out entirely from his story. He didn't want to get into too much detail with Faruk. The less the Turk knew the better, especially if this drug dealer was ever caught. Faruk couldn't reveal what he didn't know.

"He said that he was going to Italy," Faruk said, posing the statement as a query.

"That's where I am going. That is, if you will take me."

"Matt didn't say anything about that."

"He said that he was going to get you an extra pair of shoes for help-ing me."

Faruk laughed. "Yes, then you are telling the truth if you know that."

An awkward pause ensued.

"So will you? Will you take me?" Shea asked.

"It must be a big story if the Iranians killed Matt over it."

"It is. The biggest story the world has ever seen."

"I suppose you need to fly private for other reasons, too?"

Shea nodded.

Faruk didn't change expressions. "I don't need to know. But if it will take Talib down, I'll help you. If he starts a war over here it's bad for business. Besides, I don't like Persians."

Shea and Faruk shook hands. They sat in silence all the way to the airport.

84

THE SABIHA GÖKÇEN AIRPORT WAS NAMED AFTER THE FIRST FEMALE combat pilot in the world. Turks were proud of their aviation prowess and had two major airports in Istanbul alone to show off just how much they liked to fly.

The Gökçen airport was located forty-five minutes outside the city, but Ronnie the Rastafarian made it in thirty. He blazed through the airport gate and pulled up next to a stealth black jet, a Lear 85.

"I trust Matt told you that I don't transport commercial product—in the legal sense," Faruk said.

"I know it isn't cotton candy."

Faruk didn't know what cotton candy was, but he let the comment pass. "Okay, then. Let's go," he said.

Shea and Faruk got out of the van and beat a path up the jet's stairs. Ronnie unloaded dozens of crates from the van and stowed them in the jet's cargo area. He then scampered up the stairs and closed the door.

Shea was seated in the first seat facing the cockpit. The Lear only sat eight people, and the seats faced one another. The two seats behind him had been replaced by a small couch.

Ronnie went into the cockpit and sat in the pilot's seat.

"He's flying the plane?" Shea asked, incredulously.

"Ronnie? Yeah. We have a lean team. Have to, you know. Don't worry. He's a former Turkish fighter pilot." He yelled up to the cockpit. "You can fly this thing, right, Ronnie?"

Ronnie shouted back: "Like she has never been flown before."

Faruk sat across from Shea. "Matt was nervous about him flying, too. Must be a British thing."

"I'm Irish, and he was Welsh."

"Right, he told me that. *Y Ddraig Goch*, correct?"

"Yes," Shea said, understanding the Welsh words and translating. "*The Red Dragon*. That is the flag of Wales."

Faruk was happy he had remembered that and pronounced it correctly. He continued, "For the last year every week he flew with me. Always got me something. Never was late. It's strange. I just spoke with him. He didn't sound right when I called. You two must have been in trouble then."

Ronnie fired up the engines and the jet shook. Shea thought about what Faruk just said. Something wasn't right. Then he remembered: Beynon had called Faruk, not the other way around.

SHEA QUIZZED FARUK: "WHEN DID YOU SAY THAT YOU SPOKE WITH him?" He began talking louder now that the jet engines had started.

"I don't know, an hour or two ago," Faruk said.

"And you called him?"

"Yes."

"Of course," Shea thought. "That is how they knew where to find me!" He said aloud, "Faruk, get rid of your phone—now!"

"What are you talking about?"

"That wasn't Matt you spoke with. That was a SAVAMA agent. They'll trace your phone to us here."

Faruk thought back on his conversation. He had wondered why Beynon had hung up on him so abruptly. It wasn't like Matt. He was always affable. *This guy must be right.*

Faruk stepped to the cockpit. "Hold it up, Ronnie." He opened the door and tossed out his phone. "Okay," he instructed. "Let's get airborne."

Faruk sat back down next to Shea.

Shea said, "You know you could have just removed the battery and SIM card."

"I'm the trafficker, remember? I know how to evade detection. If they follow that signal, it will lead them to the runway . . . and we'll be long gone. If I took the phone apart now, they'd know. We'll trick them and buy some time."

Ronnie taxied the jet down the runway and took off, wheels up.

ZHUBIN GOT STUCK IN THE NOTORIOUSLY BAD TRAFFIC AROUND TAK-sim Square. He watched the dot on his handheld device as it went to Gökçen airport—and stopped. Either the Turk and Shea were waiting for a commercial flight, or they were escaping on a private jet, Zhubin figured. He bet the latter and called SAVAMA HQ again. He ordered them to scramble a fighter jet and monitor all air traffic leaving the airport.

Zhubin finally made it to Gökçen where he drove onto the runway and found the phone in the exact spot where the GPS indicated.

SAVAMA HQ told him of all the flights that had left the airspace over the past thirty minutes. Only one hadn't filed a flight plan. It was heading over the Mediterranean toward Greece. Zhubin knew that there would be time for the military jet to stop and get him. He gave the order in a terse command: "Shoot it down."

THE IRANIAN AIR FORCE (TECHNICALLY THE ISLAMIC REPUBLIC OF Iran Air Force) pilot was shocked to get the go-ahead to shoot down a civilian aircraft. He couldn't remember when a government had ever sanctioned such an order. Sure, the United States had threatened to fire on certain commercial airplanes during 9/11—but even then it didn't follow through on its threats. That is unless the conspiracy theories were true and the planes that crashed in Pennsylvania and into the Pentagon were shot down by the U.S. military.

In any event, the pilot wasn't going to disobey his orders. Like any fighter pilot, though, he had an ego and he was an independent thinker. At the tender age of nineteen, he also had balls. He asked for confirmation of his orders and was given them again, this time more emphatically.

Iran had a "fly over" agreement with Turkey, and the Iranian fighter pilot had been conducting practice maneuvers near Antalya. The agreement allowed flight tests over sea, not over land.

According to the Iranian flight controller, he was to intercept a Bombardier Lear Jet 85 that was on a trajectory toward the Aegean Sea.

It wouldn't be difficult to find: the Lear was flying only about fifty feet above the water. It was a sure thing that no other jet would be flying so low.

The modified F-5E Tiger II fighter jet had a maximum speed of Mach 1.8, or 1,369 miles per hour. It could intercept the Lear in less than half an hour.

RONNIE HAD FLOWN THE PATH FROM ISTANBUL TO NAPLES DOZENS of times. The path went down the middle of the Dardanelles Strait to the Northeast Aegean Islands at the bottom of the Thracian Sea. Then they'd usually bank left through the middle of the Aegean past the Cyclades to the Ionian Sea where they'd bank right up the Mediterranean to the boot of Italy.

Water. They were careful to only fly over water. And they flew low, sometimes so low that salt would spray onto the windshield.

They avoided radar screens this way and—unless they were specifically targeted—they could go undetected by satellite monitoring.

The route was circuitous. It would be far easier and faster to fly straight across the mainland of Greece to Italy's toe. The Lear 85 had a range ample enough to the lengthier route. It could fly almost 3,500 miles without refueling. It was the perfect carrier plane for the longer but safer route over the seas.

Shea had never flown in a luxury private jet before. He had chartered old planes to take him to gnarly places in Africa. He had flown on military transports and on old Russian helicopters in the Balkans. But luxury was never an adjective for any of these noncommercial flying adventures. They were uncomfortable and hair-raising journeys.

Ensconced in the Lear's plush leather seats, Shea settled comfortably into his seat.

The jet had taken off, as any plane would, nose up for ascension. Then it did what few planes would: it dove precipitously and then straightened out. Shea looked out the window and his heart jumped into his throat.

"Holy shit! Are we going to crash?" he could see the white caps of the waves below.

Faruk chuckled. "No, my friend. We have to fly low. Here"—he shut the blind—"relax. Can I get you a drink? Fully stocked bar. Anything you want."

"If you have Redbreast Irish whiskey, I'll kiss you," Shea said, not looking at Faruk, and his back pressed tightly against the seat from the jet's G-force.

Faruk smiled and he got up. He walked to the back of the plane and then appeared back at Shea's seat a minute later with a bottle and two glasses. "Here, but save the kiss for someone else."

Shea was pleasantly surprised to see that the young Turk had such an esoteric brand of pot-stilled Irish whiskey on hand. Shea didn't savor the whiskey for long—he slugged it.

Faruk sat on his armrest. "*Sláinte*, you say, right?"

"Right."

"*Sláinte*, then." Faruk downed his glass, too. He slid off the armrest onto the seat. "So, Naples. Why Naples if I may ask?"

"Going to Rome, actually. There is someone there I need to meet."

"I can help you get there. My friends have helicopters, boats, trains, even, I think."

"I thought all the trains in Italy were owned by the government?"

"My friends own the government, too."

"Mafia?"

"There is no such thing," Faruk said, smiling slyly.

That's when a fierce noise boomed overhead. The jet teetered, and then made a stark ascent. Faruk tumbled down the aisle to the back of the plane. Shea couldn't do anything. He just held on for his life.

The jet now was going straight up. It seemed as if it was going to tumble over, upside down. And then it did.

SHEA HAD KEPT HIMSELF BUCKLED INTO HIS SEAT ON THE PLANE. Faruk, however, was on the ceiling. The jet came around and flew straight again. Faruk slammed back down onto the floor. Miraculously, he wasn't hurt.

"Ronnie, what is going on?!" Faruk screamed to the cockpit, as he crawled back up the aisle.

"Wish I knew boss. Got a military jet on my tail. Had to evade. Sorry about that."

"Shit," Faruk thought. "The Greeks." They had finally gotten too close to Greek airspace and been spotted. Fucking Greek officials weren't taking any payoffs either. He didn't understand that. *In a country with so much debt, how could there be no bribery?* he wondered. Anyway, it was too late to think about that now.

"Can you lose him?" Faruk asked Ronnie.

"If I could raise him on the radio, I could lie and tell him we'd put down—and then fly back to Turkish airspace. But he isn't talking or listening. I don't understand," Ronnie said. "We aren't even close to shore."

The boom hit the cabin again and this time it was followed by a staccato. The military jet was firing on them.

"Buckle up," Ronni said. "Here we go again."

Faruk strapped himself into his chair.

The Lear was no match for the modified F-5. The military jet was probably the most famous fighter jet in the world. It was even featured in the movies *Top Gun* and *Apocalypse Now*. It was a badass machine—fast, agile, and built for attack. It had an awesome amount of firepower: two cannons in the nose capable of two hundred eighty rounds each, eight rockets, eight air-to-air missiles, and two air-to-surface missiles; as well as a variety of air-to-ground ordinance: cluster, unguided, and napalm bombs. The F-5 was twice as fast as the Lear and could easily fly circles around it.

Ronnie's only maneuver was the upside-down loop. A couple of those, however, and the fighter would get wise and wait it out "abovedeck." One sidewinder missile later and the Lear would be toast.

Ronnie was flying straight again. "Bad news," he said. "That isn't a Greek fighter jet. The tail flag is Iranian. Anyone know why an Iranian military fighter is looking to shoot us down?"

There wasn't time to answer any questions. The focus had to be on escaping. Faruk asked the obvious: "What can we do, Ronnie?"

"You can hold on. Pray if that is your thing, which I know isn't yours, Faruk. But you, mister whatever your name is, may want to take the opportunity."

"No way out of this?" Shea asked.

"Only one," Ronnie said.

90

FARUK LEANED ACROSS SHEA AND OPENED THE WINDOW BLIND. THE
Iranian fighter pilot was looking right at him. He was flying that close.

The F-5 banked right, its left wing high in the air. It would come
around and flank them. This time if Ronnie ascended, the Iranian
would just pursue; there would be no escape.

Ronnie cut back on the throttle. He knew the fighter jet would come
around fast and hard and he wanted to make sure there was as little
distance between them as possible. The Iranian wouldn't risk firing a
missile if he was right on the Lear's tail. The blowback would catch him
up in the explosion.

Ronnie descended as close to the water as he could. A few waves
crashed against the jet's belly as it skimmed the sea.

Ronnie was familiar with the F-5 model. It was a common enough
jet that Northrop Grumman sold around the world. For an American
company, it wasn't too discriminating about which nations it sold the
aircraft to. Hence, Iran having a fleet. It had an older fleet, but a fleet
nonetheless of the coolest fighter jets ever made.

The F-5 did have some technical glitches. It had a short range—less
than 1,000 miles—and its surface bombs sometimes didn't separate
cleanly from the wings. That's how so many Vietnam era jets got
scorched. Last but not least—and this was what Ronnie was counting
on—the guns of the F-5 tended to "smoke up" the windshield during
firing and often resulted in engine damage.

Ronnie didn't have to see the F-5 on his tail. He could hear and feel the supersonic jet. It was close, nose to tail, just as Ronnie had hoped. No way the pilot would risk a missile.

Ronnie braced for it. The guns exploded and ripped holes through the Lear's fuselage.

The Iranian pilot was surprised the Lear wasn't taking evasive action. Flying low over the sea was hardly evasive. Fighter pilots practiced that maneuver all the time. In fact, that was the focus of the practice runs the Iranian pilot had just been pulled from for this secret sortie.

The Iranian pilot thought the target in front of him was too easy. He wanted a real World War II–style dogfight. He decided to go easy on his first round just to make things interesting. Then he'd blow the Lear out of the sky.

But smoke filled the cockpit after he fired his first round, and one of his engine warning lights flashed. The Iranian pilot looked down at the control panel—for a second. And that is when the Lear pulled up. The wash from the Lear jet's exhaust put just enough pressure on the extended nose of the F-5 to make it dip. The smoke blocked the pilot's view, and the Iranian didn't pull up . . . in time. The pointed nose extension, which looked like a four-foot rod protruding from the front of the plane, caught the top of a wave—and fifteen tons of steel crashed into the sea. The F-5's armament did the rest of the job. It exploded in a fantastic ball of fire that Ronnie could see from a mile away. Which was about as far away as they were from the crash now.

Faruk and Shea were white as ghosts

"Lost 'em!" Ronnie exclaimed from the cockpit.

The wind was zipping through the bullet holes in the jet. Neither Faruk nor Shea spoke for several minutes. Faruk then unbuckled himself and picked up the bottle of Redbreast that had rolled under his seat. "I don't think we need glasses, do you?"

Shea grabbed the bottle and took a swig.

91

IT WASN'T EXACTLY NAPLES WHERE THEY LANDED. IT WAS A SMALL,
private airstrip near the ancient city of Pompeii.

Shea's knees were still weak as he walked off the jet and watched as
a team of men unloaded its illicit cargo.

"There's a helicopter over there," Faruk said. He pointed to a dark
hangar in the distance. "I can have it take you to Rome."

"All the same, thanks," Shea said. "But I'll take the train."

92

IT WASN'T THE FIRST TIME THAT SOMEONE HAD BEEN KILLED IN THE
basement of O'Shaughnessy's house. There was even a place for dispos-
ing of the bodies.

Behind the furnace in the corner of the basement was a hatch door.
It led to a fireplace box. A fireplace below the fireplace. The chimney
extended the entire height of the house. The bodies were burned there
along with sandalwood. The scent assured the stink of flesh wouldn't
choke the neighborhood.

It was Sunday morning and O'Shaughnessy knew that St. Peter's Cathedral, across the yard from his front door, would be burning incense for Sunday services.

He dragged the bodies one at a time into the hatch, lit the burner, and closed the door. O'Shaughnessy then showered, dressed, and walked out onto his porch.

Churchgoers were arriving for services. They all walked past his yard but none turned and looked his way.

O'Shaughnessy walked down the two wooden stairs to the small, gated courtyard area. All the homes of the block looked the same. O'Shaughnessy's was the only stand-alone house; the rest were attached. The owners of these long ago tenements painted their doors bright colors to give them a sense of distinction. O'Shaughnessy's door was always painted red.

He flicked the collar up on his peacoat as he stepped through the knee-high steel gate and turned toward the church entrance.

Steven and Mary Nolte along with their six grandchildren. The Malloys. The O'Briens. The Costigans. All were headed to mass.

Same priest said the services. Feckin' old bugger, O'Shaughnessy thought as he walked by the twin spires.

St. Peter's was a grand old cathedral. It was built in 1866 out of sandstone and was extremely fancy and ornate compared to the housing complexes that surrounded it. O'Shaughnessy hadn't been to church in decades and had no plans to attend now. Still, the building itself drew O'Shaughnessy close.

Barney Hughes, a local baker who had refused to increase his prices during the potato famine, built the cathedral. He fostered loyalty and became wildly rich. He then made a second fortune on bread and cereals and gave most of his money away.

A good portion of his dough (as the locals liked to yuck) went toward building the cathedral. Nothing had his name on it. It was a place for others to benefit from.

O'Shaughnessy was standing under the massive stained-glass window out front and remembering the last time he had attended mass inside. It was for the funeral of his sister and her husband—Michael's parents.

93

WILLIE DYSON UNEXPECTEDLY WALKED UP TO O'SHAUGHNESSY IN front of the church and snapped him out of his fog.

"Goin' in, Sean?"

"You know me better, Willie. You?"

"Not for years and for none to come. Ever."

There had been rumors, O'Shaughnessy remembered now, of Willie having been abused by one of the parish priests. Years ago. Before the revelations and the cover-ups that rocked the Vatican and the world.

O'Shaughnessy was sorry for his blunder and changed the subject. "Watcha doin' here then?"

"Was callin' on you."

"What fer?"

"Big story about a robbery out at the industrial plant. Following up on that. Kennedy twins I hear were involved. You know anything about that?"

O'Shaughnessy shook his head and spat on the ground. "Nah."

"Tommy around then?"

"What you need him fer?"

Willie just looked at him. "Come on, Sean, give me something."

"Can't give you what I don't know."

"All right then."

Willie began to walk away and O'Shaughnessy called after him. "Any news on Michael? You are in the news business after all, right?" Ever the wiseass comments.

Willie stopped. He thought about his conversation with Shea. He could use it to get more information, perhaps about the robbery. Maybe even rattle O'Shaughnessy with it.

"Matter of fact."

"He's alive then? Whereabouts? What did he say?"

"You remember anything better about last night?" Dyson timed his about-face well.

O'Shaughnessy didn't like this game, but he wanted to know about Michael. He was still a wild card in the nuclear bomb plot.

"Memory is coming back," O'Shaughnessy said.

Willie got the message. "Michael is on the run. British News chief in Istanbul was shot dead. Michael was there."

Willie hadn't given O'Shaughnessy anything more than what was already on the Internet, but it was something. "Now, about that break-in down at the docks last night?"

"All right. Fair enough. Tommy was behind it. Wanted to bring me in on it but I let him know that I wasn't going in on that game. Last I seen him. Last night."

Willie was surprised that O'Shaughnessy had given up his old friend like that. It was all the information he knew he'd get and he took it. "Thanks, I'll look into it."

He turned and walked away for the second time. O'Shaughnessy called after him again, but this time Willie didn't stop. "If Michael checks in again, I'd like to see him. Tell him that. Here. Tell him I'd like to see him back here and that I'll wait for him . . . *at home.*"

Willie turned his head to the side and gave tacit acknowledgment that he'd heard. He looked up at the church and sniffed the air. Something didn't smell right. Something stank.

94

O'SHAUGHNESSY WALKED DOWN THE ALLEY BY THE CHURCH TO Falls Road. He looked over at St. Comgall's primary school. He thought of his childhood and of the man he had grown to be, not the man he had wanted to become. He took a left and saw the influences, maybe, of why. They were displayed in giant murals along the walls that lined Falls Road: The Manchester Martyrs. The Maghaberry Prisoners. The words *Not Forgotten* in huge letters. And portraits of Bobby Sands everywhere. "*Askatasuna.*" Freedom. Indeed.

He stopped in front of Sinn Fein headquarters at the end of the road. He looked down at the gates separating this, the Catholic section, from that, the Protestant section. Division. As was he. A divided man.

A young boy ran down the street after his parents. They were all on their way to church and the young boy had fallen behind. He caught up to his parents and wiggled between them as they walked. Each took one of his hands, and they walked like that, bound, until they disappeared from his view. It was innocence and caring defined.

Family.

He saw it clearly then, the world. He saw his role and knew that he had to follow through on all the things he had done. His plan was in place. The world needed to be saved. From those who waged the violence against the weak. From those who waged the wars. And it needed a rebirth of those who saved, saviors, in their purest forms.

The models for hope throughout the ages, throughout time, hadn't changed. People had. They had lost faith and institutionalized the inscrutable and the ignoble. Times were in desperate need of changin'.

O'SHAUGHNESSY CALLED MAHMOUD TALIB FROM THE STREET COR-ner in front of the Falls Road newsstand. He punched in the code and scrambled his mobile phone so it couldn't be traced or tapped. He told Talib that the plan they had worked out together was going along perfectly. He had acquired the trigger material that he needed and would have it delivered on schedule.

Talib asked about Abramov. O'Shaughnessy lied and said that Abramov was on his way to Iran with the nuclear material.

Talib had been insistent that Abramov be in on the deal from the start. He wanted Abramov to step in and take control of Russia. Talib was obsessed with the Russian connection.

"Now you will come to make the trigger?"

"Now I will come to make the trigger," O'Shaughnessy said, and hung up.

The church bells began to ring. St. Peter's had a carillon of nine bells and they seemed to ring incessantly.

O'Shaughnessy bought the *Sunday Irish Times* and walked home.

Michael Shea's photo was on the front page.

95

NEDA WAS QUIET. SHE HAD GONE THROUGH THE FOUR STAGES OF abduction and captivity—fighting, denying, submitting, docileness. She didn't chant aloud anymore. She merely heard the words, saw them if she really tried, in her head.

"*Agnirva apamaayatanam, ayatanavaan bhavati, yo agner ayatanam veda, ayatanavaan bhavati, apova agner ayatanam, ayatanavaan bhavati.*" It meant "offer all bitterness in the sacred fire and emerge grand, great, and godly."

THERE WAS THE CAR AGAIN, A PLANE, ANOTHER CAR. SHE WAS BEING led up stairs. Other people spoke. She had no idea who they were but they sounded young. She was, though she didn't know it, at the Haghani seminary in Qom. The students were watching her as she was being led in. She was in full burka, not even a slit for her eyes.

"Who is she?"

"What did she do?"

The whispers were all around her.

If she could have answered them she would have said, *Nothing. I have done nothing. It is who I am that matters and is dangerous. Even if I told you, it wouldn't mean anything to you. There is only one person to whom my identity matters, and I will show myself to him soon. When I am led out of this darkness and my blindfold is removed. Then I shall be revealed—to the one that matters.*

Neda began to call upon a higher power to free her. The power was beyond the scope of the known mind, she believed. It was *Wahdat al-Wujud*, the unity of being. There was an ultimate truth and it would be revealed . . . in time.

She heard more voices. They invaded her silent chants and prayers. "An infidel . . ." they whispered.

Neda had arrived at the Qom seminary escorted by Ray. He had been considerate and gentle with her the entire trip from Istanbul. There had been no abuse after the torture. It wasn't Ray's job or his place to question her or abuse her further. Besides, he knew what she was in for.

It was common practice for women in Iran who were about to be executed to be raped. This was sanctioned by the imams. They wanted to ensure that a virgin didn't go to heaven. Neda was no virgin. Most of the women who were raped and then executed weren't. It was just another excuse for violence. As if imprisonment, torture, and execution weren't enough.

The imams wanted the afterlife to reflect only their kind. Few people realized just how monolithic these types of fanatical Iranians were. The name Iran was itself equivalent to the word *Aryan*.

The meaning behind the word *Aryan*, "striving for a superior race of people," had bred hostility and violence the world over. Even though "Aryan" among scholars meant "speakers of the Indo-European languages" by extension of the word's meaning, the speakers of those languages became associated with "purity."

By the end of the Second World War, the word *Aryan* had become associated by many with the racial theories and atrocities committed by the Nazi regime. Although this obviously was not its origin.

The meaning was again being corrupted, this time, ironically, by those who actually were truly Aryan by definition: Iranians, albeit fanatical Iranians.

96

NEDA WAS TAKEN DOWN INTO THE BASEMENT OF THE SEMINARY.
There was excitement among the older students. They were the ones
chosen to perform the religious ritual: "the rape of the virgin."

Sometimes a dozen or more students would be selected. They would
form a line outside the prison chamber and begin. They were doing
God's work at the command of the Ayatollah. He'd typically stand by
and watch to ensure that each boy performed. Some couldn't. In those
instances, the Ayatollah would show him how it was done.

For this particular case, Ayatollah Mesbah Yavari would not be in
attendance. He was told by Talib that a political prisoner needed to be
dealt with and interrogated. Mesbah Yavari, of course, had offered the
use of his private prison cell.

Neda was led down the stairs where she could feel the darkness of
the basement walls around her. All the sounds were muffled. She sensed
where she was—belowground—and she felt the evil all around her. She
continued to chant and pray, this time aloud. A door creaked open, and
she was pushed through it. She heard it shut behind her and all became quiet. She stopped praying and took off the burka. She looked at
it rumpled on the ground and thought of the millions of women around
the world who were forced to wear this . . . costume.

She celebrated countries like France that banned the wearing of burkas in public. She questioned how women could be subjugated as such,
and railed against those who wore their burkas proudly. She remem-

bered reading one woman's comment about how she chose to wear the garment. It was a show of modesty, the woman had said. It was a sign of religious freedom and respect. It was hardly freedom. It was the opposite. It was suppression of the worst kind.

97

NEDA LOOKED AROUND THE TINY ROOM IN WHICH SHE HAD BEEN placed. It was a six-foot by nine-foot cell. Cement walls. Cement floors. Cement ceiling. Shackles on the wall. Dried blood.

She knew what she was in for. She didn't know at whose hands she would suffer, but she knew that she would indeed suffer. Still, she felt strong. She could always go to that safe spot in her mind. She had that. *What did these people have? What did he have?*

She thought of him now. She thought of the fear he instilled. She became sad. She had failed. She would never be able to show the world the false face of evil. She had tried. She had tried along with the others, the Golden Dawn. They had known what he was attempting to do. But it was too late to stop him. Talib would assume the role of the Mahdi.

With the scroll gone and with her in prison, the only hope rested with Shea. If he could get to Balthazar and expose the fakery, there was still a chance the coming of the Mahdi could be stopped.

Shea. He had taken her by storm. She had never felt that way toward another man. It was visceral. They had nothing in common yet there was an energy and electricity between them that rose above this world and put them into another.

She was glad she had had the chance to have loved him.

"Better to have loved and lost than never to have loved at all."

Neda sat in the middle of the private prison cell. She was wearing the white tunic that Shea had given her back in Tatvan. Her legs crossed, she was in lotus position and her eyes were shut. She let her hands rest on her knees with her palms up to allow the spirit in. She chanted the fire prayer aloud.

"Agnirva apamaayatanam, ayatanavaan bhavati, yo agner ayatanam veda, ayatanavaan bhavati, apova agner ayatanam, ayatanavaan bhavati."

The door creaked open and she felt a chill enter the room. When she opened her eyes, he was standing there, looking down at her. His eyes were the same. His face had aged as well as his body. And he wore a beard.

Mahmoud Talib may have been the president of Iran and believed himself to be the Mahdi. But to Neda he would always be just one thing: her brother.

98

"Your voice was always magnificent," Talib said to his sister, Neda, as he looked down at her.

"I sang to you as a child," she said, the sadness in her voice noticeable.

"I remember. I still hear it sometimes," Talib said. His voice, too, was soft, tender.

"Do you remember the words that I sang?" Neda asked, taking her hands from her knees and clasping her fingers together, as if in loose prayer.

"Yes."

It was a lullaby:

A flower was lost and the thorn remained
A lot of oppression remained for me
A baby remained for me
This is my mate's memorial.

Since the last time the song had been sung, brother and sister had become enemies. Archenemies. Still, the line between them could still not erase the common blood that ran between their veins.

"Why didn't you listen more to the words, Mahmoud?" Neda asked, not taking her eyes from his. "A flower lost is but a thorn."

Talib looked away.

"You are foolish to believe such things."

"What have you become?"

"It's not what I have become. It is who I am. It's who I have always been."

"You are not the Mahdi."

She said it declaratively and it stung, the truth.

Talib took a step forward and without leaning over, backhanded her across the face. "You don't know what I am or what I am capable of," he said.

"Of course I do," Neda said, taking the blow without a sound of hurtfulness. It was his words that hurt most. "I know who you really are: a person so weak that his parents had to have him admitted to a hospital."

Talib moved away from her, as far as he could.

"They were visiting you," Neda continued, "when they were killed. You know that, don't you? It is the cause of your own pain, Mahmoud.

You were faking your own illness then and you are faking who you are now."

Talib hadn't been spoken to with such disrespect in years. He had forgotten what it was like. "Do you know to whom you speak?"

"Of course Mahmoud al-Ghazali. That is your given name. Remember? Does Ayatollah Mesbah Yavari know that? I foolishly believed that you had changed your name to our adopted parents when we were young out of respect for them. Then I found it was something else. You needed to say that you were from the line of Fatima to fulfill the prophecy. But our parents were not. We are from the line of Zainab, the disputed daughter of Muhammad. Not Fatima. You are a fake, Mahmoud. You are still just a weak little boy. And you'll be found out."

TALIB SLAPPED NEDA AGAIN, THIS TIME WITH HIS OPEN HAND.

"You can beat me as much as you want, Mahmoud. It won't make anything different. No matter what scrolls you uncover or what weapons you gather or what alliances you make. They can't change your bloodline, Mahmoud."

Neda was saying out loud what Talib hoped the world would never figure out. It was why he had chased her all those years. It was what she and her husband were going to expose during the elections. They weren't going to unveil a scroll. They were going to unveil Neda herself as Talib's sister.

This might have proved to do little harm to Talib politically. Who would fault the president for disowning—for surely that is what he would claim—such a radical sister? But the Golden Dawn knew the revelation would have an impact on Talib that went beyond politics; it would quash his plans of being named the Mahdi, of what amounted to being named king in the Muslim world.

According to the family tree of Muhammad the prophet, he had six children: four daughters and two sons. The boys died in early childhood. Only two of his daughters survived him, and only one of them, Fatima, was recognized by Shia Muslims as legitimate. The other, Zainab, was of disputed heritage. And unfortunately for him, this was the line from which Talib's parents were born.

Talib was about to hit Neda again when he stopped himself and began to laugh. It was a menacing laugh, a hysterical laugh.

"You are so wrong, Neda. You don't even know. I have the power to change fate. A bloodline is all that you make of it. If as you say we are all one, then the only way to clear the bloodline is to remove the bad blood. You see, if I remove you, my bloodline will be pure. It is that simple."

"But you have to kill me to do that."

"You must embrace the evil to do good. That is what the Koran says, praise Allah."

"Convenient the way you butcher the word of God to suit your needs. The Koran literally means 'that which was communicated.' Yet you interpret it for your own means and ends. You and all the ayatollahs."

"The world needs one religion and it needs me to make it so. Then there will be salvation. I am seeking a higher path for the world."

"And the Christians and the Jews and all the others?"

"They will come together, as the prophecy states."

"Not if they know the extent of your deception.

"That will never happen."

"All roads lead to Rome," Neda said, smiling.

Talib suddenly realized what she was saying and where Michael Shea was going. He had been told by Zhubin that Shea was headed for Italy. Now he knew why, and what he was going to do.

Talib raced to the door and took a last look back at Neda. "You have no idea the damage that you have done. The world needs me."

"The world will decide."

Talib left to get in contact with Zhubin. He had to tell him about Shea. If all else failed he supposed he still had the physical power to change the world. Nuclear power. But of course that was not the ultimate power he was seeking.

100

MESBAH YAVARI WAS IN THE BASEMENT CONTROL ROOM. HE HAD heard Talib and Neda's conversation. It changed everything. Mahmoud Talib had lied to him. It was a grand plan of deception. He was not the Mahdi. It was one thing to excuse the timing of the Mahdi's arrival, and it was quite another thing entirely to change the incarnation of God.

101

ZHUBIN HEARD FROM SAVAMA HQ THE NEWS OF THE FAILURE TO shoot Shea's plane down. The satellite tracking the Lear had traced it to Naples, Italy. Zhubin had no idea where Shea could be heading. From Naples it would be easy enough for the journalist to get lost. He could travel by boat to southern France, by train to Switzerland, or by car to pretty much any point in Europe. If he had the patience, he could even drive all the way to his home country of Ireland.

Border crossings were easier to do by driving. Zhubin knew this about Western countries. They put people through hell at airports, ridiculously even making them remove their shoes. But via train, ferry, or car it was very easy to smuggle guns or bombs. The border guards barely gave travelers a look.

He remembered traveling across the Swiss border from Italy once and the guards weren't even at the crossing station! Of course a person could ski from Italy to Switzerland to France, so it might be difficult to monitor all the crossings. But still.

Zhubin's intelligence data showed that the private jet that had been tracked to Naples was owned by a Turkish drug dealer, Faruk Eserol. The jet, according to the SAVAMA file that was sent encrypted to his handheld, made the same journey every week. That didn't help him figure out where Shea was headed. It was unlikely that Shea would stay in Naples. London, Belfast, or another point where Shea had a network were more likely destinations.

Shea might try to get back into Iran for the woman. But Zhubin didn't see how that would be possible. The exact nature of Shea and Neda's relationship hadn't been established. If there was something deep between them she would be a priority. Shea would try to get her loose.

Zhubin knew that he needed something, anything, to let him in on where Shea was going. He needed a new scent, a clue.

Madonna was there for him.

Rome, it was conveyed by Talib after Zhubin answered his mobile phone. Shea would be going to Rome. Talib told Zhubin to get to the Iranian delegation at the Vatican. That was where he'd likely find Shea. And it was critical that he be found. Now. The sun and the moon were set to align.

102

SHEA WAS ON THE EXPRESS TRAIN FROM NAPLES TO ROME, THE CITY of Seven Hills. He didn't have much to go on. He knew only that he had to get to Vatican City and find the Iranian delegation there. Then he had to find a guy named Balthazar.

Simple enough. *Ha.*

As the train rolled into Rome's Termini Station, Shea still didn't know how he'd get to Balthazar. He got off and walked out to the Via Giovanni Giolitti across from the Museo Nazionale where he was assaulted by taxi drivers asking him if he wanted a ride. Then he found the solution to his problem.

He navigated past the swarm of *tassisti* and was brushed up against by two little girls. They were Gypsies; cute, young teenagers. Their faces were grimy and they wore, essentially, rags. They closed the tips of their fingers and then placed them against their mouths, kissing them, gesticulating that they wanted money for food to eat. They made moaning noises. Then he felt it at the last second.

She was a pro. If Shea hadn't been expecting it, he never would have felt it at all. He had been to Rome so many times that he expected his pocket to be picked by Gypsies. They tried every time. But this young girl was the best one yet.

A good pickpocket would typically use physical contact or some type of distraction to divert the attention of their "mark." This is how the mark never feels being robbed; he or she is distracted. Also, some type of prop is usually used to hide their hands. A baby. A newspaper. A jacket draped over their arm.

But this young girl didn't use any of the usual props or pull any of the typical pickpocket stunts. Her hands were just superfast—like a magician's. Wise and skilled, she was, beyond her years.

Shea grabbed her by the wrist. The other Gypsy girls scattered. He held her arm up in the air, and she was still holding on tight to his money.

Two things typically happened when a Gypsy was caught stealing. It went one way or the other. Either the Gypsy smiled and made light of the situation, trying to charm their way out of it. "Oh, well, mister, you caught me. What are you going to do? Have me arrested? Look how young and cute I am." Smile, smile, smile.

Or . . . the Gypsy went berserk. This one chose to go nuts. She struggled madly and cried and screamed. Her hand was so grimy that it was slippery and she was able to pull it away from Shea. So he grabbed her by the back of her shirt and pulled her back to him. She continued to struggle, kicking and screaming. Finally, she bit him on the arm.

Shea slapped her hard. He took her arms and wrapped them behind her. One tussle and she would be in excruciating pain. It didn't take much for him to subdue the kid.

Shea felt bad about it. People passing by looked at him like he was a freak, but this was business. He needed her help.

It was how he'd get to Balthazar.

103

Shea escorted the Gypsy girl across the street and down an
alley past the Hotel Cherubini. The alley was deserted and it would be
impossible for the little girl to get past him to escape. She knew it.

Shea slapped her again and put her up against the wall. He needed
her to be afraid of him. It was his only power over her. Her eyes were
wide and she was frightened like an animal that had just been caged.

"Do you speak English?" he asked. She looked side to side, hoping
someone would come to help her.

Shea thought about that. Whether other Gypsies might come and
try to protect her. Or more likely the Russian scumbags that ran these
Gypsy beggars for profit.

No one appeared. He took her face in his hand and made her look
him in the eyes. *"Inglese?"*

She shook her head.

Shea spoke enough Italian to get by. He wanted her to remain
afraid of him but he also needed to bait her with something nice to
gain her cooperation. He took out some lira and showed it to her. It
wasn't much—part of the stash of currencies he always kept—but to
this little girl is was like a million dollars. She nodded and got on her
knees.

"No!" Shea yelled, disgusted that at this age she even knew what he
might be looking for sexually. He pulled her up by the hair. Now she
looked really confused.

"Come," he said. "Then you'll get this," he explained in Italian. She nodded again.

They got a taxi at the station.

She was going to help him get to Balthazar.

Or get him killed.

ZHUBIN HATED ROME. IT WAS FAR TOO BIG OF A CITY FOR HIM AND there was always traffic. For his profession, Zhubin needed maneuverability, not crowds and delays. So Rome sucked in his opinion. Big.

He had left on such short notice from Istanbul that there was no one from the Iranian mission to pick him up at the airport. He didn't think it would be a problem taking a taxi into the city from Ciampino. But it was.

The road from the airport to Vatican City took more than an hour. *Didn't these people sleep?*

He was dog-tired. He needed rest badly. He looked at his watch. Midnight. He looked up into the sky and could barely make out the moon.

Zhubin showed his SAVAMA identification to the security guard at the Iranian embassy. He went into the wing reserved for VIPs and discreet guests, such as himself. He took advantage of the hospitality.

Morning prayers weren't for another five hours. He could finally sleep. Then he'd wait for Shea to make his move.

105

SHEA SAT WITH THE GIRL AT THE PARK CALLED VILLA ADA. HE HAD
bought a soda, a slice of pizza, and some chips and watched as she
wolfed it all down. He patted the grass and motioned that she could
sleep. After forty-five minutes of sitting next to him on the little patch
of grass, she finally slept.

He watched her breathe. This was someone's child, he thought. The
world wasn't fair to some. The law of the jungle, for humans at least,
had been replaced with the law of money. Those with the least were
easy prey.

He thought about Talib's plan to come out as the Mahdi. There was
a kernel of understanding in what that fanatic wanted. Shea agreed
that there had to be a better way of existence. To be sure it wasn't radical Islam. Equality would take a revolution, he knew. If only a revolution could be done for the right reasons and not the wrong ones—for
good instead of evil. Maybe, he thought, struggling to stay awake, the
real Mahdi might come and save Earth. He could sympathize with
that kind of hope. Then he, too, zonked out.

106

SHEA SHOT UP FROM THE GRASS. THE GYPSY GIRL WAS GONE.

Damn it! I knew I shouldn't have closed my eyes—just for a second.

The *adhan* announcing *fajr*, the first Muslim prayer of the day, came exactly as the first ray of light hit Shea's face.

The Villa Ada he had slept in was the largest park in Rome. It was four hundred fifty acres, about half the size of Central Park in New York City, but a stunning display of lake, forest, and meadow within the confines of a city just the same.

The girl could have gone anywhere. Shea followed the trail past the trees and to the meadow. It was the most direct path out of the park. Who knew when she had left? But he had to try and find her. There wasn't much time. The Iranian delegation would be arriving at the mosque any minute. And it being Ramadan there would likely be a large contingent of observers besides them coming for prayer.

Shea's lucky cipher would be that the Iranian staff could be easily identified by their diplomatic plates; they'd be written in Farsi. This would make his job of filtering out Balthazar easier. That still would only chop the group to about two dozen men. To winnow that down and figure out who Balthazar was, Shea needed the girl. *Where was she?*

He walked fast, checking the bushes, trees, and small garden enclosures for any sign of her.

Shea's plan was to have her pickpocket the Iranian delegation as they entered the mosque.

To pray, most Muslim men wore loose-fitting shirts and trousers—simple attire ripe for pocket picking. Some wore fanny packs under their shirts. Contrary to what most tourists believed, these items were even simpler to rob. A zipper was never a good defense. In more aggressive circumstances, thieves sliced the pouches open with a blade.

He was almost at the edge of the park. Across the way was the giant mosque, the largest in all of Europe. Cars, buses, and scooters were lined up. Worshippers rushed in.

He heard a splash. By the pond near the old salt road, Via di Ponte Salina, stood the girl. She was feeding the ducks with the remains of the bread from the panina Shea had given her the night before.

It was a scene Shea hated to interrupt because the girl looked so happy. She was giggling loudly as the ducks gathered and flapped their wings, fighting each other playfully over the bread crumbs. They then paddled over, straining their necks for the next toss of food.

Shea swooped in like one of them and picked the girl up under one arm. "Sorry," he said. "Playtime later."

The girl submitted, and tossed the last of the bread to the ducks. They waddled after her, and she waved good-bye.

107

SHEA PLUNKED THE GYPSY GIRL DOWN BY A TREE ACROSS FROM THE mosque. Only the Viale della Moschea, or mosque road, separated them from the entranceway of the building. Security, of course, was everywhere. Whether temple or mosque during holidays, armed guards roamed the grounds of religious institutions these days. Such was the practice of religion in modern times. So much for good faith in one's fellow man.

The Iranian delegation serendipitously arrived just as Shea plopped the girl down. He watched as old man after old man got out of the vehicles with diplomatic plates written in Farsi. Balthazar couldn't be that old. He was Gaspar's younger brother, Neda had told him, and Gaspar himself was no more than forty years of age.

Finally, Shea saw what he was looking for: three young men got out of the last Iranian diplomatic vehicle to arrive. This would narrow his marks considerably. Shea pointed to them. The Gypsy girl understood. She ran to them and went to work. As she ran she wasn't thinking about Shea's money. She was thinking about playing with the ducks.

After the three younger men got out and just before the vehicle they were in pulled away another man stepped out of the door. Shea's heart sank. It was Zhubin. How had the pit bull tracked him here?

Shea watched nervously as the Gypsy girl ran up to the young Iranian men. She played her part well. She approached the first man, her fingers to her lips, and tugged on his shirt. As he was distracted, she reached up and took something from him. The man didn't feel anything. He shooed her away. She repeated the move two more times. Then she approached Zhubin.

Before she could even touch him he had her by the arm. He slapped her hand. She looked up at his face and froze. The look in his eyes scared her stiff.

Thankfully, Zhubin didn't catch the Gypsy girl in the act of thieving. He let go of her arm and shoved her away, thinking she was just another beggar child. Still, Zhubin kept an eye on her as he walked into the mosque. The girl turned and fled back across the street.

Shea read the identifications: Reza Dabir. Mohammed Kaveh. Balthazar Khaledi.

Khaledi. Skinny and pale. He stood out from the rest. And he was young, just twenty-two, according to his embassy ID. Shea could have picked him—if he had gotten up close—as Gaspar's brother even without the ID. They looked alike. About a hundred pounds difference and twenty years between them, but the family resemblance was there.

Shea realized that he'd have to tell Balthazar his brother had died. That wouldn't be easy. Still, the most difficult part of his plan wasn't emotional, it was getting the girl to put the IDs back and to pass along a note to Balthazar. The note was simple:

> *Gaspar sent me.*
> *Vatican Secret Archives*
> *Noon.*
> *Leo XIII Study Room*

108

AS SOON AS THE SUN ROSE, PRAYER TIME ENDED. PEOPLE STREAMED out of the mosque and onto the street. Balthazar and the Iranian officials were the first to leave.

The Gypsy girl knew her job and she executed it expertly. None of the young men suspected anything. They all lived in Rome and were used to begging Gypsies. The only one who noticed anything awry was Zhubin. As he left the mosque's courtyard, he noticed the girl's hand slip under Balthazar's shirt. He had seen that she was holding something, then not. She had slipped something to him!

Zhubin didn't know the man. He was a young official. But he could easily find out who the young man was when they got back to the embassy.

He watched as the Gypsy girl dodged traffic on the Viale della Moschea and headed into the trees. Then he saw him. It was for an instant, like the flick of a shutter lens on a camera, but he saw Michael Shea.

It would be futile to try and go after Shea and the girl now. There was too much of a crowd and too much traffic to contend with. Besides, he had a new person to follow. The young, pale-looking man who just stepped into the black SUV he was looking at. The one whom Zhubin assumed was just given a message.

THE IRANIAN EMBASSY WAS ALMOST DIRECTLY ACROSS THE STREET from the Pakistani embassy in the northern district of Rome. It was located in one of the more fashionable neighborhoods of the ancient city, past Monte Mario, the highest point in the city.

For security purposes, the Iranian embassy was behind nondescript hedges and a tall gate on a busy street. Unlike the flash of the American embassy mansion in central Rome along the Via Veneto, this embassy was very basic and humble. It was purposefully away from the crowds of the Spanish Steps and located closer to the Vatican. It rarely took visitors.

A long driveway brought those entering its grounds to the embassy's front door. The shuttles that took staff to and from the mosque parked at the gate. Embassy officials walked the long driveway to their offices or quarters.

Most of the embassy staff chatted as they walked. It was a clear and crisp day and none seemed to be in a hurry to get home or to work. They spoke about football (they were looking forward to the exhibition match between Roma and PAS Hamadan), politics (would Berlusconi run again for office), and pop culture (a Hollywood starlet was in town filming a movie).

Only two men walked alone. One was at the front of the pack and the other at the rear.

Balthazar was walking as fast as he could, practically running, to the embassy.

Zhubin thought he knew why.

But he was wrong.

Balthazar had to pee badly. So bad it hurt. His bladder was about to explode. A few drops escaped from his penis. He had to run. He didn't think he'd make it. He grabbed his crotch and squeezed. *Why aren't there restrooms at mosques?* he wondered as he flew in the door and headed straight to the men's room on the right side of the lobby.

He lifted his shirt, pulled down his pants, and took a whiz.

Ahh.

Glorious relief.

Balthazar looked down and saw that the zipper to the fanny pack he was wearing on his belly wasn't shut all the way. He finished his pee and tried to closer the pouch's zipper. It wouldn't fasten. It was caught on a piece of paper.

Zhubin watched as Balthazar came out of the men's room and went to the security desk where he ordered a car to take him to the Vatican. It wasn't unusual for Balthazar to go to Vatican City. In fact, he went there almost every day. He was one of the resident religious scholars, after all.

After Balthazar left, Zhubin ordered his own car.

He told the driver to follow Balthazar no matter where he went.

110

SHEA'S KNOWLEDGE OF ROME EXTENDED TO THE VATICAN. THERE had been death threats waged against the pope from a rebel group in Nigeria several years back and Shea had covered the story for British News. He had gone to the Vatican Secret Archives building to get some background information for the story and was granted access. That one time was all he needed to get lifelong clearance.

The Secret Archives, Shea knew, weren't all that secret. In fact, the word *secret* was a poor translation for the Archivum Secretum Apolstolicum Vaticanum. Secret in this case was better transliterated as "secretary" than anything mysterious. The place was meant to act as the pope's personal library, not a place to hide things.

The archive of books used to follow the pope around to his various residences because the manuscripts informed his activities and official duties. Then in 1610 they were placed in their own building next to the Vatican Library, one of the most complete libraries in the world with millions of volumes on its shelves.

The note that Shea had given to Balthazar was succinct. It named the Leo XIII Study as the meeting place as opposed to the Old Study room. The Leo XIII room was adjacent to the Vatican gardens where scholars went to smoke and snack. It would be better cover.

SHEA GAVE THE LITTLE GYPSY GIRL MORE MONEY THAN HE EVEN promised. She didn't pay attention to it, though. She was focused on the ducks. Shea watched as she skipped toward the pond again, lira in hand.

He knew the joy in her life was scant. At least for a few hours she could escape her misery, he hoped.

There but for the grace of God . . .

And he meant it.

111

THE GATE TO THE ARCHIVE WAS THE SAME AS THE ONE THAT ADMIT-
ted vehicles into the Vatican grounds. It was a busy spot. Hence, the Swiss Guardsmen—responsible for the security of the Holy See—weren't as thorough as they would be in other places. Traffic backed up.

Even though Shea hadn't made an appointment, he merely gave his name to one of the guardsmen, here, too, dressed in their wacky blue, red, orange, and yellow uniforms straight out of the Renaissance. Shea's name was on the permanent admissions list, and he was simply waved through by the guardsman, this one even sporting a silver morion helmet.

It was, really, like going back in time.

Past the frescoes and statues and the priceless oil paintings, Shea went into the Leo XIII study. He sat at one of the tables with their uncomfortable wooden chairs and small reading lamps. He picked a spot in the back of the room in front of a bookcase lined with file folders. The process was: a scholar looked up a text in the folder, put in a request for it with the clerk, and then could have it copied for fifty cents. Otherwise the clerk took a voucher for the manuscript's return. No original material could ever be taken from the Vatican grounds.

A few men in tweed jackets sat in the room. A Hasidic Jew worked in the corner with his back toward everyone. And a woman, who wore thick, framed glasses and had on an expensive-looking blue suit, sat at the communal table typing her head off. An investment banker? An attorney? Maybe the economy had gotten so bad that the big banks were looking for advice from Midas on what to do next.

Shea took a red file folder from the case and pretended to read it. The clerk behind the counter to his left didn't give him the slightest hint of acknowledgment. Ten minutes later, Balthazar came in and sat down.

Balthazar looked at all the people in the room trying to figure out who had sent him the note. When he looked at Shea, Shea gave him a nod of complicity. He then stood up and went to the stairs that led out to the Vatican gardens. Balthazar followed.

Outside, neither of them saw Zhubin standing next to a row of hedges by the library.

112

AS SOON AS SHEA AND BALTHAZAR WERE FAR ENOUGH AWAY FROM the Vatican Archive building, Balthazar asked, "Who are you? Why did Gaspar send you? What do you want?"

"Slow down," Shea said. "Take it easy." He decided to come right out with it: "Your brother is dead."

Balthazar stopped jittering and walked a few steps to one of the perfectly maintained sections of grass in the Vatican Garden. He sat between two palm trees and began to cry.

Shea walked over to him and stood. Then he, too, sat down on the grass.

"How?" Balthazar asked.

"SAVAMA" was all Shea had to say. He let the information hang there, and sink in. "He said that you were working on something in the archives that might help me. He said it had to do with the Mahdi."

Balthazar stopped crying. He became sober and serious in a flash. "What did he say to you exactly?"

"He said it had to do with the Third Secret of Fatima, whatever that is. I am a journalist and I found out that Mahmoud Talib is planning a nuclear strike. Neda and Gaspar—"

"I know Neda."

"She said that. She said Talib believes he is the Mahdi."

"Yes. We have been watching him, gathering evidence. Then we were going to announce who she was."

"Who she was? You mean he."

"No." Balthazar hesitated. "Didn't Neda tell you?"

"Tell me what?"

Balthazar looked at Shea skeptically. "Where is Neda now?" he asked.

"The SAVAMA kidnapped her. That's why I am here. You are my only hope. I need to discredit Talib. I need proof of his plans. Before your brother died, he told us to find you. I assumed it's because you can help."

Balthazar looked down. "That is what we were hoping Neda would do. But I have it. I found the connection here to the Mahdi. It is the Third Secret of Fatima."

"What do you have?"

"It's in my bag back at the study room. I can show you. The Secret of Fatima is not what the Vatican said it was. They said it was a prognostication. That was the official announcement. It was hidden, they said, to protect the pope and the public. But that isn't true. The Third Secret of Fatima has to do with the second coming of Christ."

"Gaspar said it was connected to the Mahdi."

Balthazar looked at Shea quizzically. "My friend, they are one and the same."

Shea was silent for a moment trying to digest all the information.

Balthazar continued, "The Third Secret of Fatima is the prophecy of the Mahdi. The secret is hidden in plain sight. The Mahdi is Fatima's secret. He is her blood."

"What does the Vatican have to do with this?"

"They have been waiting for the Mahdi to appear because it precedes the second coming of Christ. That is the prophecy. It will signal the End of Times. But the Mahdi must be related to Fatima. Talib is not. We can prove that."

"How?"

"Neda—"

Shea heard the thud. It sounded like a rock that had been thrown hard into mud. Balthazar's mouth remained open but no words came out.

Only blood.

113

SHEA LOOKED OVER AND SAW ZHUBIN AIMING HIS GUN AT HIM. HE dove over the fountain he was sitting next to and heard the splash from the shot. Another bullet pinged off the fountain itself. Chips of stone splattered.

Zhubin began to walk toward Shea, Terminator-style. Shea was closer to the entrance to the Secret Archives building than Zhubin was, but there was still too much open ground to cover. He'd get picked off, for sure.

Shea looked over at the entrance. Soon, he would have to risk the run. Either that or he'd be shot dead where he huddled.

The buttoned-up woman in the blue suit from the study room walked outside. She was on her mobile phone. She saw Zhubin's outstretched arm and the gun in his hand. She screamed just before he shot her.

The clerk and the other scholars in the room heard the scream and ran out. Zhubin looked at them and then back at Shea. He made a strategic decision. He ran.

Shea beat it back into the study room. He saw Balthazar's bag and grabbed it. Swiss Guardsmen came barreling through the room. Shea pointed outside: "A man out there has a gun! He shot at me!"

The scholars and the clerk ran back inside, too, when they realized there was a man on the loose with a gun outside.

Shea used the mayhem to work his way out of the Vatican. The Swiss Guardsmen were blockading the buildings. Out on the street police arrived. And Shea, quietly, walked away.

Zhubin, meanwhile, was being chased. He jumped over a hedge and across a lawn that was barricaded by a stone wall. It was a six-foot-high blockade but the stones were massive and provided good ledges. Like a practiced rock climber, Zhubin used his feet more than his hands to push himself up. His hands made it to the top. He lifted his leg to hoist himself over the ledge when he felt a tug on his foot. Two Swiss Guardsmen had hold of him. They yanked him down. And he dropped his gun.

Two more guardsmen came and subdued him, which wasn't easy. They had to fire two stun guns into his chest to get him to quit fighting. Then they cuffed him and dragged him off, ironically, to the Secret Archive building. Centuries ago one of the rooms in it had been converted to a cell. It was the first time in the twenty-first century that the cell was being used. But it could still do its job well.

Zhubin wasn't escaping anytime soon.

114

SHEA RAN ALONG THE PERIMETER OF THE VATICAN AND DASHED down a small one-way street. It was heading away from the Vatican, but Shea could hear and see at every cross street a swarm of police heading toward the Holy See. He didn't look out of place. Others were moving quickly about. A sense of panic was in the air—another assassination attempt on the pope? A bomb?—and people were quick to respond: the curious headed toward the Vatican and the cautious headed away.

Shea stopped running when he made it to the Tiber River. In a parking lot next to the Santo Spirito Hospital, he sat down on the tar and opened Balthazar's bag.

Inside he found several Moleskine notebooks. They were neatly categorized and batched in groups. A rubber band held the notebooks together in their groupings and Roman numerals indicated which batch was which. The writing was in Farsi, so Shea had no idea of the notebooks' contents.

He also found two Mont Blanc Rollerball pens and a green file folder. Inside the folder were papers copied from the Vatican archive, among other documents. Lastly, there was a photo of Balthazar and two other men. Shea recognized one of the men as Gaspar. The other, a younger man, was lean and handsome. He had a thin beard that ran along his jawline.

115

SHEA FLIPPED THROUGH THE PHOTOCOPIES. THE FIRST ONE WAS
clearly marked:

CONGREGATION FOR THE DOCTRINE OF THE FAITH
THE MESSAGE OF FATIMA

Shea read the surprisingly accessible text that began, "As the second
millennium gives way to the third, Pope John Paul II has decided to
publish the text of the third part of the 'secret of Fatima.'"

The twentieth century was one of the most crucial in human history,
with its tragic and cruel events culminating in the assassination attempt
on the "sweet Christ on earth." Now a veil is drawn back on a series of
events which make history and interpret it in depth, in a spiritual perspective alien to present-day attitudes, often tainted with rationalism.

Throughout history there have been supernatural apparitions and
signs which go to the heart of human events and which, to the surprise
of believers and nonbelievers alike, play their part in the unfolding of
history. These manifestations can never contradict the content of faith,
and must therefore have their focus in the core of Christ's proclamation:
the Father's love which leads men and women to conversion and
bestows the grace required to abandon oneself to him with filial devotion. This, too, is the message of Fatima which, with its urgent call to
conversion and penance, draws us to the heart of the Gospel . . .

The Vatican commentary was accompanied by digitized copies of the original texts and translations.

Shea read that the three secrets were a series of visions and prophecies given to three young Portuguese shepherds by an apparition of the Virgin Mary.

The three children—Lucia Santos and Jucinte and Francisco Marto—said that they were visited six times between May and October 1917 by the Virgin Mary.

The secrets revealed to them involved visions of Hell, the two world wars, and the shooting of Pope John Paul II. The Vatican took the visions very seriously and kept them under lock and key, only releasing the third secret in 2000 because of the speculation and attention it had gathered. People believed the secret involved the turning of the New Millennium and Armageddon. This was the Third Secret of Fatima.

The official version of the Third Secret released by the Vatican was that it involved the assassination of Pope John Paul II:

> The decision of His Holiness Pope John Paul II to make public the third part of the "secret" of Fatima brings to an end a period of history marked by tragic human lust for power and evil, yet pervaded by the merciful love of God and the watchful care of the Mother of Jesus and of the Church.

But Balthazar's notes showed that was a lie. The Third Secret of Fatima was something else entirely.

It was about the coming of the Mahdi.

116

ACCORDING TO ANCIENT PROPHECY THE MAHDI WOULD COME AT the End of Times to rid the world of wrongdoing, injustice, and tyranny. He was to be the redeemer of Islam, and would be related by birth to the daughter of Muhammad.

The Mahdi was to rule as long as nineteen years alongside another—Jesus Christ.

Of course Jews believed that the Messiah had not yet appeared on Earth, and Christians believed there would be a Second Coming. However, both believed in the prophecy of the Mahdi.

Shea put the commentary and notes aside for a second and rubbed his eyes. He couldn't believe what he was reading. Each page had the Vatican seal on it. The copies were clearly authentic documents. Still, they read like a piece of fiction, a thriller no less.

He read on. According to Balthazar's notes, after the coming of the Mahdi and the appearance of Christ, it would be Judgment Day.

Shea thought about the Third Secret of Fatima. The connection of name Fatima in the two prophecies couldn't be a coincidence. The Mahdi had to be from that family lineage and bloodline. It linked it to the coming of Christ. And the fire. What other weapon would pose world destruction from fire except a nuclear bomb?

"We saw an Angel with a flaming sword in his left hand; flashing, it gave out flames that looked as though they would set the world on fire."

Moreover, there was a Russian connection! That would explain the Chechens' involvement.

"Russia will be converted, and there will be peace; if not, she will spread her errors throughout the world, causing wars and persecutions of the Church. The good will be martyred; the Holy Father will have much to suffer; various nations will be annihilated. In the end, my Immaculate Heart will triumph. The Holy Father will consecrate Russia to me, and she shall be converted, and a period of peace will be granted to the world."

My God, Shea thought, these fanatics weren't crazy. There was a connection to the nuclear plot Talib was scheming.

Shea looked at the last piece of paper in Balthazar's file. His eyes grew wide. His heart sank. It was about Neda. He understood what Balthazar had been scratching at when he mentioned her name to him. It all made sense to him now. This was the proof he needed to get the story out.

There was only one journalist he trusted with it.

Shea found a newsstand that sold prepaid telephone calling cards near the Campo Marzio, the Roman district that boasts some of the most famous monuments in the world.

Looking up at the Porticus Octaviae, he called Willie Dyson. Dyson was eager to see the documents and report the story. But he added a verbal salutation . . . from Sean O'Shaughnessy. He said, "He wants to see you, Michael. Home, he said, at *home*."

There couldn't have been two more compelling reasons for Shea to get to Belfast. The question was how was he going to get there?

117

THEY LINED UP IN FRONT OF THE PRISON CELL. SIX OF THEM. THE oldest was eighteen, and this was his second time. They were preparing to rape the "virgin."

The boys tried to mask their nervousness. They spoke loudly, fidgeted, and wrestled with one another. A close listen would reveal a higher pitch in each of their voices. A close observer would see nervous ticks and a general tightness of their movements. The boys were waiting for the word to go inside. One after the other.

Talib had put Ray in charge of the violent punishment. The SA-VAMA agent stood to the side of Neda's prison cell door. He himself was waiting for the go-ahead from Talib. He checked his phone every few seconds, flipping it open then closing it, flipping it open then closing it. He, too, was on edge.

Ray hated this. He knew what they were about to do was cruel and unusual punishment. But Ray was a good soldier. He wouldn't disobey orders. And he was a good Muslim. He understood the concept of desecrating the virgin.

Still, it didn't sit well with his internal moral compass. Ray might have been indoctrinated by his religion, but no external codes could ever really rewire the internal human system—a feeling, it was—of determining right and wrong.

Ray examined all the students in front of him. Tall. Gangly. Short. Fat. Glasses. Timid. Extroverted. Introverted. They were just kids. And he had been just like them at one time. How many years ago was that?

Twenty years? More? And what had he done since? He had served his country. He had become a good Muslim. He had had myriad experiences and traveled all over the world. He had seen what was out there and what people from all different walks of life were like.

He looked at the faces of the boys gathered in front of him. He imagined what their lives would have been like had they been in a different part of the country, a different part of the world. He knew that people, children especially, were shaped by the uniformity in their lives and the institutions of culture and of government. It was difficult to break out of the boxes that family, friends, religion, and tradition set for people, Ray thought. It took ego, and a strong sense of self to break out of that conditioning.

Ray knew himself too well. He could never break out of the course that had been set for him by school and work and the duties and obligations that went along with those things. He was a sheep and he knew it. The world produced few shepherds.

Ray looked at the group of students before him and wondered if any of them would be able to break the molds set for them by others.

There was one. He stood apart from the rest of the students. He didn't partake in their carousing with one another. He was a handsome young man with a thin beard that traced his jawline.

And he was the first in line.

118

Neda listened to the seminarians' banter outside her door. They were young voices, the type she had heard just before she was led into her cell. Like the whispers.

She could have been anywhere, but she knew that she wasn't imprisoned in Tehran. Those jails were famously overcrowded.

The room she was in appeared to be more of a private cell than a prison. And the young men? What were they doing here? They kept asking who she was.

She must be in a school of some sort, she thought. For Talib to be here it meant it was a religious school. The only one she knew that he'd dare step foot in was in Qom.

So that is where he brought me.

It was ironic that Talib had brought her to a city that spoke to his falsehood, a city that was built around the teachings of Fatima, to whom he'd laid false familial claim. It wasn't even irony so much as perversion, she thought. He had perverted the good that Fatima stood for.

Fatima was considered an exemplar for Muslim men and women. She was regarded as "the Mother of the Imams," and played a special role in the Shia faith. Shia tradition held that Fatima is the judge in the hereafter.

Neda called upon a prayer, the prayer of Fatima. Then the door opened and a handsome young man walked in. She recognized him at once. He had grown since she had last seen him. He had a thin beard that traced the line of his face. It was Gaspar's youngest brother, Melchior.

"Melchior!" she said excitedly. "What are you doing here? What is going on?"

But he hushed her quickly, putting his fingers to his lips. Then they spoke in whispers, too. Just like the young boys.

"There isn't time to explain everything. I have to get you out of here, and it won't be easy. Are you hurt?" he was looking at the welt Talib left on her face after he struck her.

"No, I'm fine. Where are we?"

"In Qom, at the seminary. There are six men outside and they have instructions to hurt you . . . badly."

Neda looked at him, a serious expression on her face. She let him know that she understood.

Melchior continued, "I need you to help me with one of them. And this is what I need you to do . . ."

119

MELCHIOR KNEW THAT HE COULD TAKE THE STUDENTS HANDILY. But Ray was a different story. A highly trained SAVAMA agent would be a difficult man to take down. With five others helping him, it would be impossible.

Melchior was a martial arts expert and knew that no matter what the kung fu films would have a person believe, more than three opponents was an almost unwinnable fight. Only the movies let someone have eyes in the back of their head, perfect timing, and superhuman strength that, with the flick of a finger, could knock men out cold.

Reality was a whole different set of circumstances. Most fights wound up on the ground within thirty seconds. A pile of men could not be pinned down. Melchior needed to separate Ray from the bunch and he needed Neda's help to do it.

Neda began to scream and yell. Melchior made a lot of racket, too, slapping his hands together and grunting and groaning. He waited a full minute and then opened the cell door. He asked Ray to come inside.

"I think I killed her," he told Ray.

Ray saw Neda on the ground in the corner of the cell. She was on her back, her tunic pulled up above her knees.

"What have you done?" Ray asked.

"What I was told," Melchior responded.

Ray looked at Melchior skeptically. There wasn't a scratch on him and his clothes were still perfectly pressed. His observation skills honed from years of training, Ray knew when someone was lying.

Ray walked halfway across the room toward Neda and then spun around with his gun drawn.

It was too late. Melchior kicked the gun out of his hand and crouched low, sweeping Ray off his feet. He then twisted around and tried to punch Ray in the throat. He wasn't fooling around. These were deathblows, and Ray knew it.

Ray turned away at the last second and Melchior ended up punching the floor. Ray bucked his legs and kicked up, high in the air, keeping his shoulders on the ground. He wrapped his legs around Melchior's neck and squeezed.

Legs are the most powerful weapons of the human body. Ray could choke Melchior out in seconds. But he didn't have a tight enough lock and Melchior was able to take hold of one of his feet. He took hold of the heel with his other hand. He wrapped his leg over Ray's chest with one of his legs so Ray couldn't roll away. And then he twisted the foot with all his might. It snapped bone, cartilage, and knee joints. Ray writhed in pain and screamed out loud. Melchior sat up and closed the index and middle fingers of his left hand. He cocked his arm and jabbed Ray between the eyes, centimeters above the nose bridge. It cracked the eye socket connector and opened a soft spot to the brain. Melchior cocked his arm again, this time with just the middle finger bent—and drove his knuckle through Ray's skull.

Before he died, Ray wished that he had something more to fight for besides his own life. It might have given him the strength that he needed.

The boys flew into the room at the sound of Ray's roar. Three of them tried to wrestle Melchior down. It was useless. He knocked them all out.

Neda, by now, had risen. She was struggling with two of the younger boys. Melchior turned his attention to them and clunked their heads together. They fell to the ground without more of a fight.

Melchior took Neda by the arm and pulled her out of the cell. He locked it, and they ran up the stairs. At the top stood the old man, Ayatollah Mesbah Yavari.

120

MELCHIOR DIDN'T STOP AT THE TOP OF THE STAIRS. HE RAN HEAD on, and down, into Mesbah Yavari. The head butt was so powerful that it sent the ayatollah skidding across the floor. He landed against his door like a hockey puck slapsticked into a goal.

Melchior and Neda ran past the fallen ayatollah. They needed to make it past the seminarians' sleeping quarters to get to the staircase leading out.

They had made it past the Ayatollah's prayer hall and were just steps from the dorm area when Mesbah Yavari—shocked at the sight of a woman on his grounds, a woman whose head was bare and who wore a skimpy white tunic—called out, "*Komakam!*"

It was the word in Farsi for "help" and "emergency" all rolled into one.

The seminarians responded immediately. They teemed out of the dorm room into the hallway. Dozens of young men surrounded Melchior and Neda. She thought this would be it. An escape had been close but now the inevitable would occur. She would be killed and Talib would get his way. The world would suffer. The Golden Dawn, the secret sect whose ancient mission it was to guard the Mahdi, had failed in their sacred duty to protect the world. For more than one thousand years the Golden Dawn had waited and watched in the shadows of humanity for its judge to appear.

They had seen many imitations. In tenth-century Egypt a false prophet claiming to be the Mahdi had appeared and built the city of Cairo with help from his Berber followers. The Golden Dawn helped stage a coup that saw him imprisoned until his death. In Morocco, one hundred years later, another false prophet appeared and claimed universal leadership. He created a sultanate—until the Golden Dawn saw to it that he was killed in battle.

From India to Afghanistan to Pakistan, Somalia, and within all the Muslim world Mahdi imposters appeared throughout the centuries and the Golden Dawn struck them down, one after one—quietly, without attention. The sapient sect knew how easily someone, even a false prophet, could be made into a martyr. The world was to be kept in the dark as much as possible about the Mahdi's existence. It was no different now.

Neda had thought the secret battle was lost. But Melchior knew differently; he whistled.

121

UP THE STAIRS FROM THE OUTSIDE CAME DOZENS OF YOUNG MEN dressed in white. They faced off against the seminarians, and a battle began. Punches, kicks, elbows, and head butts. It was a clash of not only flesh but also ideology. It was an exhibition of conflict between good and evil.

Melchior protected Neda from the combat. He blocked and barreled their way through.

Mesbah Yavari was on his knees trying to stand. Some of the boys in white saw him and began to approach. The Ayatollah scrambled but couldn't find his footing. The boys saw their opportunity to "kill the king."

They ran, their arms taut, their fists clenched, and their minds focused. They could break the mighty Haghani Circle. An example of good overcoming evil could be shown to the other fanatics around the world who chose the side of darkness.

They were within a few yards of the ayatollah. He knew it was coming. He covered himself and cowered. "No!" he cried out. "No, please don't hurt me. I am just an old man." Pathetic. Their anger flared. The young men were almost on him.

The door opened behind the Ayatollah and a hand dragged Mesbah Yavari into the room just as the three young men in white crashed into the door.

Outside, Neda and Melchior were running through the courtyard. The Golden Dawn sectarians in white and the seminarians in black spilled down the stairs and followed them like the detritus of a tornado. They were out front and the world behind them was left in ruin.

The Golden Dawn had learned their own form of martial art from Sufi elders. It consisted of twirls and lightning-fast, arched blows. It was the secret movements the dervishes practiced and became a popular dance show. It was one of the oldest forms of fighting known to man and was highly effective because it capitalized on momentum. A practiced dervish fighter could create enough force to break a baseball bat in half with a kick.

The seminarians had been taught the ancient Persian form of wrestling, *koshti*. It was a rough martial art combining grappling and wrestling in various forms. The style involved grabbing hold of an opponent in such a way that he or she could be tossed to the ground; it was a Middle Eastern form of judo.

Boom! a member of Golden Dawn would land a flying kick to a seminarian's chest. Smack! a seminarian would slap down a Golden Dawn fighter to the ground.

At the seminary's entrance, Melchior turned and looked back. White on black, black on white. It was difficult to determine which side was winning. As it had been since the beginning of time, good and evil would be almost perfectly matched. The yin and the yang, the positive and the negative. Like the atom, a proton and neutron. An artificial tilt to one side would send the world off its axis. That is what the Golden Dawn was really born to prevent. They existed to keep balance.

Melchior looked up in the sky and saw both the sun and the moon. Krishna paksha.

Standing at the entrance with him, Neda was looking past the epic battle. At the window on the second floor of the seminary, Talib was looking out—and at her.

122

INSIDE HIS CHAMBERS, AYATOLLAH MESBAH YAVARI FINALLY GOT UP and dusted himself off. The three men who had come so close to attacking him were banging on the door trying to get in.

Talib turned away from the window. It was just him and his mentor in the room now.

"We must leave," Talib said. "Is there another way out?"

"We are in the hands of Allah now," the Ayatollah said.

"The Assembly of Experts," Talib looked at his watch. "The moon and the sun will become one tonight. Today is the day I shall be revealed to the Assembly. We must get to them before it is too late."

"I am afraid that it already is."

"No. My men will be here shortly. They will take care of these children. Then we can address the other ayatollahs. We can make our announcement. The pieces are in place. Our weapon will be a reality."

Mesbah Yavari sat in his thronelike chair. "There can be only one Mahdi," he said. "And as it is written, the Mahdi will be from the bloodline of Fatima."

The Ayatollah leveled his gaze at Talib. "You are not. We cannot go against the word of Allah."

"I am the Prophet!" Talib shouted. He stepped closer to Mesbah Yavari. "You know that. Since I was a child you have known—"

"Stop! I heard what you told your sister. Sister! You are not of the bloodline of Fatima, and so it will not be. The Mahdi's time has not come."

A look of hate and fire came into Talib's eyes. The truth stung him more than any pain he had ever endured. "It shall be! And I shall make it so!"

"Without my blessing, the Assembly will not hear you."

"Unless you die!"

Talib lunged at the Ayatollah. He wrapped his hands around the old man's throat and squeezed.

The door to the chamber flew open.

Outside a caravan of SAVAMA agents pulled up in front of the seminary.

123

MICHAEL SHEA HAD THE CONTACT INFORMATION THAT FARUK HAD given him in his pocket. He hoped the crazy Turk hadn't returned to Istanbul yet. He needed a private ride to Belfast.

After a brief conversation, Shea found himself on an Apache Attack helicopter. A jet crossing so many international borders would be impossible to hide. A helicopter, however longer it would take, could maneuver without having to register a flight plan. The hitch was that the Apache had a maximum range of 1,200 miles. It would have to hop from Italy to Switzerland to France, England, and finally put down in Ireland, which is exactly what it did.

Even though Faruk had pimped out the chopper with a noise-deflecting interior, Shea still had ringing in his ears as he stepped off. The helicopter had landed at Belfast Castle, the familiar landmark that overlooks the city from the slopes of Cave Hill.

Shea could see Belfast stretching out before him. But it wasn't the sight that brought him back in time. It was something else: a feeling, a feeling that he came from and belonged to this land. It was primal and tribal at once. Shea took a deep breath and inhaled the scent of the Irish greens all around him.

The whirlybird flew away and Shea walked over to the man he had called from Italy, the man who was now waiting for him by the footpath to the side of the twelfth-century Norman building—Willie Dyson.

The first thing that Shea did was hand over the file on Talib that Balthazar had put together. The greeting between the two old friends was quick.

"Glad you're home and safe, Michael."

"Home, yeah. 'Tisn't safe from what you've told me though."

They shook hands and got right down to the possibilities for the story they could broadcast.

"Wiretap is not admissible in court," Dyson said. "You know that."

"I do," Shea said. "But we aren't going before a judge. We are reporting a story. If Sean confirms what I've told you, you'll have enough to broadcast the story."

Shea was massively frustrated with the journalism system that allowed the most ridiculous and scandalous news to be disseminated but required sources and backup for the important stuff. It was why the public learned more about the sexual proclivities of public officials and celebrities than serious policy.

Dyson interrupted Shea's thoughts. He said, "I'll see if I can get anything solid on the Chechen. Confirming the information out of Rome, though, will be tough."

"I'd leave that out—the Vatican connection. We should just go with what we have: 'a source says Talib is negotiating with terrorists to acquire nuclear arms, etc.' And then as a sidebar you can get into the evidence that we have that shows Talib changed his name. The religious info can be tacked on the end, so we play the story from strong to weak."

"But people love the religious bit," Dyson said. "Conspiracy always gets good ratings, especially when it comes to the church."

"Let's not turn this into *The Da Vinci Code*, shall we. This is about real bad guys doing real bad things in the real world. Not some piece of fiction."

"You're no fun, you know that, Shea."

"That's what I'm told."

124

IT WAS SEVERAL MILES DOWN THE ROAD LATER WHEN DYSON BROUGHT up the subject of O'Shaughnessy. Then Dyson's tone turned deathly serious. "You can't kill him, Michael." He didn't need to specify whom he was speaking of.

"Can," Shea said. "Been planning it for years. Burning at me, too."

"It'll blow the story. You've got to look at the big picture. It's the world we are talking about."

Shea was silent for a minute. "Said 'can,' Willie. Didn't say 'would.'"

"Good. As long as we are straight on it then."

Shea was seething inside. He had spent the better part of a decade chasing down his uncle and trying to get him in a room all alone. He had asked himself whether he could really do it. Could he really stare his uncle in the face and pull the trigger, choke the life out of him, or stab him in the heart? Shea had various scenarios for killing. And he had come to the same conclusion no matter what bloody end he fantasized about putting to Sean O'Shaughnessy's life: "Yes, yes, I can kill him. I can live with that."

It wasn't even so much about killing his uncle as it was about stopping his uncle from killing more—so many more—people.

Shea's motive was saving the world from a dark terror. And now he knew just how dark that terror was—an abyss, a nuclear abyss.

125

ZHUBIN HAD SPENT A WHOLE DAY AND NIGHT IN AN ITALIAN JAIL. HIS interrogators tried myriad threats and an array of intimidation tactics to get him to speak. None worked.

The Italian detectives didn't get physical. It wouldn't have mattered if they had. Zhubin had said just one sentence: "Let the Iranian ambassador know that I am here." And then he handed over his diplomatic passport.

Technically, Zhubin hadn't broken Italian law. He was on Vatican property when the shootings and murder occurred. When he had revealed his identity and showed his identification to the Vatican police, they had released him into the custody of the Italian authorities. And like much of the bureaucracy in Italy, there was confusion as to what and how he could be charged with a crime; the Vatican said it wasn't pressing charges.

On diplomatic grounds, the Italian police released Zhubin with the caveat that he leave the country. He agreed to do that. Although he didn't say that he would be leaving after he visited someone in Naples.

Zhubin had plenty of time in jail to think about Shea's next move. There would be few places for him to run as a wanted man. So, like any person on the lam, Shea would rely on what was familiar, and that included a familiar network of people. Was Faruk the drug trafficker in that network? Zhubin decided to follow up on that possibility. It was the only clue he had.

126

ZHUBIN CAME ALONE AND UNARMED TO THE BASE OF MOUNT VESU-vius just five miles east of Naples. He looked up at the imposing strato-volcano that looked at a distance like an early teen female's breast—low rising and pointed.

Zhubin wondered if the volcano would erupt. It was one of the few volcanoes that regularly did and was considered one of the most dangerous in the world because of it. After all, it did lead to the destruction of Pompeii—forever casting that city in stone.

He walked quickly on the dark gravel that lined the villa's driveway. *Lava rock,* he thought as he scoped the entrance. His intel put Faruk inside the villa of a well-known mobster. And Zhubin had just stepped onto that villa's grounds.

Surprisingly, there was no guard gate or security at the villa's entrance. Zhubin walked straight down the middle of the private driveway seemingly unnoticed.

Seemingly.

Inside the security room of the villa, three thick men took rifles from a locker. Two more took up positions at the front door.

Inside, Faruk was enjoying dinner with an obese Italian man. They were eating pasta and drinking wine without any idea that a SAVAMA assassin was headed their way.

127

IT STAYED LIGHT UNTIL LATE IN THE EVENING DURING THIS TIME OF year—late summer—in Italy. Glare was a problem for Zhubin. He couldn't see in front of him, for the sun was blinding.

He stepped off the path of the driveway into the shaded patch of shrubs and trees that ran along its side. He could see better now. Just in time.

Three men were coming down the driveway with rifles in their hands. They were scanning the terrain in front of them.

Zhubin looked around to improvise weapons. The volcano had provided many.

He waited for the men to walk past him and he then quietly stepped onto the driveway behind them. He probably could have sneaked up to the house itself, but he didn't want to risk the men coming back. He needed to take care of them. Now.

The sharp-edged lava rocks were like knives or Ninja stars—extremely sharp and pointed. He caught the man on the far left from him square in the back of the head. The man fell without so much as a sound. As the second man turned, Zhubin caught him with two rocks—one stuck to the side of the man's head and the other nailed him in the throat. The third man got it straight between the eyes. Not a shot was fired.

Zhubin had one long, thin rock left. It had the sharpest edge—and he used it to slice all three men's throats. He wasn't taking any chances. He remembered a scene from an American movie. "You gonna kill someone," the man in the movie had said, "make sure they're dead." Zhubin made sure.

He pried a rifle from one of the dead man's hands, bending each finger back. And then he ran up the driveway to the front entrance of the villa. Speed would now be his advantage.

He shot the two men standing at the door without breaking stride. He crashed through the door and after two rooms found two men, one old and fat and the other young and lean, eating dinner.

Faruk and the old gangster didn't have time to register what was going on. A man was in the room holding a rifle at them. A shot was fired. Faruk didn't have time to process the liquid that dripped down his face at first either. His brain told him it was pasta sauce. Of course it wasn't. The fat old mobster's head, what was left of it, fell into the bowl in front of him.

Later, Faruk gave Zhubin the information that he needed. It came in one word: *Belfast*. He told him that Shea had gone to Belfast.

After Zhubin had left, Faruk tried to call Ronnie, his Rastafarian pilot and driver. He realized that he'd have to dial with his left hand. His right thumb was missing.

He slumped in the chair and waited for Ronnie to get him. He noticed that Zhubin had left the gun on the table, and that he had taken a cannoli.

PART THREE

"FOR OUR
OWN GOOD"

1

UP CLOSE, HIS UNCLE'S FACE HAD AGED, BUT IT WAS AS H[
remembered—cold, the eyes dead. It was all that Shea could do to re[
strain himself when he met his uncle at the door.

The house was also exactly as he remembered it, standing in th[
shadows of St. Peter's Cathedral. The small gated garden wafted smell[
that brought Shea back in time. Through the brightly colored door, h[
stepped inside.

"We ain't gonna hug?" O'Shaughnessy joked upon seeing him.

"No, we ain't," Shea said. He began to rub the back of his neck rathe[
than shake his uncle's hand.

"Why? Why invite me here?" Shea asked.

"Why'd you come?"

"To end it."

"Aih. There's the answer for us both."

"You can't follow through on sending materials to Talib, Sean. Not
now. And the Chechens . . ."

Shea wanted to get all the facts out and on the table ASAP and goad

his uncle into some type of admission. Then he and Dyson would have what they needed for their news story. Then he could deal with his uncle on a more personal level. Death was a possibility.

"Save it, Mikey. I know that you are recording this so I'll make a deal with you. I give you the story, then you turn it off. We have something private to speak about. Deal?"

Shea, at first deflated on account of his uncle's perception, nodded in agreement.

"All right, then," O'Shaughnessy said. "I met Mahmoud Talib after he contacted me about some materials he was looking for. He needed to make the trigger to a bomb, a nuclear bomb. He also needed someone to configure it for him. And that job went to me as well. Alu Abramov, God rest his soul, was also contacted. Abramov was a member of the Chechen resistance. He had a particular type of plutonium that Talib wanted. Between the two of us, we could give Talib what he needed to build a nuclear weapon. We met a few days ago in Iran, at Lake Urmia. And I think you know the rest of the story."

"Abramov is dead?"

"Yeah."

"How?"

"I had him killed is how."

Shea just looked at his uncle, dumbfounded that he would admit to everything just like that—on tape.

O'Shaughnessy continued, "Now I know what you are thinking, Mikey. Why is he telling me all this?"

Shea said, "Exactly."

"Turn that device off, or whatever it is that you got hidden, and I'll tell ya."

Shea reached under his shirt and turned off the recorder. "Done. So why, Sean?"

"Because that recording is never going to see the light of day."

2

WILLIE DYSON WAS SITTING IN HIS CAR AROUND THE CORNER FROM St. Peter's Cathedral waiting for Shea. There wasn't much for him to do. He ran through the story in his mind. It was fantastic.

One the one hand, he had sold both Shea and his uncle out. He had played them both right down the middle. Now he was about to tip the scale in his own favor. He would win the glory. He smiled wide.

The bullet came at an angle, from the side. It pierced the side windshield and put a nice-sized hole about as big as a large coin in it. The rest of the glass didn't shatter. It held in place. Walking by, a person might not even notice the window break. In fact, the parish priest who walked by didn't notice anything at all. He didn't see the bullet hole nor Willie Dyson slumped over in the front seat with blood oozing from his temple.

Dyson died not far from the place he'd been done wrong by the priest as a child. He hadn't ever been able to rest easy at night or, sometimes, even during the day since.

Until now.

Zhubin had put him out of that misery.

3

INSIDE SEAN O'SHAUGHNESSY'S HOUSE, MICHAEL SHEA WAS RUB-bing the back of his head again, but this time not out of subconscious fear; he couldn't figure out what his uncle was getting at.

"Sean, you're mad. This story is getting out. You're done. Don't you get it?"

"No, Mikey. 'Tis you that doesn't understand. First, though, I have to tell you: Tommy is dead. 'Twas him that shifted the bomb at Omagh. Burden of yours on that can be put to rest. You done the right thing."

"Sean, I saw your note . . ."

"That's right. Left it for you. Trouble was, it went all wrong. Tommy switched things."

"Sean, what are you saying? That you wanted me to call the police?"

"Aih. That was the idea. Time to own up and apologize. Work now is finished."

"Why would you want to warn the authorities off?"

O'Shaughnessy sat down in his favorite chair in the living room. Next to it was the only photo in the whole house—a picture of his sister . . . Shea's mother. He looked at it.

"Mikey, I been working with the authorities all along. Time to come clean. Did a bit of nasty business. Had to prove myself at killin'. Did. Balanced out, mostly, until Omagh. That's when things tipped— they went wrong. Had to move on to where I could do some good. That meant the world. Here was finished. People was starting to suspect things. Got to understand. That is why I could never reach out to you. Was for your own protection."

Shea was in shock. He thought back on all the acts of terror his uncle had committed all over the world. "That's impossible, Sean. I've seen the men you've killed. I witnessed the bombings."

"You saw what you wanted to believe, Mikey."

Shea thought through all the circumstances in which he had seen or thought he'd seen his uncle's handiwork.

Lima, Peru, 1992. Two car bombs killed eighteen people. One was outside the police station in Callao. Shea was there.

"Lima—"

"I came in after the fact. Took up with the Shining Path and got the fellas responsible. Disbanded the operation a bit, too."

Shea remembered reading that the Shining Path militants had been inactive after the bombing. People thought they were just gearing up again.

"Spain, the Basque letter," Shea said, referring to an extremely sophisticated bomb that had been placed inside an envelope and exploded in the face of a well-known journalist. The sophistication of the bomb had led to O'Shaughnessy, who had been traced to the Basque region and been photographed with the ETA, the Basque terrorist group that had taken responsibility for sending the letter.

"Only thing those Basques been making since has been good food," O'Shaughnessy said.

Shea went on to list Somalia, Pakistan, Israel, and North Africa. For every incident and explosion, O'Shaughnessy had an explanation.

Shea himself had to sit down. He sat on the couch across from his uncle, the photo of his mother between them.

4

SHEA COULDN'T BELIEVE WHAT HE WAS HEARING. "SO WHAT YOU ARE saying is that you have been working undercover for all these years?"

"Aih. We have a big plan, a master plan. Now you see, it has come to an end," O'Shaughnessy said.

"Who's 'we'?"

"MI6. Had them try to bring you in, too. Talib's men got in the way of that, though."

The famous terrorist Sean O'Shaughnessy was a spy—for the good guys? It still wasn't fitting together for Shea. He asked, "Omagh? . . ."

"Like I said, a dark day for us all. I'm sorry, Mikey, I know it was tough on ya. I was tough on you." O'Shaughnessy reached over and put his hand on his nephew's knee and squeezed his thigh. "But you came out good. I been watching. Even if you didn't know it, I been looking out for ya. Got your back, I did. And now I am asking you to get mine. We can't let a word of this business with Talib get out. Hear me?"

Shea thought of Neda. Was there a way to save her? He'd get to that. Instead he asked about the nukes.

"They're going through. Same with the trigger material I got for him. Talib will get them just as he ordered. Have another Chechen who is crossing the border into Iran 'round about now. Triggers will be a bit different than Talib expects. Armed them to blow on contact.

"Mikey, if Talib tries to ignite a nuclear weapon, it will blow him and his people to kingdom come. 'Tis the only safeguard that will stop him

· 342 ·

from continuing to build them. That's why this shipment has to go through. It's the only way the world will be safe," O'Shaughnessy said.

Shea had to reconcile whether his uncle was telling the truth or bluffing.

In the next moment he found out.

THE NOISE OF THE RINGTONE ON ZHUBIN'S MOBILE PHONE GAVE Shea a second's notice. And it saved his life. Thank you, Madonna.

Zhubin had come crashing through the front door firing. He shot clean through O'Shaughnessy's shoulder and grazed Shea's arm. The SAVAMA assassin had landed on the floor behind the couch. Shea scrambled to a safer area between the chair and the couch where Zhubin couldn't shoot him.

O'Shaughnessy was on his stomach, gagging on blood. Zhubin stood and shot O'Shaughnessy again, and again. With his limp arm, O'Shaughnessy handed his gun to his nephew. And Michael Shea took it. He fired off a few rounds in Zhubin's direction. It was enough to cause Zhubin to take cover. Shea looked at his uncle's eyes. They were beginning to close.

Shea couldn't see Zhubin anymore. Then Zhubin stood again. Shea couldn't raise his gun fast enough. Zhubin had a clean shot. He raised his arm and aimed directly at Shea's face. He was but six feet away.

Zhubin tried to pull the trigger but couldn't. A vision of his mother flashed in his mind again. This time he also heard her last word to him. It was a whisper. He could almost feel her breath on him. She had been that close, in his arms, when she had said it. "Why?" she had asked. "Why?"

Zhubin's arm jerked. He pressed the trigger, taking aim on the answer to that question as much as on Shea. Shea was shot in his right shoulder. His left hand, however, was still free to shoot, and he blasted off three rounds. They hit Zhubin in succession. Zhubin stumbled back, and out of sight.

The pain of the gunshot was excruciating. The bullet inside him was shaken loose by his movement and Shea began to bleed profusely. He slouched against the sofa, next to his uncle, whose breath was heaving.

The door to the house opened and a barrage of MI6 agents entered.

Before he passed out, Michael Shea heard his uncle's voice for the last time: "For our own good, Mikey." It was what Shea had remembered his uncle saying after he hit him on the back of the head as a boy. But this time O'Shaughnessy had taken away one letter, *y*. He hadn't said for *your* own good. He had said for *our* own good.

O'Shaughnessy had extended that virtue to the community, the world. And now Shea knew what it all meant; his uncle wanted good to prevail.

There was only a trace of blood in the room where Zhubin had been—a thin, red line of it that marked his escape.

6

THE DEATH OF AYATOLLAH MESBAH YAVARI WOULD BECOME SOME-thing of lore. Some said that he had hung himself before his seminary was ransacked by Zoroastrians. The myth was that he killed himself in honor before being kidnapped. Another was that he had sacrificed his own life in order to save President Mahmoud Talib.

The real story was that when his door was broken down, the three young members of Golden Dawn watched as Talib strangled Mesbah Yavari to death. The president was crazed. The old man's body floun-dered madly trying to escape death. He felt it, though, every second of it—each dying breath. In pain, he died.

Before the Golden Dawn could take Talib, his SAVAMA entourage had entered the building. The Golden Dawn had to escape, which they did. But it left Talib free.

Talib then fled back to Tehran. He shooed his wife and children out of his office at the presidential palace and took up the cause of address-ing the Assembly of Experts. He informed each of the ayatollahs of Mesbah Yavari's death and he requested an audience with the Supreme Leader.

His request was denied.

It left him no choice. He'd abandon the metaphysical power for the physical. He had all the parts that he needed now for the nuclear bomb. He'd just have to assemble it to bring the world to its knees.

7

"THE CHARGES AGAINST YOU DON'T LOOK GOOD," GABE, THE BALD, middle-aged MI6 officer said. Gabe was so nondescript that Shea could run into him on the street tomorrow and not recognize him. The man had a slight lilt to his voice, and Shea knew he was from the home country.

"Your uncle gave us some new testimony about your participation in the Omagh bombing, and as you know that incident has never been resolved to the liking of the people or the government. Besides, since your travels put you in just about every country where a terrorist action has taken place over the last decade, an international warrant is out for your arrest, and British News, your employer, would like to know, as would we, by the way, how two of its finest journalists wound up dead while in your company. Quite a bloody trail you've left behind, I'd say. And that's literal."

Shea was lying in a hospital bed in a ward God knows where. England? Ireland? Some secret MI6 compound somewhere on Earth?

He had passed out from the gunshot wounds after hearing his uncle's last words to him. Then he woke up here. And this lug wouldn't let up.

But his first thoughts didn't stray to questions about himself or his own fate. As soon as he had regained consciousness, Shea thought of Neda. How he had failed her. If Talib did ignite the nuclear bomb, as his uncle said, Neda would be taken with it. If she was still alive, Shea needed to somehow get to her. That was, if she was still alive—and he doubted that.

Gabe sensed that Shea wasn't processing or realizing the gravity of his situation or what he was saying. He snapped his fingers in front of Shea's face. "Hey, hey, hey. Paddy. You with me?"

Ah, the slang gave him away. Gabe couldn't mask that. He was Irish, and pretending not to be.

Shea then began to pay attention to the meaning behind the words themselves. For sure he was in a predicament. Without his uncle's testimony there was no evidence of the story he was working on or the nuclear deal. Without Balthazar's file, there was nothing to report about Talib either. And without Neda, a part of life/love was lost. *Where had it all gone?*

"I made a tape recording," Shea said. "When I was with my uncle. I recorded the conversation . . ." His mouth was dry as sand and he felt the pain all over his body despite the drugs that ran through his veins to keep him numb.

"Dyson, Willie Dyson. He knows what's what. We were working on a story—"

Gabe cut him off, shaking his head. "See, you weren't listening. Said two British News journalists were dead."

Shea had thought Gabe was speaking about Munjed and Matt Beynon when he had said two journalists. Now he realized something dire. Dyson's death made his situation hopeless.

Until Gabe provided him with some promise.

8

GABE'S DEMEANOR CHANGED AND HE LOOSENED HIS TIE. HE SAT ON the corner of Shea's bed. Shea was the only person in the eight-bed ward. It was so quiet he could hear his own IV drip.

"Listen," Gabe said, "I ran your uncle for the service. Knew him better than anyone in the world. He told me he was going to fill you in. Did he?"

Shea, for once, looked into Gabe's eyes. They were trustworthy. "Did," Shea answered.

"Good. See, there isn't a cut-and-dry or black-and-white solution out there to stoppin' bad things. Wars can't even be won on those grounds anymore. Just ask the Americans. There's no frontline anymore, Michael. We have to go behind them. And that means, sometimes, joining up with them, the enemy.

"Your uncle was a good soldier, best there ever was. There's no tallying all the good he done for the world. A lot of it came with some unsavory things, but that's what I'm sayin': ensnared in the web of the wicked a strand of good gets caught. We can't let that go. All's lost when that happens. They win. Can't let that be."

Shea was hoping the agent would stop being so obtuse and get to the point of his little diatribe.

"I don't follow," Shea said. "What are you going on about?"

"We need good men like you behind enemy lines."

"Me?" Shea asked, sitting up until the pain dropped him back onto the pillow.

"Take up your uncle's mantle, as it were. Be a spy for us. That's what we'd like. You have the cover now. We know you weren't involved in any of those things, but the world doesn't."

For our own good, his uncle had said.

Shea thought about the proposition. He had tried through journalism to fight for the truth. But journalism had changed. It had become more like fiction. In fact, a colleague of his had turned to writing novels. When Shea had asked him why, his friend had said, "I can report the truth better that way."

Times certainly had changed. The agent was right: there was no black and white anymore. The world was gray with sparkles of light in it once and again. Shea thought: like stars in the sky at night.

He didn't address the agent's proposition right away. He just said, "There is a woman, Neda. She is in Iran. I need you to help me get her out . . ."

THEY MET ON THE ISLAND OF MALTA IN FRONT OF THE MEGALITIC Temples, the oldest freestanding structures on Earth.

Neda had arrived first. She was wearing the white tunic Shea had bought for her. It was now washed and stitched.

Despite having taken pains to cover her bruises, they still interrupted the beauty of her face. The tenderness of the bruises from the beatings she had taken subsided. In all, she felt great and she glowed with anticipation.

Shea watched her from atop the mounds of stones that comprised the Skorba Temples. Neda stood looking radiant. The members of the Golden Dawn who had escorted her to the island now disappeared into the cavernous entranceways of the temple site. Assumably they would stand guard and watch.

The temples' architecture was all the same: an oval forecourt bordered by the temple's own facades that faced south. The facades and internal walls were made of orthostats, a row of large stone slabs that lay on end.

The MI6 contingent who dropped Shea off on the island was long gone. They had given him a week, all expenses paid, to spend with Neda at one of the seaside villas the British government still owned on the island. (The British Empire, after all, had ruled the island for some one hundred fifty years, until 1964.)

MI6 had its own spies inside Iran, and it hadn't been hard for them to track down Neda.

Shea got that unearthly feeling just looking at her. It was some type of magic.

She heard him walk down the slope and she felt it, too. The force of their attraction got stronger and stronger the closer they came to one another.

They didn't say a word. They touched and then hugged so hard and tight that from a distance they looked as one.

10

FARTHER AWAY ON THE ISLAND OF MALTA TWO YOUNG BOYS PLAYED.
They were kicking a ball back and forth.

They both had the olive skin of Middle Easterners, although one's skin was darker. He was chubby. The other, the younger of the two, was thin. Despite their slight skin, age, and weight difference, the boys were equally matched.

They were playing in the courtyard of the Chak Chak Temple. Around them stood the Secret Chiefs: the heads of every religion in the world. They each held a translated copy of the Avestan scroll found by Lake Urmia; the original they buried in the ground in the farthest corner of the apse.

The Secret Chiefs watched as the Mahdi and the Christ child played.

They agreed that it was time to unite and convert the world—from ignorance to wisdom, from hatred to love, from fear to faith, and from evil to goodness. A final order was given to the Golden Dawn.

And that evening news broke of the mushroom cloud over Qom.

11

IN BED, SHEA ROLLED OFF NEDA AND CAUGHT HIS BREATH. HE RE-
flexively reached up to rub the painful bump on the back of his neck,
but he found that it was no longer there.

He wrapped his arm around Neda, and she curled up into him.
Then he closed his eyes.